Froi of the Exiles

BOOK TWO

of the Lumatere Chronicles

MELINA MARCHETTA

Candlewick Press

This is a work of fiction. Names, characters, places, and incidents are either products of the author's imagination or, if real, are used fictitiously.

First U.S. edition 2012
Previously published by the Penguin Group (Australia) 2011

Library of Congress Cataloging-in-Publication Data is available.

Library of Congress Catalog Card Number pending

ISBN 978-0-7636-4759-9

11 12 13 14 15 16 SHD 10 9 8 7 6 5 4 3 2 1

Printed in Ann Arbor, MI, U.S.A.

This book was typeset in Palatino.

Candlewick Press
99 Dover Street
Somerville, Massachusetts 02144

visit us at www.candlewick.com

To Laura
For conversations in Ravenna
and New York playlists

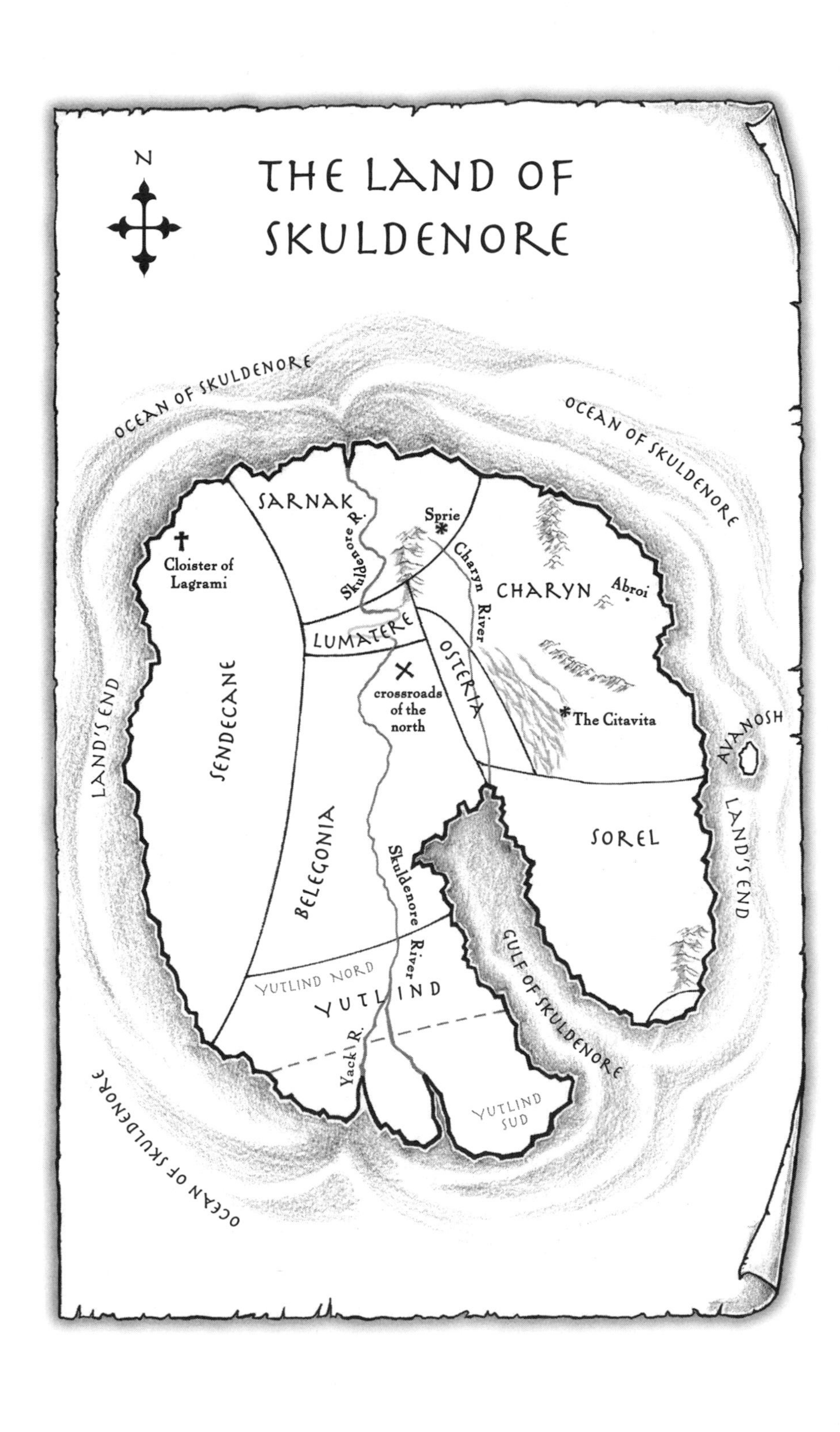
N
THE LAND OF SKULDENORE
OCEAN OF SKULDENORE
OCEAN OF SKULDENORE
SARNAK
Skuldenore R.
Sprie
Charyn River
CHARYN
Abroi
Cloister of Lagrami
LUMATERE
OSTERIA
crossroads of the north
The Citavita
AVANOSH
LAND'S END
SENDECANE
LAND'S END
SOREL
BELEGONIA
Skuldenore River
GULF OF SKULDENORE
YUTLIND NORD
YUTLIND
Yack R.
YUTLIND SUD
OCEAN OF SKULDENORE

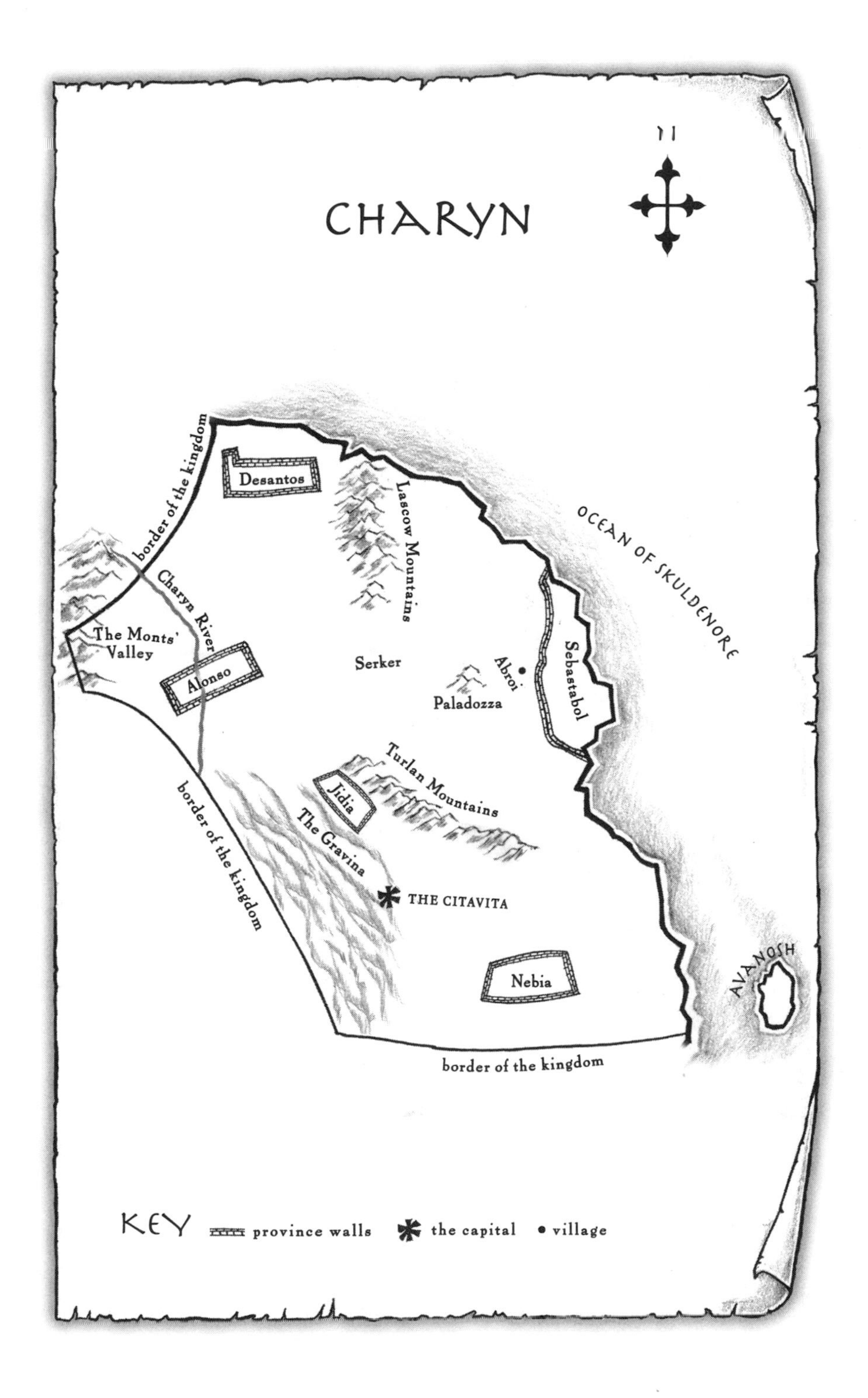

CHARYN
N
OCEAN OF SKULDENORE
border of the kingdom
Desantos
Lascow Mountains
Charyn River
The Monts' Valley
Alonso
Serker
Abroi
Paladozza
Sebastabol
Turlan Mountains
Jidia
The Gravina
border of the kingdom
THE CITAVITA
Nebia
AVANOSH
border of the kingdom
KEY
province walls
the capital
village

PROLOGUE

They call her Quintana the curse maker. The last female born to Charyn, eighteen years past.

Reginita, *she claims to be. The "little queen." Recipient of the words writ on her chamber wall, whispered by the gods themselves. That those born last will make the first, and blessed be the newborn king, for Charyn will be barren no more.*

And so it comes to be that each autumn since the fifteenth day of weeping, a last-born son of Charyn visits the palace in a bid to fulfill the prophecy. But fails each time.

They weep for fear of hurting her. But she has no tears for herself. "Come along," she says briskly. "Be quick. I'll try to think of other things, but if your mouth touches mine, I will cut it out."

Most nights she concentrates on the contours of the ceiling, where light from the oracle's godshouse across the gravina *shines into her chamber. She holds up a hand and makes shapes in the shadows. And inside of her, in the only place she can hide, Quintana sings her song.*

And somewhere beyond the stone that is Charyn, the blood of a last born sings back to her.

PART ONE

The Curse Maker

CHAPTER 1

Froi's head was ringing.

A fist against his jaw, an elbow to his nose, a knee to his face, and they kept on coming and coming, these old men, he had called them. They came for him one after the other, and there was no mercy to be had this day. But Froi of the Exiles wasn't born for mercy. Not to receive nor to deliver it.

Behind his attackers was a sycamore tree waiting to die, its limbs half dragging on the dry ground beneath it, and Froi took his chance, diving high between two of the men, his hands reaching for one of the branches, his body swinging, legs jutting out. A boot to a face, one man down, then he pounded into another before the branch collapsed under his weight. He pulled it free from the tree, swinging the limb high over his head. A third man down and then the fourth. He heard a curse and a muttered threat before the flat of his palm smashed the next man who came forward. Smashed him on the bridge of the nose, and Froi danced with glee.

Until he was left facing Finnikin of Lumatere and Froi felt the feralness of his nature rise to the surface. "No rules," they had declared, and the dark goddess knew that Froi loved to play games with no rules. And so with eyes locked, they circled each other, hands out, waiting to pounce in the way the wolves in the Forest of Lumatere fought for their prey. Froi saw a bead of sweat appear on the brow of the man they called the queen's consort, saw the quick fist come his way, and so he ducked, his own fist connecting with precision. But all it took was the thought of the queen, her head shaking with bemusement and a smile entering her eyes, to make Froi think again about where to land his second blow. In that moment's hesitation, his legs were kicked out from under him and he felt his face pressed into the earth.

"You let me win," Finnikin growled, and Froi heard anger in his voice.

"Only because she'll kill me if I bruise that lily-white skin," Froi mocked through gasps.

Finnikin pressed harder, but after a moment, Froi could feel that he was shaking from laughter. "She'll thank you for it, knowing Isaboe." Finnikin leaped to his feet. They exchanged a grin, and Froi took the hand held out to him.

"Old man, did you call me?" Perri, the captain's second-in-charge, asked behind him. "Because I'm sure I heard those words come out of your mouth."

"Not out of my mouth," Froi said, feigning innocence and spitting blood to the ground from a cut in his lip. "Must have been someone else."

Around the sycamore, soldiers of the Guard were picking themselves up, curses ringing the air while the lads in training began collecting the practice swords and shields.

"If he goes for my nose again, I *fink* I'll hang him up by his little balls," one of the Guard said, getting to his feet. Froi tried to ignore the mockery.

"Nothing little about me," he grunted. "Don't take my word

for it, Hindley. Ask your wife. She seemed happy last night, you know, with the size and all."

Hindley snarled, knowing there was no truth in the words, but the danger was in having spoken them. Froi saw the snarl as an invitation, and all hope of ignoring it failed as he lunged at the man, wanting nothing more than to connect a fist to Hindley's nose for the third time that day. Because no matter what, the taunts still stung. Three years ago, when he hardly knew a word of Lumateran, his tongue would twist around all the strange pronunciations of his new language, causing great amusement among those who saw Froi as nothing more than street scum. *Here comes the feef wif nofing to show for,* they'd taunt. Finnikin had once told Froi that the greatest weapon against big stupid men was a sharp mind. It was one of the reasons Froi had agreed to continue his lessons with the priest-king. Three years on, he had exceeded everyone's expectations, including his own.

Today they had set up their drills in a meadow close to the foot of the mountains. Finnikin and Sir Topher had business with the ambassador from the neighboring kingdom of Sarnak, and they had chosen the inn of Balconio as the meeting place.

"You're not as nimble as you used to be," Perri said as they walked toward the horse posts by the rock hedges of a Flatland farm that had long been deserted. Lumatere was filled with empty farms and cottages, a testament to those who had died during the ten years of terror, which ended three years ago, when Finnikin and the queen broke the curse and freed their people.

"He's talking to you," Finnikin said with a shove.

"No, he's talking to you," Froi replied with an even greater shove. "Because I'd probably kill a man who called me nimble."

Perri stopped in his tracks, and Froi knew he had gone too

far. Perri had a stare that could rip the guts out of a man, and Froi felt it now. He knew he would have to wait it out under Perri's cold scrutiny.

"Except if it came from you, Perri," he said seriously. "I'd prefer the word *swift,* though. And you can't say I'm not swift."

"What have I told you about talking back?" Perri's voice was cold and hard.

"Not to," Froi muttered.

He knew he should have counted. It was the rule to count to ten in his head before he opened his mouth. It was the rule to count to ten if he wanted to smash a man in the face for saying something he didn't like. It was the rule to count to ten if instinct wasn't needed but common sense was. It was part of his bond to Trevanion and Perri and the Queen's Guard. Froi did a lot of counting.

They began walking again, silent for what seemed too long a time. Then Finnikin shoved him with a shoulder and Froi stumbled, laughing.

"He's filling out more than we imagined, Perri," Finnikin said. "Perhaps it's true what they say, after all. That he comes from River folk."

"Wouldn't mind being known as a River man," Froi said.

Still nothing from Perri.

"Not as a Flatlander?" Finnikin asked.

Froi thought about it for a moment. "Perhaps both."

He saw Perri's look of disapproval.

"You can't stay working on Augie's farm much longer," Perri said firmly. "Sooner or later, you'll have to join the Guard."

The topic of where Froi belonged came up more often these days. What had begun as a roof over his head three years ago with Lord August and his family had become home. And Froi's kinship with the village of Sayles had strengthened as he toiled alongside them, day in and day out, to restore Lumatere to what it had been before the unspeakable. But Froi's place was also with the captain and Perri and the men of the Guard in the barracks of the palace, protecting the queen and Finnikin and their daughter, Princess Jasmina. Once a boy with no home, Froi now found himself torn between two.

"I can do both."

"No, you can't," Perri said.

"I can do both, I tell you!"

"You've a warrior's instinct and the skill of a marksman, Froi," Perri said. "You're wasted as a farm boy. It's what I tell Augie every time I see him."

"Lady Abian says I'm probably eighteen by now, so you'll have to start treating me as one of the men," Froi muttered. He hated being called a boy.

This was followed by another stare from Perri. Another round of counting to ten from Froi.

"I'll treat you like a man when you act like one," Perri said. "Agreed?"

Finnikin shoved him again, and Froi tried not to laugh because Perri hated it when Froi didn't take things seriously.

"When I'm as old as my father, they'll still be calling me a boy," Finnikin said. "So why shouldn't you endure the indignity of it all as well?"

"Oh, Finn, Finn, the indignity of it all," Froi mocked, and Finnikin grabbed him around the neck, squeezing tight.

At the horse posts, Froi tossed the stable boy a coin as they collected their mounts. The boy gave Finnikin a note, and Froi saw irritation and then a ghost of a smile appear on his friend's face.

"I'll ride ahead to the inn," Finnikin said.

"Not unescorted, you won't," Perri said.

"It's around the bend in this road. Nothing can happen to me from here to there."

Froi rubbed noses with his horse. He knew this argument would last a moment or two.

"Anything can happen," Perri said.

"Suppose around the bend are ten Charynite scumsters, waiting to jump you," Froi said, mounting the horse.

Finnikin shot Froi a scathing look. "You're supposed to be on my side, Froi. And how do you suppose Charynite—"

"Scumsters," Froi finished.

"How do you suppose Charynite scumsters got up the mountain and passed the Mont sentinels?"

"All it takes is for one of them to slip through," Perri said.

But Finnikin was already on the horse, trotting away.

"I'll see you at the inn," he called out over his shoulder. He broke into a gallop and was gone.

"I think he forgets his place sometimes," Perri murmured, staring after Finnikin. "He still believes he can come and go as though he's some messenger boy."

There was silence between them again as they rode to the inn. Froi watched Perri carefully. He wondered if Perri would stay mad for long. Despite most things from Froi's mouth coming out wrong, he hated disappointing Perri or the captain.

"I can take leave from the farm, Perri," he said quietly. "Especially when it comes time to travel into Charyn and do what we have to do."

Perri was silent for a moment. "What makes you think I'm taking you to Charyn?"

"Because you've taught me everything I know about . . ." Froi shrugged. "You know."

"Killing," Perri said bitterly.

"And when I'm not training with you or working on the

form, then I'm with the priest-king being taught to speak the tongue of our enemy." He gave Perri a sideward glance. "So the way I see it, *that* says you're taking me to Charyn."

Perri was silent for a moment. "You know what the priest-king says?"

"*Sagra!*" Froi cursed. He knew he was going to get another serving from Perri.

"He says that you don't have time for your studies anymore. That you think there's no merit in learning and stories."

"I've learned all I need to," Froi said. "Studies and learning and stories won't protect the kingdom, and they won't reap harvests."

Perri shook his head. "I would have given anything to be taught at your age. The priest-king says you're a natural, Froi. That you pick up facts and foreign words and that you understand ideas that are beyond many of us. Who would have thought that hidden beneath all the talking back and fighting was a sharp mind? But it means nothing to the captain or me when you show little control over your actions and words."

Froi took a deep breath and counted, making sure he didn't take it out on the horse.

"You're not training anyone else, are you, Perri?" he managed to ask, trying to hold back his fury at the thought. "Not Sefton or that scrawny fool from the Rock? They think too much. You can see it on their faces. And they'd never bear a torture. Never."

Perri looked at him and Froi saw his eyes soften.

"And you would?"

"You know me, Perri," Froi said fiercely. "You know that if you wrote me a bond and told me what to bear, I'd bear it. You know me. Have I let you or the captain down once these past three years, hunting those traitors?"

In the distance, a Flatlander was harnessed to his plow, working a field on his own. Froi and Perri held up a hand in acknowledgment, and the man waved back.

"When the time comes, we will have only one chance to get into that palace," Perri said. "There will be no room for mistakes. Their army combined is more than our entire people, and if we make the slightest of errors, there will be a war to end all wars across this land."

There was a flash of anguish on Perri's face. Froi saw it in everyone's expression once in a while, especially those who remembered life as it once was. Froi didn't feel the sadness. Despite Isaboe and Finnikin's belief that he was one of the children lost to the kingdom thirteen years ago, when the impostor king took control, Froi remembered nothing about Lumatere. All he had known was life on the streets in another kingdom, where a chance meeting with Finnikin and the queen changed his life. In a secret part of him, Froi reveled in what he had gained from Lumatere's curse. He never looked back, because if he did, he would have to think of the shame and the baseness of who he had once been without his bond. He would do anything to prove his worth to the queen and Finnikin. Even kill. It was what he had been taught to do these past years. Over and over again.

Although every Lumateran had been trained to use a bow to defend the kingdom, Froi had stood out and was handpicked by Trevanion and Perri to work alongside them. He was swift and had mastered any skill thrown his way. The first time Froi was sent into the home of a traitor with a dagger and sword, Captain Trevanion had made him vow it would not end with death. They needed the man alive. What they required was information about the bodies of ten Flatland lads who had gone missing in the fifth year of the curse under the cruel reign of the impostor king. Froi studied the information and had gone in with vengeance in his heart. This man had been a traitor, a collaborator. He had spied for the impostor king and betrayed his neighbors. In the end, Froi had kept the man alive. Barely. From the information he forced out of him, they found the remains of the lads and were able to put them to rest seven years after they were slain. If the lads had lived, they would have been a year or two older than Froi today. Despite the passing of time, the grief from the families on the day of the burials was indescribable. What Froi had done to get that confession was worse.

But the punishment of most other traitors was different. When the palace was certain beyond doubt of their guilt, Captain Trevanion and Perri would ensure that retribution was quick and out of plain sight of the people of Lumatere, who had already seen enough bloodshed.

"Don't you just want to tear out their hearts?" Froi had asked both his captain and Perri one day when they had marked a traitor from a distance and shot an arrow into his chest. That the man died quickly with no fear or pain disturbed Froi.

"You can't go around feeling too much," Captain Trevanion had explained, watching a moment to ensure that the man was indeed dead. "Because if you feel too much, enough to want to kill them so savagely, then one day you're going to feel enough to spare their lives. Don't ever let emotion get in the way. Just follow orders. Most times the orders you follow will be the right ones."

Most times.

Sometimes it was a snap of the neck. Other times a dagger across the throat or a blade piercing the heart. But it was always clean and quick. More than once they had found a small band of the dead impostor king's soldiers in hiding, deserters from his army, seeking refuge in the forest at the far corner of the western border. Many of them had fled when Trevanion and his Guard had entered the kingdom to set their people free. Although the impostor king was half Lumateran, he was also a Charynite and his army was mostly made up of Charynites. Those soldiers now filled Lumatere's prison while Finnikin and Sir Topher endeavored to prove guilt or innocence by collecting evidence and testimonials. More than a hundred prisoners had been released and returned to Charyn.

Perri and Froi came to the outskirts of Balconio, where cottages began to appear. They passed a fallow field, and Froi heard Perri murmur words that he had heard over and over again each time anyone passed a fallow field. It was a prayer to the goddess that the soil would regain its fertility. In the last days of the curse, the impostor king had set alight most of the Flatlands.

"There's talk that Isaboe and Finn will sell the village of Fenton," Froi said.

"Queen Isaboe and the queen's consort," Perri corrected.

Froi made a rude sound. "Every time I call Finn the consort anything, he wrestles me, and he's no skinny thing anymore."

"It's hard for him," Perri said quietly. "No matter how strong his union with the queen, he has much to prove."

"He doesn't have to prove himself to her," Froi said.

"But he has to prove himself *because* of her."

Froi was distracted a moment by the rotted crop of cabbage that lined the road. He leaped off his horse and crouched, feeling the soil, shaking his head at the waste of it all. This year Lord August had decided to use a water system created by a soldier in the impostor king's army. It was the only thing of worth the enemy had contributed, apart from some of the most stunning horses Froi had ever seen. But many of the Flatlanders refused to adopt the Charynite methods, despite the fact that their crops were dying.

"They are fools," Froi said, looking up at Perri.

"Don't underestimate how deeply felt the hatred is," Perri said. 'They see it as the method of an enemy, and they don't want a part of it."

"So they'd prefer that their crops die and their people half starve! I told Gardo of the Flatlands that he was a horse's arse just the other day. What kind of man wastes his crop for the sake of pride?"

"You need to refrain from insulting the villagers, Froi," Perri said, laughing. "They have daughters. You're going to have to bond yourself to one of them sooner or later."

Froi stiffened. "I have a bond to my queen." He mounted his horse and steered it back onto the road.

He heard Perri sigh. "Froi, it was a worthy promise at the time, but you can't spend the rest of your life refusing the pleasures of lying with a woman."

"Why not?"

"Because it alters nothing of the past," Perri said firmly. "You can't change who you were. If anyone realizes that, I do."

Froi looked away. He didn't know how much Perri knew. Didn't want to know, really. It brought him too much shame. Three years ago on their travels, when the queen was disguised as the novice Evanjalin, and Froi was a filthy thief they had picked up along the way, he had tried to force himself on her. On the streets of the Sarnak capital, where he grew up, the men had taught him that power was survival. The Lumaterans had spent three years trying to unteach what he knew. Some nights he woke in a sweat remembering what he had done. The queen had spoken about it only once since they entered Lumatere. It was when a member of her Guard, Aldron, was sent on palace business with Finnikin, and Froi had been chosen to replace Aldron.

"Are you sure?" he had asked her quietly as they stood at the bailey, watching Finnikin and Aldron ride away.

"That you can protect me?" she said, her eyes still out in the distance where Finnikin and Aldron were tiny specks on the horizon. "Trevanion claims there's no one better than you, Froi. But if you're asking if I'm sure you won't hurt me, then yes, I am."

Froi had felt pride and relief.

Her dark eyes were suddenly on him, and he shivered at the memory of their fierceness. "But I've told you before, I will never forget. *Ever*. And nor will you. It's part of the bond you made to me that day we freed you from the slave traders. Do you remember?"

Froi would never forget. "That if I ever harm a woman, you'll have me hanged and quartered." And she would. That he knew.

Most days, he feared that a monster of great baseness lived inside him, fighting to set itself free. Killing the traitors of Lumatere for Isaboe made sense. But killing also fed the monster. He could not bear the idea of letting that monster free among the girls of Lumatere. So Froi kept away from them.

"It's the only way of proving myself to the queen," he muttered to Perri as they entered Balconio.

"Find another way," Perri said.

Froi shook his head. "I don't trust myself."

They reached the inn, where they would wait until Finnikin's meeting with the ambassador of Sarnak was over. The village of Balconio sat on the Skuldenore River, at the foot of the mountains. It could easily have been a village of ghosts. Many of its people had died in exile. But the queen and Finnikin had decided that an inn in such a place would attract customers and give life to Balconio. They had approached the people of one of the surviving villages and proposed their plan. Froi had once heard Lord August tell Lady Abian that it was a smart decision. One day, when the gates of Lumatere were open to the rest of the land, the inn would be the perfect place for trade. Despite their wariness of foreigners, the queen and Finnikin knew that to survive they would have to do business with neighbors. This inn and the export of silver from the mines to their neighboring allies, Belegonia and Osteria, was the first step. Most nights, the Balconio Inn was filled with Monts on their way to the palace village or merchants and farmers trading their goods and skills, but this past year, the people of the neighboring villages had begun to venture out of their homes for enjoyment rather than necessity. It helped that the inn also boasted the best ale in the kingdom.

Captain Trevanion met them at the gate of the inn. He was one of the most impressive men Froi had ever seen: mighty in build, with a face that even men would call handsome. He was Finnikin's beloved father, and Froi knew they still felt the pain of having been separated from each other when Finnikin was a lad of nine. The captain had also believed for ten long years that his beloved Lady Beatriss was dead, but she had lived, and during the past three years, there had been much talk about whether they would rekindle their love.

"We're old men, I hear," Trevanion said, cuffing Froi.

Froi laughed. "If you and some of the Guard weren't old men, then being called old men wouldn't insult you so much."

"We're only some forty years, Froi."

"He calls Aldron an old man, and he's not even ten years older than him," Perri mused, looking around. "Where's Finn?"

"I thought he was with you."

"He rode ahead."

Froi watched the two men exchange worried looks and followed them into the inn.

Inside, they jostled through a crowd. Tonight it was mostly

filled with the Queen's Guard, but Froi also recognized a handful of Rock villagers and the lads who traveled with the queen's cousin, Lucian of the Monts, which meant the Mont leader was somewhere in the vicinity.

In a corner close to where the innkeeper was serving from barrels of ale, Froi saw the Monts speaking tensely among themselves. Most were cousins to Finnikin through his marriage to the queen, but Finnikin and Lucian were nowhere to be seen. Froi sensed Trevanion and Perri's unease and followed them to the bar. The lad assisting the innkeeper looked up when they approached. He was young and nervous, and it was evident that he had never come face-to-face with the captain of the Guard before.

"You're new," Trevanion said.

"Yes, sir. Just started."

"Did you recognize the queen's consort?"

"No . . . no, sir, but he introduced himself."

Trevanion looked relieved. "Where is he?"

"He's with a . . . a . . . w-w-woman, sir."

Perri, Froi, and Trevanion stared at the lad in disbelief.

"A woman?" Trevanion snapped. "What woman?"

"A woman waiting in his room, sir. She had left a message."

"What room?" Trevanion demanded, already halfway up the staircase.

Perri dragged the nervous lad along with them. "Was she armed?" Perri barked.

"What message?" Trevanion shouted.

"She said, 'Tell my king I'm w-waiting in his chamber.'"

Trevanion stopped just as they reached the top of the stairs. Froi watched the captain's expression change from fear to exasperation.

"Her king?"

Trevanion muttered his favorite string of curses. The captain had spent years in a foreign prison among lowlifes from every kingdom of the land, and at times, even the Guard flinched at some of his expressions.

A palace soldier stood outside one of the chamber doors, shrugging haplessly when he saw his captain.

"I can't control her any more than you can control him, sir," he tried to say. Trevanion pushed him out of the way, knocking sharply before entering the room.

Near the window, Finnikin stood with both hands against the wall, his head bent over her. As always, the intimacy between them made Froi ache.

"I promise you," Finnikin said. "I've already shouted at her and used a very, *very* reprimanding tone."

"I was quivering," the queen said, stepping out from behind Finnikin.

Froi hid a grin, but Trevanion and Perri failed to hide their anger.

Isaboe was dressed more for comfort than for style, but still she managed to take Froi's breath away. When he had first laid eyes on her in that Sarnak alleyway, her head had been bare. Now her hair was thick and black and fell down her back, contrasting with the deep purple of her simple dress that fell loosely, from her shoulders.

"Surround the entire inn and send away every person who does not belong to the Guard or the Mont cousins," Perri barked to the soldier outside. Trevanion disappeared with the man.

"That will make us popular," Finnikin said, his arm around his wife. "Not only have we finally decided to collect taxes, but now we're getting in the way of their drinking."

Isaboe caught Froi's eye. She grabbed Finnikin's face to reveal to Froi an already purple eye.

"You?"

Froi pointed to himself questioningly, feigning surprise and hurt.

"Where are his bruises?" she asked Finnikin.

Froi made a scoffing sound at the thought.

Trevanion returned to the room. "Where's Jasmina?"

"In the next chamber," the queen said, "and if any of you wake her, Captain, I will have to kill someone tonight."

"I need to check—"

"*No*," both Isaboe and Finnikin said.

Trevanion stared at them.

"I'll see that—"

"No," the queen said again. "You can see your granddaughter when she wakes up."

Trevanion looked disgruntled.

"She'll know it's you the moment you walk in," Finnikin complained, "and she'll think it's a game and call out 'Pardu Twevanion' all night. I've not slept for two years!"

Trevanion fixed his stare on the queen, his anger still present.

"I finished the business with the Osterians earlier than predicted," she explained with a sigh. "I thought I'd come and visit before Finnikin's meeting with the Sarnaks. Coincidentally, Lucian is also here, so I get to see my husband and my cousin. I'm very lucky in that way."

Finnikin and Froi laughed. Trevanion and Perri didn't.

"Where is Lucian?" Trevanion asked.

"Apparently checking the privy and mouse holes for Charynites."

"I'm glad you're amused about the safekeeping of this family, my queen," Trevanion said.

The queen regarded him coolly, and in an instant the mood in the room changed.

"Not amused at all, Captain," she said. "I'm never amused about the safety of our family."

Froi saw a flicker of regret on Trevanion's face.

"It's just safer for you and the child to be in the palace, Isaboe," he said, his voice softening.

"I'm sorry," she said with remorse. "But it seemed so harmless, and you know what it feels like after three days speaking about mines and goats with the Osterians. It's what keeps them protected from invasion — the ability to bore the enemy to tears."

There was a knock, and without so much as an invitation to enter, Lucian of the Monts joined them, his stare going straight to the bruise on Finnikin's face. Although not as tall as the River lads, Lucian had an imposing build and a temper to match. There was ruddiness to his cheeks, courtesy of the mountain weather, and a bluntness in all things about him that set Lucian apart from the other leaders of Lumatere. Froi remembered little of Lucian from those few days he spent with the Monts before Lucian's father died in the battle to reclaim Lumatere. But many believed he was a changed lad since. Lord Augie said over and over again to Lady Abian that he was too young to control his kin on the mountain and protect the kingdom from the Charynites.

"*Bastard*," Lucian said, turning to Froi. "Bastards, both of you. Fists only?"

"Bit of wrestling thrown in," Finnikin said. "You can't see his bruises, but I promise they're there."

Lucian had been the childhood companion of both Finnikin and Isaboe's brother, Balthazar. The two friends still spoke of the slaughtered heir to the throne as if he were there among them, but Froi had never heard them mention Balthazar in front of Isaboe.

"How's Yata?" she asked, pecking her cousin's cheek with a kiss.

Lucian sighed. "The Guard is going to have to come up the

mountain after all," he said, not wasting time. "There's been an incident."

Froi recalled the tenseness of the Mont lads downstairs. He knew it could only mean one thing. At the foot of Lucian's mountain on the Charyn side was a cavernous valley that belonged to Lumatere. Half a day's ride east on horseback was the closest Charyn province, and at the end of winter, Charynites had begun to take refuge in the caves that perched over the valley and alongside the stream. A bold, desperate few had sent messages through Lucian, asking for refuge in Lumatere. The queen declined, but the Charynites refused to go away and their numbers grew each day.

Froi saw fear on the queen's face. The threat of the Charynites was always, *always* on her mind.

"For two weeks now, we've had a message sent up from the valley through Tesadora. A Charynite, through a contact, has requested to meet with the queen or Finnikin."

"Since when does a Charynite request anything of us?" the queen demanded. "They're fortunate enough to be using our valley."

"Who is the contact?" Finnikin asked.

Lucian looked away, and Froi realized he was avoiding the question.

"Lucian?" the queen ordered.

The Mont turned back to her and still there was a moment of hesitation. "Phaedra."

The room was quiet for a moment.

"The wife you sent back?" the queen asked.

"Do not call her that," Lucian snapped.

"Watch your tone, Lucian," Finnikin warned.

The Charynite girl was an unspoken source of tension between the Monts and the queen. At the beginning of spring, the leader of Alonso, the closest Charynite province, had traveled up the mountain with his daughter Phaedra in tow, insisting on a meeting with Lucian. The *provincaro* claimed that when his daughter was born, he had entered a pact with Lucian's father to betroth their children. After almost two years of petty skirmishes between the Mont lads and the sentinels of Alonso, and talk that the *provincaro* of Alonso was out of sorts with his own king, Finnikin and Isaboe had agreed that perhaps they could use the situation to Lumatere's advantage. Lucian had been furious. The girl was said to be frightened of her own shadow, spending most of her day sobbing in the corner of Lucian's cottage. Froi had met her once. She had politely spoken to him in Lumateran about the endless rain, her pronunciation poor at times. Froi had repeated to her a lesson taught by the priest-king about what to do with particularly strange pairings of sounds. Phaedra had thanked him, and he saw gratitude and kindness in her eyes.

The Monts despised Phaedra for more than being a Charynite. Mont women were strong and walked side by side with their men. Phaedra could barely boil water. Six weeks later, the girl left. Some said that Lucian threw her out, others that she walked out herself, but this was the first time her name had been mentioned by Lucian.

"And what is Phaedra doing in an unprotected valley when one would presume she should be back in her province living with her father?"

"She works alongside Tesadora as a translator and registers the newcomers as they arrive."

Froi watched the queen pretend to be confused. He knew that Lucian didn't stand a chance in this exchange.

"Let me get this right. Phaedra failed at being a good Mont wife, but she can run a camp of hundreds of fleeing Charynites, translate for Tesadora, and has somehow managed to be affiliated with a faction demanding a meeting with my king and me?"

Lucian turned to Finnikin for support.

"Don't look at me, Lucian," Finnikin said. "Don't even try to involve me in this one."

Lucian held up his hands in exasperation. "She was useless, I tell you! Even Yata would agree."

"Why is she still in the valley?" Isaboe demanded.

Froi watched the flicker of regret cross the Mont's face.

"According to Tesadora's girls, the *provincaro* refused to take his daughter back into his home. Phaedra lives in the caves now."

The queen nodded. Froi knew that nod. It was the gesture she used when simmering with fury.

"The wife of the Mont leader is living in a filthy cave?"

"You show respect for her now, my queen," Lucian said angrily. "Yet you failed to attend my bonding ceremony."

"You married her in Alonso, Lucian." The stare she sent him was cold, and apart from Finnikin, Lucian was the only man who ever dared to match it. Isaboe and her Mont cousins did this often. All of them. They fought fiercely. Loved each other fiercely. Laughed fiercely. Finnikin said it was best to leave the room and let them shout. It would all blow over soon, but for Lucian's sake, Froi would have welcomed sooner rather than later.

"Tell the girl that I do not meet with Charynites, and if they dare make the command again—"

"I haven't actually told you the worst of it," Lucian interrupted.

The room grew quiet. Tense. Froi felt the hairs on his arm rise.

Lucian kept his stare focused on his cousin. "And may I stress that no one is hurt."

There was a deadly silence in the room.

"This morning in the valley, a Charynite took a dagger to

Japhra's throat," he said, referring to one of Tesadora's novices.

Froi leaped to his feet. He heard the queen's cry, Finnikin's hiss of fury. The captain's fists were clenched tight. Perri was gone from the room before another word was spoken.

"Japhra's staying in Yata's home for the night but insists on returning with Tesadora to the valley tomorrow."

"And the Charynite?" Trevanion asked.

"He's under guard."

The queen looked at Finnikin. Froi saw fear in Isaboe's expression that sickened him. The queen's anxiety about a possible attack from the Charynites had grown tenfold since the birth of her child.

"You go with your father and Perri," she said to Finnikin.

Finnikin looked torn. "The Sarnak ambassador—"

"I'll speak to the Sarnak ambassador," she said.

"No!" Finnikin shouted.

"And what would you prefer?" she asked him sharply. "That I travel up to the mountain and interview a potential Charyn assassin?"

"I'd prefer that Aldron take you and Jasmina back to the palace," Finnikin said. "I'll speak to the ambassador, shorten our meeting and then travel up to the mountain."

"And while you're at it, why don't you plow every field in the kingdom and check the nets in the river?" she said sharply. "Then go up to the Rock quarry and break your back working alongside your kin. And perhaps work in the mines after that."

She was no different from Finnikin. Froi knew everyone in the room wanted to say that. Both the queen and Finnikin refused to believe they had the privilege of palace life, and both could be found at any time working alongside their people during their visits across the kingdom.

"I don't want you dealing with the Sarnaks, Isaboe," Finnikin said. "Don't let me have to imagine how it will feel for you to be in their presence."

"And it feels any different for you?" she cried. "You can't be everywhere at the same time, Finnikin. I will take care of Sarnak. They are no threat to us. You take care of Charyn, and perhaps sometime this week we may be able to pass each other on the road and wave from a distance."

Finnikin sighed, and Froi watched the queen's expression soften.

"This is an attack from the Charynites, my love," she said. "Heed my words. This is the beginning."

CHAPTER 2

Finnikin watched Isaboe from the entrance of the dining hall of the inn where she sat alongside Sir Topher and their ambassador. Standing behind Isaboe was her guard Aldron, and opposite was the ambassador of Sarnak, his scribe and two of his guards.

The atmosphere in the room was strained. The ambassador of Sarnak was used to speaking to Finnikin about matters between the two kingdoms, and Finnikin was used to keeping his wife from having to deal with Sarnak after what she had witnessed there in her fifteenth year.

"Come, Finn," his father said quietly at his shoulder. "Lucian is waiting for us."

Finnikin wanted to stay a moment longer. Isaboe had faced more hostile opponents since she came to power, but this was different.

The Sarnaks waited for her to speak. Finnikin imagined that her silence spoke of an arrogance to the visitors, a sort of play to show who had the power in these negotiations. But he knew what her silence meant.

She looked up and caught his eye. It wasn't magic or curses, this thing that lay between them. It was more profound than that. He couldn't even put it into words, and at times it made him want to walk away and take refuge from the ties that bound them both.

I can do this, he read in her eyes.

You can do anything, he was saying in return. *But I wish you didn't have to.*

"My queen," Sir Topher prodded gently.

She nodded in acknowledgment. "Gentlemen," she began, her voice husky but strong. She had a habit of changing her words moments before a speech. Today seemed like one of those times.

"To be honest, these days I don't know what to say," she continued. "You see, our daughter is almost two years old, and she is speaking up a storm. I know the time will come when she'll ask questions. And I won't know what to tell her.

"When she asks why we don't sleep in the larger chambers of the palace, will I find the words to tell her the most heinous of stories? That thirteen years ago, when I was a child of seven, assassins came into those rooms and murdered my father and my mother and my precious older sisters? She'll want to know how I survived and perhaps I'll have to hide the truth. You see, my brother Balthazar and I were doing the wrong thing that night. The only truth I may be able to tell Jasmina is that her uncle would have been a great king if he had lived beyond his ninth birthday but that he died saving me from the assassins who found us in the Forest of Lumatere."

She stopped, unable to go on.

Look at me, Finnikin begged her with his eyes. *Look at me, and I'll give you the strength.*

"She'll be so sad, Jasmina will be," she continued. "You see, she likes her stories to be magical. At the moment, her favorites are about rabbits that speak and horses with wings that take her across the sky to her favorite friends in the kingdom."

A ghost of a smile appeared on her lips as she looked at the Sarnak ambassador across the table.

"You have a grandson yourself, sir?"

Finnikin watched the ambassador nod.

"They do love their tales of wonder," he said, chuckling.

"But my tale has little such wonder," Isaboe said. "I'll have to tell her that I ran for my life and wasn't there to see the days of the unspeakable that followed, but that her father recorded the events in his *Book of Lumatere,* stories of good people who turned their backs on their neighbors because they needed someone to blame. Stories of how her *pardu,* Trevanion, was accused of treason and sent to a foreign prison, separated from his son, her beloved father, who was no more than nine at the time. She'll weep for her grandfather and for the sorry truth of how he believed that his love, Lady Beatriss of the Flatlands, had died in a filthy dungeon giving birth to their dead child, moments before she was to be burned at the stake."

Finnikin heard the low intake of ragged breath from his father. Hearing his name and that of Beatriss would have told Trevanion enough despite his ignorance of the Sarnak language.

"And then the hardest part will be explaining Lumatere's curse, for curses are not the easiest things to explain to a child: how half the kingdom was trapped inside the walls, while the other half walked the land in exile for ten long years. She'll have to speak to Lady Beatriss to hear the depravity of what took place inside these cursed walls. How the impostor king and his army, trapped by the curse themselves, forced themselves into the beds of our women, hanged the children of men who chose to rebel, and burned our land over and over again."

The ambassador bowed his head. He was a good man.

Finnikin had come to realize that during these last three years of negotiations. But goodness in a man was not enough when it came to appeasing a kingdom that had lost so much.

"Both my king and I will have to tell our daughter what happened to our suffering people who traveled from kingdom to kingdom in exile. Begging for sanctuary."

Her eyes fixed on the ambassador of Sarnak, and Finnikin shuddered at the force of her memory. "Begging *your* kingdom for sanctuary, sir."

Her voice broke.

"Give me the words, Ambassador," Isaboe pleaded. "Give me the words to explain to my child the fate of three hundred of our exiles from her grandfather's village, who had taken refuge on your riverbank. Although I was there to witness it, I still cannot find the words to explain what happens when a king turns his back and allows his people to do as they please. Give me the words to describe the mass grave her father saw at the crossroads of Sendecane. What a fever camp looks like, where bodies are piled onto each other in a pit, as I witnessed in Sorel."

The tears pooled in her eyes, but Finnikin saw triumph in them as well.

"Knowing Jasmina, she'll make me repeat over and over again the story of her father climbing a rock to find me at land's end," she continued, her dark gaze looking over the ambassador's shoulder and fastening on Finnikin.

"But I know which part she'll love best. That despite all the horror our people had to endure, we found a way. How her father and I and this good man who sits by my side traveled the land searching for the captain and his Guard and my Mont cousins. How Beatriss of the Flatlands and Tesadora of the Forest Dwellers found a means from within the kingdom to lead us home and reunite our people."

There was silence, until Finnikin heard the ambassador of Sarnak clear his throat.

"We need each other, Your Majesty," he implored. "Has my king not expressed his sorrow enough? The silence between our kingdoms has gone on for too long. Let us unite and fight a more cunning enemy."

She leaned forward. "Do not bring me apologies from your king, sir. Bring me the news that the men who slaughtered my unarmed people on that riverbank have been brought to justice."

She stood, her eyes never leaving the ambassador. "Do me that honor, sir, so that one day the princess of Lumatere may befriend the grandson of the Sarnak ambassador who convinced his king that great men make amends for wronging their neighbors."

Finnikin felt his father's hand on his shoulder. He must have made a sound, for Isaboe looked up again.

Go, he read in her eyes.

Finnikin turned and walked away.

Outside, as they mounted their horses alongside Lucian and his Mont cousins, Finnikin explained what had been spoken between Isaboe and the Sarnak ambassador.

"We might have to make do with nothing more than an apology," Trevanion said quietly. "If what happened on the mountain is an attack from Charyn, we may need the Sarnaks now more than ever."

Finnikin shook his head. "We've worked too long and hard for this," he said. "She'll not weaken on the matter. Mark my words. I know Isaboe. She will not give in until the Sarnaks give her what we want."

CHAPTER 3

The Charynite was slight in build, but most Charynites Froi had seen were. His hair was worn long to the shoulders, and although he appeared to be older than Finnikin, it was hard to determine his age. His face was bruised and bleeding, and Froi knew from one of the Monts that the beating had come from Tesadora of the Forest Dwellers, tiny as she was, who now stood beside Perri with savagery in her eyes.

The wife that Lucian had sent back stood before them, trembling. She was small and plumpish with a sweet round face.

"My kinsman does not understand why you require me here, sir," Phaedra said quietly, looking up at Lucian, her face reddening.

"We speak Lumateran," Lucian said. "You speak for us. Understood?"

Meanwhile Trevanion crouched down close in front of the Charynite prisoner, studying the man with an unnerving intensity.

"Ask him the reason for the attack," Trevanion ordered Phaedra, not taking his eyes from the Charynite.

Trevanion's Charyn was weakest of everyone's in the room;

Perri's a little stronger. Finnikin had insisted that they learn the Charyn tongue if they were to travel into the enemy kingdom to kill the king. Some days, Finnikin insisted that they speak nothing but Charyn for practice, although both Finnikin and Froi would become frustrated at how slowly they were forced to speak.

Phaedra repeated the question.

Froi saw the movement in the Charynite's throat, the swallowing of fear. Nevertheless, he stared Trevanion in the eye.

"Because I had requested more than once to speak to the queen . . . or her king, and I was refused time and time again."

Phaedra translated the words.

"So you take a dagger to Japhra's throat?" Lucian asked in Charyn, forgetting his vow to speak only Lumateran.

The Charynite tilted his head to the side, looking beyond Trevanion to where Finnikin stood. "Well, it worked, did it not?"

Froi snarled, but didn't realize he had done so aloud until the man looked toward him with little fear and a slight expression of . . . Was it satisfaction? It was a long moment before the prisoner looked away.

"We don't need the girl," the Charynite said quietly, indicating Phaedra. "Most of you can understand me clearly. True?" He looked from Froi to Lucian and then finally to Finnikin. "There aren't too many men in this part of the land with hair that color, Your Majesty," he said. "And everyone knows the Lumateran queen and her consort speak the language of every kingdom in this land."

Finnikin stood coldly silent.

"Ask the girl to leave," the Charynite repeated.

"We make the demands," Lucian said. "Not you."

"Ask her to leave," the Charynite said tiredly. "For if she

hears what I say, my men will have to kill her, and they are scholars, not killers. They hate the sight of blood."

Despite the regret in the man's voice, Froi knew he spoke the truth.

Lucian called out to one of the Mont guards. "Get her out of here," he ordered. "Have one of the cousins take her down to the valley." Lucian turned his attention to the girl. "Return to your father's house, Phaedra. Once and for all. If I see you in the valley, I'll drag you back to your province myself!"

The girl walked to the entrance of the cell, turning to look at the Charynite hesitantly.

"Go," the man said gently. "You've risked enough, Little Sparrow, and we are grateful indeed."

Lucian bared his teeth. The Charynite gave a small humorless laugh as Phaedra left the cell.

"Foolish of you to have let her leave your spousal bed, Mont. If she had been given the chance, Phaedra of Alonso would have been the first step to peace."

"What makes you think we're after peace with Charynites?" Lucian asked.

"Because Japhra of the Flatlands speaks of it in her sleep."

Tesadora hissed with fury. "Don't speak her name again, or you'll be choking on your own blood."

"Japhra's a woman with worth beyond your imagining," he continued as if Tesadora had not threatened his life. But Froi saw moisture gather on the Charynite's brow and knew that Trevanion's close proximity and Tesadora's presence unsettled him more than he would care to admit.

"Some women learn to listen better when they speak little." The Charynite's eyes fixed on Finnikin again. "Did you not learn that from your queen in her mute days?"

Finnikin finally spoke. "You are pushing my patience,

Charynite, and if you make one more reference to our women, including my queen, I will beg a dagger from my kinsmen and slice you from ear to ear. So speak."

The Charynite kept his focus on Finnikin.

"My name is Rafuel from the Charynite province of Sebastabol. I'm here in the valley with seven other men." He waited a moment for Lucian to translate. Rafuel met Trevanion's stare. "I have a way of getting you into the palace, gentlemen. To do both our kingdoms a great justice.

"To kill the king of Charyn."

Froi could sense that the others were as stunned as he was to hear the words, but there was little reaction.

"And why would we trust you, Charynite?" Finnikin asked.

"Because we have something in common, Your Majesty."

"We have nothing in common."

"Not even a curse?" Rafuel said calmly.

"Sagra!" Froi muttered. Another godsforsaken curse.

Rafuel's eyes met Froi's again.

"Our curse was first," Rafuel of Sebastabol said.

"Really?" Finnikin asked, sarcasm lacing his words. "Was it worse than ours?"

Rafuel sighed sadly. "If we sit and compare, Your Majesty, perhaps I may win, but we will all be left with very little in the end."

Finnikin pushed past his father and grabbed the man to his feet, his teeth gritted. "How could you possibly win? My queen suffers with this curse."

"And so does her king, I hear."

The Charynite had the power of saying so much in the most even of tones.

"Did you not notice anything peculiar when you passed through Charyn during your exile?" the Charynite continued.

Finnikin regained his composure and shoved the man away.

"I passed through Charyn three times only. The first was when I was ten and visited the palace with Sir Topher, the queen's First Man. We were consigned to one chamber and spoke to no one. The second time was three years ago when we were searching for exiles and I can't recall a friendly chat from a Charynite back then either. And the third time, a group of your soldiers took forty of our people hostage on the Osterian border and beat up our boy," he said, pointing back to Froi.

"*Your* boy?" the Charynite questioned, his eyes meeting Froi's. "Are you sure of that?"

Tesadora flew at him, but Perri held her back.

"Why does he still breathe?" she demanded. "It's simple. Snap his neck."

Rafuel was staring at her, almost in wonder. "That's the Charyn Serker in you, Tesadora of the Forest Dwellers."

This time Perri let her go, and Froi watched Tesadora throw herself at the Charynite, her fingers clawing his face. Froi had heard stories of her half-Charyn blood, but no one dared speak of it. Perri waited a moment or two, enough time for her to draw more blood. Only then did he calmly step forward to pull her away. Froi felt an instant regret that it was over so soon. Somehow he was always drawn to darkness, and no one in the room had a darker core than Tesadora.

Rafuel continued as if his face weren't bleeding. "It is forbidden for a Charynite to speak to outsiders. Such a rule gets in the way of a 'friendly chat.'"

"Why forbidden?" Lucian asked. "What have your people to hide that we don't already know of you?"

Rafuel gave a small humorless laugh. "I could fill a chronicle of what you don't know about us, Mont. But I leave such things to Phaedra, who writes of the arrival of our people on your land with a fairer hand than I ever will." Rafuel of Sebastabol turned to Tesadora. "I see you writing your chronicles from time to time, too. Have you not noticed anything strange about the valley? All those people, hundreds of them?"

Trevanion asked for a translation. Rafuel was speaking too fast.

They turned to Tesadora, whose cold blue eyes looked even more sinister.

"What is it?" Finnikin asked her.

Tesadora shook her head. Perri let go of her arm, and for the briefest moment Froi saw her lean against him. He knew they were lovers despite a savage history between them, but like Tesadora's Charyn blood, no one spoke of it.

"There are no children," Tesadora guessed quietly. Lucian repeated the words in Charyn, and they all looked to Rafuel for confirmation. Rafuel nodded.

"Where are they?" Finnikin asked, stunned.

"They're all grown up," Rafuel said.

Finnikin advanced toward him again with frustration. "I'd prefer not to have to guess, Charynite. If you've gone to all the trouble to get me up this mountain, then make it clear to us. Speak to us as if we are as ignorant as a Charynite."

Something in Rafuel's expression flickered. "We're not all ignorant, Your Majesty," he said coldly, "and I don't know how to make it clearer to you. Our women are barren. Our men, seedless. A child has not been born to Charyn for eighteen years."

Again there was a stupefied silence as they tried to grasp Rafuel's words. Froi caught the confused look that passed between Finnikin and Trevanion.

The Charynite turned to Lucian. "It is probably yet another thing that shames Phaedra," he said. "That she believes you spoke the truth when you called her worthless all those times."

"You seem to know too much about my wife," Lucian said, fury in his tone.

"Last I heard, you denounced her as your wife," Rafuel of Sebastabol said. "So one would presume you forfeit the right to be indignant about my knowledge of her feelings."

Froi marveled at this fool's lack of fear.

"That first time I visited with Sir Topher," Finnikin said, his voice full of disbelief, "I remember children in the streets. There was one in the palace as well."

"If you were ten at the time, the youngest child in Charyn would have been six," Rafuel said. "Her Royal Highness, Princess Quintana," he added.

"I never met her," Finnikin said.

The Charynite took a deep ragged breath. "It's where the story of the curse begins. With her birth."

"We're not here for a story," Finnikin said, frustrated. "Go back to the part where you get us into the palace without betraying us."

"I want to hear what he has to say," Tesadora said flatly. "More important, your wife will want to, my lord," she said, turning to Finnikin with slight mockery in her expression.

"I thought you wanted him dead a moment ago," Finnikin said.

There was little love lost between Tesadora and Finnikin. Froi put it down to jealousy. The queen shared a bond with Tesadora, and Finnikin was envious of anyone who had a bond with the queen. Froi knew that more than anyone.

Finnikin turned to the Charynite. "Then tell us a story, Rafuel of Sebastabol, and make it quick."

Rafuel kept his eyes on Trevanion. "Could you perhaps ask your father to step back, Your Highness? I'm a small man and it's not as if he can't snap me in two from the other side of the cell."

"He's more comfortable where he is," Finnikin said.

Rafuel sighed. "The year before the birth of Quintana, the oracle's godshouse was attacked and the priestlings were murdered," he began. "The oracle queen survived, but her tongue and fingers were cut off. So she could not speak or write the truth. A young priestling named Arjuro of Abroi was absent from the godshouse on the night of the attack and was charged with assisting the murderers."

Finnikin quickly translated.

"Your priest-king is your spiritual leader, but the oracle of Charyn was more than that for us. Since the beginning of life in Charyn, most decisions made by the king and the provinces had to be sanctioned by the oracle. The oracle and the godshouse were Charyn's moral and intellectual beacons." Rafuel's eyes flashed with fervor. "You're a scholar, I hear. Then you've not seen anything until you've seen the books once translated by our priestlings. They will take your breath away, Your Highness."

"I have seen ancient books, you know," Finnikin said defensively. "In the Osterian palace. I spent more than a summer there."

Rafuel made a rude sound. "Osteria? A more tedious race of people I've never come across. I can imagine their translations. You know what we say in Charyn? That man learned to snore by being in the presence of an Osterian."

Froi could see that Finnikin was trying to hold back a smile. Finnikin and Isaboe's favorite pastime was outdoing each other with insults about the Osterians.

"But everything changed nineteen years ago," Rafuel continued. "The *provincaro* of Serker died, and his successor refused to pay taxes to the palace. The Serkers claimed that the palace was robbing them blind. The king, in turn, stationed his army outside

Serker. It was a step toward a war in which Charynites would kill Charynites, and the oracle's greatest fear was that the other provinces would take sides in such a war. The oracle ordered the king to remove his army from outside Serker, and she ordered the *provincaro* of Serker to pay his taxes to the king and swear allegiance. If not, she threatened to remove the oracle's godshouse from the Citavita and the sacred library from Serker. You could not imagine a bigger insult to the capital or to Serker.

"That spring, the oracle's godshouse in the capital was attacked, and we lost the brightest young minds of our kingdom when the priestlings were slaughtered. They were young men and women trained to be physicians, educators, philosophers. They died unarmed and savagely. On that day, every priest, priestess, and order went underground and have stayed there."

"Mercy," Finnikin said.

Froi knew that Finnikin was a lover of books and history and stories. It was Finnikin who had written the chronicles of their kingdom in his *Book of Lumatere,* which was now being added to with the stories recorded by Tesadora and Lady Beatriss. When Finnikin stayed silent, Froi translated the words.

"The palace blamed Serker," Rafuel continued. "As punishment for the godshouse slaughter, the king of Charyn razed the province to the ground. It sits in the center of Charyn and has been a wasteland ever since."

"What about the people?" Lucian asked. "Where did they go?"

"How many Forest Dwellers do you have left after the Charynite invasion?" Rafuel asked.

Froi saw the stunned look on Finnikin's face.

"No Charynite has ever claimed that the five days of the unspeakable were part of a Charyn invasion," Finnikin said huskily.

"The palace has never claimed it," Rafuel corrected quietly. "But what took place in Lumatere thirteen years ago is Charyn's shame. Mothers wept for the sons forced into the army that was sent into your kingdom alongside the man you call the impostor king. Now a generation of last-born sons weep for the stories they have heard of what their fathers did."

Rafuel's eyes met Finnikin's. "Silence is not just about secrecy, Your Majesty. It is grief and it is shame."

No one spoke. No Lumateran wanted to see worth in a Charynite. Especially not a Charynite who had taken a dagger to one of their women.

"Fifty-four," Tesadora said.

The others turned to her.

"Fifty-four Forest Dwellers were known to survive the days of the unspeakable."

Rafuel was pensive. "The number of those who survived the Serker massacre nineteen years ago is even more heartbreaking. We know there to be one for certain. The king's Serker whore. She lived in the palace at the time of the attack and is the mother of the princess, Quintana."

"The rest?" Lucian asked.

"He had them slaughtered."

"His own people?" Finnikin asked, stunned.

"Hundreds upon hundreds of them," Rafuel said. "Although there are rumors that a handful survived and have spent all this time hiding in the underground cities."

Rafuel looked bitter. "Most of Charyn sanctioned it. They wanted revenge for what took place in the oracle's godshouse. But others believed that it was the palace behind the slaughter of the priestlings. Regardless, after the carnage in the godshouse, the king took the oracle queen into the palace to protect her. Or so he claimed. It put him in good favor with the people, who were inconsolable about what had happened to their goddess of the natural world. But nine months later, on the day the king's Serker whore gave birth to Quintana of Charyn, the oracle queen threw herself out of her palace chamber into the *gravina* below."

"*Gravina?*" Finnikin asked.

"Ravine," Froi responded without thinking. The priest-king's education had been thorough, and when it came to the languages of Charyn and Sarnak, Froi was the stronger speaker, although in Finnikin and Isaboe's presence, he always pretended that he wasn't. He felt both Rafuel and Finnikin's stare and looked away.

"We don't know what took place first," Rafuel said. "The birth of the princess or the death of the oracle, but from that moment on, the fertility of the land ended."

"I don't understand. How does childbirth just end one day?" Lucian asked.

"On that day, every woman who carried a child in her belly . . ." The Charynite swallowed hard, unable to finish the thought.

Lucian, engrossed in what Rafuel had to say, shook his head with frustration. "What? What happened?"

"Can someone translate?" Trevanion snapped.

Finnikin cleared his throat and there was emotion in his voice as he repeated Rafuel's words. "On that day, every woman who carried a child in her belly . . ."

"They bled the child from their loins," Tesadora said, her voice low and pained. Perri stared at her as though someone had punched him in the gut. Tesadora took a ragged breath. "I need to see to that fool girl, Japhra."

Rafuel looked up. "Tell her—"

"Don't!" Tesadora said through clenched teeth. "You keep away from her."

A moment later, she was gone. Too many things were happening that Froi didn't understand.

"Go on," Lucian ordered Rafuel.

"When Quintana of Charyn was six years old, the first sign was said to appear, written on her chamber walls in her own blood: *The last will make the first*. The words were written in godspeak. No one but the gods' blessed is gifted with godspeak. Then on the thirteenth day of weeping—which is what we call her birthday—the king decreed that every last-born girl in the kingdom was to be marked."

"Marked?" Lucian asked, horrified.

Rafuel pointed to the back of his neck, the shackles around his wrist clattering.

"Quintana of Charyn was born with strange lettering scorched onto the nape of her neck."

"But why mark the last borns at thirteen and not at birth?" Finnikin asked.

"Why do you think?" Rafuel asked. "At thirteen, the girls were of child-bearing age."

Froi was relieved that Tesadora was out of the room for that piece of information.

"Quintana of Charyn also claimed that she was the chosen vessel after her thirteenth birthday. And that only she was meant to carry the *first* in her belly. A boy child. A king and curse breaker fathered by her betrothed, Tariq."

"At thirteen? Betrothed?" Lucian asked with disgust.

"Your *yata* was betrothed at fourteen, Lucian," Finnikin said.

"Quintana claimed that the birth of the child would take place before she came of age and if any other male dared to break the curse with a last-born female, the goddess of fertility would set Charyn alight."

"She's obviously mad," Finnikin said. "And those who believe her are just as mad."

"As mad as a queen who claims she can walk the sleep of her people?" Rafuel said boldly. "As mad as those who believe her?"

An intake of furious breath sounded off the walls. Lucian grabbed the Charynite just as Froi was about to fly across the room and land a fist to his jaw.

Finnikin stayed calm as he walked toward Rafuel of Sebastabol.

"I'd really like to know what took place, Charynite, and I'd hate to have to kill you before that moment. So perhaps you can refrain from bringing up my queen."

Rafuel of Sebastabol had the good sense to look contrite. After a while, he nodded. "Next month Quintana of Charyn comes of age. The last-born male from the province of Sebastabol will travel to the Citavita, the capital, and he will bed the princess in an attempt to plant the seed. One last born from each of the provinces has done so for the last three years. Before that, it was her betrothed, Tariq. But when Quintana was fifteen, he was smuggled out of the palace by his mother's kin after his father mysteriously died. He is the king's cousin and only male heir."

"Are they gifted, the last borns?" Lucian asked.

Rafuel was amused by the question. "They are actually quite . . . useless. They were precious to us and some were spoiled as children and others stifled. Most fathers feared the worst for their sons and they were kept out of harm's way. It's hard to find a last-born male who can use a weapon or ride a horse. The daughters are confined to the home. Some are the most frivolous girls you will ever meet, while others are the most timid and shy. I would say most of their kin are about to send them underground for fear of what will take place when the princess comes of age."

Finnikin rubbed his eyes, shaking his head. After a moment he said, "A sad tale, Charynite, but I still don't understand why you're here."

"Because you have a lad who speaks our language, who is of the same age as a last born, and who is not so useless. More important, he is trained as an assassin." Rafuel's eyes caught Froi's. "Yes?"

No one spoke. Froi stiffened, his eyes locked with the Charynite's. Froi could see that the man was hiding something. He had been trained to notice the signs.

"Gentlemen, your kingdom or mine could not have asked for a more perfect weapon to rid ourselves of this most base of kings. Your lad from the Flatlands is our only hope."

CHAPTER 4

In Isaboe and Finnikin's private chamber, away from the prying eyes of their people and the world of their court that forced them to be polite and restrained, they spoke of Charyn and Froi and Rafuel of Sebastabol and curses and last borns and Sarnak, and then Charyn again and taxes and empty Flatland villages, and then Charyn again. When all that talk was over, they stood before each other ready for the mightiest of battles, which they had saved until last.

Finnikin would describe the situation as tense. Isaboe didn't describe situations. She described how she was feeling during the situation. Then they would argue about what was less important. Facts or feelings. Tonight it was about both.

"How do you expect to rule a kingdom and be so weak in this matter?" he said, trying to keep censure out of his tone. He saw her face twitch at the mention of the word *weak*.

"Not now," she said. "Another day. Perhaps next week."

"And then perhaps the week after that and then the week after that," he suggested with little humor.

He saw the pain flash across her face.

"Do it, Isaboe. You must show strength!" Finnikin could see

her softening, and he nodded. "Now," he urged in a whisper.

Isaboe took a ragged breath before crouching to the floor. Finnikin knelt down beside her. Their daughter looked from one to the other. She had Finnikin's face and Isaboe's hair, and now that she was nearing the age of two, she was showing some of Trevanion's temperament, which was beginning to alarm both of her parents.

"Jasmina, my beloved. Finnikin and I . . ."

Isaboe's eyes met Finnikin's and he nodded at her with encouragement.

"We've had the most beautiful of beds made for you. So beautiful that every little girl in the whole of our kingdom wants to sleep in it. Tonight we thought you could sleep in the most *beautiful* bed in Lumatere, and Finnikin and Isaboe could sleep on their own. Together."

Together. Finnikin smiled at Isaboe. He was proud of his queen. Proud of them both. Jasmina meant everything to them, and he couldn't imagine their lives without this blessing. He did imagine frequently, however, sharing a bed with *just* his wife while their little blessing was asleep in another room.

Their daughter stared from Finnikin to Isaboe. He beamed at her, his shoulders relaxing for the first time in days.

Jasmina's bottom lip began to tremble.

"Do you think she's going to be smarter than us?" he asked as they lay in bed later that night. He could see the moon through the balconette doors before them, looking almost close enough to grab, and as usual, it made him wonder about all things strange and mysterious. And about how insignificant he was in the scheme of things.

Finnikin turned to see Isaboe bending to kiss Jasmina's brow as she slept between them. "Most probably," she murmured.

"Then she won't need us one day."

"What a thing to say, Finnikin," Isaboe said, "when I feel a need for my father and mother now, more than I ever have."

"True enough," he said gently. "It may have to do with such attachments belonging to women," he added.

When Finnikin added words, he always regretted it. He was regretting it now because the flames from the fireplace illuminated his wife's stare of disbelief.

"Your father lives in the chamber beside us, Finnikin. You speak to him every night and every morning, and if for some reason you can't sleep through the night, you speak to him then as well. Do you not see that as an attachment?"

She waited for his response, and he chose not to reply because then they'd get into a discussion about why Trevanion had not announced his betrothment to Beatriss yet, which would lead back to a discussion about empty Flatland villages. Then they would both fall asleep thinking of neighborless Flatlanders and Finnikin would wake up in the dark, despairing for his kingdom. Not able to get back to sleep, he'd knock on his father's door, because Trevanion didn't sleep either, and then Isaboe would win this argument.

"True enough," he said with a sigh. He could see her mind was already elsewhere and he knew exactly where.

"Sleep and don't think about it," he said. He was sick and tired of the subject of Charyn.

"How can I not?" she asked. "Barren wombs and curses. If you ask me, they've poisoned all their children."

"If only you did believe that, then we could kill the Charynite in the mountain and banish those in the valley and not send Froi into the unknown."

Isaboe turned to face him. "But you must think it's all strange?"

"Isaboe," he said, exasperated. "Unbeknownst to us, our neighboring kingdom has not birthed a child for eighteen years. How can I not think it strange?"

She placed a finger to her lips as a sign for him to lower his voice. "I know you," she whispered. "I know you're trying to find reason where there is no place for it."

"Reason failed halfway down that mountain," he said. "I think Rafuel of Sebastabol speaks sincerely."

"Then you seriously want me to consider this plan for Froi?"

"I don't think we will ever get into that fortress any other way," he said.

"It's too perfect," she said. "We want the king dead. They want the king dead. They need an assassin who is of age and speaks Charyn. We have an assassin who is of age and speaks Charyn."

She looked at him, pained. "How would they have known?" she whispered. "Do you think we have Charyn spies in Lumatere?"

They had spoken often of spies in the early days after the curse was lifted. Exiles had entered the kingdom with nothing to vouch for the fact that they were indeed Lumateran. Anyone could have been a spy. They both knew that there was still a lack of trust between those who had been trapped inside and the exiles. Regardless of the years of progress, it would be some time before their kingdom was back to what it once was.

Finnikin sighed and reached over to blow out the candle, and they lay silent, listening to Jasmina's breathing.

"I hate them," she said moments later. "It hurts to hate this much, but I do. I want them all dead, especially everyone in that cursed palace. I think of that abomination of a princess, and I want her dead as much as her father. Because I want to lie down to sleep and not imagine them coming over our mountain and annihilating my *yata* and Mont cousins first. I don't want to imagine them clearing the Flatlands, turning our river into a bloodbath, storming your Rock village. I want to stop thinking of them coming through the castle doors and doing to our daughter what they did to my sisters and my mother and father."

He felt her breath on him as she leaned close.

"Promise me, my love. Promise me that if they come through the palace doors and there's no hope, you do what you have to do. You make it quick for her so she doesn't suffer."

Finnikin swallowed hard. He remembered the first time he was forced to make Isaboe such a heinous promise as Jasmina suckled from her breast.

"Let's not talk of these things, Isaboe."

He gathered them both to him, and he felt her lips against the back of his hand. At times like this, he ached for her, but sometimes there was more between them than their daughter.

"I've never spoken of this," she said quietly in the dark, "but when we lost Froi in Sprie that first time, I didn't return for the ruby ring he stole from me. It was as if I was sent there to search for him."

Finnikin was quiet. He had always felt threatened by the bond between Isaboe and Froi. They shared a desperation to survive, and there was a feralness and a darkness about them that he envied fiercely, though he was frightened by what this might mean.

"I've questioned the intentions of the goddess these past three years, and she has whispered to me over and over again, *'You will lose him.'*" He felt Isaboe shudder. "I have a bad feeling about this, Finnikin."

He leaned over and kissed her. "And I have a bad feeling that I'll never have a moment on my own with you again," he murmured. He heard a sound coming from Jasmina, and he lay back down on his side again.

"Tomorrow," she whispered, "between me seeing the

Flatland lords about the cistern system and you placating the fishmongers about the taxes, I think we may be close to the guest closet on the third landing before I have to go off and speak to the ambassador about Belegonia and you have to speak to Beatriss about Sennington." She paused. "We'll have time."

He sighed. "So I'm reduced to taking my wife up against a wall in a palace closet?"

She chuckled in the dark.

"And why do I have to speak to Beatriss?" he asked with a groan. "I'd rather speak to the ambassador about Belegonia."

"She may not have given birth to you, but Beatriss loved you as a mother in the years she was betrothed to your father, and still does. Perhaps you're the best person to speak to her, or Tesadora if she returns to her senses and comes back up the mountain. Beatriss can't live in that dead village any longer, Finnikin."

He was pensive a moment. "Tesadora reacted strangely to the news of the Charynite. She was not surprised about the curse, and then she left all of a sudden and I could swear it seemed as though she would cry."

"Tesadora doesn't cry."

"And you should have seen Perri's face. He was quiet through our whole journey home."

She sat up and lit the candle by her bedside.

"Why didn't you ask him what was wrong?" she asked, alarmed. "If Tesadora was almost crying and Perri was stranger than usual?"

He shrugged. "What would I have said?"

She made a rude sound.

"*What?*" he asked.

"You men are useless."

Finnikin sighed. "We choose to mind our business and we're useless?"

She shook her head. "Do you know the difference between you and me?"

"An obvious one or not so obvious?"

She ignored the question. "I speak to other women about life and death and what upsets us and what confuses us and what we'd want to change in our lives. And you, my love, talk to men about what the terminology is for this." She made a strange movement with her hands.

"Is that a death blow to the nose?"

She gave him a withering look, blowing out the candle.

"That's harsh, Isaboe. We talk about more than that."

"Such as?"

"Life," he snapped. "Life . . . things. Things to do with life."

"Then have you spoken to your father about when he is going to have a bonding ceremony with Beatriss?"

He sighed.

"Because that's life, Finnikin. The life of two people very dear to me. And I believe your father is going to ruin everything by not speaking of the past. *Still* not talking about it after three years."

"Do they have to talk about the past?" he asked.

"Yes. They were lovers once. She gave birth to his babe, rest that precious soul. Yet they haven't grieved together."

"This is not your concern, Isaboe." He thought for a moment. "Although Trevanion was strangely quiet on the way home. Everyone was strange."

"I'm not just speaking for Beatriss, Finnikin. I'm speaking for Trevanion. He is your father, and in my heart, he is the only father I have. I want him to be happy, and I know that without her, he isn't."

"He's wonderful with Vestie," he said, thinking of Beatriss's daughter, who was born under horrific circumstances during the curse. "He would do anything for her."

"And I commend him for that. I could imagine how hard it would be for him to feel so strongly about another man's child. A tyrant's child. But it's Vestie who will be hurt the most, Finnikin. Find out what you can."

"Ah, so I'm not going to see Beatriss to speak about Sennington. I'm going to speak about my father?"

She pressed her lips against his shoulder.

"I've married the smartest man in Lumatere."

"And I've married the most scheming woman in the whole of the land."

She feigned a haughty sniff, moving away. "If it all seems like a scheme, I may have to withdraw my offer of a tryst in the closet tomorrow."

This time Finnikin chuckled.

"Withdraw the offer and I will dash my head against a stone wall."

CHAPTER 5

Froi took leave from Lord August's village and spent the next week in the mountains with Trevanion and Perri, interrogating the Charynite. Although the Captain hadn't confirmed for certain that Froi was going to Charyn, Froi knew he was there with them for reasons other than his skill with the Charyn language.

"It's one of the best-defended castles in the entire land," Rafuel explained to them, "and it has little to do with the Guard or soldiers and everything to do with the actual stone and structure." The Charynite drew them a picture, and Froi committed it to memory, translating the information to Trevanion and Perri.

"Ask him more about the last borns," Trevanion requested.

"First, there is Quintana of Charyn," Rafuel began when Froi asked. "She was the very last to be born to the entire kingdom on the day of weeping."

"Only her?" Froi asked. "Was there no one else born that day?"

"Then there are those born last to their province," Rafuel continued, ignoring the question. "Grijio of Paladozza and Olivier of Sebastabol, for example, were born to their provinces three days and five days prior to Quintana's birth. Tariq was born to his people a month before Quintana. Satch of Desantos was born last in his province six months before. And every girl born in the same year as Quintana is marked as a last-born."

"Gods," Trevanion muttered. "He better be speaking the truth when he claims those girls have gone to ground."

Froi repeated Trevanion's words. He saw Rafuel's teeth clench.

"Do you Lumaterans believe you protect your women better than we protect ours?" he asked.

"The captain judges Charynite men by the way they treated Lumateran women. His beloved was dragged into the beds of your men time and time again and gave birth during the curse," Froi said.

"Not my men," Rafuel said bitterly. "Mine are peaceful scholars down in that valley. And the Charyn army may have raped. That I won't deny. But it's not only our women who are barren," Rafuel said. "The seed of a Charynite male is useless. Whoever fathered Beatriss of the Flatlands' child is no Charynite."

Froi stared at him, stunned. He looked up at Trevanion and Perri. Through the mere mention of Beatriss's name, they would have comprehended Rafuel's words, regardless of the speed at which Rafuel was speaking. Perri had paled. Worse still, Froi saw the truth on Trevanion's face. The captain already knew. He would have known from the moment Rafuel of Sebastabol revealed the curse days ago.

"Ask him about their gods," Trevanion said, as if nothing had occurred.

Rafuel spent the rest of the day speaking mostly of Charyn customs and their beliefs, their produce and their gods. There were too many gods to learn by heart. In Lumatere, there was Lagrami and Sagrami, one goddess worshipped as two deities for hundreds of years. Even in Sarnak, where Froi had grown up, Sagrami was worshipped. *Sagra,* he grew up cursing. Once or twice the word would slip out in the presence of the queen, who despised the way Froi's Sarnak mentors had butchered the name of the goddess.

"It's sacrilege," she'd say coldly.

Listening to Rafuel now, Froi was intrigued by the idea that at the age of thirteen, Charynites chose the god who would guide them for the rest of their days. Rafuel's was Trist, the god of knowledge. Froi imagined he would choose a warrior god.

From the third day on, Trevanion and Perri whispered between themselves unless Froi had to convey some crucial information to them.

"Are you listening to me?" Rafuel said.

Froi nodded.

"You dip and you taste," Rafuel continued. "Not the way Lumaterans eat." Rafuel did a somewhat rude impersonation of a man hoarding his food to himself and shoveling it down his throat.

"Are you calling us pigs?" Froi asked, watching as Rafuel winced for the tenth time at the formality of Froi's Charyn.

Rafuel thought for a moment and then nodded.

"Actually yes, I am. Piglike."

Froi turned back to Trevanion and Perri, who were discussing the need for longbow training in the Rock village.

"What is it?" Perri asked Froi.

"He said we eat like pigs."

Trevanion and Perri thought about it for a moment and then went back to their conversation.

Sometimes Lucian would join them if he wasn't down in the valley, or quelling a feud or two between the Monts, or settling trade with the Rock elders who wanted a herd of cattle grazing on the mountain in exchange for the quarried stone they supplied for the Mont huts.

"You seem interested in our ways, Mont," Rafuel said the third time Lucian visited.

"Most interested," Lucian said. "Best way to find the weakness of the enemy is to understand their ways."

Rafuel sighed and returned to his explanation about the etiquette of dancing. He stood to demonstrate, the iron shackles clattering around his wrists. "Hips must beckon while arms are in the air. Never lose eye contact with your partner."

Lucian made a snorting sound. "Ridiculous. It will make Froi look like a woman."

Froi growled. "Not dancing with no one," he said in Lumateran.

"It's a seduction, Mont. Not like the dancing of Lumatere and Belegonia, where you stomp as though you're making wine."

Froi turned back to Trevanion and Perri.

"What did he say this time?" Trevanion asked, irritated.

"That we don't know how to dance."

Trevanion and Perri went back to their talk.

The Charynite taught Froi words and phrases the priest-king had failed to pass on. *Horse's arse* was Froi's favorite. *Sheep-swiver,* was another. *Sheep-swiver* or any other type of swiving worked best accompanied by a gesture.

"You speak too formally because you were taught by the holy man," Rafuel accused again and again. "The lad you will be replacing comes from my province of Sebastabol. He was raised on the docks. We're a bit on the crass side, if you ask me. And we don't speak in full sentences. Keep it short and to the point."

"When shall he be traveling from his province?"

"Shall?" Rafuel stared at him. "Are you listening to me, fool? Olivier of Sebastabol can charm. Can provide entertainment. Can irritate. But he can't say words like *shall.*"

"I cannot help sounding as if I have something stuck up my arse," Froi snapped. "Is that crass enough for you?"

Rafuel sighed. Trevanion and Perri looked over at Froi with irritation. They sighed. There would be more sighing done that day.

Most nights, Froi traveled down to the valley with Perri to watch over Tesadora and the three novices who had followed her there at the end of winter. Sometimes he would sit alone with her if Perri was out checking the stream for trespassing Charynites. The unspoken rule was that the Charynites stayed on the other side of the stream. Any attempt to cross it would be seen as a threat to Tesadora and her girls.

Froi was used to Tesadora from the early days of the new Lumatere, when she lived in the forest cloisters with the novices and priestess. She was a Forest Dweller, and no group of people had been more shunned in Lumatere. It had been her mother, Seranonna, who cursed the kingdom thirteen years ago as she burned at the stake, but those trapped inside Lumatere had come to respect Tesadora for what she had done to save their young women and help break the curse. She was a hard woman who trusted few people, especially men. Lord August always joked that he would be a fool to find himself in a room alone with her. Lady Abian, who had come to love Tesadora dearly these past three years, claimed that if Lord August found himself in a room alone with any woman, he would have his wife to fear.

"It doesn't seem as if they're going to leave any time soon," Froi told Tesadora as they sat high on a rock face, staring across the stream to where the Charynite camp dwellers had set up their homes in caves.

"I just wish they'd go home where they belong and get out of my sight," she said.

Froi stared at her. "You hate them?"

"Despise them."

"Then why are you here? You were happy with the novices in the Cloisters out in the forest."

"I'm not a priestess," she said. "It was only my place to take care of the novices during the curse."

"And this is better?" he asked angrily. "Perri has to travel almost two days to be with you. He's only seeing you every day now because of the Charynite prisoner in the mountains."

"Poor Perri doesn't have to do anything," she said, standing and holding her arms around her body to stop the shivering. Summer was fading, and the mountains and valley were the first to feel the bite of the cold.

Tesadora was tiny for a Lumateran, and her face was shaped differently from the other Forest Dwellers. Her hair had gone white from the terrors she witnessed when she walked the sleep alongside the queen during the ten years of the curse, although she was no older than Lady Beatriss. Sometimes Froi had to stop himself from staring at her. She had a beauty that could weaken men if they weren't already weakened by their fear of her.

"The queen misses you, and so do Lady Beatriss and precious Vestie and Lady Abian. At least in the forest, they were able to see you more often."

She looked at him, the shape of her eyes similar to Froi's. His were hooded and gave an impression of mistrusting the world. They were eyes not born for smiling, but for judging and being judged in return. He wondered often about the similarity. Sometimes he dreamed that Tesadora and Perri had sired him and that one day the truth would be revealed and they'd all celebrate. But then he'd see Tesadora with Lady Beatriss's daughter, Vestie, or even with Princess Jasmina. He'd see the fierce love, and he knew that whatever was said about Tesadora, she would never have forsaken her child.

"There are some things beyond our control, aren't there?" she said.

Froi was surprised to hear her words. Tesadora was controlled by no one.

"Were all the Charynites bad?" he asked quietly, thinking of the many hidden soldiers he'd come across.

She shrugged. "Most. If not bad, they were weak. One or two took a stand. A young soldier and a Charynite traveler found us in the early days and told me that the novices of Lagrami in the palace village were in danger. They helped the novices escape and brought the girls to us. Strange," she murmured. "It was two Charynites who united the cloisters of Sagrami and Lagrami."

She shuddered. "The traveler was imprisoned and they hanged the young soldier for it. In front of the rest of their army. A good deterrent, don't you think? A Charynite never helped a Lumateran again, whether they wanted to or not. Even if they weren't working against their own, they hated to be seen as outcasts. So what one did, the others would follow."

Froi thought of Tesadora's words the next day in the cell. He could not keep the hatred out of his voice. "What would you have done if you were the enemy trapped within the walls of Lumatere?" he asked Rafuel of Sebastabol.

Rafuel gave a humorless laugh. "Does it matter, Froi? What's more important is what would *you* have done?"

That day, Trevanion and Perri had asked for information about the role of the *provincari* in Charyn. Rafuel explained that they were in power until they died and then the people of their province chose either their offspring if the person was desirable, or another.

Froi absently translated, bored by the information. Rafuel droned on about their power within their province and how they differed from the nobility and how they worked hard to keep the palace out of their affairs. But in the middle of his swift lesson, the Charynite caught Froi's eye and slipped in the words, "You don't belong in this kingdom, lad."

Froi was alert in an instant. He looked back to where Trevanion and Perri sat.

"What did he say?" Perri asked.

Froi hesitated. His mouth felt dry and he could hardly speak.

"The *provincari* don't care too much for the king these days," he found himself saying.

Trevanion nodded. "We know. Once you get inside, we'll want you to find out who holds the most power among them. The queen and Finnikin want to know who helped the Charyn king plan the slaughter in our palace."

A Mont guard came to the prison door. Perri and Trevanion stood to speak to him.

Froi turned back to Rafuel. From Trevanion's calm tone, the Charynite knew Froi hadn't repeated his words.

"Why do you travel down into the valley each night?" Rafuel asked with urgency.

Froi didn't respond.

"Do you want to know why I think you're there, Froi?" Rafuel asked, leaning as far forward as he could with the iron bracelets around his hands. "Because blood sings between Charynites far from home. My blood sings to you. The blood of every Charynite in the valley sings to you."

Froi stared at him, fury in his expression. "I'm not a Charynite far from home," he spat. "I'm a Lumateran from over the mountain."

"Why is Tes—the white witch in the valley?" Rafuel asked, looking over Froi's shoulder to see if the men had recognized that he had almost spoken Tesadora's name. But Perri and Trevanion were still speaking to the Mont guard.

Froi thought for a moment. Swallowed hard.

"A worse-tempered woman I've never met, despite her beauty, which makes a man ache regardless of age," Rafuel continued, "but she's in the valley because our blood sings to her. It's out of her control."

Froi shuddered. Rafuel's words were too close to Tesadora's the night before.

"She's half Charynite, is she not?" Rafuel continued. "It's what kept her apart from the other Forest Dwellers when she was a child. Outcast from the outcasts themselves."

Froi's hands were shaking.

Rafuel's eyes shone with excitement. "My men are searching for an assassin to kill the king, Froi. But I'm also searching for the last male child born to the Citavita on the day of the curse and smuggled out of the kingdom. Most say he's a myth. But I know for a fact that he's not."

Froi stared at him, confused.

"Do you know why you seek out the white witch, Froi? Because her blood sings to you. Two Charynites far from home."

Froi's palm flattened itself with great force against the bridge of the Charynite's nose. Trevanion and Perri were on him in an instant, dragging him away from Rafuel, whose face was bloody and swelling. They shoved Froi toward the guard.

"Get him out of here," Trevanion snarled.

The silence Froi experienced as they rode down the mountain was unnerving. He prayed it wouldn't last long, but it wasn't until they reached the foot of the mountain that the captain spoke.

"What were you thinking?" Trevanion demanded, as if it had taken him all that time to quell his fury.

"I wasn't thinking," Froi said.

"He's a prisoner, Froi! He was chained. We're not savages."

Perri's face stayed impassive. "We can't let him go to Charyn, Trevanion. We can't."

Froi leaped off his horse, standing before them both. "You say I'm not ready?" he shouted.

"In might and skill, you are. Here," Perri said, pointing to his head. "No."

"I can imagine explaining ourselves years from now to the less hostile *provincari* of Charyn," Trevanion said. "'Our boy doesn't work well without instruction. He needs to be informed of his bond. Of what is expected of him. Of what is unacceptable. He has little idea how to do that on his own. He lived fourteen years as a savage on the streets of Sprie. Three years in Lumatere has changed many of his ways, but he insists on a bond.'"

"I can do this, Captain. You know that." Froi was begging.

"What if your rage is hard to control, Froi?"

"Count to ten, Captain. And then count to ten again."

"Speak to us your bond."

"Only kill those who are a threat to Lumatere. Make sure the kill is clean. Treat all women as I would the queen. Don't answer back an elder who deserves my respect. Listen with my ears and not my rage. Never act on anger. Never ever disregard an order from you or Perri."

"No spitting at the nobility regardless of what comes out of their mouths," Perri continued.

Froi bristled. "I've never spat at Lord Augie or Lady Abian."

"They're different, Froi," Trevanion said, irritation in his voice. "They've given you a home. There's no doubt that you are protective of those you care for, but it's the way you treat others that causes strife. You spat at Lord Nettice at the Harvest Moon Festival. Grabbed him by the throat and didn't let go until he turned blue."

"I didn't like the way he spoke to Lady Beatriss," Froi said, looking at Trevanion. "How could you not understand that, sir?"

"I'm the captain of the Guard, Froi," Trevanion said. "Do you honestly think it is my place to choke every man who insults those I love?"

"And he insulted the king. Your son, Captain."

"He's the consort, Froi. Not the king. There will be men who will insult Finnikin for the rest of his life. It's what happens when you marry the most powerful woman in the kingdom. But that's no reason to almost choke the life out of a man. A wise man has tolerance for such people. A wise man walks away or finds a means of changing the way they think."

Froi looked away.

"Don't turn away from me when you don't care for the words spoken," Trevanion said through gritted teeth.

Froi counted to ten in his head and turned back. "Sorry, Captain."

Trevanion and Perri exchanged a look. Something passed between them as it always did. They had spent ten out of the last thirteen years apart, yet both men could still speak so much to each other with just one glance.

"You follow the bond that only we speak to you. Not Rafuel of Sebastabol or even the priest-king who may want you to search for the hidden priests of Charyn. You do only what we instruct you now."

Froi nodded, excitement strumming his blood.

"You enter that palace. A place filled with nobility more useless than any you have ever met here. At least in Lumatere they do not rely on the queen to house and feed them. When they speak words that insult you, you keep to your bond and your mouth stays shut. As far as they're concerned, you're a witless idiot from the provinces."

Froi nodded, although he wanted to tell them that according to Rafuel, those from Sebastabol were not witless.

"You make no attachments to any other person and you never involve yourself with the plan of another. There are those living in the king's court who will always search for new blood to give their cause more weight. You do not join forces, even if they are an enemy to our enemy. You work on your own."

"As if I'd be that daft."

Perri made a sound of disbelief and dismounted, pointing a finger at Froi. "He's not ready, Trevanion," he shouted. "He can't even listen without answering back!"

Froi knew the decision could turn against him at any moment. He wanted this kill. He gripped Perri's jacket. "Let me do this for her. Let me prove to you that I'll give my life so the queen and Finnikin can live with peace in their hearts. Please. You know I can do this." He looked at Trevanion. "You know I can, Captain."

Trevanion was softening, Froi could tell.

"Thankfully, because of your bond to the queen, we do not have to remind you that bedding the princess of Charyn is not part of the plan. When it comes to her, you do what you need to do."

Froi wasn't quite sure what Trevanion meant by that, but dared not ask in case his captain thought he was answering back. He nodded all the same. What needs to be done.

"You find a way into the king's chamber. Regardless of the hatred we all feel for him, you make it quick. Make sure he is dead before you leave that room. The moment he stops breathing, you return home. The very moment. Do not look back."

Froi nodded. He looked at Perri, waiting for his blessing.

"Can you do that without causing mayhem?" Perri snapped.

"Have I ever broken my bond to you and the captain?"

"Part of the bond is not to talk back to us!" Perri said, exasperated. "You do that all the time."

"Apart from that," Froi said sheepishly.

Perri grabbed hold of his ear and pulled Froi toward him in an embrace. "You keep safe, Froi. Keep safe and come home to us."

On his final day in Lumatere, Froi said his farewells to Lord August and Lady Abian and their sons, who were the brothers of his heart. He was glad Lady Celie was in Belegonia. She would have cried, and no one enjoyed watching Celie cry.

"Where are you really going, Froi?" Talon asked. He was Lord August's oldest son and shrewd despite his younger years.

"Sarnak," Froi lied. "I'm a messenger for the queen. I know the language well."

It was the story Trevanion had instructed him to use. He looked Lord August squarely in the eye and wondered if he knew the truth. Lord August shared a strong friendship with Trevanion.

"You know where your home is," was all Lord August said before walking away.

Lady Abian kissed his cheek. She said little for once, but he saw tears in her eyes.

"When you return, we will choose that day to celebrate your eighteenth birthday," she said.

He nodded, his throat tightening with emotion. A birthday. What did the Charynite call the day their princess was born? The day of weeping.

"I'll count down the days," he said.

He went to see the priest-king next. The old man was teaching some of the younger Lumaterans in the front garden of his hovel. Froi waited for them to leave, pulling out thistles from the herb patch he had planted for the priest-king that spring. Oregano, garlic, chives, and rosemary were dwarfed by creeping thistles.

"I've told you before, blessed Barakah," Froi said when the youngsters left. "Pull them out the moment you see them, or you'll be slurping the blandest of soup."

"But they're so beautiful in color," the priest-king mused, getting to his feet and straightening his back with a groan.

"And what happened to the chair I made you?" Froi asked, frustrated, looking around at the hovel. When Rafuel spoke of the godshouse of Charyn where the priests and priestlings once lived and learned, Froi could not help comparing it to this shack in a meadow. Once, the priest-king of Lumatere lived in a grand shrine-house in the palace village, but the blessed Barakah claimed to have been another man back then.

"You need to move to a bigger home. Did you know that in Charyn they used to have schools for priestlings, taught by those less powerful than you? They'd learn about the Ancients, become the scribes of the people, learn how to be physicians."

The priest-king chuckled and beckoned Froi to him so that he could lean on his shoulder. "Let's walk a moment or two, lad," he said.

Froi propped up the old man, frustrated by his stubbornness.

"Anyway, I thought you said learning was a waste of time," the priest-king said.

"We don't want the Charynites being better than us."

They walked an overgrown path through the small meadow that looked over the outskirts of Lord August's village. Even if the priest-king agreed to build a larger house, the land surrounding it would be too small to make a proper impression. Froi knew Finnikin's dream, but he usually fell asleep while Finnikin was speaking about it over and over again. Finnikin dreamed of a library filled with the greatest books Lumatere ever saw, in a school where holy men and scholars from Belegonia and Osteria would come to teach as guests. It was the queen's dream as well.

"We're going to lose our smart ones like Celie to Belegonia," she said. "We need a school for them."

Froi felt the priest-king's stare. He knew the time was coming for him to say his good-bye. He didn't want the priest-king asking where and why he was going. Then he'd have to lie again, and this blessed man was the first person to treat Froi as an equal.

"Can you sing me the Song of Lumatere?" Froi asked quietly.

There was a ghost of a smile on the priest-king's face. "I've said it once, and I will say it again: there is a song in your heart, Froi. You must unleash it or you will spend your days in regret."

"I'll sing for no one," Froi said stiffly. "And if you don't want to sing it, you just have to say!"

The priest-king leaned forward and pressed a kiss to Froi's brow. A blessing. "Stay safe, my young friend."

Froi gently placed his hands on the fragile man's arms. "I will see you in less than a fortnight, blessed Barakah, and we'll do something about this garden."

In the palace courtyard, Perri fitted him with scabbards for his daggers and short sword.

"This was made especially for you," he said, placing one of them across Froi's shoulder blades. "A beautiful hide, indeed. Look." Froi saw his own name engraved in the leather, and whether it came from Perri or Trevanion, or the king or queen, it made Froi feel proud. Apart from Isaboe's ruby ring, Froi had never owned anything in his life.

"You mightn't be able to get weapons into the capital, but keep it safe."

Froi looked up and saw Isaboe standing alongside Sir Topher, watching from the parapet. Even from here, he saw sadness in his queen's eyes. A sadness of spirit. He knew Finnikin would be feeling exactly the same.

Later, Finnikin walked with him until they arrived at the gates of the palace village. "Do you ever think of that day with the slave traders of Sorel?" Finnikin asked quietly.

"I think of it all the time," Froi said.

"I was going to kill you," Finnikin said, a catch in his voice. "You were begging me, remember?"

Froi couldn't speak. In his whole existence, it was the only time he had ever lost hope. He would have preferred to die that day rather than be sold as a slave in Sorel. He had counted on Finnikin being accurate with his dagger from a distance. But he had not counted on Isaboe wanting him to live. Not after what he had tried to do to her.

He sensed Finnikin's sadness and didn't want to leave Lumatere with the memory of it.

"Then you both argued." Froi grinned. "About my name."

Finnikin chuckled. "Your mouth was split. I was sure you were calling yourself *Boy*." He feigned a grimace of displeasure. "Did she have to be right?"

"She did have a point. Who'd name a babe a nothing name like *Boy*?"

Froi looked back up to the palace and then at Finnikin. "Why won't she see me? I can't leave without her blessing."

"She's afraid to bid you farewell. You mean everything to us, Froi."

"I do this for you and her. I will do anything for my king and my queen."

Finnikin smiled sadly. "But Isaboe and I are just two people, Froi. You need to want to do it for the kingdom."

Froi saw tears in his king's eyes, and they embraced.

"Kill this beast who has brought so much despair, and come home to us safe, my friend."

* * *

It was Perri who accompanied him to the mountain that night. From there, Froi would travel through the valley and pass the province of Alonso, where he would meet Rafuel's contact. They would travel for days, and at the foot of the ravine outside the capital, they would be introduced to a man named Gargarin of Abroi, who had answered the request of the *provincaro* of Sebastabol to travel to the palace with the last born.

When they began their ascent, Froi heard the beauty of the priest-king's voice across the land, and the song inside Froi that he refused to sing ached to be let loose. What had frightened him most about Rafuel of Sebastabol was that his stories had made Froi's blood dance. They had given him a restlessness. A need to be elsewhere, to search for a part of himself that was lost. But what he feared was that the search to find answers would take him away from this land of light. That once he left, he would never find his way back home.

In the Flatlands of Sennington, Lady Beatriss heard the song and sowed seeds into a dead earth that refused to yield. Her beloved daughter, Vestie, sat on the veranda, waiting for Trevanion, who had kept away these past days. In the distance, she saw two more of her villagers take leave with all their possessions for the more fertile land of their neighbors, and a loneliness and dread gripped Beatriss more fiercely than in those wretched years when the kingdom was torn apart.

In the valley between Lumatere and Alonso, the wife Lucian of the Monts had sent back camped in a cave between her father's province and her husband's mountain. She recorded the names of her people and learned the ways of the Lumateran healers. Most nights her shame burned bright and she longed to return home. But she pledged to herself, and to the goddess she had chosen to be her guide that one day Phaedra of Alonso would be something more than the object of the Monts' ridicule and Alonso's failure.

In the mountains, Lucian stumbled to his empty cottage, his body weighted by the weariness of leading a people who had little respect for him. He wondered what his father would do, if he lived. A fair man, Saro was, who had tried to teach Lucian to see the worth in every man and woman, regardless of whether they were the enemy. But Lucian was not his father, and deep inside of him a desire burned bright each night. A desire to steal away down the mountain and cut the throats of every Charynite who slept in the valley. Including that of the wife he had sent back.

Part Two
The Reginita

CHAPTER 6

Lumatere had always been a feast for Froi's eyes. Even during the years of little rain, it was a contrast of lush green grass and thick rich silt, carpeting the Flatlands and the river villages. But Charyn was a kingdom of rock and very little beauty. Here, the terrain was a rough path of dirt, pocketed with caves and hills of stone. Sometimes the dry landscape was peppered with wildflowers or the mountains of rock were shaped like the ghouls and spirits painted in the *Book of the Ancients* Froi had seen in the priest-king's cottage. Wind holes had been carved out of the caves, and from afar they resembled the sockets of eyes.

Rafuel and the priest-king had instructed Froi that most of the Charynites had migrated to the kingdom from all corners of Skuldenore. The only original inhabitants had been the Serkers, who had now disappeared, although stories existed of underground cities where Serkers and other nomads were in hiding from the king and plotting their revenge.

Stone, stone, rock, stone, and more stone.

Froi met his guide outside the province walls of Alonso, the birthplace of the wife Lucian had sent back. It was a province bursting with unwanted newcomers, a place on the brink of war within its walls. These days it accommodated its desperate neighbors from the smaller provinces all but wiped out by plague and drought. Froi suspected that the *provincaro*'s marriage of his daughter to Lucian had little to do with a promise between two men and more to do with a need to make use of the Lumateran valley.

Apart from the capital, which was known as the Citavita, there were six provinces left in Charyn, each one of them large, powerful, and containing the most fertile land in the kingdom. There were also a handful of mountain tribes or nomads who kept very much to themselves. Rafuel had explained that if a clan chose to stay outside the major walls of a larger province, there was always the threat of the palace riders collecting their young men to be part of the king's army or taking their last-born girls. At least in the provinces, people were protected by the *provincari*, who still had power against the king. The palace's greatest fear was that the *provincari* would unite their armies against the king, but after the annihilation of Serker, no *provincaro* was willing to take that chance.

The guide's name was Zabat from the province of Nebia, east of the capital. He spent much of his time not looking Froi in the eye, which was never a good sign.

"You have a strange name," Froi said as he changed clothing and became Olivier of Sebastabol. The trousers were uncomfortable, tighter than he was used to wearing, and the doublet jacket worse. But he liked his buskin, and he fastened the laces up to his knees, relieved that there was at least one article of clothing that didn't make him feel a fool.

"Strange in what way?" Zabat demanded.

"Different from Rafuel and even the princess Quintana."

"Those of us from Nebia hail from the kingdom of Sorel.

Hundreds of years ago, mind you. You'd think everyone would get over that fact, wouldn't you? We have as much right to Charyn as anyone else."

"And who says you don't?" Froi asked.

"Those from the province of Paladozza," the guide said, seemingly on the defensive. "And anyone from the Citavita. They all came from the kingdom of Sendecane during the time of the Ancients. Just like most of the Lumateran Forest Dwellers and those from the Rock."

"Charynites and Lumaterans don't hail from the same place," Froi scoffed.

"Do you have women named Evestalina? Bartolina? Celestina? Men named Raffio?"

Froi didn't reply.

"All from the same place," Zabat stated flatly. "Nothing changes. Names stay the same. So do traits."

The time Froi enjoyed best was when the terrain was flat enough for a gallop. It meant he didn't have to listen to Zabat's voice drone on and on.

"And really, who put Rafuel in charge? I ask. Does he look like a warrior to you? . . ."

Or when they came across a herd of mountain goats and their bleating drowned out Zabat's voice. But all too soon it would begin again.

"Did he say I was a priestling? Doubt that. What? Do you think they're better than the rest of us because they're gods' touched? Gods' touched." Zabat made a rude sound. "It's all I've heard my whole life. The gods' touched or the last borns. There's always someone more special than us ordinary folk."

Apart from such distractions, there was little around Froi to take his attention away from Zabat's complaining. The world outside the provinces was nothing more than brown tufts of grass and stone. Miles upon miles of land had been either overgrazed or was too far from water to carve out a living. Suddenly he could understand the overcrowded Alonso and the desire for Charynites to keep inside the province's walls.

"And if you ask me . . ."

No, Froi didn't ask him.

"The Serkers were the worst," Zabat continued. "Their people built the first library, as well as the largest amphitheaters in Charyn, so weren't they the greatest in the land in their own eyes? I say it's a good thing that Serker is now in ruins."

Later, Froi dared ask what the shapes in the far distance were. A mistake.

"The province of Jidia," Zabat replied as they began to travel down a ridge that would lead them to yet another mountain of stone.

"Because really, who cares if the Jidians built the first road to the Citavita? Do we have to hear about it for the rest of our lives?"

Froi bit his tongue to stop himself from speaking. Two days with Zabat had taken its toll. Worse still, their trail into the base of the ravine would soon disappear and they would have to leave their horses behind. On foot, Zabat's voice was closer to his ear, so Froi practiced an internal chant taught to him by the priest-king.

"Some people say they see the gods when they perfect this chant," the blessed Barakah once told him. Froi would be grateful enough if the gods chose not to visit but managed to have Zabat's tongue ripped out and fed to the hounds that guarded their realm instead.

When they reached a wall of rock that seemed to go as far as the eye could see, they tethered the horses to be collected on Zabat's return. Froi followed Zabat into a tunnel through the stone, so narrow that he felt the breath robbed from him. That thousands upon thousands of years ago someone had cut their way through this rock seemed unfathomable to Froi. On the other side, he found himself following Zabat into a gorge with a steady stream of water pouring down from the mountain of rock high above. Where they stood, trees and reeds grew along the bank, but surrounding them on both sides loomed granite walls, blocking the light from the sun.

"The base of the *gravina,*" Zabat explained.

Froi peered ahead of him to see how far he could see downstream. Zabat tapped him on the arm and then pointed up.

"The Citavita is up that way."

"You expect me to climb that?"

"Farther downstream, you will still have to travel up, and the path is even more treacherous. It's not as bad as it looks."

This was to be the meeting point with the man they called Gargarin of Abroi. The plan so far had worked as Rafuel had predicted. Rafuel and his men had come across the news weeks before that Gargarin of Abroi, after an eighteen-year absence from the palace, had been granted an audience with the king. Upon hearing the news, Rafuel had sent a message to Gargarin under the guise of the *provincaro* of Sebastabol, asking the king's former architect to escort Sebastabol's beloved last born to the province. The real lad's name was Olivier, and his party would be apprehended and kept prisoner in the rock caves outside his province, where Zabat would ensure their safety. Olivier and his guards would be released unharmed when Froi had done what he was sent to do. As far as Gargarin of Abroi knew, he was doing the *provincaro* a favor and had no inkling that he was accompanying an assassin into the palace.

Farther downstream, Zabat stopped and looked up at the cave dwellings that formed part of the *gravina* wall.

"Hello there," Zabat hollered, dropping his pack to the ground. "Hello, I say again."

Froi heard Zabat's voice echo over and over again throughout the gorge. Wonderful. The gods had found a way of multiplying the idiot's voice.

"Hello there!" Zabat hollered again. And again the echo. *"Hel-lo!"*

"Do you honestly believe I didn't hear you the first time?"

Froi swung around and saw a man stepping out from one of the caves. He had cold blue eyes, stark pale skin, and the blackest of hair. He would have been no older than Trevanion and Perri, but was slight in build and limped, with a staff in his left hand. He wore a coarse gray tunic, which hung on his thin frame, and loose frayed trousers that seemed to have seen better days. His shoes were no more than cowhide tied onto his feet. Rafuel had spoken little of Gargarin of Abroi except to say that he lived as a recluse, preferring his own company. Zabat held out a hand, and Froi prepared to do the same. The priest-king had told Froi of the custom of shaking hands. In Lumatere, men embraced or held up a hand in gesture. In Sarnak, there was a bow of acknowledgment between people. Froi did not understand the shaking of a hand. He had seen it only once or twice in the most polite of circumstances. On his last night in the palace, he had practiced with Finnikin. It ended in an arm wrestle that then had them both rolling around Isaboe's feet as she nursed Jasmina and murmured to the princess about the idiocy of men.

"Sir Gargarin?" Zabat questioned.

"Just Gargarin." The voice was clipped and cool.

"May I present to you Olivier of Sebastabol."

Froi held out a hand as Gargarin of Abroi turned to him. The man flinched, a quick expression of shock on his face. No, not shock. Horror. When Gargarin refused to take his hand, Froi let it fall to his side, biting back fury. He felt studied. Judged. *Remember your bond,* he told himself. *That when you feel rage, you count to ten. You don't spit. You don't pound a fist into the face of the other. Count to ten, Froi.*

"You're from Sebastabol?" Gargarin questioned, disbelief in his voice.

"Yes, sir." Both Zabat and Froi spoke at once. Had they already failed? Froi had imagined they would encounter problems at the hands of the palace riders in the Citavita. Instead, it seemed that this scholar with his cold stare had already seen through them.

"Where are the rest of his guards?" Gargarin asked, indicating Froi with a toss of his head.

"It's just me, sir," Zabat said. "There has been a change in circumstances," he continued firmly. "The *provincaro* of Sebastabol has sent word that I escort Olivier only this far. I'm to return as soon as possible."

"A change indeed," Gargarin said, eyeing them both suspiciously. "Why would a last born be sent into the palace with no guard?"

"These are tense times, sir. The *provincaro* will be visiting the Citavita on the third week of this month for the day of weeping, and he will need his guard."

"Last I heard, the *provincaro* of Sebastabol was unable to travel to the Citavita for the day of weeping, and I've been to Sebastabol enough times to know that the *provincaro* has more than one guard anyway. So what makes you so special, Zabat? Are you gods' touched?"

Froi groaned. Another woeful tirade from his guide was sure to take place.

"Olivier has a good understanding of swordplay," Zabat

said. "And, frankly, I don't think one has to be gods' touched to be able to do everything these days. I've managed to get as far as I have without a talent to my name."

Gargarin of Abroi stared at Froi. Zabat was already dismissed.

"No last born has a good understanding of swordplay," Gargarin bit out. "The last borns have been taught to keep out of harm's way for no other reason but that Charyn cannot afford to lose them."

"I would like to think of myself as unique among lads," Froi said.

Too formal, idiot, he told himself.

There was no reply from Gargarin. Just the same penetrating stare.

"We camp the night and leave at first light," Gargarin said, walking back into the cave. "And if for some fool reason you are carrying weapons, heed my warning. They won't let you past that drawbridge with so much as a toothpick."

Froi made sure to keep his distance from the man who would act as Olivier of Sebastabol's chaperone. He set up his bedroll outside, despite the cold night, preferring to sleep away from the others. When Zabat disappeared, off to relieve himself by the sounds and smell of things, Froi climbed up the path of stepping stones that would eventually lead to the top of the *gravina.* Close by, he found a large rock, more like a low narrow cave, its outside roof etched with the image of a fan bird. Froi removed the scabbard and short sword from across his shoulder and the two daggers at his sleeve. He took the queen's ruby ring from his pocket but couldn't bear to part with it and so placed it back inside the hidden pouch of his trousers. He crawled on his belly and secured the weapons at the rim of the cave before crawling out again.

When Zabat returned, Froi was already by the stream. "He knows we are lying," Froi whispered. "Can we trust him?"

Zabat looked back at the cave dwelling that Gargarin had disappeared into. "Who knows? Those born with brains think they're above the likes of us."

"I like to think I have a bit of a brain myself," Froi said.

Zabat ignored him. "Gargarin of Abroi was not just an architect but one of the king's advisers in the palace at the time of the godshouse attack nineteen years past. I don't know which way he is aligned, but it doesn't matter. He can get you into the palace."

"What else do you know about him? Rafuel didn't go into much detail," Froi said.

"All I know is that at the age of sixteen he was palace-bound at the same time that his priestling brother was godshouse-bound. He was considered a genius, and at the age of twenty-five, he disappeared and has not been seen in these parts for the past eighteen years."

"Why did he leave if he was so precious to the king?"

Zabat was silent for a moment. "His brother was the priestling arrested for treason and imprisoned after the oracle godshouse slaughter. Some say that Gargarin of Abroi was ashamed of his brother's actions. They say he left the Citavita because he felt himself unworthy of the king's respect. Whatever the reason, he was considered a traitor to the palace. Only now has he been allowed to return."

"And what do others say? Others such as Rafuel?"

"Who knows what Rafuel believes?" Zabat muttered. "There is much he doesn't tell us."

Froi knew he was going to receive another tirade of self-pity.

"I need more than that," Froi snapped.

Zabat shook his head, refusing to respond. Froi stepped

closer, threateningly. "If you're going to send me with him to do Charyn's dirty work, then have the decency to tell me what he's capable of!"

"He's a hermit. Refuses to align himself to the provinces. But they all want Gargarin."

"They all want *him*?" Froi asked with disbelief. "A cripple?"

"Every single *provincaro* in this land. He's designed waterways and was the architect of a cistern system in the province of Paladozza that helped them during the years of no rain. He knows the history of this kingdom and this land better than any priestling. Stranger still is the fact that he is not gods' touched."

"How is it that he's not aligned to a province?"

"He was born in Abroi. A place that no province will claim as theirs. It's a wretched village between Paladozza and Sebastabol. The people there have been breeding with each other for so long because no one else will have them. A favorite saying in the kingdom is that a sheep turd has more intelligence. The only things of worth that Abroi has ever produced are the twin brothers Arjuro and Gargarin. One was gods' touched, the other an architect. Inseparable for the first half of their lives, enemies ever since."

Froi couldn't help but shudder each time he heard the word *Abroi*. After what Rafuel had said to him, was it too much of a coincidence that Froi's name shared the same sound as a Charyn backwater?

"I've heard that the names of Charyn men rhyme with the place they were born," he lied, fishing for some sort of truth.

Zabat made a rude sound again. "Are you a fool? Do we look like Osterians? They need to rhyme everything so they can remember which goatherd village they come from. Karlo from Sumario. Florence from Torence. Tinker from Stinker."

"You're making that up," Froi scoffed. "There's no such place as Stinker."

"What would you know?"

"The Sarnaks are worse," Froi said, relieved that he was no Froi from Abroi. "They like to blend two names into one."

Zabat looked at him questioningly.

"Jocasto from Sprie?" Froi tried.

Zabat thought for a moment. Shook his head.

"Casprie," Froi responded.

"Ridiculous."

Froi tried not to agree. It had taken him years to work out the strange logic of Sarnak name games.

"Lester of Haybon?" Froi continued. "Go on. You'll never guess." He enjoyed the look of stupidity on Zabat's face as he tried to work it out.

"Straybon," Froi explained.

Zabat scowled. "Give me another. I'm beginning to see the pattern."

"Ah, yes, a pattern." Froi lied this time. "What if our man Straybon was from the town Fletcher? The Sarnaks wouldn't want to waste three words ordering a bow and arrow, would they?"

Zabat was lost, his face twisting as he tried to work out the puzzle.

"Stretcher," Froi announced.

Zabat shook his head with disbelief. Froi nodded, solemnly.

"He's making a fool of you," they heard a voice say behind them.

Froi leaped to his feet. Gargarin of Abroi's eyes were drawn to where Froi's hand had reached for a weapon that was no longer there. Their eyes met for a moment before the man limped toward the stream.

"Do you believe his priestling brother betrayed the oracle to the Serkers?" Froi asked quietly, watching Gargarin.

"It's dangerous to believe otherwise," Zabat muttered.

Early the next morning, Zabat woke him.

"It's time for me to go," he said.

Froi yawned, thrilled to be leaving him behind.

"Are you clear on the instructions, Lumateran?" Zabat whispered.

Froi nodded.

"In Rafuel's letter, he says that your captain has reassured him that the kills will be clean. We're not savages. But it's important they are dead."

Froi was suddenly confused. He sat up, his back aching. He tried to clear his head from sleep. "*They?* You mean *him,* the king."

Zabat cast his eyes down.

"And her."

"And who?" Froi snapped. "Who is *her*?"

When Zabat didn't answer, Froi snarled ferociously enough for the man to step back.

"The king's spawn," Zabat said.

Froi stared at the man. "The princess Quintana?"

"You are squeamish about killing a woman?"

"It's not part of my bond."

"She's to die," Zabat whispered. "She cursed the kingdom."

"I said it's not in my bond," Froi said firmly.

"Then you misunderstood your bond. Do you honestly believe your queen wants Quintana the whore to live? After what her father, the king, ordered thirteen years ago, when he sent those assassins into Lumatere."

Froi thought of Trevanion's words. Not to bed the princess, but to do what was to be done. Is this what he had meant?

"Rafuel said nothing of—"

"There are many who agree that Rafuel does not give orders," Zabat said.

They both turned at the sound of Gargarin of Abroi shuffling out of his cave house.

Zabat held up a hand in a wave. "I'm off now, Sir Gargarin," Zabat called out.

"Devastating, to say the least," Gargarin muttered, looking up at the gray sky.

Zabat stared back down at Froi. "I will say it again, lad. You misunderstood your bond. Your queen and her consort want Quintana the curse maker dead."

CHAPTER 7

It took almost two days to climb the ravine to what was called Upper Charyn. It had taken longer because Froi was slowed down by Gargarin of Abroi's limp and half-dead arm. Most of the time, Froi would reach higher ground and wait, taking in the walls of stone that seemed to close in on him from the opposite side. He understood flatlands. He understood forests and rivers and mountains, even rock villages. What he didn't understand was how anyone would want to live in the base of a ravine, except for the purpose of fishing in a stream. But, then again, as he watched this half-crippled man tackle the climb, Froi was beginning to suspect that Gargarin of Abroi was no ordinary sane man.

The path up the *gravina* was marked with surprises. Stones that infrequently became steps to their destination would disappear into a backbreaking climb. Near the top, at its steepest point, Froi gripped a ledge and held a hand out to Gargarin, yanking him up by the cloth of his undershirt, dragging him over the jagged stone until they both lay facedown, catching their breath.

"You tore my shirt, idiot," Gargarin muttered, wincing from pain, his dark hair matted to his forehead.

"Pity. Never seen a finer piece of woven cloth," Froi said, gasping.

When he stood, Froi was breathless to see the great depth they had left below. Up so high, the jagged walls of the *gravina* looked unrelentingly cruel and there seemed nothing to soften the grayness of the stone. But somehow Froi saw a beauty to it that was different from the monotony of the flatland that now spread before him. At least caves and gorges brought an aspect of intrigue. Here in Upper Charyn, he was back in a world of unrelenting tufts of dull-brown grass, gnawed to its edges by overgrazing such as he had seen on the road from Alonso.

He watched Gargarin hobble to the side of the road and feel the dry earth in his hands. Moments later, Gargarin stood and threw the dirt to the ground in anger.

"Idiots," he muttered. "*Idiots*."

It was the only word Froi would hear for the rest of the day. They traveled in silence, and Froi's dislike for Gargarin of Abroi increased with every step the man stumbled.

That night, they set up camp under a star-speckled sky, one that Froi felt he could almost reach out and touch. He'd not seen anything like it since his time with Finnikin, Isaboe, Trevanion and Sir Topher in the grasslands of Yutlind Sud. With Gargarin of Abroi sitting silently before him, he missed those moments of their journey more than ever.

"Do you think it was the Serkers?" he asked Gargarin abruptly when the silence almost forced him to break his bond and strangle his companion.

Gargarin looked up. Through the flickering flames, Froi could see there was no question in Gargarin's eyes. He knew exactly what Froi was asking—whether it was the Serkers who had killed the oracle queen and priestlings. He merely looked annoyed.

"You're bored, are you?" Gargarin asked. "You don't have Zabat to play word games with, so now you're going to riddle me about the past?"

"Actually I am bored and it's not a riddle," Froi said. "It's a question I have every right to ask if I'm going to travel to the Citavita and break a curse that began with the Serkers."

Perhaps Gargarin of Abroi was bored as well, because he chose to respond.

"Pick a province that the rest of Charyn despised because of their arrogance, and use them as the scapegoats. Every kingdom needs a scapegoat for one reason or another. The Yuts have their southerners, and the Lumaterans had their Forest Dwellers."

Froi flinched to hear his homeland named.

"The Forest Dwellers were murdered by . . . the man they refer to as the impostor king, the way I hear it," he muttered.

"Because the Lumaterans allowed it to happen," Gargarin said flatly.

"If you say the Serkers are scapegoats, then you're implying that the Serkers were not capable of brutality?" Froi said.

"I'm not implying that at all."

"The *provincari* say—"

"The *provincari* will believe anything that will keep their provinces safe," Gargarin interrupted coldly. "Why would they want to believe anything else but that the Serkers murdered the priestlings and tortured the oracle? What's the alternative? Believing the attack came from the palace?"

"They're dangerous words you speak, Sir Gargarin," Froi said.

"Truth is dangerous and I'm not a 'sir.'"

The next morning, they continued on the path that ran alongside the edge of the ravine. The walls of it had widened until Froi could barely see the other side. He felt as though he and Gargarin were the only two people left in the land, that at any moment they would topple off the edge of their world, never to be seen again.

Throughout the day, he tried again and again to make conversation with Gargarin, but the man refused to speak.

"Did I do something to displease you in another life?" he finally asked.

Gargarin continued walking. When Froi reached out and gripped his arm, Gargarin swung around, breaking free viciously and stumbling. Froi went to grab him, and they both toppled to the ground. As they lay there a moment, Froi felt the man's eyes bore into his. *I know you,* the stare seemed to say. *I know the evil of your core.*

"I don't care what you think of me, cripple!" Froi said. "I answer to a more powerful bond. To people I respect."

"A bond? Men with bonds are controlled by the expectations of others," Gargarin said, his cold tone cutting. "Men with bonds are slaves."

Froi jumped to his feet, counting again and again. "Be assured that once inside the palace, I won't breathe in your direction," he snarled.

"Good to hear," Gargarin said, struggling to stand. "Because my promise to your *provincaro* was that I would only escort you into the palace. I've given enough to this kingdom."

The road to the capital dipped and rose and then dipped, and when it rose again, the Citavita appeared before them across a long narrow timber bridge. As Rafuel had promised, the walls of the ravine came into view again, mightier in height than Froi had seen on their journey so far. They traveled across the bridge of the Citavita, with its planks swinging and swaying. Through the mist, Froi saw a tower of uneven rock in the distance, but as they traveled closer, he realized that he was looking at a cluster of dwellings carved out of the stone, perched atop each other precariously, as if about to spiral into the chasm below.

Against the dirt-colored capital was the white of the castle. Froi saw turrets higher than any he had ever seen before. But looming even higher over the castle battlements was another rock.

"What is that?" Froi asked.

"The oracle's godshouse," Gargarin responded.

"What's keeping it from toppling down?" Froi asked, trying not to sound aghast, but aghast all the same.

He heard Gargarin of Abroi's ragged breath. "That would be the gods."

After they stepped off the bridge and onto the more solid ground of the Citavita, they began the steep climb on a winding road that wrapped around the rock of dwellings. Froi couldn't tell where one home began and another ended and realized that the roofs of the houses were the actual path to the palace.

Lining the winding path, people worked silently selling their wares, but it was clusters of men, their heads bent low in whispers, their eyes promising malevolence and spite, that Froi noticed the most. These men were no different from the thugs he had answered to on the streets of the Sarnak capital. In Sarnak, these men had, in turn, answered to no one. Froi could tell that the Citavita's street thugs were armed and he could have pointed out every concealed weapon. He itched for his own.

When they finally stood in front of the castle gates, he understood why no one had ever entered uninvited. Isaboe's castle in Lumatere was built to provide a home to the royal family. It was only recently that Finnikin and Sir Topher had sat with Trevanion and an architect from the Lumateran Rock village to discuss the extra security measures required for their young family and their kingdom.

But this castle was built for defense. Froi stared up at the soldiers, their weapons trained on them. The soldiers stared down at him. Up close, he could see that the castle was built on its own rock, a fraction higher and separate from the rest of the Citavita. Although it was a narrow space between the portcullis and where they stood, there was no moat surrounding it. Instead there was a drop into the *gravina* separating them, which seemed to go on forever. Rafuel had given him a strange description of how the *gravina* narrowed in a serpentine fashion past the palace and godshouse of the Citavita.

"Gargarin of Abroi?" a voice rang out toward them.

Gargarin raised his hand in acknowledgment. The drawbridge began to descend across the space, stopping where Froi and Gargarin stood. Once on the bridge, it was a short but steep climb to the gate. On each side, a thick braided rope provided a place to grip firmly. Gargarin's staff fell to the steel beneath their feet, and he struggled once, then twice, to retrieve it.

Waiting for them at the gate stood a man of Gargarin's years, his hair longish around the ears, his mottled skin covered with a coarse, fair beard. He was all forced smile and Froi caught a gleam of pleasure in his eyes as Gargarin continued to struggle for his staff.

Froi picked it up instead.

"Put your arm around my shoulder," Froi ordered, and for the first time since they had met, Gargarin didn't argue. Froi wondered what it did to a man of Gargarin's age to be hobbling like an old man.

"Welcome back, Abroi's Gargarin," the man at the portcullis greeted. There was mockery in the way he spoke the words. Froi remembered what Zabat had said. That Abroi had produced nothing of worth but Gargarin and his brother, the priestling. Perhaps this man's words were a reminder to Gargarin of where he came from.

"May I present to you, Olivier, last born of Sebastabol. Olivier, Bestiano of Nebia, the king's First Adviser."

Froi held out a hand. But Bestiano's attention was already drawn back to Gargarin. Last borns seemed insignificant to the king's adviser.

"The king wept when I told him the news, Gargarin. That the brilliant one who left us too soon is back in our midst."

"When one hears there is a price on their head, they tend to feel quite uninvited," Gargarin said politely.

Bestiano made a scoffing sound. "You exaggerate."

Gargarin held up the scrolls. "I come bearing gifts. Perhaps my way of buying forgiveness for my long absence."

"Only you would consider words on parchment a gift," Bestiano said smoothly. "Eighteen years is a long time. You may have to offer him your firstborn if you truly want his forgiveness. Or your brother."

Froi watched Gargarin stumble, saw the flicker of emotion on his face.

"Then it's true that he has returned to these parts?" Gargarin asked flatly. They entered the barbican and, up above, Froi saw at least ten soldiers standing beside the murder holes, just as Rafuel had described. On the ground, four soldiers approached and searched them thoroughly. Froi noticed that they were more careful with Gargarin. They studied his staff and patted his entire body.

"I could bend over if you prefer," Gargarin said, his voice cool, staring at one of the men. "Perhaps you weren't thorough enough."

Froi was beginning to feel better about Gargarin. The man seemed to dislike everyone, not just him.

Bestiano led them into a bustling courtyard, past the barracks where soldiers trained with practice swords. Two men carrying large vats pushed past them and disappeared into a doorway to their left. Froi imagined it must lead to the cellar, according to the sketches Rafuel had shown him in Lumatere. There was bellowing from kitchen staff—between the cook and one of the serving girls by the sounds of things—and when Froi wasn't competing with servants for space, or tripping over the young man sweeping the courtyard grounds and the not-so-young page handing Bestiano a message, he found himself surrounded by livestock.

"Your brother took up residence in the oracle's godshouse a year ago and refuses to meet with the king," Bestiano said, watching Gargarin closely. "It is the king's greatest desire that there be peace between the palace and the godshouse after all this time. It's what the people of the Citavita want."

"What's stopping you or the king from entering the godshouse and dragging my brother out? It's not as though you haven't done it before."

It was a taunt, and despite Froi's short hostile history with Gargarin, he was intrigued.

"Let's just say that the king has become a superstitious man and our only surviving priestling is not to be touched. The king is frightened of consequences from the gods."

Gargarin's laugh was humorless. "From what I know of the gods, they seem quite considerate and only send one curse to a kingdom at a time."

Bestiano forced another smile. "From what I know of your brother, no one can irritate the gods more."

Despite the politeness, the tension between the two men was strong. Froi would have liked nothing more than to see where it would take them, but his attention was drawn toward a figure standing half concealed at the entrance of the first tower to their left. Her tangled hair was so long, it seemed to weigh her down, forcing her to raise her head when peering.

Bestiano shushed her away with an irritated hand before turning back to Froi and Gargarin. "It's best that you go to your chamber before dinner."

The king's First Adviser walked away, and they followed a guard into the first tower, where the girl had disappeared. Froi saw her again, looking down from the stairwell, but each time they climbed closer to her, she would turn and disappear.

When they reached the second floor, they followed the guard down a dank narrow corridor until he stopped at the first of two doors.

"Yours," the guard said.

"Mine?" Both Gargarin and Froi said at once, exchanging looks.

"Both of yours."

"Both?"

They stared at each other again. Froi couldn't imagine that his expression was any less horrified than Gargarin's.

"There's been a mistake," Gargarin said patiently.

"No mistake, sir."

Gargarin made no attempt to enter the room. Instead he studied the ornate design of the timber door, a bitter smile on his face.

"What's your name?" he asked the guard.

"Dorcas, sir."

Dorcas would have been around Rafuel's age. He had a look Froi knew only too well. The look that said he understood nothing if it was not spoken as an order.

"Well, Dorcas, I think it's best that you place us in separate chambers, and I'd prefer not to have this one," Gargarin said.

"Not my decision to make, sir."

"Bestiano's idea, I suppose?" Gargarin asked, and Froi heard a quiet fury in the question.

"My orders are to take you to this room, sir. Both of you."

Dorcas walked away, and Froi waited for Gargarin to enter the room.

"Bad memories?" Froi asked.

Gargarin ignored him and finally reached out to open the door. "It's not your place to ask questions that don't concern you. It's your place to do what you've come here to do."

"And what is it, according to Gargarin of Abroi, that I have come to do?"

The cold blue eyes found Froi's. "If you want a demonstration, I would advise you to go down to the stables and watch what the serving girls get up to with the farriers."

Gargarin entered the room, and Froi followed. It was small, with one bed in the center, doors leading outside to a balconette and nothing else. Froi hated being cold and couldn't imagine a guest room in Isaboe's palace without a giant fireplace and rugs warming the chamber. Gargarin poked under the bed with his staff and pulled out a straw trundle mattress.

"You take the bed."

"No, you take the bed," Froi said. "I do have a conscience, you know."

"And I prefer to sleep on the floor," Gargarin snapped. "So plunge that fact into your conscience and allow it to rotate for a while. Until it hurts."

Froi walked to the doors that opened to the balconette. Across the narrow stretch of the *gravina,* the outer wall of the oracle's godshouse tilted toward them.

"Is it that they don't like me or that they don't like you?" Froi called to Gargarin inside.

Beside their own balconette was another that belonged to the room next door. After a moment, the girl with the mass of awful hair stepped out onto it. She peered at Froi, almost within touching distance. Up close she was even stranger looking, and it was with an unabashed manner that she studied him now, and with great curiosity, her brow furrowed. A cleft on her chin was so pronounced, it was as if someone had spent their life pointing out her strangeness. Her hair was a filthy mess almost reaching her waist. It was strawlike in texture, and Froi imagined that if it were washed, it might be described as a darker shade of fair. But for now, it looked dirty, its color almost indescribable.

She squinted at his appraisal. Froi squinted back.

Gargarin appeared beside him and the girl disappeared.

"I'm presuming that was the princess," Froi said. "She's plain enough. What is it with all the twitching? Is she possessed by demons?"

"Lower your voice," Gargarin said sharply.

"Does she know what they think of her out in the provinces?" Froi continued. "That she's a useless empty vessel and that they call her a whore?"

After a moment, the girl peered out from her room again.

"Well, if she didn't before, she certainly does now," Gargarin muttered.

That night, the great hall was set up with three trestle tables joined together to accommodate at least sixty of the king's relatives and advisers. Froi had met most of the advisers, each titled according to their rank.

"Why would you want to be the king's Eighth Adviser?" he said to Gargarin as they were escorted to their chair by the king's Seventh Adviser.

"Once upon a time Bestiano was the king's Tenth Adviser," Gargarin replied. "If you stay long enough, you get rewarded."

"And what were you back then?" Froi asked.

"A fool," Gargarin said flatly. "With a bond."

Froi was placed beside the strange princess, who was dressed in the most hideous pink taffeta dress, bunched up in all the wrong places.

"Good evening, Aunt Mawfa," she called out, her voice indignant where indignance wasn't required. "Good evening, Cousin Robson."

No one responded to her greetings. Most belonged to what Finnikin would have called the vacuous nobility and droned on and on about absolutely nothing worthwhile.

Froi was hungry and before him were steaming platters of roasted peacock, salted fish, pastries stuffed with pigeon meat, and the softest cheese he had ever tasted. He had been warned about the flatbread of Charyn and watched the way the others gathered their food with it.

But what caught his attention was most people's reaction to Gargarin. He seemed to be the man everyone wanted to speak to.

"Interesting talk in Paladozza, Sir Gargarin, of the *provincaro*'s plans to dig up his meadows to capture rain," one man called out from the head of their table.

"Not a 'sir,'" Gargarin corrected, "and not so strange at all. I was disheartened to see the outer regions of the Citavita today. I drew up plans for water catchment here long ago, yet they seemed to have gone astray," he continued, his attention on the king's First Adviser.

"Would you contemplate visiting Jidia to speak to Provincara Orlanda when you leave here?" another asked.

"No, he's to visit Paladozza this winter," a man spoke up from the end of their table. "Is it not what you promised the *provincaro,* Gargarin?"

"Indeed."

Gargarin kept his head down. Something told Froi that Gargarin was making no plans to go anywhere. The talking had caught Bestiano's attention, and he watched Gargarin carefully. Enviously? Was Gargarin a threat to Bestiano's role as the king's First Adviser? Gargarin hardly noticed. Once or twice, Froi caught Gargarin looking at the strange princess Quintana, while the princess blatantly stared in turn at Froi throughout the entire meal, with little apology or bashfulness.

As Rafuel had explained, the Charynites gathered their food with soft breads to soak up the juices and wipe their plates clean. The princess chose to share Froi's plate. Froi liked his food all to himself; it came from years of having to fight for his own. Worse still, the princess made a mess around the dish. Her hair fell into the plate often, and Froi was forced to flick its filthy strands away more than once. She resorted to leaning over to grab pudding from the plate of a whining duke who had called the servant over four times already to fill his cup of ale, complaining in a loud whisper that there was wine as per usual on the other side, but not theirs. When Quintana spilled food for the umpteenth time, the Duke of Who-Cares-Where grabbed his cup and slammed it hard on the table, catching the tips of her fingers. "Beastly child."

Bestiano excused himself from where he sat and walked down to them, tugging the princess by the sleeve of her dress. "Perhaps you can show Olivier to your chamber," he hissed. "Make yourself useful rather than making people sick to their stomach, Quintana."

One of the women tittered, putting a hand on Gargarin's shoulder. "She's no more useful in the bedchamber."

Gargarin moved his shoulder away.

The princess smoothed down the creases in the awful gown and stood, beckoning with a gesture for Froi to follow. Froi stared at the food before him, reluctant to leave it behind.

"Good night to all," she called out. No one looked up except for Gargarin, and the noise of the big hall continued as though she had never spoken.

The princess continued her farewells down the shadowy narrow passageway lit only by one or two fire torches that revealed a guard in every dark crevice.

"Good night, Dorcas."

"Good night, Fekra."

"Good night, Fodor."

Some muttered under their breath. No one responded. But she greeted them all the same.

Froi used the time to take in the various nooks and crannies and count each guard he passed.

When they reached their quarters, Quintana stood at his door and waited. He wondered if she was expecting him to perform tonight.

"I'm very tired," he said. He yawned for effect.

"Do you not have something to tell us, Olivier of Sebastabol?" she asked in an indignant whisper.

He tried to think of what he should say. Was there something Rafuel had left out in his instructions?

"Perhaps tomorrow we can go for a walk down to the Citavita," he said pleasantly. Dismissively. "How about that?"

She shook her head. "We prefer not to leave the palace."

"We?" Froi asked curiously, looking around. "We who?"

After a moment, she pointed to herself.

"What's the worst that can happen if we go for a walk around the Citavita?" he asked.

"We could come across assassins, of course," she said, as though surprised he wouldn't think of such a thing.

"Of course."

She studied his face for a moment.

"How is it that you don't know much, Olivier of Sebastabol?"

He shook his head ruefully. "Exhaustion turns one into a fool." He bowed. "If not a walk around the Citavita tomorrow, then a walk around the palace walls will have to do."

He shut the door on her before she could say another word.

Early the next morning, a sound from outside the room alerted Froi. The mattress below was empty, and from where he lay, he could see out onto the balconette, where the sun had just begun to creep up. There Gargarin stood, staring across the *gravina*. Froi couldn't see much in the poor light, but when he looked across toward the godshouse, he saw the outline of a man on the balconette opposite and suspected it was Gargarin's brother. A moment later, Gargarin turned and hobbled back inside.

As Gargarin stood at the basin and splashed water onto his face, Froi stepped outside, curious about the priestling. He marveled once again at how the godshouse could sit so high on a piece of tilted granite, promising to plunge toward them at any time. Froi began to turn away, but suddenly he felt ice-cold fingers travel down his spine. He swung around, his hand grabbing at the fingers, and saw that it was the princess, leaning over the cast iron of her balconette and reaching toward him, standing on the tip of her toes.

Her stare was cold and it made him flinch, but he saw fear and wonder there, too.

"You are indeed the last born," she said, her tone abrupt. No indignation now. "It's written all over you."

Froi didn't respond. He could only stare at her. It seemed as though he was facing a completely different girl. She had the same dirt-colored hair and eyes, but her stare was savage.

"You'll have to come to our chamber this night," she said.

Froi could have sworn he heard her snarl in disgust at the thought before she turned and disappeared into her room.

"Our?" he questioned, and for the first time since he had left Lumatere, Froi wondered what he had gotten himself into.

The day went from bad to worse. Gargarin of Abroi was in a wretched mood, and they almost came to blows over an ink pot that Froi spilled on the man's papers. Not that it was Froi's fault. If it wasn't Gargarin's staff tripping Froi, it was his scrolls and quills laying everywhere or his muttering filling the small space of their chamber.

"Let's make a pact, Gargarin. I keep completely out of this room today and every second day, and you do the same on the other days."

"What are you waiting for?" Gargarin said, without looking up from his work.

Froi spent the rest of the morning avoiding the princess, who had returned to being the indignant girl who had escorted him to his room the night before. Everywhere Froi turned, the princess was there. Peering. Staring. Squinting. At every corner. From every height. It almost became a game of him watching her watching him.

Later that day, he hovered around the well, which seemed the perfect place for talking rot and finding out vital information from people whose ancestors had spent too much time breeding with each other. The king's very simple cousin, for example, pointed out that the tower Froi could see from where he was standing was the prison and currently held only one prisoner. "The rest of the scum are kept in dungeons close to the bridge of the Citavita," the man explained.

"And the king?" Froi asked.

"We try not to refer to him as scum out loud," the cousin whispered.

"No, I mean, where is he kept?" Froi said.

The king's cousin shrugged. "I've not seen him since the last day of weeping."

Froi looked around hastily, not wanting to be obvious about his scrutiny. There were five towers as well as the keep. He had seen the Duke of Who-Cares-Where walk into the keep and knew for certain that if the man didn't get wine at his table, then there was no possible way he slept in the same compound as the king. So apart from the tower Froi shared with Gargarin and the princess opposite the godshouse, and the prison tower alongside of theirs, that left the third, fourth and fifth towers as possible locations for the man Froi had been sent to assassinate. He knew that if he could get up to one of the battlements, he'd at least have a better view of the entire fortress. But as he excused himself from the king's cousin, he walked into Dorcas.

"Just the person I was looking for," Dorcas said, full of self-importance. "I have a message."

"For me?"

"The banker of Sebastabol is passing through on a visit to Osteria," Dorcas advised. "He would like a word. Apparently your families are acquainted."

Froi's heart began to thump against his chest. Less than a day in the palace and his lie was about to be discovered.

"Did you hear me?" Dorcas asked.

"You mean Sir Roland is here? In the Citavita?"

"Sir Berenson," Dorcas corrected, his eyes narrowing.

"Oh, you mean Sir Berenson the banker, and not Sir Roland the baker?"

"Since when is a baker a 'sir'?" Dorcas asked.

"In my father's eyes, he is," Froi said, nodding emphatically. "'Yes, yes, that man deserves a title,' Father says every time my mother comes home with a loaf."

Dorcas didn't seem interested in stories about bakers. But Dorcas was intent on following instructions.

"He's in Lady Mawfa's sitting room in the third tower," Dorcas said. "Run along."

"The third tower?" Froi asked, eliminating it as the King's residence. He had watched Lady Mawfa the night before whispering gossip to anyone who came close to her. He couldn't imagine the king sharing his residence with such a parrot.

"Are you sure it's not the fourth tower?" Froi tried. "Didn't you say he was visiting the king?"

"I didn't say that at all," Dorcas said, irritated. "And he won't be staying for long, so run along, I say."

Froi had to think fast. Dorcas wasn't moving until he did, and Princess Indignant had just revealed herself from behind the well, beckoning Froi with an impatient hand. Then he heard the tapping of Gargarin's staff and saw the man limping toward the steps of their tower. Froi took his chance.

"The proud fool," he said to Dorcas, clucking his tongue and shaking his head. "I've told him again and again to rest. *Gargarin!*" Froi called out, before running toward him. He reached Gargarin halfway up the steps to their chamber and placed an arm around his waist to assist him, despite the fact that Gargarin neither wanted nor needed help.

"What are you doing?" Gargarin growled, trying to pull

away. They both balanced unsteadily on the spiral steps.

"I'm here, nothing to worry about," reassured Froi loudly, waving Dorcas away as the guard approached, looking slightly concerned.

"Do you need assistance, sir?" Dorcas asked Gargarin.

"Did I ask for it?"

"No, sir," Dorcas said.

Regardless, Froi dragged a fuming Gargarin up the rest of the steps, causing them both to trip forward. Froi turned back to Dorcas, mouthing, *"Too proud,"* rolling his eyes, and shrugging haplessly. "I'll take care of this, Dorcas."

Dorcas watched them for a moment, holding up a hand of acknowledgment to Gargarin, whose teeth were gritted. When Dorcas descended the steps, Gargarin struggled to pull free of Froi with a fury that almost had them both tumbling down.

"Are you an idiot?" Gargarin hissed. "Let go of me *now*."

"You look pale. Let me just get you to our chamber," Froi said. *So I can avoid seeing Sir Berenson the banker,* he added to himself.

"I was born pale! I'll die pale!"

At the top of the steps, Gargarin finally broke free and hobbled away.

"I thought the room was mine for the day," he said as Froi followed him to the chamber.

"A decision I regretted the moment I left the room," Froi said. "I can't bear the idea of you staggering around tomorrow with nowhere to go."

Gargarin stared at him coldly. "A decision I have *not* regretted agreeing to. *Go. Away*."

Froi spent the rest of the day in the stables avoiding the princess, the banker of Sebastabol, and Dorcas. As Gargarin had predicted, he was given a lesson or two by the stable hand and scullery maid about mating, as well as picking up a few choice words that the priest-king hadn't covered when he taught him the language of Charyn.

When he arrived back at his room that night, feeling anything but amorous himself, the princess was standing outside her chamber. Waiting. The cold stare was back.

"You are certain you have nothing to tell the *reginita*?" she asked sharply.

"The who?" he asked.

She thought for a moment, her mouth twisting to the side. It was the strangest type of contemplation he had ever seen. She was waiting for something, and Froi couldn't understand what.

Unimpressed, the princess beckoned him into her room with an arrogant wave of her hand. Her chamber, much like Froi's and Gargarin's, was simple, with a bed in the center and no fireplace in sight.

She began to undo the hooks that fastened her dress.

"Perhaps we started off on the wrong foot," Froi said. "I don't want this week—"

She stopped for a moment. Squinted. "A week? What needs to be done should only take one night."

What needs to be done.

Froi would need more than a night to understand the intricacies of this palace and to do what he was sent to do.

"And here I was becoming so attached to your sweet disposition." He beat his breast with pitiful exaggeration. "If I go tomorrow, I'll never have a chance to know you."

Her brow furrowed, as though she didn't quite comprehend him. Despite it all, he didn't want to be cruel. If he was to do what he was sent to do, he didn't want to feel anything, even hatred or dislike. But he pitied her. The way she spoke about herself as if she was another. The way her court dismissed her. Isaboe of Lumatere was loved. Adored. Isaboe knew who she was even when she took the name Evanjalin for all those years.

"You're not what we expected," she said, and there was disappointment in her voice. "They promised us more."

There was something so strangely matter-of-fact in the way she spoke. Froi fought hard not to react and choked out a laugh.

"They?" he asked. "Bestiano and your father?"

She stepped out of the dress and pulled off her slippers, leaving her in only a white cotton shift that reached her knees.

Froi pulled the shirt over his head, inwardly rehearsing what he would tell her. How his inadequacy prevented him from planting the seed.

She stopped undressing for a moment, confused. "What are you doing?" she asked. "You don't need to remove your shirt." She indicated his trousers, pointing a finger.

This time, Froi sighed and made an exaggerated show of untying the string around his trousers while she lay down, raising her white nightdress to the top of her thighs, but no further.

Froi shucked his trousers and knelt on the bed. *Buy time, Froi,* he told himself. His hand traveled up her legs, his fingers gentle. She pushed them away, and there was that unrelenting stare again.

"Do you not know what to do, fool?"

"I know exactly what to do," he bristled.

"Then be done with it. Hands are not required."

"Should your pleasure not be part of it?"

"Pleasure." She shuddered. "What a strange word to use under such circumstances. We're swiving, fool."

"That's a filthy mouth you have there, Princess."

She caught his eye. "Don't tell me you're a romantic," she said. "What would you like to call it? Making love?"

"I just want to make it easier," he said honestly. "It's not in me to be tender, and I don't want to hurt you."

"I'm not looking for tenderness," she said, turning her head to the side. "Just haste, and if your mouth or fingers come near me again, I'll cut them off."

But Froi could only remember his bond to Isaboe. *You never take a woman if she doesn't invite you to her bed, Froi.* During the years it had changed to, *I'll never bed a woman again, my queen*. He had wanted her to know that the bond came from his free will and not her order. Although this moment with the princess was sanctioned, he felt like a demon.

"I can't continue if it's not what you desire," he said quietly, wanting her to turn back to look at him.

"What has desire to do with it?" she asked, cold fury in her voice. "If you would prefer a moment to conjure up passion, I'll turn my back and you can use your hand on yourself and think of another."

Froi spluttered with disbelief.

He stalled again, placing a hand gently on her thigh, and for a moment he saw wonder in her eyes. Until he realized that the wonder came from whatever lay above him. He twisted his head to see her holding up a hand to make the image of a bird on the shadowed ceiling.

And he knew he couldn't go through with the mating. If he was going to do what he was sent here to do, he couldn't feel pity or compassion or even desire. Not that he felt desire. How could he with this squinting ball of hair? Froi knew what desire felt like. He fought it daily. His bond to Lumatere was to rid them of the enemy, not to bed their abomination, their curse, their despised princess. He regretted not asking Trevanion what he meant by the words, *What needs to be done*. What did he mean for Froi to do to the princess?

"Begin," she said, turning back to look at him, and when he shook his head, she slapped him hard across the face. In an instant he had her body straddled, trapping it between his legs.

"I'm not a whore and nor are you," he hissed, "so don't treat us so. And next time we do this, I'd like a bit more involvement from you, Princess. I don't like to feel as though I'm *swiving* a corpse."

He saw the snarl curl her lips, and the base savage inside of him was excited by the burning malevolence he saw in her eyes. But he leaped out of the bed, pulled on his trousers, and slammed the door behind him.

Bestiano stepped from the shadows. "Is it done?" he asked.

"No. I'll have to return tomorrow."

The next morning, Froi watched a party of men on horseback ride out of the courtyard and prayed the banker from Sebastabol was among them. When he thought he was safe, he ventured to breakfast, starving from having missed out on food the night before.

"Sir Berenson was disappointed to have left without seeing you." Quintana was at his shoulder the moment he walked in. She was wearing the same awful pink dress that she had worn the first time he saw her, and every other time, come to think of it. Froi decided it was either her favorite dress or the only dress she owned. The latter was ridiculous for a royal, so he settled on the former. It was obvious she had bad taste. She was back to being Princess Indignant, all earnestness and incessant talking. It actually relieved him to see her in this mood.

"Sir Berenson left?" he asked, looking around the room for the best candidate to sit beside. Perhaps Lady Mawfa with all her gossip would be helpful to him today. "Already? Without so much as a good-bye?"

"He said he asked for you all night," Quintana said indignantly.

"I searched for him high and low." Froi feigned a hurt expression. "It's always the same," he said, searching for an audience. "Despite being a last born, I will never receive the same respect as my cousin. If I were Vassili, rest assured Sir Berenson would have made the effort to find me."

Froi was placed opposite an elderly cousin of the king, who picked at the dry pieces of skin between his fingers and put them on the table beside Froi. Next to Froi were Gargarin and Quintana, who insisted once again on stealing food from his plate. He slapped her hand away more than once.

"Do you have something to tell us?" she whispered in his ear.

Froi gritted his teeth. He didn't know what part of her he disliked more. The cold viper or this annoyance.

Suddenly he felt Bestiano's attention from the head table. "What are you both whispering about?" the king's First Adviser asked.

Froi pointed to himself questioningly. "I was just wanting to say how becoming the princess looks in that gown. The color is perfect for her complexion," he lied.

Her response was a shocked squint. She tilted her head to the side in confusion, as though contemplating whether Froi's words were a compliment.

"Quintana," Bestiano called out. "One responds to a flattering remark."

The princess seemed wary. "We're not the recipient of many compliments, my lord, so we're unsure about its sincerity."

There was no bite in her tone. Just confusion. Froi realized too late that he had picked the wrong person to play with and was beginning to feel uncomfortable about what he had started.

Gargarin of Abroi kicked him under the table as a warning.

"Say thank you, Quintana!" Bestiano barked.

"We cannot offer thanks because I doubt Olivier's earnestness," she said. There was anxiety in her voice, as though she didn't know what to do under the circumstances.

"Say thank you," Bestiano repeated.

"It's not necessary," Froi said. "It was an attempt at humor between us and—"

"Say. Thank you!"

The room was suddenly quiet. The princess was trembling but shook her head and spoke as though rehearsing a speech. "We only say thanks if we feel gratitude, and the *reginita* does not believe—"

A fist came down on the main table. Froi saw her close her eyes and flinch.

"Enough of the reginita."

Froi watched as Bestiano made his way toward their end of the table. Froi stood to step in the man's way, but Gargarin pulled him back into his seat just as Bestiano dragged Quintana out of her chair by her hair and pushed her out of the room.

"It has a greater effect on morale when the girl takes her meals in her chamber," Froi heard one of the ladies say. The others went back to their breakfast as though the incident had never taken place.

"Are you happy now?" Gargarin asked, quietly furious.

With a shaking hand, Froi picked up his tea and drank.

A little while later, he walked to her chamber, practicing a sincere attempt to make amends. If he wanted to know more about her father's whereabouts, he'd have to try to make things right with her. A part of him also felt guilt. He imagined that Bestiano had the authority to give her a blasting worse than any Froi received from Perri. But when he arrived at her chamber, the door was locked.

"Princess," he said, knocking. "Your Highness. Open up. I know you're in there."

There was no response. Froi entered the chamber he shared with Gargarin, then opened the doors out onto the balconette. It was a short distance between the two chambers and despite the depth of the *gravina,* it was an easy jump. Froi climbed onto the wrought iron of his balconette and leaped, landing comfortably on hers.

He looked inside the room, his hands ready to knock at the glass.

But he recoiled in horror.

Later, when he couldn't get the image out of his mind, he tried to work out what had made him sickest. Was it the way Bestiano would trap her hand in his grip, stopping her from making shapes in the nonexistent shadows over his head? She didn't look as though she was struggling, but there was something dead in her eyes, so unlike the squints and inquisition or the coldness that had followed Froi around since he first stepped foot in the palace.

He turned away, taking deep breaths of air.

Across the *gravina* in the godshouse, he saw someone standing at the window. But a moment later, the man was gone.

CHAPTER 8

What would Lucian's father have done? About Orly's prized bull? And the Mont lads running riot? And the Charynites in the valley? And the wife he sent back? And the fact that everyone in the kingdom had an opinion of what Lucian of the Monts was doing wrong? What would he have done about the loneliness that woke Lucian each day before dawn?

Except this morning, when it was Orly's neighbors who woke Lucian before daybreak to tell him about the bull running riot across the mountain.

"Every night, Lucian. Every single night that blasted idiot of a bull gets out, and if I see it again, I'll kill it," Pascal said when Lucian managed to pull the animal out of Pascal's wife's rose garden.

"You'll do no such thing, Pascal," Lucian said with much patience. "I'll speak to Orly."

Splattered with mud and bleary-eyed, Lucian dragged the bull back to Orly.

"Do you honestly think I wouldn't check and recheck the latch each night, Lucian?" Orly said as they studied the pen to determine how the bull could have escaped. "Do you honestly think this bull stood on his hind legs and unlatched the gate himself? Find the culprit and lock him up with that Charynite, or I'll find him myself and cut off his legs so he'll be running away from me on his stumps."

"You'll do no such thing, Orly," Lucian said, looking from owner to bull. They strongly resembled each other, and Lucian didn't want to cross either of them. He waved to Orly's wife, Lotte, hoping to make a dash for it, but Lotte wanted to stop and talk.

"He's awfully precious about that bull, Lucian," she said with a sniff, as they stood outside the cottage watching Orly sing soothing words to the bull. "He won't even allow my Gert to breed with his Bert. Enough is enough, I tell him."

Gert was Lotte's cow, and Lucian knew this because when both cow and bull went missing they would hear, "*Gert*, Bert, *Gert*, Bert," hollered in a singsong through the mountains at any time of the morning; Lotte's high-pitched *Gert* followed by Orly's grunting *Bert*.

"Honest to our precious goddess, Lucian, if he doesn't change his ways I'm going to pack up my things and go and live with your *yata*."

"You'll do no such thing, Lotte," he said. "Orly wouldn't know what to do without you."

"Fix this, darling boy," Yata said later, handing him a mug of hot tea. "Because if Lotte comes to live with me, I'll pack up my things and move down into the valley with Tesadora and the Charynites."

"You'll do no such thing, Yata."

"You know what I say," Pitts the cobbler said as Lucian handed him a pair of boots to mend. Pitts waited for Lucian's response, and despite the fact that Lucian didn't think a response was required, he responded all the same.

"What do you say, Pitts?"

"I say, it's one of those thieving, stinking, gods-less Charynites down in that valley. Round them up, I say, and I'll fix them all for you."

"I'll do no such thing, Pitts." Lucian sighed. "And I think they have more gods than we can poke a stick at."

Then there was the matter of the lads who snuck down the mountain for half the night and were too tired to work for their ma and fa most the day. Lucian had faced them all that afternoon and tried to look stern.

"We want to keep an eye on Tesadora and the girls," his cousin Jory said. He was fourteen years old this spring, a thick-set lad with a stubborn frown and the leader of the lads.

"And what is it you do down there?" Lucian asked. Jory was his favorite and showed great promise as a fighter.

"Make sure they don't come up here and rape our women because theirs are so ugly," another cousin said, and the lads laughed.

"Men don't rape women because their women are ugly," cousin Jostien said, but there was a protest at his words. "That's what my fa said! He says that inside their hearts and spirits they are nothing but little men who need to feel powerful."

"I'll tell you what else about Charynite men is little," another called out, and they all tried to outdo each other with their boasts about their own big 'swords of honor.'"

There was something about the lads and their words that made Lucian uneasy, but lads were lads and he had walked away, firmly reminding them that work was not going to be done with all of them standing around.

Most days he went to see the Charynite, Rafuel. A calmer man he had never encountered, despite the circumstances of his imprisonment.

"Can I at least have something to read?" the Charynite asked.

"Strangely, we don't have many Charynite books on the

mountain," Lucian said, sarcasm lacing his voice. "And we're not here to make your life more comfortable."

Usually he checked the prisoner's shackles for infection around his wrist and ankle.

"You don't have someone else to do this?" Rafuel asked. "One would think a Mont leader had better things to do."

"A Mont leader does have better things to do," Lucian murmured, not looking up from his task, "but every man and woman on this mountain who volunteers to check your shackles is usually armed with a dagger and my queen is very particular about who gets the pleasure of stringing you up if Froi doesn't return, Charynite."

And then it was late afternoon and the day had passed with nothing really being accomplished. That was Lucian's problem. It's what plagued his thoughts as he traveled to check on Tesadora and the girls. Lucian hadn't spent three years failing. He had spent three years accomplishing nothing.

But the journey down the mountain calmed him, despite his day. As a child, Lucian had traveled with Saro to the closest Charynite province of Alonso no more than three times, but the valley between them had always fascinated him. Lucian caught sight of the gorge below. On the side where the mountain met the stream was woodland and a world that looked easily like Lumatere. But on the other side of the stream was a strange landscape of caves perched high. Thousands of years ago, when there were no such things as kingdoms named Lumatere and Charyn, travelers from Sendecane had settled here and carved their homes out of the granite made soft by rainwater over the ages.

But then for hundreds upon hundreds of years, the valley was uninhabited. The settlers either moved west to Lumatere, or east to Charyn. Because the stream belonged to the mountains, the valley was said to belong to Lumatere, and the boundary between both kingdoms was determined farther downstream, where the water became a trickle.

In the accounts collected by Tesadora and the girls in their chronicles, most of the cave dwellers claimed that they had once belonged to the smaller provinces of Charyn. These provinces had been all but destroyed during the years of drought and plague. Some of the larger provinces had gone as far as building a wall around their region. It was to protect their people from both the king and the threat of being overcrowded by their landless neighbors.

Now here these people were, living off the fish in the stream and supplies sent grudgingly by the province of Alonso and weekly bread sent down from Lumatere. Lucian knew the *provincaro* of Alonso kept these people fed so they wouldn't return to his province and cause him more misery among his people. But he also knew that his father had enjoyed a strange friendship with the *provincaro*. Would he have helped Sol of Alonso in spite of everything?

"What would you have done today, Fa?" Lucian whispered, because sometimes he truly felt his father on this mountain slope. "About Orly and especially the lads? Would you have backhanded them with their talk of rape and women? Or are they just lads being lads?"

Lucian tied up his horse at Tesadora's campsite, where a large tent was pitched between a thicket of trees. If not for the branches, those in the caves would be able to see where Tesadora and her girls slept at night. It made him furious just to think of what the men could do by merely crossing the stream.

He reached the stream and could see the Charynites up in their caves looking down at him suspiciously or lining up to have their details recorded by Tesadora's girls. Farther along,

Phaedra of Alonso was bent over in what looked like a vegetable patch and was speaking to a man and a woman.

"Tell them not to plant their seeds, Phaedra," Lucian barked out. "They're not here to stay, so there's no need for scattering them."

Phaedra and the couple stood up for a moment, and he watched as Phaedra spoke to them. They crouched back down again. Cursing, Lucian crossed the stream, knee-deep in water. When he reached them, Phaedra stood there, cowering as usual.

"Luci-en, this is Cora and her brother Kasabian."

Cora and Kasabian seemed the same age as his father had been when he died.

"Lucian," he corrected with irritation.

Cora gave Phaedra a shove, and Phaedra retrieved a piece of parchment from her sleeve and passed it to Lucian with a trembling hand. He read it, shaking his head.

"You want grain? Why, when we give you bread?"

"We'd like to make our own bread, Lu-cion . . . cien . . . shen." She turned away miserably, and the woman nudged her again. "Yours is strange and round. Ours is flat. And if we could grow our own herbs to make pastes, we'd be most appreciative. Your food is making us ill. All those turnips."

"It's fine for a Mont," he said. "And how many times do I have to say no planting!" he snapped as he watched a number of others squat at the vegetable garden that looked a ridiculous mess anyway. These people knew nothing.

"They're not planting," Phaedra said. "We had set up a number of vegetable patches along this stretch, but . . ."

She stopped a moment.

"But what, Phaedra?" he said. "Speak. It's as though I'm talking to an idiot!"

The man, Kasabian, spoke quietly. Just one word.

"What did you say to me?" Lucian asked, stepping forward and towering over him.

"What I said was, 'Enough,'" Kasabian said quietly. "Enough."

With a withering look, Lucian made sure the man knew who had won this round. He walked away, toward Tesadora and the girls. While two of their companions recorded the names of those standing in line, Tesadora and Japhra beckoned the people to where they could be checked for illness. The Charynites were cautious and looked frightened.

Lucian held out his hand for the Charynite chronicle of names and particulars. He counted two hundred and forty-four people so far, and knew that each day more would arrive, looking haggard and weary, not a smile among them. Most had found a cave and kept to themselves, including Rafuel of Sebastabol's men.

"Does he look suspicious to you?" Lucian asked Tesadora, who was quietly studying the weathered face of an old man who stood before her. Tesadora was said to know the symptoms of almost any ailment by looking in someone's eyes and at their tongue.

"Well, I'm not sure what suspicious looks like," she said bluntly. "Sometimes when you come down the mountain and stand behind those trees, you look suspicious."

"Are you aware these people can almost look into your campsite, Tesadora?" he said. "From up there." He pointed to their caves.

"Almost," she murmured, looking closely into the man's eyes. "But not quite. It's why I chose that particular tree to pitch our tent under at the beginning of summer, so—"

"So you don't trust them, after all," he said, feeling slightly victorious that the stubborn Tesadora was admitting it to him.

She pointed to her mouth and poked out her tongue, and the man in front of her did as she instructed.

"So I wouldn't have to hear you or Perri or Trovanion or anyone else tell me that these people can see into my campsite." She looked at him. "And still you stand here and waste my time."

"What about Rafuel's men?"

"They can't see into my campsite either."

"I mean, have they come out yet?" he said, quickly losing his patience.

"No, and I'm not climbing up to them. If you want to know anything, speak to your little bride. She's quite the popular one in this camp. If she was any more cheerful, she'd make us all ill."

Tesadora turned her attention back to the old man before her.

"Give him a blanket, Japhra," she said quietly. Japhra placed a blanket around the man's shoulders, and he walked away.

"Do you give everyone a blanket?" Lucian asked, watching as Japhra had to almost drag the next woman to Tesadora.

"Just those who are dying," Japhra said when it was obvious that Tesadora had already dismissed him.

Lucian was livid. "If he's contagious, he can't stay in the valley," he hissed.

Tesadora's stare was hard. "The only thing contagious around here at the moment, Lucian, is fear and ignorance. The Charynites are afflicted with one and the Monts with the other."

She waved him away with irritation. He added her to the list. What would his father have done about Tesadora in the valley? Would he have ordered her back to where she belonged, in the Forest of Lumatere? Would he have spoken to Perri and said, "Take care of your woman; she shouldn't be down here among these strange people"?

"It's getting dark," Lucian said to Tesadora. "Finish up what you are doing here and meet me on our side of the stream."

He walked away. "Phaedra!" he barked. Still the idiot girl stood with the brother and sister at the mess of a vegetable patch. She looked up, and Lucian pointed to the other side of the stream. "Now."

Phaedra stood, brushed the dirt from her hands and dress, and walked toward him. Kasabian followed, and Lucian stared at him with irritation.

"Mont," the man called out. "Can we ask?"

"No," Lucian said. "No grain. We hardly have enough for ourselves. I can't promise you anything."

The man shook his head.

"No, lad—"

"And I'm not a lad," Lucian snarled. "I'm the leader of the Monts."

Kasabian took a moment to think and then nodded. "Then you are just the person I need to speak to. As the leader of your people, could you please ask your lads to refrain from stomping through our vegetable patches?"

Lucian looked over Phaedra's shoulder to where a woman joined the sister, Cora, and bent beside her to work.

Kasabian's eyes were stony. "And could you ask your lads to refrain from relieving themselves in the stream? It's your stream, I know, but it is also a stream used by our women. We mean no disrespect because it is probably not an insult to do so in front of your Lumateran women, but to have men relieve themselves in front of a Charynite woman is an insult for us. Your lads frighten our women, Mont leader. All I ask is that you speak to them."

The man's voice was soft, much in the way of Rafuel's. Maybe it was a weapon to speak in such a way. All his life, Lucian had never heard his father raise his voice. He didn't have to.

And because Lucian was shamed, he walked away.

CHAPTER 9

Froi spent the morning with the kitchen staff, who were a chatty lot. They were accepting of his presence among them, and he enjoyed their company, perched on a stool, watching.

"If you weren't a last born, you'd be one of us," a pretty girl with a wicked chuckle told him. She grabbed one of his cheeks with two fingers. "Nothing special about this face, eh?"

"Face don't need to be special," another joked. "What's between his legs has to work its magic."

There was more laughing as they kneaded the dough and hammered at the cheese. Two of the servants walked in with a side of salty bacon on their shoulders.

"The king must be the most grateful man in the world to have such food served to him," Froi said. He had been in the palace for three days and was no closer to working out where the king was hidden.

"Oh, we don't cook for the king," the pretty girl said, popping a piece of pork on Froi's plate. He was enjoying not having to share his food with anyone and wolfed it down hungrily.

"He has his man for that," an older woman said, "and I thank the gods every night of my life, I do. Imagine if something got into his food. Bad enough that we were almost blamed for what happened to Princess Useless."

"Someone tried to poison her?" Froi asked.

"You'd think that if someone was going to try, they'd get it right," another muttered.

It wasn't that Froi found it strange that someone would try to kill the princess, but that the servants spoke about it so openly, without fear of retribution.

"Do you ever see the king?" he asked, wiping his plate clean with a piece of flatbread.

"Saw him last day of weeping. He doesn't come down to the main hall no more. They say he's mistrustful of just about everyone. Except Bestiano."

Froi closed his eyes a moment, wanting to get the image of Bestiano in the princess's chamber out of his head. Suddenly the food he had consumed churned in his stomach.

"You're pale, lad," the older woman said, pushing him along to make room for the grain sacks.

He waved off her concern. "Does no one here refer to it as her birthday?" he asked.

They all stopped working a moment to look at him.

"It was the day we wept," the cook said coldly. "Don't know how you feel about it in the provinces, but here in the Citavita, it's the day of weeping."

Birthdays were the greatest of celebrations in Lumatere. Froi would know. He had never had one, but everyone else drove him insane with suggestions about what to buy the queen or Finnikin or Lord August. He knew that here in Charyn, the day of weeping had some other kind of political importance, however.

The portcullis had been raised more than once that day, to let in a parade of livestock and wooden casks containing the best wine in the region. The pretty servant girl explained that the *provincari* visited each year for the day of weeping, and the king wanted them to be impressed by what the Citavita had to offer the week after next.

"Always thought it would be over by the time she came of age," the cook said quietly. "Work that magic between your legs, lad, or there'll be no Charyn to speak of one day."

On his way back up the tower to his chamber, Froi found Gargarin stooped on the narrow stairwell, his body pressed against the wall. When Gargarin heard his footsteps, he stumbled to his feet, sweat bathing his brow. Only then did Froi notice the blood seeping through his shirt.

"Who did this to you?" Froi demanded, trying to hold him upright in the narrow space. "Was it Bestiano?"

He kept a step above Gargarin to accommodate them both. When they reached the second level, Froi placed his head under the man's shoulders and walked him up to their room. Once inside, Gargarin hobbled to his bed, trying to shuffle through the contents of his pack with one hand while the other held the wound. "It's nothing. A scratch," Gargarin said, his voice weak.

Froi ignored him and forced Gargarin to sit. Slowly Froi peeled the shirt from where the source of the wound seemed to be. He looked up at Gargarin in disbelief. "You don't seem the type to provoke dagger attacks."

Gargarin fumbled through the items in the pack, but Froi pushed aside his hands and reached for a piece of flannel. He went to the water pitcher, dampened the rag, and began to clean the wound.

"Something tells me you've done this before, Olivier of Sebastabol."

"Who, me?" Froi murmured, trying to see how deep the wound was. Gargarin flinched.

"Get up," Froi ordered. Gargarin obeyed. He was in too much pain not to. Froi removed the sheet from the bed and tore strips from it. He ordered Gargarin to sit and began to wind it around his midriff.

"It's not so deep," Froi said.

Gargarin didn't respond.

Froi waited for an explanation, but there was none.

"Tell me who did this," Froi said.

As though nothing had occurred, Gargarin shuffled to the desk and sat down. He untied the ribbon around his manuscript and bent his head to study the pages.

A dismissal. Froi walked to the desk and sat on Gargarin's work, refusing to move.

"What?" Gargarin snapped after a moment.

"You have a wound," Froi said. "Is it such a common occurrence that someone attempted to murder you?"

"Someone's always attempting to murder someone in Charyn," Gargarin muttered. "And if you don't get off my sketches, you'll be next."

Froi stood and retrieved Gargarin's pages, but instead of handing them back, he studied them.

"You draw ditches?" he asked.

He read the word *Alonso* at the top. The sketch showed meadows sprouting ducts of water in different directions.

He stopped himself from commenting. He couldn't let on to Gargarin that Olivier of Sebastabol knew anything about the land, even though Froi was a farmer at heart. More important, he didn't want to have anything in common with this man, except for the chamber they shared.

Froi flicked through the rest. "Is that a garderobe for the

palace? You don't think the king's eighteen advisers are happy enough shitting into the *gravina*?"

Gargarin laughed. It was short but sincere. "There has to be a better way in the Citavita than throwing sewage out on the street to be swept down into the *gravina*," he said.

Froi made himself comfortable on Gargarin's desk. He handed over a sketch of a wheel in water.

"Explain that to me," Froi said.

While Gargarin of Abroi was speaking of capturing rain and of waterwheels, he didn't seem so distant. He was smart; Froi could see that. Although Finnikin and Isaboe and Sir Topher and even Celie of the Flatlands were among the smartest people he had ever met, Gargarin was different. He knew little of other languages and failed in charm. But from the conversations Froi had listened to at dinner, he could see that Gargarin knew the land and the law, and he knew Charyn's history and the agreements between provinces. What Froi had first believed to be a sense of superiority, he had come to understand was awkwardness. Gargarin of Abroi did not like people. He trusted no one and preferred to keep his own company. Regardless, Froi had witnessed those who wanted to gain Gargarin's attention in the great hall and had seen that Bestiano was threatened by this crippled, broken man.

He watched the pencil in Gargarin's twisted grip as the man went back to his scribbling.

"Going to see the princess," Froi said when it was clear their talking was over for the day.

Despite wanting to avoid a repetition of the night before, there was a part of Froi that was desperate to see how she was faring. It wasn't that he cared about her, but he cared that the heinous scene he had witnessed that morning with Bestiano had been prompted by his actions.

"Do you have an aversion to using doors?" Gargarin

muttered as Froi went out to the balconette.

"I have an aversion to Bestiano knowing exactly when I pull down my pants and pull out my—"

"Enough said."

It was quiet in her room. At first he believed it to be empty, but then he heard the breathing. A moment later, he felt an arm around his neck and a dagger to his throat from behind.

"That's the best you can do?" he scoffed. "Point the tip of a dagger under my chin?"

"We thought you were an assassin," she said in the strange indignant voice. He was relieved. He had little time for Quintana when she was in her cold savage mood.

"We?" he looked around.

She pointed to herself.

"And that's how you protect yourself from an assassin?" he demanded, removing the dagger from her hand. "If you really want to be successful, you give yourself five seconds to kill a man. In one second," he said, positioning her before him with her hands on both his shoulders, "you place a knee between the intruder's legs, and with great speed and force you make sure that he is left . . . legless."

"Legless?"

"In so much pain, Princess, that he can hardly hold himself upright."

"Second," he said, placing the dagger in her hand, "you plunge it into the side of his body and twist. Right about here."

"And then," he said, guiding her hand that held the dagger, "to make sure he's dead, you take it from one ear to the other across the throat and you press hard and make sure he's bleeding."

She was contemplating what he said. He could see that from the concentration on her face.

"Think you can do that?" he asked.

For a moment she didn't respond, and then she asked, "Is this part of the plan, Olivier?" There was excitement in her voice.

"I don't know what plan you're talking about," he said.

She looked disappointed for a moment and then nodded with determination.

"You'll have to creep in again," she said. "But not straightaway. The *reginita* needs to be surprised."

"Oh, she's here, is she?" he mocked.

He left the room, climbed onto the wrought-iron trellis, leaped onto his balconette, and returned to where Gargarin was still at his desk.

"It would probably be a good idea if you lay down a while," Froi said. "From what I've heard of dagger wounds, the loss of blood catches up with you."

Gargarin ignored him. Froi was becoming used to it.

A short while later, Froi quietly leaped back onto the princess's balconette and crept inside.

This time when he tiptoed into the room, he felt an arm come around him instantly, the tip of a blade under his chin.

"See, now you're irritating me," he snapped, pushing her away. "Wrong place for the blade! All it will do is make a hole. Did I not tell you that already?"

She refused to look at him. "One more time?" she suggested, her eyes downcast.

"Are you pretending to be meek?" he asked.

She looked up at him, pleased, and nodded. "Did it not work?" she asked in her practical tone.

"No."

"We were trying to impersonate Aunt Mawfa when she looks at Sir Gargarin. We've not seen that look on her face before, so there's been little time to practice."

"You practice being Aunt Mawfa, do you?" he asked.

"Oh, all the time. It's very important for us not to be noticed, and no one notices Aunt Mawfa."

Back in Froi's chamber, Gargarin looked up at him when he entered.

"You're making me dizzy," he muttered.

"That would be the dagger wound. I'm going to insist that you sleep on the bed tonight. I'll take the floor."

The next time Froi crept into the princess's chamber, she had improved slightly and managed to draw blood.

"Again?" he asked. She went to nod and then shook her head.

She walked to the bed and lay down, as she had the night before, and lifted her shift to the top of her thighs. Froi lay beside her, contemplating how many nights he would have to go through this charade.

"You need to be atop of me," she instructed.

Froi sighed and shifted himself closer to her.

"You need to remove your trousers."

Froi thanked her politely for the instruction. The moment his body touched hers, she did as she had the night before. Her hand left her side and reached over his head. Froi twisted away from her to study the shape on the wall. It made him think of Bestiano capturing her hand.

"What is that?" he asked quietly.

"A bird."

He rolled away from her and lay back, staring at the ceiling.

"You can do what you have to do at the same time," she said quietly. "It won't interfere."

She shivered.

He reached over and smoothed her nightdress down past

her thighs and pulled a sheet over their bodies. "Why can't they put a fireplace in here for you?" he asked. "It will only get colder in the weeks to come."

"Bestiano says it will teach me to be strong," was all she said.

"Bestiano needs to be taught a lesson."

She looked surprised by his words and he had to remind himself that he was Olivier of Sebastabol and not Froi of the Exiles.

"Show me how it's done," he said, holding up his hand to the wall, trying to imitate the image she had made.

Quintana made a clicking sound of irritation and reached over to adjust his fingers. "Or else it will look like a rabbit," she said, and he heard exasperation in her voice.

"Oh, we couldn't have that."

He practiced for a moment. "I saw a low cave at the bottom of the *gravina* with the prettiest picture of a fan bird etched on it," he murmured, trying to give his bird a tail like that of a fan.

"Do you want me to show you a bull?" she asked.

"No," he said. "Let me think of how to make one myself."

He looked at his hands in the shadows and thought for a moment, hiding his middle fingers. She reached up and tried to alter them, but he slapped hers away, irritated. He tried another movement. She made a sound of approval. But then a light flickered across the *gravina* and she leaped out of bed, creeping to the window.

"What is it?" he asked, grabbing his trousers and beginning to dress.

She peered out. "It means Gargarin's on the balconette."

From where they stood, Froi couldn't see Gargarin next door, but he saw the dark shape standing at the godshouse balconette across the *gravina*, the priestling illuminated by a lantern he held in his hand.

"It's what the brothers did last night, and you've seen them first thing in the morning. One comes out first and then the other. They don't speak. They haven't for such a long time, you know." She opened the balconette door. Gargarin was exactly where she said he'd be.

"Sir Gargarin, is it true that my mother Lirah took a dagger to your chest today?" she asked, as though it was the most natural thing to ask.

A woman knifed Gargarin. Froi was intrigued and impressed.

"True indeed," Gargarin said.

"Thankfully she missed your heart."

"Many have said it's in the wrong place anyway, so it was a blessing for me," Gargarin said.

"*Poor Lirah.*" Quintana shook her head with dismay. The way she said the words was very dramatic, as though she was in pain.

"Poor Lirah? What about poor Gargarin?" Froi said. "How did this happen?"

"Gargarin went to see my mother, Lirah, who's imprisoned just there across the way," she said, pointing up to the prison tower beside them. "Lirah managed to retrieve a dagger from her guard and plunged it into Gargarin's chest."

Quintana's tone was as matter-of-fact as the one she used to instruct Froi on how to make shadow puppets.

"Never thought you were the type to summon such passion from a woman, Gargarin," Froi said.

But Gargarin wasn't listening, and Froi followed his gaze across the *gravina*.

"Blessed Arjuro!" Quintana called out with a wave, as if greeting a neighbor. "Blessed Arjuro," she called out again, just in case he hadn't heard her holler the first time. Blessed Arjuro was either deaf or rude.

She sighed with disappointment. "I call out to him each

morning, Sir Gargarin, and he gestures with his finger but won't say a word."

"Gestures?"

Quintana imitated what she saw, and Froi laughed.

"That's not a gesture," Gargarin said. "That's just Arjuro."

"He was imprisoned here when I was a child," she explained to them both. "When I was six years old, they took him out of the dungeons and chained him to a leg of my father's table."

"Where is your father?" Froi asked boldly. "I've not seen him at all. An introduction would be most appreciated."

"Some say my father's not even in the palace," she said, nodding at his surprise. "There are assassins everywhere," she added in a whisper, but her attention was back on the priestling, Arjuro.

"Back then, Arjuro was needed to translate the words from the *Book of the Ancients*. My father and Bestiano believed it could break the curse of the last borns. I'd come to visit often in the days they allowed me to see my father." She waved to Arjuro again but was ignored. "I don't think he remembers me, Sir Gargarin."

"I can't imagine him forgetting, Princess," Gargarin said gently.

Froi stared across the *gravina*. If Arjuro of Abroi had been chained to a desk in the king's study, he would know the chamber intimately. He could be the best chance Froi had to get inside. Below where they stood, Froi could see a piece of granite, a natural extension of the stone wall, jutting out from the palace, extending almost halfway across the *gravina,* as though a hand were reaching out to touch the godshouse wall. As dangerous as it looked, Froi knew it wasn't impossible to leap from the granite and catch hold of the trellis opposite. But Froi also knew that he would never be able to attempt such a leap in the dark. He would have to wait for the early morning.

* * *

Back in the princess's chamber, Froi lay down beside her and blew out the candle. "Don't feel much up to anything tonight after all this excitement of Gargarin being knifed by your mother."

"My mother, Lirah," she corrected.

"Yes, that's what I said."

"Then it's best you return to your room. We're not used to waking up with someone in our bed."

Froi thought of Bestiano outside. Was he waiting for Froi to leave so he could enter?

"Might just stay here for a while." Froi knew it would change little. Bestiano would still come to her chamber long after Froi had left the palace.

The princess didn't argue and he heard her shallow breathing and realized that she was asleep.

He woke to a hand splayed across his face and a quiet little snore. He picked up the hand and placed it back on her side of the bed, only to notice a white jagged line across her shoulder. He reached over to touch it, and she flinched, suddenly awake and moving away.

"What happened there?" he asked, trying to ignore the fact that he was facing the mood of Quintana the ice maiden and not Princess Indignant.

Her stare was hard, her eyes no longer a strange brown, but the color of basalt.

"Dagger," she said.

He tried not to show his surprise. "It's a pretty impressive wound. Want to see mine?" He began to pull up his shirt.

She made a face of irritation. "You're not trying to show me something I don't want to see, are you?"

He revealed the scar on his chest that he received the year before when one of the traitors attacked. She stared at it and then shrugged and showed him an even more impressive scar on her upper thigh.

"Clumsy girl," he reproached, reaching out to touch it. She gripped his fingers and twisted them, nearly breaking one.

"Let go or you'll force me to say ouch," he said calmly.

"Not clumsy at all," she said, letting go, and this time she sounded insulted. "Out of the sixteen assassination attempts, only eight managed to leave a scar," she added. "Although I do swear that my hearing hasn't been the same since the ninth assassin hollered, 'Long live Charyn,' in my ear. You'd think that if someone is going to kill you, they'd be quiet about it."

He waited for the laugh to tell him that it was all said in jest. But there was none. The ice maiden did not have a sense of humor.

"Sixteen?"

She showed him the remaining scars quickly, practically, and in the order they were received.

"Were you scared?" he asked some time later, after a pathetic attempt to match his scars with hers had failed. Quintana of Charyn's body was a map of hatred.

This time she stared up at him. "What a question to ask. Of course we were scared, you fool. How can one not be scared facing death?"

Froi saw anguish in her expression.

"It's not in us to be brave. We're not the bitch queen of Lumatere whose people worship her for her bravery. But I'll tell you this, Olivier. If the gods can keep us alive until we birth the curse breaker, then we will die without shame. What is it you called us on Sir Gargarin's balconette? Useless."

He was suddenly uncomfortable at the memory of his cruel words, but he had no idea how to apologize for them without being ripped apart by her stare.

Instead, he leaned on his elbow and looked down at her, not

quite sure how to speak his next words.

"Does . . . Bestiano believe that the last-born male will provide the seed?"

She didn't speak aloud, but he caught a grimace and her lips curled with hatred. *"I'm trying. I'm trying,"* he thought he heard her mutter. It was as though something or someone was in control inside her.

"Or does he believe any man can break the curse?" Froi persisted. "Last born or not?"

He marveled at her resolve not to look away, and his heart began to batter against his chest because there was something so dark in her stare. Froi would always, *always* be drawn to darkness.

"Bestiano is a man," she said, her tone frigid. "And no man we have ever encountered in this palace believes that another can best him."

He ignored the "we."

"So Bestiano believes . . . that perhaps he can sire the first-born if you are indeed the . . ." He shrugged, not knowing the word to use.

"Vessel," she contributed. She studied him.

"We thought you were sent for one purpose," she said, "but now we realize you were sent for another and, as per usual, the gods refuse to give us warning of their plans in advance. So if you are asking me whether I believe the last will make the first, then yes, I do. Now more than any other time. You and I are the last. It's written all over you. It would make matters much easier if you did what you had to do."

"And the other lads?" he asked awkwardly. "Before me."

"What about them?"

"Were they kind?"

She thought for a moment. "Well, you know them all except for the third, from Nebia, but we don't talk about him."

"Why?"

A strange expression crossed her face. "They say he's in a madhouse, you know."

"Because he was frightened by the palace?" Froi asked.

She shook her head. "Not the palace," she said quietly.

Was the insipid last born from Nebia frightened by the princess abomination of Charyn? Froi read it all there in her expression. Not self-pity, but self-loathing. Is that what she thought Froi's reluctance was about?

"I'm not scared," he said, refusing to look away.

"Nor was Tariq." Her expression softened. "He was my betrothed and my first. He was supposed to be the one and only last born to share my bed. His father was my father's heir if a son was not produced, but then Tariq's father died suddenly when we were fifteen and the people on his mother's side smuggled him out of the palace. They suspected someone was trying to poison him."

She gave him a bitter smile.

"That's how a whore was born," she said. "Without Tariq to fulfill the prophecy, you last-born lads of the provinces had to do."

"I know the lads feel that they let you down," he said, not knowing any such thing. Rafuel had mentioned that the last borns were acquainted and corresponded.

"Grijio constantly writes about it," Froi lied, "and Satch goes on and on every time I see him and Tariq—"

"You've seen Tariq?" she asked, surprised.

Froi gave himself a mental beating. Of course, you haven't seen Tariq, you idiot. He's in hiding.

"I'm only imagining what Tariq thinks through his letters . . ."

"To Grij?"

He nodded. "Grij passes on everything Tariq writes. You know what he's like."

"Very discreet, as I remember," she said.

"No one's discreet when it comes to me," he boasted. "I could charm the truth out of the goddess of secrets."

"There's no such thing as the goddess of secrets."

He prayed to the goddess of fools that it was the end of the conversation.

"You're the last of four lads," she said, her eyes piercing into his. "So, yes, Olivier, she does know what they think of her out in the provinces," she added coldly, repeating his words to Gargarin on the balconette.

"Eavesdropping is rude," he said.

She stared and he matched it, refusing to look away.

"I'll make a pledge to you, Princess or Reginita or whoever you choose to be today," he said. "Let's call it a . . . bond. That when you invite me to your bed, for reasons other than a curse or someone else's demands, then perhaps I will—what is it we Charynites like to call it?—plant the seed."

"Tariq and Grij and Satch warned me of you," she said bitterly. "'Everything is a jest to Olivier,' they said. But they promised me a lad of worth. 'You can trust him with all your might, Princess,' they told me."

She shook her head and Froi saw sadness.

"Oh, to go a day in my life not lied to by the gods or so-called friends."

When the sun rose, he wasted no time. The moment Gargarin and his brother completed their morning ritual of staring at each other across the *gravina,* Froi crept out of Quintana's bed.

He climbed over the balconette and grabbed on to the protruding granite, one hand at a time on the ancient stone, his legs dangling. When he reached the end of the stone, he took a moment to survey the distance between himself and Arjuro of

Abroi, who now stood at the balconette of the godshouse, watching. Froi stared into the abyss below and shuddered. Slowly he lifted himself, his mind trying hard to control the shake in his legs until he was standing on the thin piece of granite. Before he could lose his nerve, he leaped across the *gravina* and gripped the ledge at Arjuro of Abroi's feet.

The priestling seized him by the scruff of his neck and pulled him over the latticework of the balconette, and Froi lay there for a moment. When he looked up, he saw Gargarin's face with an unkempt dark beard. It seemed even stranger in contrast to the fair skin both brothers shared.

"I've never seen two men with the same face."

The priestling grabbed Froi's hair and pushed back his head for a closer look. His breath reeked of ale, and Froi could see it had been some time since he had bathed. But before the other man could hide it, Froi saw the same expression of horror he had witnessed on Gargarin's face.

"Where did they find you?" Arjuro of Abroi rasped.

"Depends on who you think I am."

"You're shit from Abroi."

"Charming," Froi muttered. "It's a pleasure meeting you as well."

Arjuro's intense study of Froi was done in silence.

"You know what they say about you over at the palace?" Froi asked slowly, raising himself to his feet, although his heart was still pounding from the leap.

"Couldn't care less what they say about me over at the palace."

"You're a fool to return to the Citavita and dangle yourself in front of the king."

A sinister smile curled Arjuro's lips. "I knew something was coming. Didn't want to miss it for the world." He gave Froi another appraisal before walking inside.

The room was large and rectangular. On the far side was another window that allowed in an abundance of light. Froi had heard it was called the Hall of Illumination and he could understand why. Through its brilliant light, he could see that the walls were covered with strange writing that did not resemble any lettering known to Froi. The black of the ink was a stark contrast to the white of the wall.

In the center of the room was an altar, but apart from a table close to the window facing the palace, the room was bare. Froi imagined that once there would have been many long benches filled with scribbling priestlings awed by the wonder of the Ancients' books. It was in this room that Arjuro cut a lonely figure.

Arjuro sat down and stabbed at a piece of cheese with his dagger. He took a swig of ale from a jug. "What do you want?" The question was followed by a burp.

"Quintana speaks of you fondly, and I just wanted to make your acquaintance."

"Never met her in my life."

"Well, she seems to think you have."

"And she seems to be the maddest girl in Charyn, so who are you going to believe?"

It was where the two men of Abroi differed the most. In the way they spoke. Gargarin was clipped and cold and quiet. Arjuro grunted, barked, growled. Froi found himself understanding Arjuro better than his brother.

He studied Arjuro's face, fascinated. It was Gargarin, but not Gargarin.

"Staring's rude," Arjuro said.

"So is speaking with your mouth full and not sharing your food," Froi responded.

Arjuro pushed forward some bread and handed him the bottle.

"At this time of the morning?" Froi asked.

"At any time of the day, I say."

Froi kept his eyes on the priestling. "Where I grew up, they crushed the skulls of babes born from the same loins on the same day. Gods' cursed, they would say."

Arjuro looked up, his eyes narrowing. "They only do that in the kingdom of Sarnak."

Suddenly, a thought entered Froi's head that was so strange, he almost felt foolish speaking it aloud. "There's two of her, isn't there? The princess?"

It could be the only answer. That like Gargarin and Arjuro, there were two Quintanas.

"More than two, I say," Arjuro said, looking over Froi's shoulder out the window. "Up here," he said, pointing to his head. "I've counted three."

"There's two," Froi argued. "The one who called out to you the other day, 'Blessed Arjuro, blessed Arjuro.'"

Arjuro winced. "She's the one who annoys me the most. The other demands in that cold voice, 'Priestling, the *reginita* requests an invitation to the godshouse at your convenience.'" Arjuro shook his head, muttering, "At my convenience."

"What's a *reginita*?" Froi asked, dipping his bread into the oil and dried herbs before him.

"A little queen." Arjuro stared over Froi's shoulder again and pointed. "That's the one I like best."

Froi turned and choked on the bread. He leaped out of his chair, but Arjuro grabbed him and made him be still. "Don't move. We don't want our mad princess going into the *gravina* just yet. Wouldn't want to take that opportunity away from someone else."

Froi stared out the window to where he could see Quintana straddling the granite he had stood on earlier. He knew in an instant that in this mood she was all rage. Teeth. A sneer. A snarl. He could have sworn she was one-part wild animal.

"Slowly," Arjuro warned as Froi calmly walked to the balconette.

The look she directed at them both was one of pure blazing fury.

"That's a side of her I've only seen glimpses of," Froi whispered, intrigued.

"Oh, that's not a side," Arjuro said. "That's a whole person. She perches herself out there once in a while. If she is Lirah of Serker's daughter, then that's all Serker savage there, bundled up into a ball of hatred toward all men. Looks like you've joined the list, Olivier of Sebastabol."

Froi watched Quintana get to her feet and the hairs of his arm stood tall. "Sagra!" he cursed, stepping closer. "Get down, you fool girl."

Arjuro was there behind him. "That one wants to die. Whatever's down there is beckoning her to jump."

But Quintana, or whoever was standing there balanced on the granite, wasn't looking down into the abyss. Her stare went straight to Froi.

"Come inside," the priestling ordered. "She'll go away."

"And if she falls?" Froi asked, unable to take his eyes off her.

"Well, she hasn't so far without your help, and she can't leap across here as you did. So it's either down in the *gravina* for her or sidling back to where she came from. I presume the others living inside her head convince her to return. It's the same thing each time. Sometimes I want to shout out, 'Jump, you little abomination!'"

Froi stared at Arjuro. "You're not like other holy men I know."

"And how many holy men would a last born from Sebastabol know when no more priests are left inside the province walls?"

Froi didn't respond. He turned back to look outside and saw Quintana standing on her balconette. Relief washed over him.

"How's my brother faring among all that insanity?" Arjuro asked quietly.

Froi shrugged. "He's not much into confiding."

"Why is he struggling to walk this morning?"

"Lirah of Serker took a dagger to him."

Arjuro grimaced. Froi recognized the expression as one he had seen on Gargarin's face.

"What does my brother have to say about the fact that the girl's prophecy has not come to be?" Arjuro asked.

"Why don't you ask him yourself?" Froi suggested. "Perhaps holler across to his balconette this evening?"

Arjuro stared at him.

"It may bring much-needed color to both your cheeks," Froi continued. Arjuro's stare suggested that Froi was bantering with the wrong person.

"He says that the gods have forsaken Charyn," Froi said.

Arjuro gave a short laugh of disbelief. "The gods have not forsaken Charyn. The gods love Charyn. Where else can they shit, if not Charyn? It's the purpose of this kingdom. To be the place where the gods shit."

Froi was surprised by the words. "You've lost hope in the gods."

"No. The gods lost hope in me. Long ago."

Froi sighed. If Arjuro wasn't going to be a source of information for him, perhaps he would be a source of entertainment.

"I've got to go. Can I use your entrance into the Citavita? Getting over here is far easier than returning the same way."

"Out there you'll be dealing with the street pigs," Arjuro said.

"I've not seen any pigs out there."

"I've not seen any pigs out there," Arjuro mimicked. "Who are you trying to fool with your fancy talk, you little shit?"

Certainly not the last priestling of the Citavita.

Arjuro walked out into a dark corridor, and Froi followed him down a winding stairwell that seemed to go on forever.

"They call themselves the street lords," Arjuro said. "The less Citavitans see of the king, the more powerful the street lords become. It's in the nature of humans," he added bitterly. "The need to be ruled by tyrants."

"Do those of the Citavita have faith in the princess producing an heir?" Froi asked.

"The princess is not going to produce an heir," Arjuro said. "The princess is insane. Perhaps insanely brilliant, because her delusions have managed to keep her alive all these years."

They passed one of the landing windows, and Froi saw the stone buildings of the Citavita outside.

"They'll kill her, you know," Arjuro said quietly. Froi heard regret in his voice.

"Quintana?"

Arjuro nodded.

"The street pigs?"

Arjuro shook his head. "She'll come of age this month and mark my words, she'll go over that balconette. 'It's an accident,' Bestiano will cry. 'At her own hands,' he'll claim. Why keep her alive when it is clear she isn't the one to break the curse? At first, the people will be stunned. Then relieved. Quintana the curse maker is dead. Perhaps it will mean the end of a barren era for Charyn."

"What does Bestiano hope to gain from her death?" Froi asked.

"A peaceful reign for the king. Bestiano has all the power he wants while the king lives. He'll begin to scour the land for last-born girls and bring them to the palace on the off chance that one of them produces the first. You can imagine the rest."

Froi was still reeling from the threat to Quintana. "So Bestiano will take over one day?"

Arjuro shook his head. "The *provincari* would never let a commoner rule. Bestiano will do anything to secure an heir, but only one he has control over, so he can continue enjoying his power. Unfortunately for him, the heir, Tariq, will never acknowledge him."

"Then who will Tariq choose as his First Adviser if he ever comes to power?"

Arjuro's eyes caught his, but then he looked away and suddenly Froi understood.

"Gargarin?"

Arjuro refused to respond, and they continued down the dark steps in silence.

At the bottom, the priestling unlatched the iron door and then removed a key from his sleeve and fixed it into the lock.

"Can I ask you something?" Froi asked.

"Can't promise I'll answer," the priestling said.

Froi hesitated. Would his question reveal a weakness in him? "When Gargarin first saw me, he reacted in much the same way you did," Froi said. "No one else has. Who do I remind you both of?"

"Someone we despise beyond understanding," Arjuro said flatly with no hesitation. He said little else, and Froi knew the discussion was over.

Arjuro pushed open the door, and they both squinted when the light poured in.

"My brother . . . he's the best man to ask," Arjuro said.

"Ask what?"

"I'm figuring that a lad with eyes like yours could have been sent by the hidden Serkers to kill the king. So talk to my brother."

Froi didn't respond for a moment. *Remember your promise to*

Trevanion. Trust no one. "I don't know what you're talking about. And if I did, what would I ask Gargarin?"

Arjuro looked past Froi to the cluster of cave homes below. "Twenty-five years ago, a young lad from Abroi with nothing to his name but a brother who was gods' touched impressed the king with his drawings and plans."

Arjuro watched Froi for a reaction. "He was sixteen at the time and the envy of every ambitious adviser employed by the king."

"Gargarin worked on the palace when it was built?" Froi asked.

Arjuro shook his head. "No. Gargarin was the architect. He knows every hidden tunnel, every mouse hole. The only thing he doesn't know is how to break out of an unbreakable prison."

Froi stared at Arjuro and then gave a laugh of disbelief. "Who are you people?"

It was a steep descent over the roofs of cave dwellings from the godshouse to the Citavita. At times, Froi could look into the homes beneath his feet, where entrances were dug out of the ceilings and the smell of bread from ovens wafted through the air. Still, it was a secluded area of the capital, and under the piercing glares of those they called the street lords, Froi felt less than safe with little means of protection.

He could see that the street lords spent much of their time sitting and watching. The men sat on the uneven roofs of the cave houses, studying the palace below and the godshouse above. Unlike the farmers, who dragged oxen up the backbreaking path, or the women, who stumbled with armloads of linens, the street lords did nothing much at all but sit around looking threatening.

"Friend," one called as he passed, and Froi itched for his dagger that lay buried in the cave at the base of the *gravina*.

"You," the man called out again. "I'm talking to you."

A leg went out, and Froi stumbled. Counted to ten.

"You came out of the godshouse, but we didn't see you go in," the shorter one said.

Froi would never understand the sameness of the world. Thugs or street lords or thieves were all the same, whether they hailed from Charyn or Sarnak or even Lumatere. Some of the wild orphans, as these kinds of people were called in Lumatere, had returned over the past years to cause havoc after too many years on their own. Trevanion put them straight into the army and trained them to exhaustion. "If they're going to hate, it may as well be for the good of Lumatere," he'd say.

"The priestling rarely gets visitors, so care to explain," the first man said.

Froi knew they would watch him travel back down to where the palace drawbridge met the Citavita. He knew he couldn't lie about where he was heading.

"Messenger," he muttered, keeping it simple, remembering what everyone seemed to say about how too perfect his Charyn sounded. He took another step, but a hand snaked out and grabbed Froi's arm.

"I'll ask again, friend. You came out of the godshouse, but we didn't see you go in."

"Well, that's the thing," Froi said politely. "You're not actually asking a question. More of a statement." He looked at the man and then stared at the hand on his arm. "So what is it you want to know?"

The man's companion laughed.

"How did you arrive at the godshouse?" the street lord asked, retrieving a dagger from a scabbard at the waist of his trousers and tracing it across Froi's cheek.

Froi turned and pointed to the space that could still be seen between the tip of the godshouse across the *gravina* to the palace.

"I jumped. I wouldn't advise it. Not good for the innards."

The street lord grabbed him by the collar and dragged him closer, his foul breath fanning Froi's face.

But suddenly a hand reached between them.

"So you're attacking priestlings now, are you, Donashe?" Froi heard Arjuro mutter. He was dressed from head to ankle in a black cape and cowl, his eyes and pale face barely visible.

The street lord stepped back, and Froi saw fear in his eyes.

"He said he was a palace messenger," the man Donashe said, looking away from Arjuro as though any moment he would be cursed.

"My messenger," Arjuro corrected. "To the palace." Froi felt the street lord's eyes on him. Arjuro poked Froi's arm, and glared.

"Did I not order you to hurry on and repeat my exact words to those in the palace?" Arjuro asked Froi. "That I'd swive a goat before I'll ever step foot in that heap of dung."

"Must I, blessed Arjuro?" Froi asked pitifully. "For those of us from the godshouse are well known for swiving goats and I'd prefer not to give them weapons of ridicule."

Arjuro shook his head. "Idiot," he muttered, walking back up the path to the godshouse. But Froi had seen the ghost of a smile on his face.

Froi gave a wave to the street lords and turned to walk away.

"I never forget a face," Donashe warned.

"Oh, neither do I, friend," Froi said. "And that is a promise."

Getting back into the palace wasn't quite as simple as getting out had been.

"I'm a guest of the king," Froi called to where he could see two soldiers standing behind the portcullis. "A last born. Olivier of Sebastabol."

Nothing. The soldiers stared between the grates but refused to speak.

"I arrived here with Gargarin of Abroi four days ago. Call Dorcas if you don't believe me, because I'm telling you, if anything happens to me, you'll pay the price. Recognize a threat if you have brains in your head."

Although Trevanion's instruction would have been for Froi to get himself back into the palace any way he could, he knew that landing in the palace prison tower was not one of them.

"You'll feel like fools when the king's adviser hears about this," he said as they opened a door and tossed him in. It was a fall of a few feet before he hit the ground. If Gargarin was truly the architect, Froi would have to thank him for planning a prison chamber built in such a way.

The room was as long and wide as the length of Froi's body. Apart from the door up high, there was a window that was big enough to crawl through, but the threat of climbing out and plunging into the *gravina* below was the perfect deterrent for anyone wanting to leave.

Later, he heard the key in the lock and stared up to see a guard and then Quintana peering over his shoulder.

"We're friends, Fekra and I," she said as the guard lowered her down with a grip on one arm.

"Ten minutes, princess," Fekra muttered. He let go of her arm, and Quintana fell onto Froi with very little finesse.

"Do you want to meet my mother, Lirah?" she asked matter-of-factly.

"Not exactly, no. I want you to go fetch Gargarin and get me out of this hole."

"Gargarin doesn't make the decisions."

She looked out the window.

"*Poor Lirah*. She's been imprisoned for at least twelve years, you know."

"Yes, yes, poor Lirah."

"Although I'm sure she is still taken to my father's chamber from time to time. *Poor, poor Lirah*. He still considers her his whore. Lirah says it's all about power and that the king never feels more powerful than when he's swiving Serker."

Quintana pointed toward the low ceiling. "She's up there. It's why my friend Fekra allows me to use this dungeon when it's empty. So I can see my mother, Lirah."

Froi could easily see that Fekra wasn't a friend of Quintana's, accepting bribes of food and ale and turning a blind eye only because there was no way in or out of the palace from this tower. But it did mean that Quintana and her mother had found a way of speaking to each other whenever the dungeon was empty.

"Lirah! Lirah!"

Froi's head rang from Quintana's high-pitched indignation.

"Sometimes," she explained to Froi, as though he had asked, "I have to call out more than once because she's on the roof. She has a small garden up there, you know. There's no way down, of course, except for lunging to her death."

"Why is she imprisoned?" Froi asked.

"She tried to kill someone, poor Lirah."

Poor Lirah indeed. She went around trying to kill people and seemed to be a failure at it.

"Lirah. Lirah." Quintana snaked her body out the window, her feet flailing mid-air. Froi caught her around the waist.

"You're going to fall to your death, idiot girl."

After a moment, Froi heard another voice.

"Who's there with you?"

"Just a last born, Lirah! We thought he was here for some other purpose, but he is the one. It's written all over him."

Quintana turned back and beckoned to him. Froi sighed. She moved aside, and he squeezed in, poking his head out and straining to look up.

The face that looked down at him from the window was not what he expected and, like an idiot, he stared. Agape. She was beautiful, but when it came to freezing a man with a death stare, Lirah of Serker could beat Gargarin and Quintana the ice maiden in the blink of an eye.

"Don't trust him," he heard Lirah of Serker snap. "He's savage stock if ever I've seen it.

Froi bristled and listened to ridiculous talk from Quintana to Lirah about Aunt Mawfa's moon eyes for Gargarin. Suddenly Fekra was at the door above them, lowering a rope, with Dorcas appearing beside him.

"The princess only."

"Can you call Gargarin, then?" Froi demanded, watching Dorcas hoist Quintana up.

"The king's adviser says you must stay here for the time being. To teach you a lesson."

"Didn't know it was a crime to leave the palace, Dorcas."

"It's not," Dorcas replied. "It's a crime to threaten the king and your words, 'What do you think I'm going to do? Get into the king's chamber and slice him from ear to ear?' were a provocation."

"Dorcas, it is in me to jest."

"And, Olivier, it is in me to obey orders."

Quintana's face reappeared over Dorcas's shoulder. "Oh, he's very thorough about the rules, Olivier. He's never let my father or Bestiano down in that way."

"Good for you, Dorcas. I pray to the gods that I can follow your example more readily."

The door shut, and Froi had a feeling he would be in this room for quite some time.

CHAPTER 10

Lady Beatriss arrived at the Flatlands' meeting hall at the same time as Finnikin and his entourage. She looked for Trevanion, knowing he would be there as part of his son's Guard.

She had found him distant these past weeks, and it worried her. During the early days when the kingdom was reunited, they had danced a strange dance around each other that spoke of never being able to return to the lovers they had been. Ten years apart was too long, and the events that had taken place during that time could not be forgotten. But during the spring this year, things had changed.

It was on the night of the Harvest Moon Dance, when Beatriss felt his eyes on her from the moment she had crossed the bridge into the palace village. Vestie, as usual, had run for him, throwing herself into his arms. Who would have known that Trevanion and her daughter would share such a bond, but it was a joy to watch. That night at the celebrations, the Queen's Guard were impeccably dressed for the occasion, with their boots polished and purple sashes around their waists to match the colors of the queen, wearing short coats that looked stylish and much too attractive to every woman in their presence. And Beatriss noticed. That's how she knew that things had changed within her. Because now she noticed every single woman who looked at the captain of the Guard. But that night, he seemed to have eyes for no one but her and the days of denial were long gone, for she met his stare with her own. When he offered to escort her and Vestie to Sennington, it was there in the hallway of Beatriss's home as she took her daughter out of his arms that he bent down and kissed her for the first time in thirteen years, and if it wasn't for the child that was pressed between them, she could imagine where that kiss would have gone.

Since then, he had found any opportunity to stop by for supper or a ride around the village. They spoke of fallow fields and his son's family in the palace and this brave new Lumatere, and although she was desperate to speak of the past, Trevanion refused.

"The past is not important, Beatriss. We don't look back."

In the palace village, she heard the whispers and suspected that he would ask her to be his wife soon, and she had practiced her response. Yes. And then a yes again.

But something had changed in the last few weeks. He visited less frequently, and when he did, he seemed distant. Try as she might, Beatriss could not understand what words or event had changed things between them. The last time they had spoken, she told him her fears of no longer being able to keep her villagers fed. Beatriss had inherited Sennington upon her father's death, the year before the curse, and from that moment on, she'd ensured that her people were looked after, even during the ten years of terror.

"We'll speak of it when I return," Trevanion had assured her. He had been off to escort Finnikin to Balconio for a meeting with the Sarnaks. She knew there had been an incident in the mountains with a Charynite that day. A week later, Froi had been dispatched to Sarnak, according to one of her villagers who was courting a girl from Froi's village of Sayles. Beatriss suspected that something had happened on the mountain to change everything.

Today, Trevanion seemed a stranger except for the familiar rumble of his voice in her ear. "They're waiting for you, Beatriss," he said quietly.

Inside, the Flatland lords were already seated. Beatriss found a place beside August. He took her hand.

"Abian says she's not seen you for some weeks, Beatriss."

"There is too much work to be done," she lied, squeezing her friend's hand.

She avoided looking across the table to the others. Lord Freychinet, Lord Castian, and Lord Artor had been in exile during the ten years and were said to have deserted their people to live comfortable lives in foreign courts. Lord Nettice, who had been trapped inside the kingdom, had acted even worse, but Beatriss couldn't bear to think of those days. She felt humiliated to be in the presence of these people. Although she had never spoken the words aloud, she despised them. None more than Lord Nettice. She felt a blackness come over her until suddenly a hand was on her shoulder and a kiss on her cheek. She knew it was Finnikin. In the short years Beatriss had been his father's betrothed, before the unspeakable, she had mothered the boy and loved him as her own. He had always been a child of great substance and here he was leading them with their beloved Isaboe.

Finnikin walked around the table, winking as he caught her eye before sitting down.

"Well, I think it's obvious why we are here," Lord Freychinet said. "There's the matter of Fenton and the matter of Sennington. So let's not waste time."

Beatriss stiffened. "Sennington? What has my village to do with today's meeting?"

Lord Freychinet stood without responding, disregarding the presence of the queen's consort. Beatriss sensed Trevanion's fury at the lack of respect shown, but Finnikin seemed unperturbed.

"Split Fenton between its two neighboring villages," Freychinet demanded. "And collapse Sennington."

Beatriss fought to hold back a gasp and heard a sharp intake of breath from August behind her.

"Only two of her small fields yield a crop, and it's not enough for her and her village to survive on," Lord Freychinet continued. He turned to Beatriss. "So sell the southern paddock to Sayles and the northern paddock to me and count your losses. If Nettice and I are to split Fenton for the good of this kingdom, we'll need your workers."

"My workers?" she asked, horrified. "They are my villagers, Sir Freychinet. Not my workers. They have minds of their own, and if they choose to accept your offer of a home on your land, then there is no one holding them back, but I will not—what was the word?—*collapse* my village, just because you need them working your land."

"Work it yourself, Freychinet," August said facetiously. "It's surprising the effect it has on your villagers' morale to have you working among them."

Lord Freychinet shook his head with disdain. "Sometimes I believe you still think you're in exile, August, and that there is no true difference between you and your peasants. Your father would be rolling in his grave."

"Oh, I count on my father rolling in his grave over and over again," August said. "If anyone deserves an uneasy sleep for eternity, it is a lord who doesn't lift a finger to take care of his villagers."

Finnikin cleared his throat. "Let us begin with my confusion, Lord Freychinet," he said, his tone even. "You see, I'm not quite sure who 'her' is. 'Her small fields' and enough for 'her and her village.'"

There was an awkward silence.

"Lady Beatriss of the Flatlands," Lord Freychinet responded.

"Then I think it may be in your best interest to refer to the Lady Beatriss by either her title or her name, if she ever invites you to."

Finnikin's voice was hard. "Is that understood?"

"Yes, my lord."

"Good."

Finnikin looked down at the pages in front of him. "I know how much of a stickler you are for protocol, Lord Freychinet, and unfortunately there is no mention of the topic of Sennington here before me, so Lady Beatriss's village is not up for discussion during this meeting."

Finnikin looked up. "Perhaps if you allow me to take over proceedings, we can discuss the village of Fenton."

He looked around the room, taking in all of its occupants. "Fenton will be sold."

"Sold?" Lord Nettice bellowed. Beatriss flinched at the sound of his voice.

"It's what Lord Selric wanted," Finnikin said. "His surviving villagers will all receive a profit from the sale."

"Ridiculous," Lord Freychinet said. "And who informed you of Lord Selric's *want,* my lord? His villagers? Was it their decision?"

"No, actually I do believe it was the decision of my wife," Finnikin said matter-of-factly. "You remember her, don't you, Lord Freychinet? The queen? Tallish. Dark hair. Not the type to say things twice, so when she speaks the words, 'Tell them that if they have a problem with my decision, I may be forced to look into the crimes against my people that took place while my lords turned their backs,' I tend to take them to heart."

He was no longer Little Finch, Beatriss thought with proud sadness. Here was a man born to lead alongside his beloved queen.

"If you want to look at behavior during the ten years, perhaps you should be looking at others," Lord Castian said with a cough, his eyes meeting those of Beatriss. "According to Nettice here, not every woman was as virtuous as they claim."

Beatriss heard August's hiss of fury. She dared not look up at Trevanion. The hairs on her arm stood tall, and she felt her stomach churn.

Finnikin's eyes were a cold gray as they stared from Lord Nettice to Lord Castian and then back to Lord Freychinet.

"You push my patience, gentlemen."

"What of Fenton?" Lord Nettice said, smart enough to bring the conversation back to its agenda.

"Fenton will *not* be given to any of you. The village now belongs to the palace. If you want Fenton, you buy it at a fair price," Finnikin said. "And the survivors of that village will have the right to stay on and work for whoever buys it if they please. If not, they can take their share and set up home elsewhere in the kingdom."

He looked around the room, his eyes cold, his teeth clenched. "Is that clear?"

* * *

Outside, Trevanion caught up with Beatriss, gripping her arm.

"What was that?" he asked, fury lacing his words. "Have they spoken to you in such a way before? Has that dog Freychinet slandered you behind your back?"

No, he has actually done it to my face, she wanted to say to him. She shook free of his grip.

"It's about the past," Beatriss said bitterly. "The past is not important, remember? We don't look back."

CHAPTER 11

Hours passed, and eventually Froi supposed that Gargarin was not going to appear. The boredom made him want to beat his head against the stone. He tried to imagine the Flatlands and its never-ending sky, and sitting with Lord August at the end of a backbreaking day, a mug of ale in his hands and a sense of satisfaction in his heart. But the strength of such imaginings only worked when he was actually under a never-ending sky in the Flatlands and not in a dungeon in a stone palace dug out of a mountain in the middle of a *gravina,* inside a godsforsaken kingdom.

He looked out of his window and craned his head to see the one above. It was a short distance up, but at least Lirah of Serker had the roof garden, which was a whole lot better than what Froi had. Before he could talk himself out of it, he removed his boots and hoisted himself up onto the windowsill. He climbed out to stand on the ledge with his face pressed to the outer walls, his fingers feeling for grooves, his toes gripping stone. Slowly he made his way up to the window above. Despite the short distance and Froi's expertise, according to Trevanion, in climbing all things impossible—all things impossible took on new meaning when there was nothing beneath him but unending space and the promise of death.

"Sagra!" he muttered, perspiring. Finnikin had once boasted that the stone he climbed to find Isaboe in Sendecane was beyond anything Froi had conquered, and Froi had said he would find a grander stone one day and challenge his king to a battle.

"Battle of stupidity," Isaboe had said. "They'll have to summon me to identify your splattered pride. They both look the same, I'll say."

Not a good thing to be thinking of, Froi. He reached Lirah's window, fingers gripping any furrow he could find.

He fell into the room headfirst. It was much bigger than Froi's cell and was furnished with a cot, books, and a fireplace. On the wall, he saw that someone had sketched the image of a newborn babe, and beside that another of a child of about five or six. A mad one, judging by the hair and the savage little teeth. He could only imagine that it was Quintana as a child, her eyes blazing as she held up a thumb and its two closest fingers. Another image was of Quintana, younger than she was now, perhaps fourteen or so. It was a good resemblance.

There was a door to the left of the fireplace and then a narrow stairwell up to the roof, where a hatch lifted to give more light to the space. Froi climbed up the steps and found himself in a roof garden that afforded him a view of the entire Citavita. A figure knelt at one of the flowerbeds.

When she stood to survey her work, he could see that she was tall, almost boyish in her form. Lirah of Serker, the king's whore. He couldn't determine her age, but if she was Quintana's mother, he imagined her to be somewhere later in her thirty years. Her hair was thick and long and the color of mahogany. Her eyes were a deep gray and their shape made Froi think of

Tesadora, although the women looked nothing alike. Serker eyes, Rafuel had said, and the type of beauty that made a man ache despite his age. Froi knew the moment Lirah felt his gaze on her, and she looked at him with a cold penetrating stare.

"I wouldn't plant that there," Froi said.

She studied him suspiciously.

"I planted some . . . back in Sebastabol. They don't like the areas out of the sun."

Froi felt studied. It was a habit these Charynites had. Lirah's Serker stare was hard and vicious.

"Olivier of Sebastabol," he said, bowing.

She gave a laugh of disbelief. "You have the eyes of a Serker, Olivier of Sebastabol."

"Those from Serker no longer exist."

"This one does, and she recognizes the eyes of a Serker lad."

"Between you and Gargarin, and Quintana when she's in a mood, I'm beginning to feel most unloved in Charyn."

This time, she flinched. Was it at the mention of Gargarin's name?

"In Charyn?" she asked. "You speak as though you've just arrived in your own kingdom."

"I meant in the Citavita," he corrected.

Froi looked out. The battlements of his tower seemed close enough to leap across. But the towers he suspected to be the king's were too far away.

"Have you used force with her?" she asked bluntly.

Froi bristled. "What makes you think I'm the sort who uses force?" he demanded.

"Because I grew up with Serker pigs such as yourself. It's in the blood," she spat.

"And is it in the Serker blood for the women to be whores?" he taunted.

"Oh, we're all whores in Charyn, Olivier," she mocked in return. "In some shape or form."

She went back to her planting, and he watched her dig into the soil and press the roots of the plant down.

"It will die, I tell you," he snapped. "I know the *cratornia*. It will not survive in so small a plot." She looked up, surprised, and after a moment, she pulled it out slowly and deliberately, then held it up. He searched the garden and pointed.

"By the bristle tree," he suggested.

She shook her head. "So he knows his bristle trees," she said, half to herself. But she refused to look up again. One would think she'd crave company, but Lirah of Serker seemed to want him to disappear.

"You'd best be gone," she said, dismissing him. "I can imagine that the climb down is worse in the dark."

Froi was kept prisoner until the next afternoon and on his release was confined to the chamber he shared with Gargarin.

"Happy that you irritated Bestiano?" Gargarin asked, not looking up from where he was scribbling furiously.

Gargarin's sketches carpeted the floor and were strewn all over Froi's cot.

"You couldn't come and release me?" Froi grumbled.

"Why would I want to do that when I had peace and quiet for at least a day?"

Gargarin discarded yet another page with frustration, dipping his quill into the ink pot to begin again.

"You may as well tell me about them," Froi said. "You know you're dying to."

A moment passed and Gargarin looked up. After seeing Arjuro, Froi found it strange to face this man.

"You know much about water, I presume?" Gargarin asked.

"Because a lad from the shipping yards of Sebastabol would be an expert."

"Ships? Water? There's a strong connection in my mind. Anyway, what's there to know? Charyn's cursed. You either get too much rain and it floods the plains, or not enough, which causes drought."

Gargarin studied him, eyebrow raised. "You? As in the rest of Charyn and not you, Olivier?"

"Words," Froi scoffed. "Are they so important?"

"Isn't the princess waiting for you?" Gargarin said.

"Which one? I've now met them all," he said, studying the maps and plans on his cot. Froi had never seen such a grand plan. Water meadows, larger than he had ever seen, and giant human-made rivers and lakes. He came around to where Gargarin sat and looked over his shoulder.

He pointed to an area beyond the planned water meadow. "What about these villages?"

"The floodings of the last couple of years have crippled the farmers," Gargarin said. "Before that, we had years of drought. The gods are determined that nothing is to grow in Charyn, and I'm determined to challenge them on that. We need to find a way to harness this water in the rainy season so we can use it during the drier months. If we build troughs to collect the rainwater in the drier areas, the soil could stay moist all year long."

"So you send it in different directions."

Gargarin nodded. "We set a watercourse. It's in the books, Olivier. In the books the Ancients wrote." The man's eyes shone with excitement. "They are hard to translate, but not impossible. If they could do it thousands of years ago, so can we."

"What would make them easier to translate?" Froi asked. "The books of the Ancients, I mean."

Gargarin's expression closed again.

"The gods' touched have a better chance. I can only understand so much."

Someone such as Arjuro, the gods' touched priestling. Froi looked down at where the goose quill was twisted around Gargarin's fingers.

"You speak; I draw," Froi instructed.

They fought the whole afternoon. Gargarin spoke too fast and would change his mind the moment Froi drew his instructions, but Froi kept up, and when they were finished, he had never seen plans with such ambition and . . . hope. He wanted to steal them away in his pack and return with them to Lumatere, place them in Lord August's hands and say, "My gift to you for giving me a home."

That night he couldn't go through the ritual with Quintana of feigning impotence or listening to prophecies about seeds needing to be planted, so he remained in his chamber.

"You spoke of a bond," Gargarin said in the dark as they both lay in their beds. His voice was soft, but there was a powerful resonance to his voice. It made Froi forget the limp and the awkward arm.

"You don't believe in them?" Froi asked.

"Not bonds drawn up by other men. I write my own bond."

"What if I trust those other men with all my heart?" Froi asked quietly.

Gargarin sighed. Outside, the shadows played across the *gravina* onto the godshouse wall.

"Dorcas was taken out of his province when he was thirteen. He's been here eighteen years and knows nothing but how to follow a bond to his king and Bestiano. He trusts them with all his heart."

There was silence for a moment.

"I fear I'll die at the hands of someone like Dorcas. A man

with no ideals of his own, but another man's bond to follow," Gargarin said.

"I fear that I will do something to bring harm to those I love," Froi said. "So I follow their rules to ensure that I won't."

"But what if you bring harm or fail to protect those you don't know? Or don't love? Will you care as much?"

"Probably not."

"Then choose another bond. One written by yourself. Because it is what you do for strangers that counts in the end."

The next morning, as Froi watched the ritual between the brothers across the *gravina,* he felt a fierce affection for the two fools.

He followed Gargarin for the rest of the day. He wasn't in the mood to face Quintana, and he decided to wait until Princess Indignant reappeared. That morning at breakfast, her stare had been cold, and after meeting Lirah, Froi understood where the coldness came from. He noticed that when the cold Quintana appeared, there was no upheaval over breakfast. Yet, apart from a snarl escaping her lips once or twice, no one seemed to notice the change. Except for him. It was this point that he found unsettling. Princess Indignant irritated him, amused him, exasperated him. But cold Quintana unsettled Froi. The beat of his heart would skip in her presence.

So he followed Gargarin, despite the fact that Gargarin did not want to be followed.

"My duty was to bring you as far as the palace," Gargarin snapped when they reached yet another twisting flight of stairs that opened up to a small alcove. From there they could see up to part of the battlement of the next tower. Lirah's prison. From this angle, Froi realized it was indeed an easy leap from their own tower to her garden.

"Go," Gargarin murmured, looking upward. "Away."

Froi wasn't one for taking instruction. "I could get up there, you know. Except she's probably the worst-natured woman I've met."

"And you've met Lirah, how?" Gargarin asked.

"Remember when you left me rotting in that cell two days ago? Well, I climbed out the window and up to hers."

Gargarin stared at him. "And what kept you attached to the walls? Magic?"

"The gods," Froi mocked.

Gargarin settled himself against the wall and continued to look up, as though waiting for some type of apparition that could appear at any moment.

Froi sat beside him and couldn't help but notice the bend in Gargarin's elbow, the way he had clutched the pencil in the chamber the night before, the limp he walked with.

"Were you born that way?"

"No," Gargarin snapped. "And rude of you to ask."

"Born this rude. Can't help myself."

Gargarin stared at him, and Froi thought, perhaps imagined, that he saw a glint of humor in the man's eyes. But soon enough, Gargarin's gaze was drawn back to the prison tower.

"You're not one to pine over a woman, so what is this about, Gargarin?"

"A desire to die with peace in my heart," Gargarin said quietly.

"And when are you planning to die?"

There was silence for a moment.

"Tell me what takes place in the Citavita," Gargarin said, and Froi felt as though he was changing the topic. "With the street pigs."

"That's what Arjuro calls them, too," Froi said. "If they're such pigs, how did they come to have so much power? They look as though they own the Citavita."

Gargarin shook his head with a grimace. "Six years ago,

when we were plague-ridden. That's how things get power. When a kingdom is at its most vulnerable."

Froi knew of the plague. It had claimed the lives of a Flatland lord's family. Lord August and Lady Abian had built a shrine to the goddess on the edge of the first paddock of the village to remember those who had died, including Lord Selric of Fenton and his wife and daughters. "If we forget who we lost," Lady Abian would tell Froi and her children, "then we forget who we once were, and if we forget who we once were, we lose sight of who we are now."

Froi felt a twinge of guilt that he hadn't thought of his Flatlands family for days.

"What happened during the plague?" he asked Gargarin.

"People began dying, and the palace riders raided the fields of crops and livestock and anything else they could get their hands on, so the king could barricade himself in the palace with only those he trusted. Beyond the Citavita, it was even worse. The provinces refused to give sanctuary to those who lived outside their boundaries and many of them overflowed into the Citavita, bringing disease with them. It was how the street lords were born. Theirs was a fury that came from dead sisters or wives who had thrown themselves to their deaths from the despair of barren wombs. But during the plague, it festered as they watched the oxen carry their cargo of grain and seed into the castle from the fields outside."

There was bitterness and anguish in Gargarin's voice. Froi wondered how he could ever have thought Gargarin cared little for anyone.

"At first the street lords found a way to bring some kind of stability where there had been theft and violence, neighbors killing neighbors for food. Sadly, the people failed to see that the street lords were always going to want something in return. Later, with the plague over and a third of our people dead, the palace tried to take control of the Citavita again. It appeared that the street lords had lost some of their power, but it was only on the surface. Today they still have a hold on the people because the people have no one honorable to hold on to. But make no mistake: those men who roam the streets are as greedy and corrupt as"—Gargarin looked around to see if anyone was listening—"those here in the palace. In one breath they say they despise the king; in another the pigs are paid a handsome sum to be Bestiano's eyes and ears in the Citavita. The street lords fear little. It is a foolish man indeed who fears little."

"They're scared of your brother," Froi said. "I can't understand why. He's nothing but a drunk with mad eyes."

"He is gods' touched," Gargarin said. "That's enough to scare any of us. Some believe that it could have been those touched by the gods who cursed Charyn or that by imprisoning the last priestling of the oracle's godshouse, the gods were punishing the palace. Both beliefs led back to one person: Arjuro."

"Is that what you think?" Froi asked, and it surprised him how much he cared what Gargarin thought. "About who cursed Charyn?"

Gargarin swallowed. "I think the curse of the last born came from more than one person. I think the power of it came from hearts filled with wrath and love and despair and betrayal and that even the gods are confused about where it came from and how to mend it."

Gargarin turned to him. "It's not safe in the Citavita, Olivier," he said quietly. "The street pigs are out of control. I'd advise you to get out of here as soon as you can."

"They'll never enter the palace," Froi said.

"There's not a huge difference between not letting them in and the street lords not letting us out. I fear for the *provincari* who will be here within days. They risk their lives."

"Why come, then?"

"They're invited to the palace every day of weeping to discuss Charyn's futureless future. But I fear that the street lords are more powerful than the palace has led the provinces to believe."

"So Quintana's not delusional in believing that everyone is out to kill her?"

Gargarin's eyes bored into Froi's. "You ask a lot of questions for an idiot," he said.

"Is that what they call me outside my province?"

"Emphatically. Olivier the idiot."

"I'm charmed, to say the very least. I've never had a title."

This time Gargarin laughed. Froi smiled at the sound. Lumaterans weren't known for their sense of humor, and Froi found himself in trouble half the time when they didn't understand his.

"Is it true that she's mad?" Froi asked.

The grimace was back on Gargarin's face. "True enough," he responded. "But if you should believe anything, believe that everyone is out to kill her, Olivier. Her only delusion is the belief that she'll break the curse."

"Then why am I here if everyone believes that she's delusional about last and firstborns?"

"Because the king doesn't believe she's delusional. Because the king is frightened by his own child and is convinced that she's mad. When a mad princess whose birth cursed a kingdom states that the gods have spoken, prophesying that she's the last who will make the first, the king takes heed of her words."

"Do you believe her?" Froi asked.

"No," Gargarin said, his voice sad. "But I would like to. Something I can't explain tells me to. But reason steps in the way." He looked at Froi, sadness etched in his expression. "She comes of age next week," he said in a low voice. "Once she's proven to this kingdom that her prophecy was a lie, Bestiano will convince the king to find another way to break the curse."

"And how will they go about convincing Her Royal Delusioness that she's not the last to make the first?"

Froi flinched at the intensity of Gargarin's stare.

"Mark my words: that girl will not live beyond her coming of age. It's best that you get out of the palace before that happens."

It was the second time in so many days that Froi had heard these words, and they chilled him to the bone.

Later, when nothing came from their study of Lirah's roof, they returned to their chamber. Froi picked up the sketches scattered all over the floor.

"This is something Charyn is . . . we are," he corrected himself, "known for." Froi looked at Gargarin. "A Lumateran once came through Sebastabol," he lied, "and told the story that despite how barbaric the Charynite soldiers were, they introduced one vital form of water use that saved part of the Lumateran Flatlands."

Gargarin stared at him, waiting.

"The rainwater was collected by the placement of sliced animal bones around the entrance of a home. When it rained, the water ran down the grooves of the bones and was taken into a cistern under the house. Then during the dry season, they'd build pipes made of animal hide to run from the cistern into the fields."

There was silence from Gargarin, and Froi turned to him questioningly and saw the man look down.

"Simple, but worthwhile," Froi said. "Don't you agree?"

Froi watched a smile appear on Gargarin's face. It was strange and twisted and reluctant, but it was also sincere and almost shy, which was strange coming from a grown man.

"In my third year in the palace as a young man, I drew up the plans for that system of water capturing. It heartens me to think that Charyn had something worthwhile to offer Lumatere.

Froi sat up, amazed. "You?"

Gargarin nodded, suddenly uncomfortable with the attention. "In Abroi, where I grew up, I saw people suffer and children die because we had so little water and, most years, no crops to speak of. It's strange that in a single kingdom, there can be an abundance of gifts in one province and little in another. Have you ever been deprived of food, Olivier? As a last born, I doubt it." Froi looked away. He couldn't remember a day in his life as a young child when he wasn't deprived of food. It only served as a reminder of what he had to do to keep his stomach full.

Gargarin sighed, standing up and straightening his back.

"Are you in a hurry to complete these plans because you have a meeting with the king?" Froi asked.

"Not yet, but I'll see him soon, and then my work will be done." Gargarin looked away. "If anything happens to me, can I trust that my drawings will get into the hands of De Lancey of Paladozza?"

"What can possibly happen to you?"

"Can you promise without irritating me?"

"Why would you trust me?"

The awkward bend of the head was there again. "I don't know," Gargarin said honestly. "But I do."

Froi shook his head. "How about I give you my word that I won't let anything happen to you instead?"

He had no idea where those words came from. He wasn't here to protect Gargarin or any of them. He was here to kill a king. But deep down he realized that he wanted to impress this man. That despite their first meeting and Gargarin's hostility toward Froi, he reminded him of Lord August and Finn and Sir Topher combined. At strange moments, he imagined introducing Gargarin to them all.

That night, Froi was allowed to attend dinner. Bestiano stared at him from where he sat at the head of the table, as though practicing to be the king himself. Froi gave a polite wave of acknowledgment.

He was assigned a place sitting with a cluster of the women Quintana had referred to as the Aunts. Their heads were bent, and they were speaking rapidly, furiously.

Suddenly Quintana was beside him.

"I searched for you all day," she said, and he could see that she was back to her indignant self, all breathless and irritated.

"I was avoiding you."

Princess Indignant seemed oblivious of any type of malice directed toward her. Sometimes it made him want to be even crueler. To punish her for doing nothing to stop herself from getting killed. Isaboe would have fought to survive.

"You can sit on our right," she instructed. "Aunt Mawfa will bore you senseless."

"Really?"

"Yes. The moment Aunt Mawfa speaks, everyone falls asleep. It has to do with the pitch of her voice."

She nudged him. "Look at her shoes," she whispered, pointing under the table. Froi humored her and ducked his head under. Lady Mawfa had plump little legs that barely touched the ground and a pair of silly pointy shoes with red bows.

Froi sat back up again. "She had them sent from Belegonia," Quintana said in a hushed tone. "They are said to have belonged to the first goddess who walked the earth."

Froi looked under the table again and sat back up.

"Not possible. I've been told that goddesses are a practical bunch," he said. "They'd never have tolerated the red bows."

She covered her mouth, laughing. A truly ridiculous laugh, all snorts and giggles.

"Quintana!" Bestiano shouted out to her. Froi stiffened. The last thing he wanted was for Bestiano to drag her out of the hall. Froi looked at her and put a finger to his lips to quiet her.

"Ask her something," Quintana whispered. "Ask her about the weather, and you'll see what we mean. When she speaks, no one listens. It's why we've chosen to be like her. We don't get into half as much trouble."

He studied Quintana, waiting for the announcement that she had been jesting the whole time. That she was an "I" and not a "we." But she swung her eyes to the side and flicked her head toward Lady Mawfa, and for a moment he wanted to laugh. He turned and politely asked Lady Mawfa about the weather.

Lady Mawfa responded in an indignant voice that was high-pitched but as hushed and dramatic as one reporting the enemy at the gates of the Citavita. The only part of Quintana missing was the squint.

". . . and it's all suffering for my joints. Poor, poor me."

Froi choked out a laugh, thinking of Quintana's own dramatics when reporting on events. *Poor Lirah. Poor, poor Lirah.*

A moment later he felt her lips to his ears. "So have you fallen asleep yet?"

Although the princess's indignant tone had not changed, all of a sudden everything else seemed to.

Froi had no idea what lay beneath all the incessant chatter, but there was more to her than even the cold unsettling Quintana and the savage he had caught a glimpse of outside Arjuro's window.

"Have you?" she asked again.

"At about the time she spoke of the dew on her windowsill."

Quintana covered her mouth again, snorting. Bestiano barked out her name, but Froi grabbed her hand and pulled it away. And there were those teeth, small and crooked in parts. Froi was slightly charmed, snorts and all.

"Let's get out of here," he whispered, dragging her to her feet.

CHAPTER 12

Finnikin was crouched on the rock of three wonders surrounded by the children of his mother's village. They stared back at him, wide-eyed and full of awe, and he found himself swallowing a lump in his throat. This rock would always remind him of Balthazar — Lucian's adored cousin, Finnikin's beloved friend, Isaboe's brother and savior, and once the heir of Lumatere. But since the birth of his daughter, the rock also had Finnikin thinking of his mother.

When he had lived here as a child, he rarely imagined Bartolina. His mother had died giving birth to him, and her spirit had failed to reveal itself to Finnikin, despite the fact that Aunt Celestina sensed her all the time and even Trevanion had mumbled about days when he felt her presence. But in these past years, Finnikin had dreamed of his mother often, especially when he brought Jasmina with him to visit his people.

Aunt Celestina wept each time, embracing both Finnikin and Isaboe. "Thank you, my darlings. Thank you for returning to us the image of my beloved sister."

Little Bartolina, Jasmina was called by the Rock villagers. Of course, she loved the attention. He had noticed in her first attempts at speech, she had referred to herself as Jasmina of Bartolina. Whenever she spoke the words, everyone would clap at the sweetness of her voice. So Jasmina of Bartolina would repeat them over and over again until Isaboe would smother her face with kisses. "Enough, my love," she would say, laughing.

Each time Finnikin returned to his Rock village, the elders would beg him to tell the children a story from the chronicles he had collected for the *Book of Lumatere*. Sometimes he'd tell them tales about the kingdoms beyond. If any good had come from the exile and entrapment of their people, it was that the world became bigger than Lumatere's walls. One time, he told the children of a great waterfall in Sorel; other times he told them about the jungles of Yutlind Sud or the bazaars of Belegonia.

"Your Highness, Your Highness," they called out that day, their arms waving for his attention.

He pointed to a sweet little girl.

"Is it true that our goddess of blood and tears carried the Flatlands to the Rock?"

There was a scoffing sound from the boy beside her, who Finnikin suspected was her brother.

"You're an idiot, Clarashin," the boy shouted at her.

"Fa says the goddess carried them," she bellowed at the boy, grabbing his hair and yanking hard.

Finnikin stepped in and pulled the two apart, settling the girl beside him. She placed an arm around his shoulders, boldly staring out at her brother. Finnikin dared to look at Jasmina, who was sitting on the lap of a young cousin, squirming. He had noticed that every time one of the children embraced him or clutched at his hand, his daughter's eyes would narrow. She wasn't much for sharing, he had come to realize. On certain occasions, she grudgingly allowed Vestie to enjoy Trevanion's affections, only because she believed that Vestie belonged to her as well. Finnikin, as far as she was concerned, belonged to both Isaboe and Jasmina. But Isaboe was all hers. If there was one thing he and his daughter shared, it was the desire to be the only person in Isaboe's life. He stood once more and stepped into the crowd of children, holding out his arms to her, and she fell easily into them.

"It's one of my favorite stories," Finnikin told the children when he was settled again, Jasmina in his lap and Clarashin by his side. "Do you want to hear it?

There were shouts of "Yes, please!"

Finnikin turned to Jasmina, who seemed most impressed by the shouting. "Do you want to hear it?"

She nodded solemnly, and everyone laughed. He looked up and caught Isaboe's smile. She was standing with the elders and Aunt Celestina, who had earlier hinted that perhaps Jasmina could stay a night on the rock alone when she was no longer fed at the breast. Isaboe saw that as a reprimand. Finnikin saw it as the right moment to walk away and not get involved.

"Well, it's a strange story, but the strangest of stories are the best to tell," he said. "And sometimes the saddest.

"You see, quite some time ago, long before the gods walked the earth, there was a war in their world between two great gods. Many were slain or lost their homes, and the realm of the gods was all but destroyed.

"Some say it was the blood of one god and the tears of the other that formed the mouth of the Skuldenore River, and others say that a songbird lapped up a drop of those tears and blood and sprinkled it on a piece of land to its south."

"Lumatere!" they all shouted.

Finnikin shook his head. "Not for a very long time. For it was once a strange place, broken into four pieces, each one of them surrounded by vast bodies of water. There were the

Mountains. The Forest. The Flatlands and . . ." Finnikin feigned a frown. "What could I have possibly forgotten? I'm sure there were four."

"The Rock," the children shouted. *"The Rock."*

"Ah, of course. The Rock," he said, hitting a hand to his head. "How could I forget the Rock? Anyway, out of the soil of the Flatlands, where the songbird had sprinkled the blood and the tears of the gods, a girl grew from the earth, and we now know her as the goddess of blood and tears. Sagrami and Lagrami."

"But they're two people, not one," Clarashin retorted.

"Well, that depends on what you want to believe," Finnikin said, looking up at Isaboe. Their decision to worship the goddess complete in Lumatere had been met with hurt and fury. "But whether she is Lagrami or Sagrami or the goddess complete, no part of her is better than the other, nor is anyone who worships one better than the other."

He looked out to the children. "Understood?"

They nodded solemnly.

"Let's get back to our young goddess," he said. "You see, she was very sad. Each night, while she slept with her head pressed into the very earth she had come from, it would whisper to her that once, long ago, it belonged to the Rock and the Forest and the Mountains. So one day, the little goddess of blood and tears began to drag the Flatlands all the way to the Rock."

Some of the children had heard the story before. Others looked at Finnikin in wonder. He nodded.

"She was that strong?" Clarashin's brother asked.

Finnikin nodded. "But she did get help," he conceded. "Luckily, the river of blood and tears felt a strong kinship with the girl and allowed her to use the Flatlands as a barge to sail upon the river. But the little goddess of blood and tears was not satisfied. Because look what she saw," he said, pointing.

The children stood and on tiptoes they stared out as far as their eyes could see.

"The Mountains?" one asked.

Finnikin nodded. "The goddess had to find a way to join them, but it was not going to be as easy as before. The river was able to help again, but it was much harder with two parts of the land now. So she placed the Rock on her back, tied a rope around the Flatlands, and dragged them both over her shoulder to the Mountains. It took days and months and years and more years, and by the time she was finished, the girl was now a woman. She could have settled in the Mountains with her friend the river, and the Flatlands she had been born from and the Rock she had come to love. But what of the Forest? The songbird would return to her over the years and tell the most magical stories about the Forest. About its beauty and power and how the ancient trees would whisper to the wind.

"One day, the god who had wept the tears that had partly made the goddess was returning from another war in their realm, when he saw a kingdom in our land of such beauty and light. This time he wept and wept and wept from the sheer joy of it, and that's how the river of tears that began in Sarnak and flowed into Lumatere actually became long enough to run through the land of Skuldenore. Lumatere was so rich that the gods chose it as a place to live, and it came to be that they walked the earth and left their mortal children behind to rule the world."

"I used to love that story," Isaboe murmured later that night as they lay side by side in Aunt Celestina's home. "There were times in exile I was so full of despair, I thought I'd end my life from the sheer loneliness of it all. But then I'd think of the little goddess. If she could live by herself in this kingdom for all those years, so could I. If she could carry the kingdom on her back, I could too."

And Isaboe did, Finnikin thought, gathering her to him.

"Remember when Lucian, Balthazar, and I would playact the goddess's voyage?" He chuckled.

"Yes, very amusing," she said. "At least Celie was always chosen to be the Rock and was fortunate enough to be carried on Lucian's back. I always had to be the Flatlands, dragged along by my hair."

"And Balthazar would stand on a barge and pretend to be the river."

He laughed again and he felt her eyes on him in the dark.

"I do love it when you laugh, my love. I don't hear it enough." There was sadness in her voice.

"Do you hate living in the palace?" she asked quietly.

Finnikin sighed. "You ask me that every time we're up here," he said. "Have I ever given you reason to believe that I don't enjoy my life with you?"

He expected her to laugh off his question, but she didn't.

"You go strangely Rock-native when you're here," she said instead. "There's a rumbling in your voice, and your shoulders don't seem so stiff."

"And you go all barefoot and primitive when you're up there in the Mountains with your feral cousins," he said.

"Do you hate living in the palace?" she asked again.

His hand traveled up her nightdress. "Do you want to know the truth?" he murmured, then pressed a kiss to her mouth. "About what I was thinking today?"

"No, I don't think I do."

"Well, here it is. I was thinking how wonderful it would be

if Jasmina and you and I lived in Lumatere all alone in the same way the goddess of blood and tears did."

She laughed at that. "And your father? Wouldn't you want him there as well?"

He thought for a moment and sighed. "Yes, and my father."

"And you'd want Aunt Celestina. And your father would want Beatriss, and Beatriss would want Vestie, and I would want Yata, who would want Lucian and all her sons and grandchildren. And in the end . . ."

"In the end, things would be exactly as they are now," he said, his fingers lightly trailing against her skin. She shivered from his touch, and he moved to cover her body with his.

"Quietly," she murmured, knowing that being the leaders of their land meant they were never left completely alone. There was always someone outside their chamber guarding them. Over the years, they had learned the art of loving each other in silence. For some reason, tonight he resented the need to contain their sounds, but he captured her cry with his mouth on hers, felt the nails of her fingers sink deep into his flesh, and gave thanks that there was no frailty in this queen of his.

Later, when they were half sated and he could taste the salt in the dampness of her skin, he pressed a gentle kiss to her throat.

"Don't ever ask me again if I hate living anywhere with you and Jasmina," he said. "This rock reminds me of the boy I was, and being with you in the palace reminds me of the man I want to be."

"Not just any man," she whispered. "A king. Mine."

CHAPTER 13

After a week in the Citavita, all Froi had achieved in his mission to Charyn was the suspicion that the king lived somewhere in the vicinity of the fourth or fifth tower. He knew he had to act fast. In less than a week, the *provincari* would arrive for the day of weeping and the guards in the palace would double. But what competed most with the task at hand was Froi's fascination with two brothers separated by a *gravina,* a princess with two people living inside of her, and a woman imprisoned for twelve years whose only contact with her daughter was a holler from a window.

The days that followed began in the same way. Each morning Froi would test himself, lying in Quintana's bed after pleading tiredness or inventing an illness attributed to the body part important in the art of planting seeds. He would play the game of trying to work out who she was from the moment her eyes opened. Princess Indignant always, *always* woke in fright. She'd squint and nod and mutter, *"There's a man dying in Turla."* On the other hand, Quintana the ice maiden was always cold and usually called him fool. If his body was anywhere close or touching hers, she'd snarl, and he came to understand that the savageness appeared with her, rather than Princess Indignant and could be witnessed in the curl of Quintana's lips and a glimpse of slightly crooked teeth. But something always seemed able to soften her. Froi would see it happen before his very eyes. The nodding. The "Yes, yes, I'm trying!" Whether he wanted to admit it or not, his heart would pound with excitement every time he saw the madness.

Princess Indignant also loved nothing more than spending her time watching the ritual between the brothers from Abroi, Gargarin and Arjuro.

"Blessed Arjuro? Can we come visit?" she called out from her balconette, trying to capture Arjuro's attention with a ridiculous wave, just in case he had lost his hearing.

Arjuro ignored her.

"Do you think he went mad in the dungeons?" she asked.

"Not in the dungeons," Gargarin said quietly.

"Do you think he loved Lirah beyond life itself?"

Silence. Froi looked over at Gargarin, watched the lump in the man's throat move as he said, "No, I don't."

"I think you're wrong, Sir Gargarin," she said.

"Gargarin," he corrected. "No 'sir.'"

"When I woke that time after Lirah took me to search for the oracle, Arjuro was there."

"The oracle?" Froi asked.

"We searched for her in the lake of the half dead. *Poor Lirah.*"

And there was Aunt Mawfa again. "Oh, my *poor bones,*" the woman had whispered while stuffing herself with the fattiest part of the piglet that morning.

The princess prattled on. "I was six, Sir Gargarin. They were all frightened because of the godspeak that was coming from my mouth. I wrote it on the wall, you know. With the blood from my wrist. My father was desperate for Arjuro to decipher it and they dragged him into the room from the prison tower and I'll not forget his face, Sir Gargarin, when he saw Lirah half dead on the wet ground. He fell to his knees and wept, I tell you, gathering her in his arms. As if Lirah were the most beloved of women."

Froi saw Gargarin's knuckles clench as he leaned on the balconette.

"What were you doing with blood on your wrists? Why was Lirah half-dead?" Froi asked, alarmed.

Gargarin elbowed Froi into silence.

"I always believed blessed Arjuro would return for her, Sir Gargarin. I've prayed to the gods that he would. More than I've prayed to the gods for myself. But then they released him in my eighth year and he disappeared for so, so long."

"You have a good heart, *reginita,*" Gargarin said gently before walking into his chamber.

The princess stared after him as if she were trying to determine his meaning.

"That was actually a compliment," Froi said.

"What about when you told me about my dress that morning?"

Froi didn't want to think of what he witnessed that day.

"Not a compliment," he said, contrite. "Being rude, I was. You've got awful dress sense, so don't ever believe anyone who tries to tell you otherwise. But that," he said, pointing inside his chamber. "That was the real thing."

He saw her face flush and she held a hand to both cheeks for a moment, as though surprised by the heat. Then she disappeared inside, and Froi wondered if she went in there to cry.

And then there was Lirah. It wasn't as though Froi was half in love with her, but there was a force at play whenever he saw her. An ache he could not comprehend. He convinced himself that he liked her garden more than her, and so one day he found a more convenient way of visiting her rooftop prison from the battlement of his tower. Froi would break into a run, sailing through the air, his legs eating the gap between the two towers, his arms outstretched as though they would grab him space, his grunt muted by the shouts from the other side, until he landed on the opposite battlement, almost, but not quite, securely on his feet. The first time, when he stood up, brushing the debris from his trousers and inspecting the damage to his arm, he turned and saw the combination of awe and horror on the faces of Dorcas and the soldiers on the opposite roof.

"Are you an idiot, or an idiot?" Gargarin hissed, watching Froi climb back down to their balconette one time.

"The first one. I really resent being called the second."

Thankfully, the fool Dorcas didn't try to stop him, because there didn't seem to be orders preventing the guest of one tower leaping over to visit the prisoner of the opposite tower. And Froi noticed each time that the battlements of the fourth and fifth towers were guarded by twice the number of soldiers of any other in the palace. Froi needed to find a way inside them.

Meantime he made use of his time with Lirah, although she wasn't much one for talking, and most of their gardening was done in silence.

"Tell me honestly," he demanded on a particularly boring day in the palace when he visited three times. "In the how many years that you've had this garden, has the petunia ever survived beside the tulip?"

Sometimes, without a word, she'd relinquish a plant to him and Froi would choose the best place for it to flower.

He found out little through Lirah. She asked of Quintana each time. Over the years, the king had allowed them in the same room only once, seven years after Lirah's imprisonment, when Quintana turned thirteen and her first blood came. "That's when they decided to whore her to Charyn," she said bitterly.

Since then, Quintana and Lirah had only seen each other from the dungeon windows. The three images of the princess on Lirah's prison wall now made sense. They showed the first time Lirah saw her babe, the last time before imprisonment, and the one and only time they had been in a room together between then and now.

"Were you in love with Arjuro?" he asked.

As usual, she didn't stop what she was doing and refused to look his way. "Why do you ask that?"

"Because you're both . . . I don't know. Savage. Cruel."

"Are you trying to flatter me?"

He laughed. It was the first attempt at humor that Lirah had made. She turned to him, as though surprised by the sound.

"Well, you both seem the kind who would find each other in a crowded room," he said.

Her study stayed intense until she went back to her digging. "Arjuro prefers men to women."

"Oh," he said, surprised for a moment. "Well that makes sense, come to think of it. I can't imagine a woman putting up with that stench."

"Yes, well he always did have an aversion to bathing."

"But that doesn't mean you weren't in love with him."

She wiped her brow with the back of her hand and it left a mark of dirt.

"I can safely say we despised each other."

"Why?"

Lirah didn't respond, and then Froi understood. "Ah. You loved the same man."

"You could say that," she said quietly, and he knew that he had asked too many questions and that if he didn't stop, she'd go back to her silence.

"When I return home, I'll find a way to send you lavender seeds," he said when the sky began to darken and he knew he'd have to leap back.

"Lavender? In Charyn?"

He waited a moment.

"About Quintana—" he began, but she cut him off.

"I don't answer questions about Quintana to strangers."

"I'm forced to share her bed," he said. "How can I be a stranger to her?"

"You ask that of a whore?" Her eyes flashed with anger, but Froi saw pain there too.

"Is it true that there's more than one living inside her head?"

"Are you asking me if she's mad?"

He didn't respond.

"Do you know what those in the palace say?" Lirah said. "That the king should have tossed her the moment she was born."

Lirah shuddered at the sound of her own words.

"Was she always so strange?" Froi asked.

"You find her strange?" she said harshly. "When as a child she managed to separate parts of herself and make them whole beings? Each situation requires a different Quintana. But she survived. In this cesspit. That's not strange or mad." Lirah sent him one of her scathing looks. "It's pure genius. Do you think she was like you or the rest of the last borns? You may not have been born into wealth, Olivier of Sebastabol, but you've been pampered by your province and your mother and father all your life."

"Wrong person to say that to," he said quietly. "Anyway, aren't you convinced I'm from Serker?"

She looked at him closely. "You're orphaned?"

Froi didn't respond. "Regardless, Quintana wasn't orphaned. So it can't have been that bad for her. She had the king, and she had you, her mother."

Lirah's laugh was bitter. "The king? Have you met the king? A more degenerate man doesn't exist in Charyn or the land of Skuldenore. The only thing the gods did right was to instill a fear in him of his own daughter, because if they hadn't, his wickedness would have shattered her body and her mind."

Froi's blood ran cold. In Lirah's mind, Quintana may have escaped the depravity of her father, but he knew she hadn't managed to hide from Bestiano.

"The gods gave her you," he said. "That must count for something."

Lirah gave a laugh of bitter disbelief. "Do you know why I'm here? In this prison?"

"You tried to kill someone. Apart from Gargarin. Was it a man you were forced to bed?" And then a thought came to him. "Sagra! You tried to kill the king?"

She shook her head.

"There are not many places to hide a dagger when you're taken to the king's chamber as his whore."

Froi stared at her. Wanted to tell her he understood. Wanted to confess the depravity in his own life on the streets of the Sarnak capital as a child. But there was too much shame. Girls were small and helpless. Boys should be able to protect themselves, no matter how young or slight in build.

She stood, brushing the dirt from her shift.

"What do you think of the cold one? The one that seems to be in charge?" she asked.

Froi shrugged. "I like it better when she's not around me."

Lirah collected her pots and string and walked toward her prison. "She's the one to fear. She'll make you do things that break your heart."

* * *

When it came time to visit Arjuro at the godshouse again, Froi didn't have the nerve to leap over the *gravina*. The first time had been enough. Arjuro kept the window to the balconette shut and the curtain drawn most days, but Froi was patient, and one morning he intruded on the brotherly ritual. "Arjuro! I'm knocking on the door at midday," he shouted. "Be sure to open for me."

Gargarin stared at him with disbelief. "Does the word *street lords* not mean anything to you?" he asked.

"Two words, not one. *Street. Lords*. Care to join me?" Froi asked. "As far as they're concerned, I'm the priestling's messenger."

Arjuro, of course, didn't play by the rules, and Froi was forced to hammer the door for what seemed hours.

"Didn't think you'd be back here," the priestling muttered, bleary-eyed.

"Why wouldn't I when there's so much fun to be had in the Citavita?" Froi said. "This what you're looking for?" he asked, holding up a cask he had stolen from the cellars. The priestling was drunk, his eyes bloodshot and swollen. They studied Froi fiercely.

Froi followed him up the dark space. He'd lost count of the steps and almost understood Arjuro's reluctance to open the door. When they reached the Hall of Illumination, Froi walked to the balconette, where he could see Gargarin watching them from across the *gravina*. Gargarin didn't usually stand out on the balconette at this hour of the day, but Froi suspected he was there to see what Froi was up to.

"Last night I dreamed of the three," Arjuro said over his shoulder. "Did he?"

"I don't understand."

"Gargarin, myself, and a third who didn't live. Throughout my life the third has returned to me in my dreams, and he has returned to me these seven nights past. I wager if you ask my brother, he'll say the same."

"Is it because you have the same face? Do you dream the same things? Sense each other?"

"It's because of the third. He haunts us when he needs to. He was born dead."

"Arjuro, you're not making sense," Froi said.

Arjuro was quiet a moment, as though he regretted speaking.

"Tell me about the third," Froi persisted.

"Our poor mother was a girl of fourteen. She refused to believe the third was dead and kept him in the cot alongside Gargarin and myself. Placed him on her breast as if he lived and had the life in him to suckle. Until flies and maggots crawled over us. It's what our father used to say. 'You should have been choked by the maggots and flies that shared your cot.'"

"He was a charming man," Froi said, repulsed.

"Is," Arjuro corrected. "He's still alive. A madman, frightened of anything strange, and three babes with the same face was too strange for him. So he told all in Abroi that there was only one."

"How could he do that if two lived?"

"By hiding us in a hovel underneath the cottage. When we were four and old enough to work the farm, he would take us out to work one day at a time."

Froi could not understand what Arjuro was saying. He placed a hand over the cup to stop the priestling from pouring another drink. Arjuro looked at him and flinched. "You have the face of a cruel man, Olivier of Sebastabol."

"But it's in me to be kind," Froi said. "Talk."

Arjuro pointed to the cup, and Froi removed his hand.

"We had one name. The word for 'nothing' in the Abroin dialect. Dafar. Nothing. One day I was Dafar and my brother stayed in the hole. The next day he was Dafar and I stayed in the hole."

Froi was breathless. "Madness," he whispered.

Arjuro nodded. "We named each other. Gargarin is not a Charynite name. I liked Arjuro. Gar and Ari." Arjuro smiled for a moment. "They were two adventurers in the year one hundred who wrote tales claiming they had gone beyond the Ocean of Skuldenore."

Arjuro swallowed a cupful of wine, soaking his beard.

"There was never a time when my brother wasn't taking care of me. It was Gar who always had the plans to protect us from our father. I received the gift of godspeak when I was six years old, and Gar and I clutched on to each other with such joy that day. The walls of our hovel were filled with words of wonder. Blessings from the gods, wisdom from the Ancients. Gargarin's time would come soon, we'd tell each other. We could not imagine a gift bestowed on one and not the other. What it took others months to learn, I could do in a moment. Read. Write. Translate for the gods. I wrote the symbols and taught Gargarin, for only the gods' touched could read the raw words written by the gods themselves, and in Abroi we had the oldest caves in the kingdom. And we waited for his gift and waited, telling ourselves we would escape from the swamp of Abroi the moment it came. But it didn't. Gargarin had not been chosen."

Froi saw tears in Arjuro's eyes, as though the moment he remembered had taken place just the day before.

"Our father, being an ignorant man, was frightened by intellect and reason. And he was even more frightened by what could not be explained. He believed he could thrash it out of me, this gift that had others in awe." A flash of pain crossed Arjuro's face.

"Gargarin always had a solution. 'If we can take turns being Dafar, then we can take turns being you,' he'd say. So we would share the beating."

Arjuro's eyes were fierce with self disgust. "I let him."

All Froi's young life he had prayed to the gods that someone would share the beatings and his pain. If anyone understood Arjuro, he did.

"One day, when we were ten years old," Arjuro continued, "Gar packed a saddlebag. He took my hand, and we walked four days to Paladozza. People stood agog by the side of the road, for they had never seen our two faces together. But Paladozza was a dream. The second capital, they called it. The godshouse was full of learned men and women, and Gar demanded a meeting with the priestess. 'My brother is gods' touched,' he said. 'Take care of him.' He then walked all the way back to Abroi."

"You lived apart?"

Arjuro nodded. "Every night I spent away from home, I dreamed of three babes. I knew I was dreaming of my brothers, one dead and one alive, until I could no longer stand being away from Gar. I walked four days back to Abroi to be with him. I told him about the dream, and he had dreamed the same.

"Finally, the *provincaro* of Paladozza came to Abroi and took us both. The priests were desperate to have me in their godshouse school. Despite the fact that our father tried time and time again to drag us back to Abroi, we found peace in Paladozza. Gar was the *provincaro*'s servant boy and I went to school, but we still managed to see each other every day. We were treated with the same respect as the *provincaro*'s son, De Lancey. Everything I learned, I taught Gargarin. At sixteen I was sent to the Citavita to begin my time as a priestling in the godshouse. Gargarin gave up the *provincaro*'s offer of land and prosperity to stay close to me and he found himself work in the palace that once sat at the entrance of the Citavita where the bridge ends. Gar was the king's errand boy."

"How does an errand boy end up being one of the king's trusted few?" Froi asked.

"Because whether it was the *provincaro* of Paladozza or the king of Charyn, Gargarin of Abroi was not easy to ignore. Within a year at the palace, he had drawn designs that everyone he met marveled at. They said that one day this lad would be the king's First Adviser." Arjuro's words were slurred. "They began building the palace across the rock, the most impenetrable royal dwelling in the whole of the land. Years later, when it was complete, the palace made the king feel like a god until he believed he had the status of one. And then this godshouse was raped."

Froi leaned forward to stare into the man's eyes. "I don't think for a moment that Gargarin believes you betrayed the priestlings, Arjuro," Froi said. "You can't possibly believe that."

"You don't want to know what I saw," the priestling said, his voice hoarse.

"Was it the slaughter?" Froi asked.

Arjuro shook his head, stumbled to his feet, and pushed Froi away.

"If I could tear out my eyes to stop what I saw on the day of weeping, I'd do it over and over again."

"Quintana's birth?" Froi asked, confused. "But you were imprisoned, Arjuro. You couldn't have seen anything."

"I saw everything," Arjuro said, his voice hoarse. "But ask me nothing of that night."

Froi followed him down the dark passage. "Then I ask why Lirah is imprisoned."

The priestling's shoulders collapsed. Froi could tell he didn't want to answer that question either.

"For an attempted murder," Arjuro said quietly.

"Who?" Froi demanded.

"Her daughter."

CHAPTER 14

Phaedra watched her Mont husband carefully. She had been sitting on his side of the stream awhile now. It was unnerving not to have her people around, especially in the presence of the white witch.

"So answer the question," the white witch said. "Are your people not coming to see me about their ailments because they think they will be banished from the valley if I find something wrong with them?"

"They're frightened of you," Phaedra blurted out. "Curses frighten my people, and so do Charynites of mixed blood."

"Well, I'm glad I didn't have to beat that out of her," Tesadora muttered to Lucian.

Phaedra had never met a more frightening woman. She noticed that even the Mont lads feared her and ventured near only when they knew the white witch was farther downstream.

"We need to know about whether Rafuel's rebels have heard from their messenger," her Mont husband said. He didn't seem worried about the ailments of her people and was impatient with the white witch's questions.

"I beg your pardon, my lord," Phaedra said, her eyes studying the patterns of dirt on the ground inside the tent.

"I've told you before, I'm not your anything," the Mont said coldly.

She nodded. "I beg your pardon, Luci-en." She winced, knowing she said it wrong. "If I did know something, I'm not certain why you think I'd tell you."

She caught Tesadora and the three other girls exchanging surprised expressions.

"What I'm trying to say . . . is that my allegiance is not with you. It's with them. It's why they don't tell me anything. They fear that you and your Guard and the white witch, and perhaps the Charynite king's riders, if they come to the valley, will attempt to torture it out of me."

"The white witch?" one of the novices asked. "Is that what they call you, Tesadora?"

Tesadora shot Phaedra a look that narrowed her eyes even more. "I've been referred to as worse."

"We don't torture," Lucian snapped. "You mistake us for Charynites."

The white witch made a strange sound of disbelief. "Of course we torture."

Lucian looked at the white witch and then at Phaedra with irritation.

"We would never torture *her,*" he said. "That's what I'm trying to explain."

"I'd torture her in a moment." The white witch spoke as though Phaedra were not standing before her. "If she knew the fate of Froi and was holding it from us, I'd relish the torture."

Phaedra dared not look at the older woman. When she had lived in the mountains during her marriage to the Mont, she had heard stories of what this white witch had done to a man who had been taken to the cloisters where she once lived with the novices. The man had been in pain, complaining of stomach cramps, and the witch had sliced him from chest to navel and left him open to die while his family watched. Worse still was the story that it was the mother of the white witch who had cursed Lumatere while burning at the stake.

"But if I was to know that your kinsman Froi was safe," Phaedra said, "I would tell you. Without torture."

Phaedra chanced a look at the Mont. She imagined that once, when his father lived, he would have been a kinder lad and full of warmth. But she had not seen that side of him, and when he insisted that she return to her father earlier in the year, she had been relieved to be far from him.

"I need to go back up the mountain," he said, getting to his feet, and she could hear weariness in his voice.

One of the girls clicked her tongue with dismay. "Whether you reach the mountain tonight or early tomorrow won't make a difference, Lucian. Stay."

He shook his head. "My father never spent a night away from his people."

He mounted his horse, and then he was gone, leaving Phaedra on the enemy side of the stream with the white witch staring at her in the dark.

"You'll never find your dwellings across the stream," she said. "You'll sleep here tonight."

Later, when everyone slept, Phaedra was awoken by the sound of a horse. She had heard the same sound from her side of the stream on other nights and had wondered who would ride down the mountain at such a time. She heard a shuffling at the entrance of the tent and then the flap was pulled back, revealing the Lumateran Guard they referred to as Perri the Savage. In the light of the moon she could see the hideous scar across his crown, saw his cold dark eyes search the room. Phaedra whimpered. She was a fool not to believe that it had been a plot all along. They had sent the most brutal of the Guard to deal with her, after all.

She watched him creep stealthily across the space, and she squeezed her eyes shut, praying to Ferja, the goddess of courage.

"What was that sound?" she heard the Savage whisper.

"Probably the wife Lucian sent back," the white witch responded sleepily. "Thinking you're going to torture her."

He snorted. "After more than a week without a break and a day on the road?"

Phaedra heard the rustle of clothing being removed.

"You were a fool to come without resting," the white witch said quietly.

"I'll find time to rest when you come home," he murmured, and Phaedra's face was aflame as she heard sounds that had little to do with torture and more to do with pleasure.

"We have a home, do we?" the white witch asked.

"I'll build you one."

This time it was Tesadora who sighed. "Sleep. You're too tired to be of any use to me tonight."

He chuckled and soon they slept and Phaedra was comforted that such a man would build a woman a home. That such a woman would speak words with tenderness.

She was forced to spend a second night on the Lumateran side of the stream, translating her chronicles of the Charynites who arrived each day in the valley for Tesadora and the novices.

"I hope you're not promising them anything," Tesadora snapped from her bedroll as the others slept.

"It wouldn't matter if I did," Phaedra said. "Charynites don't trust promises."

The next morning, she woke to a party of people arriving with more soldiers than she had ever seen. They came with women and children and some of the Mont girls she remembered from her time in the mountains. She felt uncomfortable with their stares and would have done anything to be on her side of the stream. The women who sat in the tent were dressed for the cool mountain air. Phaedra could see that they were women of wealth. She had no idea how to determine the age of a child after seeing so few in her life, but the smallest was a tiny cherub with the grayest of eyes, her hair covered by an oversize cap. She stared solemnly from her mother's lap. The other little girl was older and so beautiful, it made Phaedra's heart ache.

"What a strange way to live," one of the younger Monts said, coming into the tent after having observed Phaedra's people across the stream.

"No different from the trogs up on Finnikin's Rock," Tesadora said.

It was a noisy room of talk and giggles and hushed gossip. Tesadora laughed heartily at what the young woman with the gray-eyed child had to say. There was love among these people, and, as always, Phaedra felt so far removed and lonely from everyone, even her own.

The conversation among them changed constantly and finally settled on the Charynite camp.

"They're so dirty," one of the Mont girls said. "I tell you, I spent a day helping Tesadora, and I could barely stand the stench when I stood beside a group of women."

"Constance," a fair-haired girl warned.

Then there was silence, and the Mont girl's eyes flickered to

Phaedra. Phaedra's face felt as though it were on fire. So many eyes suddenly on her, pity in some. But what shamed her more were the stares from the children.

"The wife Lucian sent back," she heard one of them explain in a whisper.

"Spent two whole weeks crying when he first brought her to the mountain," another said.

She heard hisses of *"Shhhh"* and *"Enough!"* The stares continued and then more silence, so much of it that even the Lumaterans looked uncomfortable.

"They escaped through the sewers," Phaedra said quietly.

Phaedra felt the eyes of every person in the tent on her. Although she had never been called outspoken, she had an awful habit of speaking out of nervousness. "Enough now, Phaedra, my sweet," her father would say.

Still no one spoke.

"They were imprisoned in the province of Nebia," she said, her voice small and insignificant. "The woman Jorja and her daughter Florenza. Jorja's husband, Harker, had information about a number of Serkers who are said to live underground, and Harker was arranging to have the Serkers smuggled to the province of Alonso. What he didn't know was that his contact was a spy for the palace."

Enough now, Phaedra, my sweet.

"His wife and daughter found this out only after they were arrested in Harker's place. They escaped through the sewers of their city."

Phaedra looked at the Mont girl who had spoken. "That's why you could barely stand the stench of them. Because they escaped through the shit of their people to save the life of Harker and twelve Serkers."

Phaedra caught the wary stare of the young woman with the gray-eyed child.

Enough now, Phaedra.

"If you believe us to be filthy demons, then it is wrong of you to bring your precious babes into danger," Phaedra said, looking at the woman and her child. "If they were ours, we'd never place them in harm's way."

The young mother stared back at Phaedra with fury. She stood, placing her daughter on her hip. "Now I have Charynites telling me how to bring up my child!" she said, before walking out.

The fair-haired young woman stood instantly to follow, but another took her hand. "Let her go, Celie."

"I meant no offense," Phaedra said, hanging her head with shame.

A handsome woman with kind eyes shook her head. "She's tired. Leave her."

"But, Lady Abian, someone should go to her," one of the Mont girls said.

Lady Abian smiled ruefully. "In my early days with Celie, Augie's mother persisted in telling me what to do all the time. The poor queen may not have a mother-in-law, but every person in Lumatere has something to tell her about how to rear a child."

Phaedra turned away in horror. She had insulted Queen Isaboe of Lumatere.

"Finnikin's great-aunt told her that she should no longer have Jasmina in their bed," the one named Beatriss said. Phaedra had heard of her. Once, she had been betrothed to the captain of the Guard.

"And that Jasmina is too old to still be at the breast," a Mont girl joined in.

"Well, I have to agree there," said another.

The women chatted on, and Phaedra was forgotten. She slipped out of the tent and looked between the trees to where the queen stood with her consort's arms around her. Phaedra recognized him from the day in Rafuel's cell. They were speaking to the captain, who had the little princess sitting on his shoulders. The little princess pulled her *shalamon*'s ears, and it was strange to see the captain laugh.

Phaedra watched as her Mont husband arrived from the mountain. He dismounted and walked toward the small party. He tugged the queen's cap over her eyes, and the queen of Lumatere laughed. Phaedra saw a beauty that she had not recognized in the tent. Secretly, she had always felt shame that her Mont husband's cousin had not thought Phaedra significant enough to visit on the mountain. Or invite to the palace.

"They meant no harm," she heard Tesadora say at her shoulder.

Phaedra walked away, scrubbing away tears, not realizing that she was crying. She was tired of feeling shame. She was tired of feeling helpless all the time.

"Did you hear what I said?" Tesadora asked, gripping her arm.

"They say we're dirty," Phaedra cried, pulling free. "Luci-en says we're useless. Your queen says we're murderers. I overheard the Mont lads say we should be rounded up and set aflame. We're barren. We worship too many gods. Our bread is tasteless. Our faces are plain. We cry too much. Our fathers abandon us. We don't understand kinship. We're pitiful!"

Phaedra shook her head. "If your people mean no offense, they should not speak their thoughts out loud in front of their children, Tesadora. Because it will be their children who come to slaughter us one day, all because of the careless words passed down by their elders who meant no harm."

Tesadora stared a moment, and then a ghost of a smile appeared on her face.

"Strange things happen when we stand face-to-face with our enemy, don't they, Phaedra of Alonso?"

Tesadora leaned forward and sniffed at Phaedra's clothing.

"Why, you're not so dirty after all." She smiled mockingly. "And you just called me Tesadora, so that must mean I'm not the white witch anymore."

The queen returned to the mountain with her consort that night, but the others stayed. Phaedra had not been dismissed, so she spent a third night on the Lumateran side of the stream. She had little desire to sleep among the women in Tesadora's tent and chose to sleep under the stars in a bed of leaves, feeling lonelier than she ever had in her life.

She was awoken in the morning by the sounds from across the stream in the camp. During the night, someone had placed a blanket over her, and she now folded it carefully to return it to the tent. The Lumaterans were already awake, and soldiers of the Guard, including the captain, were swarming the forest.

She approached the others, who were pottering around a fire, being served tea by Tesadora's girls, when suddenly Tesadora stopped, staring in the direction of the stream. She stood and then her eyes met Phaedra's.

"Something's wrong," she said.

Phaedra listened a moment. It was unnaturally silent. The world of the cave dwellers seemed to have stopped.

"Trevanion!" Tesadora called out.

The captain and his Guard were there in an instant. "The stream," Tesadora said.

Phaedra and Tesadora followed the Guard. The silence could mean only one thing, that someone had arrived unannounced.

Perhaps it was the riders from the Citavita searching for last borns.

They reached the stream and came to an instant halt. Across the water, every camp dweller stood staring back at her. No, not her. They were staring at the little girl the Lumaterans called Vestie, who stood beside Lady Beatriss of the Flatlands. In the eyes of her fellow Charynites, Phaedra saw so much wonder and despair.

Lady Beatriss held her daughter's hand while the captain stood beside her. They would have been a striking couple in their youth, and Phaedra had heard that it was Lumatere's sadness that these two had still not announced a bonding day.

Lady Beatriss turned to Phaedra and Tesadora questioningly.

"We came to splash some water on our faces," she said quietly. "Please speak our sorrow if they are insulted that we used the stream."

Phaedra shook her head, unable to speak. The Mont girls arrived and stared across at the Charynites, bewildered.

"Do we have mud on our faces?" one asked. "The way they're staring is strange."

Celie of the Flatlands looked at Phaedra for an answer.

"Phaedra?" she prodded gently.

Phaedra's face burned from the attention. "When Luci-en first took me up to the mountain, I cried for days and weeks," she said, "every single time I saw a child. I had not seen one before, and I suddenly understood in my whole being what drove our people to madness. For the beauty of a child took my breath away."

The Lumateran women looked confused.

"Have they not told you? Your captain and his men?" she asked. "It's part of our curse. We've not birthed a child in Charyn for eighteen years."

Celie of the Flatlands and the Mont girls gasped in horror.

Lady Beatriss caught her breath, her eyes wide with shock. She stared up at the captain, who looked away.

"You're pale, Lady Beatriss," Phaedra said.

Lady Beatriss held two hands to her face.

"It's been a tiring trip," she said. Phaedra could see she was lying. Even Tesadora looked away.

A moment later, Lady Beatriss seemed to have recovered and she held out a hand to Tesadora. "Would you accompany me across the stream?" she asked. "I'd like to make their acquaintance."

"You're better off with Lucian's wife. They think I'm going to curse them."

Then little Vestie held a hand to Phaedra and she took it, her skin tingling at how small and soft it felt.

"They're very withdrawn, so please do not take offense at their ways," Phaedra explained. "I'm trying to find a way to have them all speak to each other, but they tend to keep to their own dwellings. The vegetable patches have worked to bring them together to a certain degree."

"I'm sure you'll think of a way," Lady Beatriss said.

The journey down the mountain was silent, and Beatriss found it hard to swallow. It was as though something sour was lodged in her throat and she could not release it. Trevanion rode beside her and more than once she tried to speak, but the words failed.

When they reached the road that passed through Sennington, she clicked at her horse to stop.

"You don't have to come in," she said to him. "I'll take her." Vestie had insisted on riding with Trevanion and had fallen asleep in his arms.

"I'll carry her inside," was all he said.

They rode down the path through the village and past the

cottage of Jacklin and Marta. Beatriss saw all their worldly goods packed onto their mule, and her heart sank. They had come to her only days before, heartbroken to have to say the words that they could not stay in Sennington. They had been offered work in Lord Freychinet's village. Their departure would mean that Beatriss's village was now down to fifteen people. Three years ago, there were forty-nine of them, all determined to put the past behind and work tirelessly on the crop. But the crop had failed to yield for three years, and it was selfish of Beatriss to keep her village tied to a dead soil.

When they arrived back at the long house, Trevanion followed her into Vestie's room and she watched him place her daughter on the bed before he followed her down into the kitchen.

"Ask me," she said quietly.

He didn't respond.

"It's what you have wanted to do since you found out about the Charynites. So ask me."

He stood, dwarfing his surroundings, as he always did in her mind. When she was a young woman, his presence had consumed every part of her. She couldn't bear being with him in a room because everyone in it disappeared from existence, except for him. Even parts of her disappeared.

"I have to go," he said quietly, walking out of Vestie's chamber and down the stairs.

"Ask me," she cried. "Ask me something. You never ask me of the past, and without questions, I can't speak, Trevanion. These unspoken words choke me inside."

He looked at her, shaking his head with despair at not being able to release the words himself.

"What do you want me to ask you, Beatriss?" he said, anguish in his voice.

"Who her father is. It must have been the first question to

pass through your mind. If the Charynites have not produced children, who is the father of Vestie?"

But Trevanion did not ask and did not speak. Whatever had happened to him in exile had broken a part inside of him that she could not mend.

Instead, he turned and walked away and left Beatriss standing alone in her kitchen. It had always been her favorite part of the house. Here, during those long ten years, she had cooked for her whole village. They had stayed united because of it. When people supped together, they shared more than food, regardless of their station in life. She stared at the large pot that was able to feed so many, and knowing what she had to do, with a deep regret in her heart, Beatriss sat down and began to pen a letter to Phaedra of Alonso.

CHAPTER 15

Froi waited in the courtyard of the palace to visit the Citavita. It had been ten days since he had arrived in the palace, but it felt longer. At times, it seemed as though he couldn't breathe from the weight of the stone walls surrounding him. The Citavita, at least, provided him with some kind of reprieve and a certain fascination. He had become accustomed to coming and going these last few days, and although there was not one specific hour when the drawbridge was raised, he spent most of his time on the lookout. Today he felt Bestiano's eyes on him, staring down from one of the upper walkways. Froi bowed respectfully, but there was no response from Bestiano.

From behind him, he heard the horses come out of the stables, and as suddenly as the drawbridge was raised, more than a dozen palace riders rode past Froi toward the gates, followed by a heavily armed horse-drawn carriage. He stepped aside, curious about who was inside, and when the carriage rolled past him, he heard the name "Olivier!" spoken with a whimper.

"Quintana?" he said, following it down the drawbridge as it lurched and rolled away. "Are you in there?" he shouted. He continued to trail the carriage down the wall of the Citavita, but it was too narrow a stretch of path to share with the riders and the townspeople. Froi pressed against the rock to stop himself from being crushed. He recognized Dorcas riding close to the carriage and broke into a slow run to keep alongside the guard.

"Dorcas," he shouted. "Where are you taking her, Dorcas?"

"Soothsayer," Dorcas replied. "It's a custom each year before the day of weeping."

"A custom to do what?" Froi snapped.

Dorcas was irritated in the way he was always irritated when Froi spoke. "To rid her of the curse. Best you go back to the palace. You ask too many questions."

"Because you don't ask enough, Dorcas, you fool. She's scared."

"King's orders."

From the tops of caves and the road above, the Citavitans stopped to watch. Their stares were bitter. "Whore!" one shouted, and threw a rotten apple at the carriage. "Demon!"

Froi followed the entourage farther down the road, watching the carriage totter close to the edge. It was too tight a fit on the narrow track, and he imagined both horses and carriage toppling over the side at any moment. But halfway down, they stopped at the entrance to one of the cave houses and Quintana was taken into the soothsayer's cave under a pelt of rotten fruit and fury from above.

Outside the cave, the palace soldiers stood guard, their attention on the roofs above. Froi watched merchants pack up their goods nervously, whilst others stared from the street lords to the soldiers, tensely waiting.

"The carriage is blocking the road, friend," one of the street lords called out to the palace riders. "There's a herd of cattle behind you that don't take too well to following orders."

Although the street lords were few in number, the palace

riders were smart enough to look wary. A moment later, the carriage jolted forward and it became impossible for the rider to see what was taking place on the narrow crowded road.

Froi heard cries from inside the soothsayer's cave and then silence. Chants and then silence again. A warbling sound caused the horses of the carriage to lurch forward. Inside the cave, another cry was followed by silence. Froi could see the horses champing at the bit, and he moved close enough to the carriage to note the driver's white knuckles gripping on tight. But the large herd of cattle was urged ahead by the street lords and began to push both horses and carriage to the edge of the cliff road.

"You're going to have to let the horses go!" Froi shouted up to the carriage driver, who stood up to look behind and was jolted again. Froi leaped up beside him, stared back at the road, and saw the herd of cattle gaining on them.

Froi shoved the driver off the carriage before the fool was forced over the side into the *gravina,* carriage and all. He then climbed up to release the mounts as they tossed their manes with fury. The driver was back on his feet in front of the horses, working on the second harness. Less than a moment after the horses were released, the carriage went hurtling over the side, crashing against the rocks in the abyss below.

On this narrow stretch of rock, Froi watched cattle, soldiers, street lords, and horses jostle for space. Inside the soothsayer's cave, there were screams and crashes, and the next moment, Froi saw a figure come racing out, her hair drenched and tangled. But Froi wasn't the only one to see her. From the flat roof of a cave above, a street lord noticed her as well. The man leaped down and landed close to Froi's feet. Without a second thought, Froi caught him with a fist to the temple, knocking him down.

As Froi raced down the winding road after Quintana, he

caught glimpses of her hair, but bend after bend she would disappear, until he reached a stretch where she seemed to have vanished altogether. He imagined that she was either heading down toward the bridge of the Citavita or was inside one of the caves teeming with vendors who were taking refuge. But then, at the entrance of a cave beside him, Froi heard the rasp of heavy breathing coming from behind a trio of baskets overspilling with threads and fabric.

"Quintana," he whispered.

The breathing stopped a moment.

"Olivier?"

He searched behind the baskets and found her there. Her hair was plastered to her face, the front of her repulsive pink dress damp. Froi crouched beside her.

"Couldn't you have worn something less noticeable?" he muttered.

But she was too shaken and miserable to respond. He studied her closely, not knowing whether he was dealing with Princess Indignant or Quintana the ice maiden.

"What did she do to you?" he asked.

She looked weary, shaking her head. He settled beside her, hearing the sound of horses' hooves hitting the hard ground outside the cave. After a moment, she placed her head against his shoulders and Froi felt a tenderness toward her.

"Sometimes . . . sometimes keeping alive is too tiring," she whispered, wringing her hands.

Before he knew what he was doing, he pressed his lips against her brow. "Don't ever say that. *Ever*."

He looked back to the entrance cautiously. A woman stood stirring a large pot with a paddle. Froi smelled saffron. He watched the woman drop a piece of cloth into the dye and retrieve another that had been soaking. On flat stones behind her, he could see a basket of cotton tunics, waiting to be dipped into the pot.

"Wait here," he said.

While the woman had her back turned, Froi grabbed one of the tunics and a scarf, and crept back to where Quintana was hiding.

He helped her remove the hideous pink dress.

"Close your eyes," she said.

Froi stared at her, bemused. Sharing beds and lifting her shift to her thighs and dropping his trousers to his ankles was normal, yet here she was, bashful.

He closed his eyes, and when she was dressed, he wrapped the scarf around her head and took her hand, leading her into the cave.

"It's best we stay here for a while."

Quintana was much too intrigued by her surroundings to complain and accepted the circumstances with her usual aplomb. If her eyes weren't prone to squinting, she would have almost looked wide-eyed with fascination. In a corner, a woman sang a song so pure that it made something inside Froi ache.

"What is she singing?" Quintana stood transfixed, her hand close to her ears, as if she wanted to capture the sound in her fist.

"I don't recognize the language," Froi said. "But it's a pretty melody."

She looked at him, surprised.

"What would you know of such things?" she asked.

"Well, if you'd really like to know, I can sing a pretty melody or two."

Froi wanted to cut off his tongue for saying the words. Except for when working alone on the Flatlands where no one could hear, he hadn't sung out loud since he was a child in a Sarnak marketplace.

He pulled her away. They were still too close to the cave entrance and not far enough away from the fury of those outside. But Quintana had seemed no safer with the palace riders. Was she any safer with Froi?

Farther along, a man juggled three apples, taking a bite from the same one at intervals until it was nothing more than its core. Quintana studied him with a sort of wonder beyond anything Froi had seen on her face before.

But she was drawn away by the cries of a woman in the folds of the cave. Froi followed her to where a couple embraced, the man's body pressing his lover to the wall, his hands concealed under her dress. Froi held out a hand to pull Quintana away, but he heard a snarl from her and suddenly she leaped onto the man's back, grabbing him by the hair, pounding his head once against the stone wall. The woman screamed, and the man twisted and turned to throw Quintana from him. But she held on tight, and Froi saw her face, saw her small, slightly crooked teeth, savage in shape.

He grabbed her around the waist and forced her from the man's back, only to feel a painful kick to his shin by the woman.

He took Quintana's arm, and they escaped through the labyrinth, choosing paths randomly.

A tunnel led down to a lower level of the caves, and Froi dragged her toward it, climbing down first, his feet and hands pressing into the indents of the narrow space to keep his balance. When he reached the ground, he held up his hands, then clasped her around the legs and settled her before him.

"Are you a madwoman, Quintana?" he whispered furiously after they both had caught their breath.

She pointed up the tunnel. "Did you not hear her crying?"

Froi looked around guardedly. Men stared from small dank corners and music rang in the distance through the pocket holes of the cave.

He leaned forward to whisper, "She was crying from pleasure."

Quintana shook her head fiercely. "That's a lie."

"No. It's the truth. People enjoy touching each other. Holding each other. Mating. Since the time of the Ancients, lovers have enjoyed it."

Even in the half-lit space, he saw her expression of disgust.

"Is that what you tell yourself, Olivier? To make yourself feel better about what you're doing to a woman. Do you convince yourself that she's enjoying herself?"

Froi bit back his fury. And his shame.

"And what of you?" he said coldly. "Lifting your nightdress in your chamber, convincing yourself that it's a sacrifice for Charyn when it's nothing more than a need to ease your loneliness because no one in this godsforsaken kingdom cares whether you live or die!"

He regretted the words the moment they left his mouth. She stepped away and he tried to hold out a contrite hand to her, but she would have none of it.

"Ease my loneliness?" she asked bitterly. "If I wanted to ease my loneliness, Olivier, I would have asked my father for a kitten, not whored myself for Charyn."

She turned and ran, and he caught her shift, hearing it tear. "Don't draw attention to yourself," he said, but she pulled free.

He lost her twice, each time catching a glimpse of her in another nook or alcove.

At last, when he believed he would never find her, there she was in a huddle of musicians.

The music they were playing was accompanied by a wailing sound that seemed to beckon all that was untamed and buried deep within. Strange instruments twanged with every pluck of the strings, accompanied by the flicker of fingers across a hide drum. The man's voice was rich, reverberating off the cave walls. Froi could tell he told a sad tale. But then the music changed in tempo and a woman with wild eyes spun and spun again, her arms raised high, and Froi was dizzy with the speed and the beat and the wails and grunts until the woman collapsed to the ground, a mass of sweat and deep breaths.

He saw Quintana then, her eyes bright with excitement. Perhaps it was the Serker in her that sang to him. Lirah's Serker blood. Whatever it was, it seemed to awaken something in Froi that he couldn't understand. That he didn't want to understand. Not with Quintana.

And then the woman on the ground rose and the music was all things enticing. In the small crowd, she caught Quintana's eye and held out a hand, and then the princess or *reginita* or savage, or whoever she was, danced. It was as if she knew this dance in the deepest core of her, and when she opened her eyes, Froi saw the Quintana who had sat on the piece of granite between the palace and godshouse that day he had watched with Arjuro. The savage in her was a beacon to all things raw and base inside Froi. Her hips swaying, her eyes closed, her hands slowly twisting and turning above her head. It was as Rafuel had said. It was a dance of seduction, and somehow in this dank cave with the half-mad princess of the enemy, Froi was seduced. He walked between the dancers and took her face in his hands and kissed her, his tongue sparring with hers for only the slightest moment before he heard the snarl escape her lips and felt a sharp pain. He wiped the blood from his mouth where she had bitten hard.

"Do that again and I'll make sure you bleed like a stuck pig," she hissed.

He clenched his fist. *Remember your bond, Froi,* he said to himself. He counted to ten.

The music slowly strummed to nothing, and he felt bereft without it. Saw that she did too. Caught the tremble in her body as she came back from wherever she had been in her head. Froi reached out a gentle hand and drew Quintana to him, pressing their brows together.

"In a kinder world," he whispered, "one I promise you I've seen, men and women flirt and dance and love with only the fear of what it would mean without the other in their lives."

She was silent for a moment, but stayed with her head pressed to his.

"Lirah says it's a sport of blood," she said. "A dance between men and the women they own. What cruel lies you tell, Olivier of Sebastabol."

He took her hand and they traveled deeper into the cave's core, following the sound of cheering into a small crowded space.

Froi sat down beside a group of men playing cards, pulling Quintana down beside him. This was a game he knew, one he had mastered on the streets of the Sarnak capital.

"You in?" a man barked, half his teeth missing, which was always a warning not to join a game.

Froi pointed to himself and then shrugged, nodding.

The man with thinning hair snapped his fingers and held out a hand, and Froi fished a handful of coins from his pocket. The man dealt, and Froi studied the cards he held in his hands.

"Sir," he heard Quintana speak.

Froi turned to her, a finger on his lips, but Quintana was staring at the dealer, creases furrowing her forehead.

"You forgot your card, sir." It was Quintana the Indignant.

There was a hiss of fury from the other players. Froi tensed, then relaxed when he realized Quintana was not in danger. The men were staring at the dealer.

"Don't know what you're talking about!" the dealer said.

"There," Quintana said, confused that he was unable to see. She reached over to touch the dealer's sleeve.

The other players stared at her. Was it a game this creature was playing, pretending innocence and confusion at the sinister workings of the world?

They threw their cards down in disgust.

"You're out of play, Aesop. Out!"

Someone pushed the coins toward Quintana.

"They're yours, miss."

Another man began to shuffle and deal, and he had a new admirer in Quintana, who watched him carefully, grinning a crooked smile each time he stared down and winked at her.

"Did you see what he did with his eye?" she whispered in Froi's ear.

"He likes you," Froi said.

When each man had their cards, Froi felt her at his shoulder, studying the hand. He tried to push her away, wary of what she would reveal to the others by her reaction.

"What's your name, lad?" one of the players asked.

He hesitated, realizing he couldn't use Olivier in case someone knew of the palace visitor.

"Froi," he responded, knowing it was safe to use the name here.

"Well, Froi. A good game is a fast game."

The men grunted in agreement.

"That means he'd like you to be quick in placing down your card," Quintana explained.

He looked at her and then laughed.

"What would I do without you?" he said.

Later, Froi led her through the caves, quickening his step when he realized they were being followed. When he pushed Quintana into a crevice and turned to face whoever it was, he saw it was a woman.

"I know who she is."

Froi ignored her.

"You're a fool to have her out here," she said. "You know the most base of men will soon come for the last-born girls and use them as whores to produce the first."

Quintana stiffened beside Froi.

Froi tried to push her behind him again. The woman thought Quintana was a last born, not the princess.

"It's against the law," Quintana said coldly. "The prophecy says that only the *reginita* can break the curse. Only her. Not the innocent."

The woman clicked her tongue with regret.

"And what happens when Her Royal Uselessness comes of age?" she asked. "I tell you, they'll come for the last borns." She turned to Froi. "You take care of your girl."

"Always," Froi murmured, grabbing Quintana's hand and turning away. Suddenly they faced another — a man bigger in build than any Charynite Froi had ever seen.

"I'll smuggle her out of the Citavita," the man said fiercely. "What have you been waiting for?"

Froi felt Quintana take a quick breath beside him. She stepped away from Froi, but he pulled her back.

"And who are you, sir?" Quintana asked.

"I'm Perabo. The keeper of these caves."

The man held out his hand to Quintana. "You know it's safe to come with me."

"She knows nothing of the sort," Froi said, "and if you don't step back, I'll break that hand in places you didn't think there were bones."

Quintana stared from Froi to the man and then to Froi again, and there was sadness in her eyes.

"It's not my time to go, sir," she said to the keeper of the caves. "Not yet."

The man's eyes bored into Froi's.

"There are those of us who treasure all last borns," the keeper hissed. "If something happens to her because of you, I will feed every bone of yours that I break down your throat."

It was late when they reached the palace entrance, and this time there was no need for calling out. The drawbridge was lowered, and two of the soldiers approached, then dragged Froi back with them. The courtyard was illuminated by torches. Gargarin stood behind Bestiano and the rest of the advisers and riders. Dorcas's face was swollen, either a gift from the street lords or punishment from the palace for losing the princess. Bestiano approached, and his backhand caught Froi across the face.

Gargarin pushed past the advisers, and one of the riders pulled him back and Froi saw him wince in pain.

Count to ten, Froi. Your work here is yet to be done. You've not even had a glimpse of the king.

"The palace risks a war with both Sebastabol and Paladozza if anything happens to the last born," Gargarin called out, a warning in his voice.

"What makes you think anything will happen to him?" Bestiano said pleasantly before turning to Dorcas.

"I think a night in the dungeon should arouse him enough to be of service to the princess tomorrow."

Later, on the hard cold ground of the cell, when the world seemed so still that it was as though Froi felt the heartbeat of every man and woman in Charyn, he heard the soft singing coming from the opposite tower. It wasn't the high-pitched purity in Quintana's voice, nor the fact that she recalled every word to a sad song she had heard only once today in the caves of the Citavita, sung in a language she had never known. It was that he knew that voice, had dreamed it over and over again in a lifetime of rot and misery, and Froi wanted to weep. For he knew he would break his bond to his queen not just with his body but also with his heart.

When he climbed through Lirah's window that night, she was lying on her cot, reading. He was surprised that the Serker whore could read. As he watched her engrossed in the words on the page, he recognized that the manuscript she held was from Gargarin's collection. Did that fool of a man bribe her guard to pass on the books he treasured?

"Do you feel nothing for her?" Froi asked accusingly. "Is it why you tried to kill her?"

She stared up a moment and then turned her attention back to her reading. "That took you long enough to work out," she said coolly.

"Do you feel nothing for her?" he repeated.

"I feel pity. Satisfied?"

At that moment, Froi hated her more than when Arjuro had revealed the truth of Lirah's crime.

"And you?" she asked, putting the manuscript down. "What do you feel, Serker savage?"

Froi fought hard not to react to her words. "I'm just intrigued," he said. "I'm wondering what it is that you're good at. Your skill in drowning children and attacking scholars with a dagger is poor," he added cruelly.

Her smile was bitter.

"Well, I must be good for something. The king has kept me alive for long enough."

"I want to know about the brothers from Abroi," he demanded.

"I loathe the brothers from Abroi," she said coldly. "That's all you need to know."

"No, I need to know more, Lirah." Froi had come to realize that somehow the clue to where the king was to be found was connected to Lirah, Gargarin, or Arjuro.

His eyes were fixed on Lirah's. Trevanion referred to this as a gnawing war, where you sit and stare at your opponent as though gnawing away at their souls. Lirah was not one to look away, but Froi could see that she wanted him to leave. So she spoke.

"Arjuro was a priestling. A greater deviant the godshouse has never known, but he was the only person who could twist the oracle around his little finger. His brother, Gargarin, was the king's prized protégé, cold and remote toward all except his twin and . . ."

She stopped. Froi waited.

"And you?" he asked.

Lirah ignored the question. Froi walked to the cot and grabbed the manuscript from her hands. He walked back to the window and held it outside threateningly. He could see the rage in her eyes.

"Talk," he snapped. She refused to.

Froi took a chance and tore out a page, inwardly asking Finn and Isaboe for forgiveness. They loved words and books. They sent messengers far and wide to find manuscripts as gifts to each other.

Without waiting another moment, he tossed the page out the window.

"You dog," she said with a bitter shake of her head.

"Talk."

She walked to him and took the manuscript, clutching it close to her body. They both knew he could take it from her in an instant, but he waited.

"For too long the wisdom and intellect in this kingdom came from the teachings of those in the godshouses," she said. "Some believed that the palace could be just as progressive and that the newly crowned king was the one to bring about the change. One of these believers, a lad who had been raised in Paladozza, traveled to the Citavita with his brother. He had the plans and drawings to prove that Charyn could be as mighty as Belegonia. He and his brother had spent years deciphering the books of the Ancients, discovering farm methods and surgical techniques that proved the brothers' genius.

"The king was impressed with the lad, but he also wanted the gods' touched priestling brother to serve him because he already had a reputation for being the best physician the Citavita had seen. But despite the wealth the king promised, the priestling was not interested in being solely in his service. More important, the oracle of the godshouse was not going to hand over her most gifted priestling to the palace."

Lirah looked up at Froi a moment, but she seemed far away.

"Everyone believes the downfall of Charyn began with the godshouse slaughter and the sacking of Serker, but I know it began with the battle between the oracle and the king over Arjuro of Abroi."

Froi couldn't fathom such a thing. Arjuro was a drunk with no hope. How could he have ever provided Charyn with anything?

"Despite the tension that was brewing between the oracle's godshouse and the palace, the brothers from Abroi refused to involve themselves. They began and ended the day greeting each other across the *gravina*. When they walked through the

Citavita together, people would stop in awe. They were beautiful to look at, with their dark curls and fierce blue eyes. They may have come from nothing, but they held a fascination for those around them. The king tried to do everything he could to use them to his advantage. He believed that if Gargarin spoke to his brother and his brother came to be the physician in the palace, then Arjuro would also convince the oracle to sanction any plans the palace had to wrest control from the *provincari*. But the brothers made a pact to never allow the godshouse or the palace to come between them."

"How did you meet the brothers?"

"I first made Gargarin's acquaintance in the palace."

It seemed difficult for Lirah to say Gargarin's name.

"We spent a lot of time in a cave the brothers called theirs at the base of the *gravina*."

"I know it," Froi said, thinking of the first time he saw Gargarin.

"De Lancey of Paladozza would be there too. It was all quite primitive at times," she said quietly. "They were strangely raw in their youth."

"And then?"

"And then the godshouse was attacked, supposedly by the Serkers. It was a massacre. Forty of the priestlings were killed. One day later, the palace riders found the oracle with Arjuro of Abroi in the cave I spoke of. He claimed that he had not been present in the godshouse on the night of the massacre and had returned to find the carnage. He had found the oracle queen maimed, violated, and close to death, and he had sworn to do anything to protect her."

"How did the palace know where to find him?"

"He was betrayed. De Lancey did it without realizing."

"De Lancey of Paladozza?" Froi asked, surprised. He was the son of the *provincaro* who had taken the brothers into his home.

"They were lovers. Whatever De Lancey did, I'm sure he's regretted it. After the capture, the palace held Arjuro in the godshouse on his own. Said it was a sound punishment to keep him chained inside the Hall of Illumination where most of the slaughter took place. During the next nine months, Gargarin was allowed to visit him. He never believed his brother was responsible and worked tirelessly to have him released."

Lirah looked up at Froi, anguish in her eyes.

"But ambition is an ugly thing, and on the night of the last born, the king asked Gargarin of Abroi for the allegiance he had always desired from his prized pet."

"What type of allegiance?" Froi asked, his blood beginning to run cold.

"The type that ensures a man must sell his soul."

Lirah walked away, her back to him, and Froi saw her stagger. If it were anyone other than Lirah he would have held out a hand to her. But Lirah did not seem the type of woman who invited help from any man. When he could see that she was composed, he walked around to face her.

"What did he do, Lirah?"

"Unbeknownst to the people of Charyn, the king ordered Gargarin to kill the oracle and the child she bore. To toss them out of the palace window into the *gravina* as though they were garbage."

"What?"

"And the king's guards dragged Arjuro to the balconette of the godshouse, chained him there, and made him watch. It's why Arjuro has never spoken to Gargarin again. That, and the fact that Arjuro spent more than eight years in the cell below this one for supposedly conspiring with the Serkers."

"Is that what you believe?" Froi asked. "About the Serkers?"

She shook her head. "Never. If anyone knows the immoral

habits of the Serkers, I do. But I would bet the life of this kingdom on the fact that no Serker would enter the godshouse and desecrate it. They may have resented the oracle over the years for instructing them on how to live their lives, but they would never have despoiled the godshouse. The Serkers were begot from the Ancients. No province was more devoted to the gods."

"Gargarin couldn't . . . I don't believe you, Lirah."

She studied him carefully and a cruel smile crossed her lips. "Oh, I see," she said bitterly. "Gargarin of Abroi bewitched you, did he? Don't worry. He's done it to the best of us."

"I'm bewitched by no man," Froi said furiously.

"Then why are you here asking questions?"

"Because I needed to know whether he is worth saving."

Lirah stared. Froi saw something flare up in her eyes.

"Saving? Aren't you here just to plant the mighty seed of Charyn?"

"I'm not here to plant a seed, Lirah, and if anyone can tell me about the king's chamber, you can."

Suddenly Lirah grabbed his face viciously.

"Who are you?"

Froi was silent a moment.

"I'll find a way to set you free," he said quietly. "There's a cloister in the kingdom of Sendecane. At the ends of the land. You take her there," he ordered. "She can live in peace, and this kingdom can forget her. This land can forget her."

"And what makes you think that I would protect her? I tried to drown Quintana, remember? I'm the scum of this earth in your eyes."

"She's your daughter. There's no greater bond than between a mother and her child."

Lirah of Serker laughed with little humor. "Let me tell you a truth, Serker savage," she said. "And then I want you to leave and not come back. I gave birth to one child on that wretched night. He was a boy child, torn from my loins and given to Gargarin of Abroi to toss from the palace window into the *gravina* below. I woke up with the oracle's bastard in my arms. Quintana the wretched. Quintana the curse maker. Quintana the whore."

There were tears of fury in the woman's eyes. "And she gnawed at my breasts day after day, screaming for her own mother, because that savage babe knew the truth. That I grieved my son until I had nothing left inside to give to her. So when you slit Gargarin of Abroi's throat, you tell him. Tell him that on that cursed night, he didn't murder the son of the oracle. He murdered mine."

CHAPTER 16

Froi crouched by the side of the bed, waiting. He wanted to be the first thing Gargarin saw when he woke. Wanted to see the fear. He had been trained by Trevanion to watch for the signals that showed the difference between a man sleeping and awake. He saw the flicker on Gargarin's face, and a moment later Froi held a hand to the man's neck.

"I could snap it in an instant."

"Then why didn't you when you had a chance?" Gargarin asked.

"Because I wanted to hear the truth from your mouth first."

The silence stretched without a flicker of emotion on the other man's face. Gargarin of Abroi could do uncomfortable silence better than anyone Froi knew. Even Perri.

"I never took you for a murderer," Froi said bitterly.

Gargarin sighed, as though a truth was revealed that had been waiting a long time to reveal itself.

"There are rules, even among the most base of men," Froi hissed. "I've done things that shame me still, but if I killed a newborn babe, I'd dash my head against a rock rather than live one moment with such blackness staining me."

Gargarin refused to look away. "I did what I had to do, and I have no shame. And I'll not explain myself to you. I'll not explain myself to those who refuse to listen to the truth but still judge me. And if I had to do it again, I would not change a single thing that took place that night. Nor would the oracle expect me to."

Froi shoved him away, trying to block out the voice in his head that told him to forget his bond and kill this man.

"Do you know how easy it is to snap the life out of a body?" Froi asked. "Especially one that is broken?"

"Then do it," Gargarin hissed. "Or are you as gutless as the rest of Charyn?"

"Olivier!" It was Quintana, from outside on the balconette. *"Olivier, are you in there?"*

Froi's eyes were fixed on Gargarin's. Deep down he had believed in the boy named Gar who had kept his brother safe all those years. Who had walked four days with no food to bring young Arjuro hope. It was what made Froi want to kill him: the knowledge that Gargarin had sold some part of himself to a darker desire. But Gargarin's action had nothing to do with Lumatere's safety, and Froi knew it was not part of his bond to take this man's life. Yet Froi wanted to cause pain, and he pressed cruel fingers against the dagger wound Gargarin had received from Lirah. His only pleasure was watching the man wince.

"Olivier!"

"Your time will come," Froi warned.

Quintana stood on her balconette, and Froi climbed onto its latticework and leaped, landing at her feet. He saw that her face was flushed with excitement.

"I've been waiting for you all night and day," she said.

Froi shivered. He realized that the words came from Quintana the ice maiden. Realized, as he felt his face heating up, that the idea of this Quintana waiting for him with excitement spoke to parts of him he believed to be dormant, and then she winked.

"Did I do that right?" she asked. Her smile was lopsided, and he saw a glimpse of the teeth.

And Froi imagined that he would follow her to the ends of the earth.

They sat cross-legged on the bed, facing each other, and she began to deal the cards with a speed and skill that surprised him.

"I practiced," she said. "I have a good memory for detail."

He leaned forward, tilting his head to the side, a hand to his ear. "Say that again."

"I have a good memory for detail," she repeated.

"You do, do you?" he questioned mockingly. "Not 'we'? Not the *reginita*? Not the princess? Not the other? So what name should I use?"

For a moment, he thought he was losing her back to the coldness. She looked away, refusing to say her name, then she began to shuffle.

He was impressed and surprised and, more than anything, he was intrigued. He was growing to enjoy the way her eyes squinted and her mouth twisted as she concentrated hard. Sometimes he heard her murmur, "Hmm, yes, I know," and he wanted to creep inside her head and join in her madness.

She snapped her fingers twice, mimicking one of the card players from that day in the cave dwellings. "Where are your coins?"

He choked out a laugh. "We're not playing for coins. You may know how to shuffle, but that doesn't mean you know how to play."

She reached over to the trinket pouch on her bedside table and took out the coins she was given in the cave. She placed them before him and began to study her cards.

"Remember, the same suit is more powerful," he explained.

She looked up at him, annoyed. "Why would I forget that?"

"Because you've only watched three rounds."

"I told you, I have a good head for details. I can tell you the name of every person in this palace, and if a new palace appeared and one hundred people were introduced to me, I'd remember their names as well."

"Wonderful," he murmured. He took his time studying his cards. "That should come in handy if you're ever fighting for your life. And you can sing as well. Beautiful voice, by the way."

"I can play with apples, too," she said.

He looked up, confused.

Quintana put her cards down and climbed over him. Decorum was not quite her forte.

She picked up three apples from the plate by his side of the bed, and concentrating hard, she began to toss them in the air with such precision that he wondered for more than the first time what else lay buried inside Quintana of Charyn.

"Slightly impressive," he said, feigning indifference.

"And you can do better?"

The first skill taught to a boy on the streets of the Sarnak capital was the ability to juggle. He could do it with his eyes shut. He took the apples from her and did just that. When he opened them, he caught the last apple in his hand and took a bite. She reached out, and he held it away until she straddled him to grab it from his grip. She leaned over him, but with their loins almost joined and the dip in her nightdress revealing a glimpse of round full breasts, Froi's control over his body failed.

Suddenly she jumped away, staring at him with fury.

"Well, you can't climb all over me and expect it to just lie there," he said, trying to fight the pain of his arousal.

Quintana watched him carefully. Then she settled back, shuffled the cards, and dealt them out as though nothing had happened between them.

"A good game is a fast game, Froi."

His head snapped back in shock. "What did you call me?"

"That was the name you gave the dealer."

He couldn't explain it to himself. How it felt to hear her speak his name.

Froi dragged his attention back to his cards, annoyed. He didn't want to feel whatever he was feeling for her. Or for anyone in this castle. He thought of Gargarin in the next chamber and how Lirah's words had made him sick to his stomach. What was it about Gargarin and the whore and the priestling and this strange princess that made him care when he was trained not to?

"Arjuro says he was never in the palace," he murmured, discarding a card and taking another.

"Well, who are you going to believe? Me or a drunk?" she asked.

"You're not exactly considered the sanest mind in Charyn."

"I'm going to win this round, so I'd advise you to give in now," she said, reaching over for his coins. Froi slapped her hand away.

"I do understand the concept of bluffing, Quintana." He looked at his cards, quite pleased with what he saw.

She sighed and threw in a few more coins.

"I take great offense at being considered insane," she said.

"There are three of you," he reminded her.

Her eyes flashed with anger. "First, there are not three of us at all. And what of you? One moment a fighter, next minute an idiot who doesn't heed warnings that he's going to lose?"

"So you're admitting there's more than one of you?" he asked.

"I'm not admitting anything at all, and I'd advise you to show me your cards now."

"Show me first," he ordered.

She turned her cards and pressed them close to his face, and he moved his head back for a better look.

"I did warn you," she said coolly, collecting the coins and placing them in a trinket pouch.

Froi was put out. "Would I have won if I played the *reginita*?" he sulked.

"She's the one with the better memory," Quintana said, then lay back on her pillow. Again it was as though she was resigned to her fate rather than anticipating it. Froi wanted the anticipation. He craved it.

"Are you going to plant the seed, or should I just blow out the candle and say good night?" she asked with a weary sigh.

"Do you come to me willing?"

He waited, praying to the gods that the answer was yes.

Quintana blew out the candle and said good night.

She woke him later. A distracted look on her face, her hair all over his eyes. Froi pushed it aside with irritation.

"Yes, I know. There's a man dying in Turla."

"Why in the name of the gods would Arjuro deny knowing me?" she asked.

"You got it all wrong anyway," he muttered, willing himself back to sleep. "He was never in love with Lirah because he was having a dalliance with De Lancey of Paladozza."

"De Lancey?" she said, horrified. "Have you seen De Lancey? He's the most handsome man in the land. He would never have a dalliance with Arjuro. Arjuro looks as though he hasn't bathed since childhood."

Froi pointed to his face. "Eyes closed. It means I'm trying to sleep."

"For some reason he is lying to you," she said. "Indeed he was in love with Lirah."

Froi sighed and opened his eyes. Her lips were pressed together in a grimace.

"Why have you made Arjuro and Gargarin your business when you were sent here for other purposes?" she asked.

"I was sent here to swive you. Your word, not mine. Seeing it's not your true desire, I've turned my attention to the lives of the brothers from Abroi and Lirah. It's helped with the boredom."

He wondered how much she knew of Gargarin's hand in the oracle queen's death.

"Do you love Lirah?" he asked quietly.

She studied his face. "Despite the fact that she's not my mother?"

He wasn't surprised that she knew; he was surprised that she admitted it to him.

"How is it that she spoke to you of such things?" Quintana asked.

"Oh, you know. She opened her mouth and words came out."

She clicked her tongue with irritation. "We have an understanding with Lirah," she said.

"So we're back to 'we,' are we?" he asked. "Sometimes this bed gets too crowded."

He turned away. "I'm going back to sleep. Send one of the others to wake me up later. I like you the least."

She didn't speak after that, but he sensed that she was awake and as much as he tried, he couldn't keep himself from turning to face her. He felt her breath close to his.

"Is it because we're not beautiful?" she asked.

"What?"

"That you don't want to save us . . . or plant the seed."

Froi inwardly groaned.

"In the books of the Ancients," she said, "the princesses are always beautiful and they always get saved and men always want to swive them."

At least if there was yearning in her voice, Froi would see it as an invitation. But there was only curiosity.

"I'm going to say this once and once only," he said. "Are you listening?"

"Only this once," she responded, and he couldn't help smiling.

"In the world outside this palace," he said, "men and women don't go around speaking of planting seeds and swiving."

"What's it called in the outside world, then?" she asked.

"It's not spoken of. It's just done. It's felt. I personally have nothing against the word," he said with a laugh. "But if you spoke it aloud, you would be judged."

He thought for a moment, suddenly registering a word she had spoken a moment before. *Saved.* He reached over and touched a thumb to her face. But she flinched and pushed his hand away.

In all her talk of last borns and seed planting, none of the Quintanas had ever spoken of being saved. He couldn't help thinking of the fear in her expression outside the soothsayer's cave. The weariness in her voice when she spoke to him of staying alive. Then there were her words to the woman in the caves. *The prophecy says that only the* reginita *can break the curse. Only her. Not the innocent.* Why would she not consider herself innocent?

Worse still, he couldn't get the words from Arjuro and Gargarin out of his mind. That she would not live past her coming of age.

"Go to sleep," she said after a while. But Froi couldn't sleep.

Too many questions were plaguing him. Why would Arjuro deny knowing Quintana?

In the early hours of the morning, he heard Gargarin leave the adjoining chamber. Froi had spent enough time with the man to know that aside from being forced to attend breakfast and dinner each day, and sitting against the wall of the second tower and watching Lirah of Serker's rooftop prison, Gargarin didn't leave his chamber.

Froi dressed quickly and crept out of Quintana's room, cautiously following Gargarin down the tower steps. Instead of exiting into the outer ward of the castle, Gargarin disappeared to where the cellars were. Keeping a discreet distance, Froi trailed him through rows upon rows of wine racks and down into a lower basin accessed through a hole dug into the ground. Gargarin struggled to lower himself into the narrow space. His hands, dependent on his staff, fumbled against the cavity wall, and Froi heard muttering and cursing that reminded him more of Arjuro than his brother.

The vertical tunnel led to a burrow so low in height that Froi stooped most of the way. He heard the tapping of the staff and in the distance could see the bobbing of light coming from an oil lamp that Gargarin must have stowed away. Farther along, the tunnel tapered and turned and narrowed. Finally, he saw Gargarin lift a grate and extinguish the lamp. Then there was nothing but black and the quiet sound of breathing. Gargarin climbed the stones up into whatever lay above and disappeared from sight.

Froi waited a while, his heart hammering. Had Gargarin inadvertently led him to the king? How long had Gargarin secretly met him this way? Who were they keeping the truth from? Was it Bestiano? Froi remembered what Arjuro and Lirah and even Bestiano had admitted about the king's prized pet.

That he had been ambitious. Froi knew that if he was to find both men together, he would kill them. The king first and then Gargarin.

After a while, he followed Gargarin up the grate, then climbed into an alcove with a small altar that served as a prayer cubicle. Gargarin's feet were a short distance away from Froi's head and the man was gazing down into what could only be the king's private solar. From where he was, Froi could see frescoes richly decorating the wall, the eyes of the gods staring down at him in judgment. He heard the sound of heavy footsteps and voices below.

"The *provincari* and their people have arrived, Your Majesty," one of the riders said.

More footsteps. Froi suspected that they belonged to more soldiers by the sounds of swords clanging as they walked. Suddenly there was a movement before him, and he watched Gargarin place a hand in his pocket and retrieve a dagger. A cold fist seemed to grip Froi's heart. *Idiot*. Gargarin was not there to meet the king. He was there to kill him.

Silently, Froi placed a hand over Gargarin's mouth.

"You'll never get out of here alive, Gargarin," he whispered, wondering why he even cared.

Gargarin tried to shove him away, his movements furious.

He pulled Gargarin back to the grate and forced him down the hole. Froi followed closely behind. In the narrow tunnel he watched as Gargarin wearily rested his head against the stone.

"Lean on me," Froi said. "Lirah's dagger wound must have triggered spasms."

"Really. You're gods' touched, are you?"

Froi ignored the mood. "Not sure whether you noticed that I saved your life, fool."

"Not sure whether you noticed that I didn't ask for saving, idiot!"

Gargarin was still clutching the dagger in his hand.

"And where did you manage to get hold of that?" Froi asked.

"I'm not here to answer your questions."

"Then what are you here for, Gargarin?"

Gargarin stumbled away, his movements even more awkward in his fury. Froi grabbed him by the coarse woven cloth of his shirt, but Gargarin pulled away again.

"Is this where you break your bond and kill me slowly?" he asked.

"Not today," Froi said. "I'm feeling too inquisitive."

"About?"

"You. Your brother. The whore," he provoked.

Gargarin stopped and Froi walked into him. There was no room in so narrow a space for Gargarin to turn, but Froi saw the whipcord fury in the hands against the wall, the way they tightened on the staff and the dagger.

"You watch what comes out of your mouth," Gargarin warned coldly. "Lirah of Serker was thirteen years old when she was sold to this godsforsaken rock. She deserves no one's scorn."

Froi reached forward and pounded the hand holding the dagger into the wall. Gargarin's fingers convulsed and let go.

"You're nothing but a pathetic shell of a man who can hardly hold a weapon, let alone a woman such as Lirah of Serker," Froi said, picking up the dagger.

"A pathetic shell of a man?" Gargarin asked. "Is that what you call those from wherever you come from who don't have power in their stride?"

Suddenly Gargarin twisted around, slamming Froi against

the wall, the staff under Froi's chin, the space so narrow they could hardly breathe.

"See, now we're speaking the same language, Gargarin," Froi said, excitement making his blood pound. They struggled for a moment until Froi had the upper hand, his arm pressed against the other man's windpipe. "If you answer my questions, I promise I won't snap your neck," Froi said.

Gargarin was silent.

"Waiting for the nod."

"Well, you're not going to get one. What's your name?" Gargarin demanded.

"Doesn't matter what my name is," Froi said, irritated. "I'm the one asking questions."

"There's something you need to know about me," Gargarin said in an even tone. "Despite the wretchedness of this body, I stopped being frightened of thugs sometime in my youth. The only people who frighten me are those who are smarter, and thankfully in this palace, there aren't many of those, so I've managed to find some peace in this wretched life of mine."

"Would you consider me smart for wondering how you would possibly know where the king's chamber is?" Froi asked.

"Because I once lived in the palace, idiot."

"You lived here eighteen years ago, when his chamber was in the keep. Twelve years ago, he was moved to the fourth tower. It's where your brother was chained to his desk. Not the kind of information they hand out readily around here."

Gargarin's expression was bitter.

"But perhaps your brother wasn't chained to the king's desk. At first I thought he was the grumpiest, meanest man in the land of Skuldenore. Who wouldn't want to wave to Quintana, especially when years ago he wept while clutching her and Lirah in his arms, as though he was in love with Lirah? But, despite the fact that Lirah's face makes one ache, Arjuro prefers the company of men in his bed, although these days I don't think anyone is enjoying Arjuro's presence in their bed. Then, when I asked Arjuro to describe the king's chamber where he spent two whole years chained to a desk, he claimed never to have been there. Said the *reginita* was lying. Perhaps she was lying. Deep down, I think she's telling a story or two."

"You have a lot of time for thinking. Is that what you do back wherever you come from?" Gargarin asked.

"Am I right?"

Gargarin's eyes flickered with some sort of triumph. "And what would you say if I told you I've worked you out?" he asked.

"Be my guest," Froi said. "I could do with some entertainment."

"You're an assassin made up of the garbage of this kingdom. You have Serker eyes and you have the face of scum from Abroi. I should know. I grew up among it. We're probably related—most of Abroi is—and the reason I don't look like the rest of you inbreds is because my brother and I took after our mother, who came from a nomadic tribe of pig-ignorant Osterians, who thankfully were blessed with refined features, but little else. You were taught to speak Charynite in the classic way, probably by a priest or a scholar, and you've spent some time in Sarnak because when you curse, you say *Sagra,* and only that kingdom butchers the name of the Goddess Sagrami. The fact that you pronounce your *z* with an *s* sound tells me you lived among the Sarnaks, and you end your sentences on a high note, which means you've spent some time with the Lumateran River people."

Gargarin waited. "Did I get any of it wrong, whatever did you say your name was?"

"I didn't," Froi said, impressed. "Anything else you'd like to add, you lying scum?"

"I don't lie. I just kill women and babies, remember?"

Froi pressed him harder into the stone. "How could you jest about such a thing?" he said.

He felt Gargarin search his face.

"What's your name?"

"Olivier of Sebastabol."

"Tell me something, Olivier of Sebastabol. Was the other Olivier murdered to fulfill what it was you were sent to do?"

Froi hadn't given the other lad a thought since he had entered the Citavita.

"If I knew what you were talking about, I'd say no. Why kill an innocent lad, regardless of what an idiot he is?"

There was relief on Gargarin's face.

"Tell me, Gargarin of Abroi, did you throw the oracle queen and the babe from the balconette?"

"Yes, I did," he said. "And no, I didn't. I'll swap my truth for yours."

Froi shook his head.

"Who sent you?" Gargarin demanded.

"Why would I tell you that?"

"Because I think we want the same thing."

Froi remembered Trevanion's warning about not trusting those with the same desire to kill the king.

"You and I are not the same, Gargarin. I would never take the life of a babe."

"Is that what Lirah told you? Arjuro too?" Froi's grip loosened and Gargarin broke free, hobbling away as though he wanted to put the greatest of distance between them. "At least Arjuro saw events that tricked his eyes. Lirah made her decision based on hearsay," he said bitterly.

Froi wanted to inflict as much pain as possible. Gargarin was every man he trusted who had turned his back or betrayed him on the streets of the Sarnak capital.

"Makes no difference to me, because a child died that night," Froi said, coming up behind Gargarin. "But it makes a difference to her."

He placed his mouth close to Gargarin's ear so that he would hear the words whispered for the rest of his days. "You killed Lirah's son, Gargarin. They swapped the babes."

Gargarin stopped, shook his head as though to rid himself of a thought that seemed incomprehensible. He managed to turn and face Froi. This time it was Froi who wanted to look away because the stare was a force beyond reckoning. Gargarin stumbled back over uneven ground. Froi leaped forward to grab him, but Gargarin pushed him away and still he stared. Froi didn't see sorrow in the man's eyes, but he saw something. Confusion, perhaps. Was that hope? Gargarin swallowed hard.

"Wherever you've come from, leave this place and never return," he said hoarsely. "Please."

The plea was the last thing Froi expected to hear.

They were both silent as they walked out into the courtyard. Something Froi could not put into words had taken place in the bowels of the castle that had left them both shaken.

Around them, the courtyard was a beehive of activity. Servants swept the ground with vigor, and the castle cooks carried a roasted pig on a spit toward the smaller drawbridge that led to the inner ward. Suddenly they found themselves face-to-face with Bestiano.

Gargarin passed the man without a word, but Bestiano's hand snaked out and grabbed Gargarin by the arm.

"The king has finally agreed to see you," the king's First

Adviser said coolly. "He felt it was best to do so with the *provincari* here."

Gargarin looked back to where Froi stood. Froi saw his eyes glance toward where he knew the dagger was hidden in Froi's pocket. The fool wanted it back.

"And what of me?" Froi asked. "Don't last borns meet the king?"

"You," Bestiano said, forcing a pleasant tone, "will travel home tomorrow with the *provincaro* of Paladozza. I especially asked him as a favor on behalf of the absent *provincaro* of Sebastabol."

Froi knew that in the early hours of the morning he would have to return to the tunnel and do what he was sent here to do.

A parade of riders entered the courtyard through the portcullis. The *provincari*, Froi suspected, here for the day of weeping. Froi turned to walk away but saw Quintana standing by the gatehouse, peering out between the riders, into the Citavita below. He knew without asking that she was searching for him, believing him to have leaped to Arjuro's godshouse.

She turned, her eyes finding Froi's over Bestiano's shoulder.

"Get out of that filthy sack, you stupid girl," Bestiano grated. Quintana had taken to wandering through the castle wearing the calico shift Froi had stolen for her in the caves. It made her look even more ordinary. Even more human than the peculiar princess in the hideous pink dress.

When Froi heard Bestiano's footsteps retreat toward where the *provincari* were dismounting, Froi approached her.

"You're going tomorrow," she said quietly. "Without having planted the seed."

Froi tried to hide his frustration. Deep down he wanted her to be of a sound mind, but each time she mentioned the planting of the seed, he knew she was nothing more than a half-mad girl.

"If you fulfill the prophecy," she said, "we will let you kiss me."

"A kiss is the prize?" he asked sadly. "Even more than giving me the rest of you? It should be the other way round, Princess. In the real world, it's called courting. You let a lad kiss you and then you offer him more."

"Let me tell you something, Olivier," she said with tears of sorrow in her eyes, "this is my real world."

Gargarin approached, returning from greeting the *provincari*. He was headed to their tower but stopped when he caught Quintana's expression.

"Has Olivier said something to distress you?" he asked gently, noticing the tears in her eyes.

"He has a wicked tongue, Sir Gargarin."

"Pity it's not in our power to cut it out, then," Gargarin said. "The *provincaro* of Paladozza would like a word," he told Froi.

Froi looked back to where the portcullis was still raised and the drawbridge down.

"I've someone to meet," he muttered, walking away from them both.

Froi hammered on the godshouse door for what seemed an eternity. He was always wary on this quiet part of the rock, away from the noise and business of the Citavita.

He stared into the peephole the moment he heard Arjuro slide it across. After a moment, the priestling opened the door and stepped aside. Froi watched him look down toward the palace.

"I suppose the *provincari* have arrived?"

Froi didn't answer. Arjuro shut the heavy door, pushing his weight against it before placing a piece of timber across the length of the entrance.

They stood silently in the dark.

"Did you swap places?" Froi asked.

Arjuro met his eyes. He didn't pretend not to know what Froi was saying.

"In a way."

"In what way?" Froi demanded.

"In the way where I beat him to a pulp and walked out of a prison as Gargarin of Abroi and the real Gargarin stayed locked up for eight years as the priestling Arjuro."

"Oh," Froi said quietly. "That way."

Arjuro was holding a bottle in his hand. He took a long mouthful. He looked worse than Froi had ever seen him. They both sat on the cold hard stone of the stairs.

"Lirah told me the truth. About what Gargarin did all those years ago."

Arjuro didn't respond.

"Is there any chance—?"

"No," Arjuro said, as though he knew what Froi was asking. "I saw him do it. You've seen the distance between the godshouse balconette and yours. They shackled me to the railings outside mine, and they made me watch. First he tossed my beloved oracle, then her child."

Froi's heart sank.

"It was Lirah's child," he told Arjuro quietly. Respectfully. "They swapped the babes."

Not even a day's worth of ale could numb Arjuro from those words.

"Gods," the priestling muttered, hammering his head against the wall. *"Gods. Gods. Gods."*

Froi grabbed him, taking the bottle out of his hand. Suddenly, a thought seemed to cross Arjuro's mind.

"Then the princess . . ."

Froi nodded. ". . . is the oracle's daughter."

"Well, that makes sense. There was no one madder than the oracle."

"Was it quick?" Froi asked. "The way they died, I mean?"

"I could see the oracle was already dead. The struggle had already taken place inside the chamber. Same with the babe."

Arjuro took the bottle from Froi and was back on his feet, trudging upward. Froi sometimes forgot that the brothers were no older than Trevanion and Perri and Lord August. But they walked like old men, as though the weight of evil stood on their shoulders.

Arjuro stopped at a landing that led to cell after small cell. Froi followed him into one of the rooms and watched the priestling collapse onto the cot, the bottle hitting the ground, shattering into pieces. "They made me watch," Arjuro repeated over and over again. "They made me watch my brother kill innocence and goodness that day."

"And what of you, Arjuro? What of your innocence or guilt? Who was it that betrayed this godshouse to the Serkers the year before?"

"There was no betrayal by me and no attack by Serker," the priestling said.

Froi sat on one of the cots, waiting. If he had to, he would wait all day.

"I had fought with the oracle. I always fought with the oracle. It's what she loved about me. I was her favorite, you know."

Froi pushed the shattered glass out of the way and stepped closer.

"I went to meet De Lancey. He was visiting from Paladozza, and one thing led to another and we spent the night together. When I arrived here, I found the horror. All dead, but her. Men and women I adored. Most no older than twenty-five. The oracle couldn't speak or write because they had cut off her tongue and fingers. I knew that we couldn't stay, so I took her across the bridge and we traveled down into the *gravina* to the cave house I shared with Gargarin. I left a message for De Lancey at the inn. He joined us the next day. Told me I was insane for suspecting the palace. In those days the king could do no wrong in his eyes. De Lancey believed that by keeping the oracle away from the protection of the palace, I was placing her life at risk. Said I was to leave her in the cave and that he would send a message to the king to advise him where to find her. He would pretend that the Serkers had left her there on the way back home so I would not be accused.

"But De Lancey was too cowardly to do it himself and sent the farrier from the Citavita. When the farrier's headless corpse was found in the town square, De Lancey realized the truth and went home to Paladozza. I think he's been plotting against the palace ever since."

"Why didn't you leave her there?"

"Leave her?" Arjuro asked, tears in his eyes. "She was my beloved oracle. I left her once, but not again. If they were going to take us, they'd take us together. But the king had a different plan and locked me up in the godshouse, keeping her in the palace. The only thing that brought me comfort was that they allowed me to see my brother."

Arjuro shuddered.

"Nine months later, I never wanted to see him again. He came straight to see me after the murder on the balconette. Wanted to explain what I had witnessed. I begged him to remove my shackles because they were cutting into my wrists. He agreed and I took my chance."

"And you never looked back."

"You always look back," Arjuro said bitterly. "Always. And

If you don't, the gods look back for you. But from that day on for as Charyn knew, Arjuro of Abroi was a prisoner of the king for the next eight years."

"So it was Gargarin who cried for Lirah when she tried to kill herself and Quintana?"

Arjuro nodded.

"He doesn't love easily, my brother. He loved me and he had a strong affection for De Lancey of Paladozza and De Lancey's father, who was the *provincaro* at the time. Women flocked to him, beautiful women. At first I thought he was like me and preferred the company of men in his bed. Men pursued him with the same passion as women. But nothing. It was as though he was in his own world of thoughts and inventions and books."

"Why Lirah?"

"Who knows why Lirah? Back in the days it was safe to travel between the godshouse and palace, we would all venture out to a vineyard across the bridge or down to the base of the *gravina.* De Lancey and I were scathing about Gargarin's choice of her. It was our jealousy, of course."

"You were jealous that Gargarin had Lirah?" Froi asked with disbelief.

"No. We were jealous that Lirah had Gargarin. Cold, cold Lirah, who was bitter toward all men, loved my brother with all her heart. It made me hate her even more, because I knew this union was not one of the flesh. She hated the touch of men. He barely tolerated the touch of anyone. I couldn't bear the idea of him loving someone as much as he loved me."

Froi could never have imagined that Gargarin, Lirah, and Arjuro had such a fierce capacity to love.

"They waited eight years to release him. The *provincari* warned the king that as long as the last priestling of the godshouse was kept captive, the curse would hold and the kingdom would stay barren. So they released the man they believed to be Arjuro of Abroi ten years ago. The king feared the gods then more than ever."

Before Froi could question why, Arjuro said the word.

"Lumatere."

Froi flinched to hear it. He could only imagine that the king was full of fear because he had sent the impostor king and his soldiers to Lumatere and they had been trapped for three years by Lumatere's curse.

"What did the palace think happened to Gargarin all those years ago?"

"That he deserted his king on the night of the last borns out of his own fear and shame at his brother's betrayal of the palace. Gargarin was considered a traitor for years, you know, and there was a bounty on his head. And now he has returned with a plan to save the kingdom, to remind the king of how brilliant he is."

"Not quite," Froi said. "I think your brother has plans to kill the king."

Arjuro shook his head. "Madness," he muttered. "Madness."

And there it was. Despite everything the priestling had witnessed, he still cared for a brother capable of such treacherous acts.

"Where did you hide all those years?" Froi asked.

Arjuro looked away, perhaps from shame of his betrayal or the horror of memory.

"You don't want to know that, lad," the priestling said hoarsely.

"Yes, I do."

Arjuro shook his head. "Get out of the Citavita, Olivier of Sebastabol. Take your cruel face and your questions with you and leave me to the misery of this cursed existence."

CHAPTER 17

Lucian called together the Monts in the meeting place of Yata's house. It was the home he grew up in with his father, but three years past, he had decided it was best for Yata and her sisters to live there and for him to find a smaller cottage.

He hadn't called many meetings in his time as leader, but he had spent too many sleepless nights thinking of what Kasabian had told him by the stream, and he knew it was time to speak to the lads and their families.

"So now the valley is theirs," his cousin's wife, Alda, snapped. "That is all it takes. They arrive on our doorstep, and we allow them to restrict our lads from entering land that rightfully belongs to us."

There were sounds of disgust around the room, and Lucian tried to make eye contact with anyone who might take his side. Perhaps his cousin Yael or his neighbor Raskin.

"They damaged much-needed produce, Alda," Lucian said with patience. "They pissed in the stream in front of the women."

Some of the Monts laughed. Alda stood. Now she had an audience, and Lucian knew he was in trouble.

"And you're telling me," she said, looking around for support, "that *you* never once crossed the river from Osteria to Charyn in the ten years we were up in those hills? That *you* never once destroyed Charynite property or relieved yourself in the river."

Lucian sighed. "That was different."

There was a chorus of disapproval at his words.

"How different?" Alda yelled. "How were you different from our lads?"

He thought a moment. "Different in the sense that our Charyn neighbors in the hills of Osteria were part of their army. But our Charyn neighbors now are exiles themselves. Can I remind everyone that we took that hill in Osteria without the permission of the Osterians, yet they allowed us to stay?"

"How dare you compare," Alda shouted.

"Lucian, our people were in exile!" Miro, his father's dearest friend, said. "These people aren't."

"And may I also add that our lads were not interested in the valley until the Charynites moved there," Lucian said.

"You started this," Alda said. "By going to Alonso and returning wed to that idiot Charynite girl. A disgrace to the memory of your mother, Lucian. A disgrace, and it's made us the laughingstock of the kingdom. *'The wife Lucian sent back,'*" she mimicked. "Do you hear them mocking Lord August of the Flatlands or the elders of the Rock village in such a way?"

Lucian clenched his fists with rage.

"The pact was made between my father and hers, and I honored it in my father's memory," he said, fury lacing his words.

"Says who?" his cousin Gwendie called. "Who heard of this pact except for the girl's father? You're gullible, Lucian. And weak, and you believe anything the enemy says. Shame on you."

"Shame," the others shouted.

"Your father died at the hands of a Charynite," Alda hissed. "Shame on you."

She walked out with her sons in tow.

"Give him a chance," Yael called out. He was Jory's father, and regardless of what was said tonight, Lucian knew Jory would have his ears boxed by both his ma and fa when he got home.

"We've given him enough chances," Pitts the cobbler said. "What has he done to keep the enemy from the foot of our mountain? Nothing! He can't even find the culprit behind Orly's bull going missing every night. How hard is that, Lucian? It's a bull with more brains than you have."

Lucian's eyes met Yata's, and he saw pain there. *Please don't be disappointed, Yata. Please,* he begged silently.

He swallowed hard. "I stand by what I say. I don't care what you think of them. I didn't think I cared what I thought of them. I still don't. But I care what I think of us, and when one of their men gave me a lesson on how they would like their women treated . . . well, it shamed me. And it made me realize that I did care and that Saro would be horrified?"—his eyes met Jory's—"and disappointed that our lads would treat the women of any kingdom in such a way. You may say shame on me for believing what the enemy says, but I say shame on all of us if we condone the behavior of our lads."

There was silence a moment.

"The lads do not enter the valley," he said firmly. "And if any of you have issue with my ruling, I will send a message to beloved Isaboe and have this mountain put on curfew."

He pushed past the crowd and left the courtyard.

Phaedra of Alonso sat by the stream that evening and wrote a letter to Lady Beatriss of the Flatlands. It had been a week since a horse and cart had arrived from the village of Sennington with a letter and a gift.

Phaedra had read the letter to Kasabian and Cora as they studied the object at the back of the cart.

"What does it all mean?" Kasabian asked.

"Well, here in her letter, Lady Beatriss writes that she used to cook for her village, but she no longer needs it and I should put it to good use."

It was an oversize clay pot, which took three men to remove from the cart and place on the ground.

"There," she said, pointing where a campfire was set up beside the stream.

"What are we going to do with it?" Cora asked.

Phaedra thought a moment. "I think we'll make pumpkin soup." She looked up at the caves where some of the camp dwellers were staring down at them. "And invite the whole village."

Later that day, Phaedra crossed the stream with a bowl of soup in her hands and held it out to Tesadora, who sat with the girls cooking trout over an open fire. Tesadora studied it.

"I don't eat orange food."

"That's silly," Phaedra said, wondering where she got the courage to call Tesadora silly. "You eat green food and red food."

"Orange is a ridiculous color for food, I say."

"I'll have a taste," the Mont girl named Constance said. Somehow Tesadora had inherited two Mont girls who had come down one day with Phaedra's Mont husband and never returned home. "I'm sick and tired of fish."

Phaedra held out the spoon, and the girl slurped it, making a face. "Something is missing."

Constance jumped up from where she sat and searched around their herb garden before coming back with a small leaf that she began to shred, stirring it into her soup. Constance tasted it again and nodded with approval, handing it to Japhra.

"Strange," Japhra said. She didn't speak much. Phaedra had heard someone say she had a gift when it came to cures, but that the Charynite soldiers had broken her inside.

Japhra held it out to Tesadora. "I've seen you eat carrots," she teased. "They're orange."

Tesadora took a spoonful of the soup and swallowed. "Tomorrow we'll show you how a soup is made," was all she said.

The next night, even Rafuel's mysterious men had left their cave and Tesadora's herbs gave a fragrance to the soup that had the more reserved Charynites coming back for seconds.

"You're sure I'm not poisoning you?" Tesadora called out to one of the camp dwellers who had refused to see her. "Because if I'm not poisoning your food, perhaps you can come and see me about that open sore on your arm."

The night after that, they made a fish stock that caused much flatulence and even more laughter.

And so it was that Lady Beatriss's boiling pot became the reason the cave dwellers came out in the open and began to speak to their neighbors. Phaedra drew up a roster, and each night it was a different person's turn to cook, and sometimes she'd see them venture over the stream to speak to the Lumaterans about recipes. Later, Phaedra completed her letter and showed it to Cora.

"Ask her if she has any need for her bread oven," Cora demanded.

But Phaedra did no such thing, and it was only after she sent the letter through her Mont husband that she wondered what had possibly happened to Lady Beatriss's village that would mean she no longer had use for the pot.

Lady Beatriss read Phaedra's letter in the palace village three days later. She was there with Vestie, collecting some fabric for a dress she promised to make her for Princess Jasmina's second birthday. She could see outside the shop to where Vestie was speaking to some of the children, but the next moment Vestie was running off and Beatriss looked out to see her daughter fly into Trevanion's arms. He was with two of his Guard.

Beatriss went outside, but she took a moment before she approached and acknowledged them all politely.

"We'll speak later," Trevanion said to his men, dismissing them. Her eyes caught his and he looked away, his attention on Vestie. But Beatriss had seen the dark flash of desire she recognized from their years together.

"Is the cart close by?" he asked quietly, taking Vestie's hand.

"Just at the smithy," Beatriss said.

"I'll walk you there."

Beatriss didn't have the strength to argue.

"A piggyback," Vestie pleaded, and he bent down so she could climb on.

As they walked alongside each other, Beatriss felt the coarseness of his arm beside hers.

"You don't seem yourself," he said, and she heard regret in his voice.

"I'm not quite sure I know who myself is anymore," she said sadly. Who was Beatriss of the Flatlands without her village? Without her sorrow? Without Trevanion of the River?

When they reached the buggy, he lifted her up to the seat of the cart and she felt her lips against his throat, heard his ragged breath. She would have given anything to hold on a moment longer. When she was settled, he hugged Vestie to him and placed her beside Beatriss.

"The queen speaks of having Vestie come stay and help with Jasmina. She's becoming a handful."

"It's the age," she said quietly. "Tell the queen we'll speak of it soon."

She rode away, all too aware of how long he stood waiting. Vestie waved until her arm was weary, then was quiet for most of the journey.

"Is there something wrong?" Beatriss asked, staring out at the village of Sayles where a plow team was at work preparing one of the fields for planting. Even the awful smell of cow dung in the air was progress. A richly fertilized field would produce a good crop, and Beatriss could not help comparing the emptiness of her village to this one.

"Mama?"

"Yes, my love."

"What's an abon . . . abobination?"

"A what?" Beatriss said, looking down at her daughter. Sometimes Beatriss thought she'd never see anything so magical as her child's face. It made her think of the poor cursed Charynites. How strange it was to feel pity for a people who had been the enemy for so long.

"Abobination."

"You mean abomination. Why?"

"Kie, son of Makli of the Flatlands, called me one today. He said . . . He said I don't have a father and that I'm an abob . . . abomination."

The air seemed to whoosh out of Beatriss's body, and she steadied herself, fighting not to react.

"It's something bad, isn't it?"

Beatriss forced a smile. "He was just being silly, my love."

But Beatriss could not allow it to rest and that afternoon, when Vestie was learning her letters with Tarah, she rode her horse to the home of Makli, whose farm was in Fenton. Makli and his family were exiles, and Beatriss had had little to do with them since the kingdom was reunited. She knocked firmly on their door and waited. When Makli's wife, Genova, answered, the woman looked taken aback.

"Lady Beatriss," she said politely.

"I was wanting to speak to both you and your husband," Beatriss said firmly, trying to keep the quiver from her voice. How many times had she heard Tesadora mock her in the days when they first became friends? "How can you fight the world with a quiver in your voice, Beatriss of the Flatlands?"

Makli came to the door and stood behind his wife. "Is there a problem, Lady Beatriss?"

"Actually, there is. Your son spoke a word to my Vestie today. He called her an abomination, and I presume that a wee boy would not know such a word without having heard it from an adult. A boy his age would not understand the absence of a father in my child's life unless he heard it spoken in his home."

"I'm not sure I like what you're accusing, Lady Beatriss," the woman said stiffly.

"And I'm not sure I like hearing my daughter ask me what such a word means," Beatriss said, and there it was. The quiver. "And I would ask you to refrain from speaking my business in front of your boy or I will report it as slander."

She walked away. Report it as slander? Was there such a thing? Would she go to Trevanion and Isaboe and say, *Makli of the Flatland has slurred my name in front of his family, and I want him banished from the kingdom*?

"I don't like your threat, Lady Beatriss," Makli called out.

"Leave it, Makli," his wife said. "Come inside."

"Don't come here again threatening us. Someone like you," Makli said.

Beatrice stopped in her tracks and turned around, then walked back up to their cottage door.

"Someone like me?" she asked.

Makli pointed a finger at her face, and his wife pulled him back.

"I say that if she is the daughter of a Charynite," he hissed, "she is an abomination, and if she is the daughter of a Lumateran, then you are a liar. Those of you who were trapped inside always believe you had it worse, but what are we to believe?"

"How dare you!" she cried.

"I dare because good people like Lord Selric and his family lost their lives in exile," he shouted, "and no one celebrates their bravery or thinks to take care of those who have survived in Fenton."

"Enough, Makli," his wife said.

"Yet all we hear of is how brave those trapped inside were. Brave Lady Beatriss. Well, perhaps brave Lady Beatriss was not as virtuous as they say. Perhaps she spread her legs for every Charynite or Lumateran who sang her praises."

Beatriss slapped his face with a cry, and it stung her hand. Makli's wife closed her eyes a moment, an expression of regret on her face.

"How could you possibly want to compete about who suffered most?" Beatriss said sadly. "For if you want to covet that prize, take it! Take it, but don't bring my child into your bitterness."

Later, Beatriss sat on the front step of the long house with Tarah and Samuel.

"Perhaps one more time," she said quietly to Samuel. "We'll try one more time, and it may just be the three of us. If it doesn't work, I'll have to let you both go."

"We'll go where you go, Lady Beatriss," Samuel said. "There's plenty of work in town, so if you go to town, we'll be there with you. But if you say let's try one more time, then we'll work these fields one more time. And if you say ten more times, then we'll work the land ten more times."

Beatriss looked away, fighting tears. She gripped their hands.

"I'm forgetting what the truth is, friends," she said.

"We were here, Lady Beatriss. We saw it all, so when you forget what the truth is, you come to us and we'll remind you."

In the days that followed, Beatriss could see the sadness on her child's face as more of their neighbors left the village.

"I was thinking of a special treat, my love," she said to Vestie one morning. "You could go to the palace and stay with Isaboe and Jasmina."

"And Trevanion?"

"Of course."

And on the day Vestie left, the blackness inside Beatriss was so fierce that she didn't have the strength to get up the next morning. Or the morning after that. Or the morning after that.

CHAPTER 18

That night, his last in the palace, Froi was stuck beside two dukes complaining about the scarcity of food at their end of the table, despite the bounty placed before them. They whispered that the *provincari* were to blame. The *provincari* in turn looked uncomfortable in the palace surrounds. The leaders of the provinces didn't have the useless look of the nobility, but they did exude power, and Froi could understand the king and Bestiano's need to keep them happy. These men and women had purpose and they had strength. United, they had once been a force against past kings. Divided, they had helped cause the misery that was Charyn today.

Gargarin was sitting beside one, a handsome man whose eyes seemed fixed firmly on Froi with the same horror and disbelief Froi had first seen on Gargarin's and Arjuro's faces. Froi knew without being told that the man was De Lancey of Paladozza.

"They're nothing, I say," the king's inbred cousin hissed in Froi's ear. "Nothing. Do they have a title? I daresay not."

Quintana sat with the aunts, and it was obvious by the hideous lime-green dress she wore that Bestiano had managed to wrest the calico one from her. In his pocket, Froi found a piece of parchment from Gargarin's scribbles. He folded it into a shape most like a rabbit and asked for it to be passed toward her.

After much grumbling and scoffing, it reached Quintana's place. She stared at it a moment and then looked over to his table. Froi saw a glimpse of her teeth.

Later, he returned to the chamber to speak to Gargarin about the events of that morning. Froi hid Gargarin's dagger under the mattress and waited awhile for the man to return, but his thoughts were too much on Quintana and before he could stop himself, he walked out to the balconette, climbed, and took the leap. From outside her window, he saw the flicker of light from where she was blowing out the last of the candles. When she saw him standing on the balconette, she walked to the doors and opened them. She was about to say his name, but he held up a hand. He couldn't bear hearing "Olivier" coming from her lips. Not tonight.

"First I'm going to use my hands, and then I'm going to use my mouth," he said, "and then you are going to teach me to be gentle, and I'll show you that not all men share your bed because it's destined by the gods or written on the stone walls of this prison of yours. I've never had a lover and nor have you. So let's be the first for each other."

He caught her face between his hands and kissed her hard.

But she stepped away and he saw the hesitation in her eyes.

Wait, Froi. Wait.

"I don't come to you pure," she said.

"Not interested in purity. Only willingness."

She backed away from him to the end of the bed, and his heart sank, already guessing her next move. Lying down and pulling her nightdress up to her thighs, asking him to undo the string to his trousers. But instead, slowly she lifted the garment over her head and stood before him, and he stared at the fullness of her. He lifted his shirt above his head and held out a hand, drawing her to him, his body veiling hers from whatever it was that made her face flush red. Then he lifted her to him, felt her legs clasp around his waist as he knelt on the bed, laying her down. Gently he placed his hands on her knees and drew them apart, pressing his lips against her inner thigh.

"What are you doing?" she asked, trying to raise herself.

"First, I thought I'd show you what a pity it would be if they cut off my wicked tongue."

When Froi woke in the early hours of the morning, she was watching him. He raised himself, pressing a kiss to her mouth.

"Happy birthday," he said.

"It's the day of weeping," she corrected. She slipped out of bed and placed her cotton shift over her body. She seemed in a hurry.

"My father's agreed to see me," she said quietly. "Before he sees the *provincari*."

"It's too early," he said, not quite meeting her eye, knowing that by the time she saw her father, he would be dead at Froi's hand.

She continued to put on her clothes without a word.

"You need to get a dress from Aunt Mawfa," he said, needing to buy time. "You can't go to see your father in that."

Quintana looked down at her dress and then back to him, nodding. Then she was gone and Froi realized with an immense sadness that he would never see the princess of Charyn again.

When he reached the cellar, it was crowded with servants, chatting with urgency. Dorcas and another soldier were overseeing the activity.

"What are you doing here, Olivier?" Dorcas asked.

"You've been demoted, I see, Dorcas."

"A proper lesson for losing the vessel," Dorcas responded.

"She's a girl, Dorcas. Not a vessel."

Froi knew he'd have to wait. Quintana and the *provincari* would see the king, and then in the confusion of the *provincari*'s exit from the palace, he'd take his chance.

Returning to the chamber he shared with Gargarin, Froi saw the rolled-up plans. They were tied neatly by a ribbon with the words *De Lancey of Paladozza* attached, and all Froi could think was that the idiot Gargarin was off to see the king without his plans. Until he remembered that Gargarin wasn't an idiot. Froi gripped the mattress and felt for the dagger, but it wasn't there. He bit back his fury. An ice-cold finger of dread ran up his spine. He grabbed the drawings and ran down the tower stairs into the outer ward, dodging servants and soldiers. He saw Gargarin heading to the fourth tower, pushing past those who stood in his way. Froi bolted toward him.

"At it again, are we?" he hissed into his ear.

Gargarin didn't respond and kept on walking toward the soldiers guarding the king's tower.

Froi gripped his arm, forcing him to slow down. "You'll fail!"

"You want the glory, do you? To go back to whoever sent you and claim the kill was yours?"

"No," Froi said with frustration. Three of the palace soldiers walked by. Froi and Gargarin nodded in their direction and continued without looking back. "But I can do something you can't. If you can convince them to let me through with you, I can do what we both set out to do and get us out of this palace alive."

"Getting out of here alive isn't part of my plan."

Froi pushed him into a small hidden alcove in the wall, trapping him. "Listen to me, Gargarin. I've been trained to do this. You haven't. Take your drawings, build your shit holes, but don't give up your life for this."

A hint of a smile appeared on Gargarin's face. A softness unlike anything Froi had seen in his expression before. "Where did you come from?" he asked, but it seemed a question Gargarin was asking himself and not Froi. "Will you do something for me?"

Froi shook his head.

"I'll ask you anyway," Gargarin said. "Give these designs to De Lancey of Paladozza. They also contain a letter of instruction to Tariq, the heir. If there is anarchy in the Citavita, promise me this."

"I'm promising you nothing, Gargarin. Tend to your own instructions and leave me to mine."

Gargarin continued as though Froi hadn't spoken. "Take my brother and Lirah out of the Citavita. Perhaps to Belegonia or Osteria."

Froi was shaking his head, pushing the plans back into Gargarin's hands.

"It's all I ask of you."

"Who are you to ask anything of me?" Froi asked.

Gargarin was silent for a moment. He went to speak, but an ear-piercing scream echoed through the palace. Then more screams and shouts.

Froi raced out into the courtyard. "*Quintana!*"

Above, between the fourth and fifth towers, Froi could see the *provincari* and their people disappearing down the stairs that would take them to where he and Gargarin stood.

Once outside, the *provincari* hurried toward them. "Gar! Gargarin," De Lancey of Paladozza called out.

When they reached Froi and Gargarin, the *provincari* were all speaking at the same time.

"Stop," Gargarin shouted. "One at a time."

"Bestiano's killed the king," the *provincaro* of Desantos said.

"What?" Gargarin said, disbelief in his voice.

"Where's the princess?" Froi asked.

They heard more screams from the tower above, then shouts and orders.

"Where is she?" Froi demanded, grabbing hold of a man.

"She arrived to visit her father before us," one of the *provincari*'s scribes said rapidly. "She demanded to see him alone, but Bestiano would not allow it. He would not allow any of the *provincari* to see him. He claimed the king had changed his mind. But the princess refused to listen, becoming hysterical, screaming, *'I need to see my father on my own. Search me now.'* The *provincari* insisted that Bestiano allow her to see the king on her day of weeping. They were frightened by her madness. One of the king's Guard stepped forward to search her, and when he was satisfied, the princess ran into the chamber with Bestiano in tow and not even moments later we heard her screams. Heard her shout, *'Bestiano has killed my father!'*"

Gargarin spun around, taking in those crowded around them.

"Go!" Gargarin ordered the *provincari*. "Get out of the palace. If Bestiano has control of the riders, he'll hold you all as hostages to your provinces. Go now."

"What—?"

"Now!" Gargarin ordered. "Take only whatever you have with you and get out of the palace. Arjuro will give you sanction in the godshouse." He shoved Froi forward. "Take him."

Froi pulled away, shaking his head. He had to find Quintana.

"Go!" Gargarin yelled.

The *provincari* hurried away except for De Lancey of Paladozza. Gargarin forced the rolled-up parchment into his hands.

The man shook his head. "We leave together, Gar."

"Go," Gargarin begged. "You need to prepare Tariq. Take him under your protection."

De Lancey hesitated one moment more, and then, with a backward glance, he hurried away.

Froi and Gargarin made it as far as the entrance to the fifth tower, where they were met by Dorcas and another guard.

"You're to return to your chambers, Sir Gargarin," Dorcas said, agitated. Beads of sweat poured down his face.

"Whose orders, Dorcas?" Gargarin asked.

"Bestiano's, sir."

"What's going on?" Gargarin demanded. There was no response, and Froi wondered if the guard knew as little as they did.

The moment they reached the chamber, Froi raced out onto the balconette.

"Quintana!"

He leaped over to her balconette, but he could see that her chamber was empty. Froi climbed back to where Gargarin was standing.

They heard a key in the door and raced toward it, but were too late. Froi hammered at the door. "Dorcas! Dorcas, find the princess!"

But there was no response, and Froi kicked at the door with frustration.

"Why kill the king now?" he asked.

Gargarin shook his head. "It makes no sense," he said. "It makes no sense at all."

It was the longest of days. The waiting and the pacing and the fear for Quintana tore Froi up inside. *Please let her be alive.* Sometimes he pounded at the door, bellowing the name of every guard he could remember. *Dorcas. Fekra. Fodor.* And all the while, Gargarin wrote like a man possessed, quill not leaving paper until late that afternoon when they heard the voices crying out from across the *gravina*.

"Gargarin!"

"Gar!"

Froi ran to the balconette, Gargarin hobbling behind him.

Arjuro, De Lancey, and others stood at the godshouse balconette.

"Bestiano rode out of the palace with the riders," De Lancey called out.

Gargarin and Froi exchanged stunned looks.

"You need to find a way out, Gar. The palace is unguarded, and the street lords are beginning to enter. They—"

Suddenly a body flew out of the window above Froi and Gargarin's. Screams could be heard from inside the chambers surrounding them.

"Gods," Gargarin gasped, searching above and below before Froi saw him look across at his brother. Arjuro's eyes were wide with horror, and then more bodies flew past them, faces contorted, screams eaten by the air below.

"They're starting at the top," De Lancey shouted, wincing as another body of a soldier bounced off the wall of the godshouse. "Get out, Gargarin. Get out."

"We are locked in," Gargarin shouted back. He spun around, searching for an answer, and before Froi could argue, Gargarin grabbed him and shoved him toward the wrought iron of the balconette. "You've done this climb before. Get to Lirah's garden and have her let you in. When the street lords reach the prison tower, they'll release whoever's in there. Tell them you're both prisoners of the king."

Froi nodded. "We can both—"

"No," Gargarin said. "No time. You know I'll never be able to climb a step. You do this now. You don't argue. They won't kill a prisoner in the king's tower. I don't know how much time it will buy you, but it's better than finding you here."

"But you—"

"They may use me to bargain, but they will kill you in an instant. Go."

Froi was shaking his head. The plan was bad. The plan meant Gargarin would die and Froi would never be able to find Quintana.

"The princess . . ."

"Is in all probability dead," Gargarin said flatly. "And if she's not, she will be soon."

On the other side of the *gravina,* Arjuro and the *provincari* watched anxiously.

"Save yourself and take care of Lirah," Gargarin said, his voice hoarse. He gripped Froi by the shoulders.

"Tell her . . . tell her that the babe they placed in my hands was smuggled out of the palace to the hidden priests. Tell her that if I knew it was hers, I would have found a way for her to know so she would not have suffered all these years."

Froi stood on the balconette, his eyes fixed on Gargarin.

"Go," Gargarin pleaded. "I'm begging you. Keep safe. Keep her safe."

Froi heard the crash of the door and in an instant he leaped up to catch hold of the latticework of the balconette above their chamber. A moment later, the street lords were outside, one of them holding a hand to Gargarin's throat. Froi held his breath, praying they would not look above.

There was shouting from the other side of the *gravina*. "We'll pay a ransom," De Lancey shouted. "We'll pay a ransom!" But Gargarin and the street lords disappeared inside the chamber.

On Lirah's tower garden, Froi hammered at the door. "Lirah! Lirah!"

He heard a fumble for the lock, and the door was pushed forward.

"What's happening?" she asked, and he saw the fear in her eyes. "All I hear is screaming and when I stood on the roof . . ."

She shook her head, and he imagined what she had seen. "We're going to have to wait for them to open the door," Froi said. "We'll say we're both prisoners of the king, but do not tell them you are Lirah of Serker."

Lirah nodded.

"Where is she?" Lirah asked. "Where did you hide her?"

Froi looked away. He couldn't find the words and he saw the slow realization on her face.

"Where is she?"

They heard another scream disappear down the *gravina.* Froi grabbed her hand and pushed her back inside her prison cell, but Lirah pulled free viciously, as though reason had left her.

"You were supposed to save her. Quintana! Where is she?"

Froi covered Lirah's mouth with his hand and she bit hard. Stunned, he stepped back.

"Coward. Bastard. You were supposed to save her."

Froi shook his head.

"Go back and search for her!"

"I can't," he said through gritted teeth. "Gargarin said—"

She slapped him hard across the face, hissing through her teeth. "Thank the gods you're motherless, you piece of worthless garbage, for no woman would stomach such a coward for a son."

Froi's face smarted for more reasons than the slap. "Don't let me say words I regret, Lirah. Gargarin said this is the best way."

"Don't speak his name to me," she cried.

"He said to tell you, Lirah! That he smuggled your son out of the palace eighteen years ago. Give yourself that reason to live."

"And you believe his lies?" she asked, half-mad with fury.

They heard the sound of a key in the lock, and a man stepped in calmly, wiping the blood of his dagger onto his trousers. Behind him, Froi could see the lifeless body of Lirah's guard. She gave a small cry. Froi pushed her behind him.

"We're prisoners of the king," Froi said, thanking Sagrami that it was neither of the street lords who would have remembered him from outside the godshouse. "The king's Third Adviser took a liking to my sister here, and when I tried to defend her, he arrested us both."

The man's eyes were greedily fastened on Lirah. Froi itched to take the dagger from him, knew he would do it easily, but they needed this man to accompany them out of the palace if they were to survive. The man beckoned them along. Gargarin's plan could work. Being the king's prisoners would perhaps set them free. Froi and Lirah stepped over the guard's body, and Froi felt her body tremble beside him. On one of the landings between the levels of the tower, Froi caught the desperate eyes of two of the dukes, who were on their knees, hands to their heads. In the courtyard, some of the servants were being released into the Citavita. The street lords carried cases of ale and wine from the cellars, smashing the bottles after they emptied them down their throats. Out in the barbican, four soldiers stood with their heads to the wall while a street lord paced back and forth behind them, a dagger in his hand. The last thing Froi heard as he passed them was the sound of the first soldier choking on his own blood.

At the portcullis, the street lord who had escorted them grabbed Lirah, bunching the skirt of her dress in his hands. So close to the entrance, but still not free.

"We live with the soothsayer," Froi said. "You know where that is? Come visit us this night. My sister will be most grateful if you do."

Lirah nodded, and the man hesitated a moment, a salacious smile on his face at the promise of what was on offer. He let go of Lirah, and Froi took her hand and hurried away. But just as they reached the drawbridge, drops of blood splattered at their feet and Froi stared up in horror at the body of a man hanging from the battlement, his throat cut, his body bludgeoned. Reaching out to drag Lirah away from the grisly scene, Froi caught the expression of bitter satisfaction on her face and he knew that the street lords had found the king's body to flaunt to the people.

The king of Charyn was indeed dead. What was it Trevanion had instructed? "The moment he stops breathing, you return home. The very moment. Do not look back." *Run,* Froi told himself. *Run down to the bridge of the Citavita and leave this place behind.*

But the pull of Gargarin's and Quintana's fates was too much, and Froi took Lirah's hand, breaking his second bond to those he loved, in as many days.

They arrived to find a crowd of people gathered at the godshouse door, begging to be let in. Froi recognized a *provincaro*'s guard at the entrance.

"There is no room," the guard shouted, shoving the crowd back. "No room."

Froi pushed through, closer to the door, his fingers digging into Lirah's hand, determined not to let her go. He caught a glimpse of Arjuro inside the foyer. The priestling stood behind the guards, searching anxiously over their shoulders.

"Arjuro! Arjuro!"

Froi climbed onto the back of the man before him. "Arjuro!"

Arjuro pushed past the guard and pointed toward Froi. A moment later, one of the guards shoved his way through the crowd and grabbed Froi and Lirah, dragging them inside.

The door was latched shut behind. The small foyer was packed with not only those who had escaped the palace but also the people of the Citavita, fearing for their lives.

Froi hurried past Arjuro and raced up the stairwell all the way to the top, dodging floor upon floor of people. When he reached the Hall of Illumination, it was filled to the brim, but he shoved his way to the balconette, where only the brave stood watching what took place across the *gravina*.

"Have you seen her? The princess? Or Gargarin? Have you seen him?"

And the only good news for a day so bleak was that Quintana and Gargarin had not been tossed into the *gravina* below.

Yet.

CHAPTER 19

Pale faces, stunned by the carnage they had witnessed, studied any newcomer who entered the room. The main hall was filled with those from the streets of the Citavita who had taken refuge in the godshouse, as well as the *provincari* and their guards and advisers. Alone in a corner, Arjuro caught Froi's eye, and Froi saw wretched misery in the priestling's expression. They had spent most of the day watching the macabre scene taking place on the balconettes across the narrow space between the godshouse and the palace. The palace scribe had asked for Froi's assistance, pen and parchment in his hand, as he identified those hurled into the *gravina* below.

"Who was that?" he asked Froi as they looked on.

"The king's cousin from Nebia," Froi replied, recognizing the body of the simpleton who had spoken to Froi most often in the palace.

Sometimes the scribe would stop a moment to throw up over the balconette before calmly returning to his task. "Cyril of Nebia, would you say? No, no, Chabon of Sebastabol."

When there was little to be seen in the darkness, they returned inside and spent the rest of the night crowded in the Hall of Illumination with hundreds of others.

"Are we safe here, De Lancey?" a woman asked.

Froi looked up to study the boy who had grown up alongside Arjuro and Gargarin. The lover who had betrayed Arjuro. A more unlikely pair Froi could never imagine in his life. Even under the dramatic circumstances, De Lancey was all perfection and charm, his skin bronzed, his garments tailored to perfection, while Arjuro's stark white skin contrasted with his dark torn hair and beard. The black robe that covered him from neck to ankle was grubby and shapeless.

"Best that you ask that question of the priestling," the *provincaro* replied in his smooth voice, pretending to study something nonexistent on the wall, as though it were the most natural thing to do under the circumstances. Arjuro refused to respond to the woman with anything beyond a grunt. Despite his forced benevolence, most in the room seemed wary of him and kept their distance.

"It's best we all leave and return to our provinces," De Lancey said. "At least we are safe there, with armies to protect our people."

There was a chorus of agreement, but also dismay.

"What about the people of the Citavita?" a woman cried. "You care only for your own provinces and leave us to this carnage. Who rules Charyn when you return to the safety of your walls?"

"And what would you have us do?" De Lancey said calmly, but Froi heard restrained anger in his voice. "You've all seen what happens the moment a king dies and his men desert their post. The ignorant take over. Savages killing their own people. Innocent people."

"Those who live in the palace aren't innocent," another shouted from across the room. "They deserve what they get."

There was uproar at those words.

"We were in the palace," De Lancey of Paladozza argued. "On province business. Do I deserve to die? Do the other *provincari*? And do you know who else was visiting the palace? Gargarin of Abroi."

Froi watched the feverish whispers. "Yes," De Lancey confirmed. "How soon we forget men who have worked for the good of Charyn."

"What about the princess?"

It was Lirah's voice. Froi had lost sight of her the moment they entered the godshouse. But here she was asking the question that no one else dared to ask. There was an uncomfortable silence, and most looked away. Froi heard the words *the Serker whore* whispered, but Lirah seemed to care little for their scorn and curiosity.

"With these savages, one does not negotiate with a list," De Lancey of Paladozza said coolly. Dismissively. "We speak one name. Gargarin's. He has the trust of almost every *provincaro* in this kingdom. Tariq of Lascow has stated that Gargarin is his choice as First Adviser if Tariq is ever to be crowned king."

There was more fierce discussion, more anger.

"Tariq knows nothing of the world. He's been in hiding since he was fifteen."

"But he is the legal heir, and at this moment, he's our only king. Gargarin knows enough to guide him. Both are aligned to no province, and that fact in itself will satisfy every one of us *provincari*. We return home, combine our armies, march into the Citavita, and place Tariq on the throne with Gargarin alongside him."

There was approval for this suggestion, the first sign of calm.

"And what of Quintana?" Lirah demanded again. "You can't leave her in the palace to die!"

"Your daughter is worth nothing," a man called out.

"If she had broken the curse, at least we could have forgiven her for something," Provincara Orlanda of Jidia said. She was a handsome woman who had fawned over Bestiano and Gargarin the night before.

"She's our last born," Lirah said.

There were hisses and fury directed at Lirah.

"Our lives have been ruined because of her," Orlanda spat.

"Your spawn, Serker bitch," a woman Froi didn't recognize shouted.

"Her birth. Her lies. Her failure to break the curse," another joined in, advancing on Lirah.

"If we choose between Gargarin of Abroi and the princess, we choose Gargarin," the ambassador for Sebastabol said.

Despite his anger toward her, Froi pushed through the crowd of people to Lirah, but Arjuro was there before him, grabbing her arm.

"Come," he said to both of them.

Froi felt De Lancey's eyes following them from across the room.

"It's best that you keep your mouth shut, Lirah," Arjuro said, shoving his way through the crowd.

"It's best that I take my leave, priestling," Lirah said coldly.

"It's not safe for you among the street pigs, Lirah," Froi snapped. "Don't be a fool."

"It's no safer here," she said quietly as they reached the door, where De Lancey of Paladozza stood, blocking Froi's path.

"Would you like to know who has taken refuge in this very godshouse?" De Lancey asked Froi smoothly.

Froi ignored him, stepping aside and following Arjuro and Lirah into the dark corridor. They stopped a moment as Arjuro lit the lamps that lined the wall. But De Lancey was on their heels, followed by four of his guards. Froi saw a flash of fear cross Lirah's face, heard Arjuro's curse as the priestling grabbed Lirah's hand, leading her to the steps that would take them to the levels below.

"Stop a moment," De Lancey ordered.

"Remember whose place this is, De Lancey," Arjuro warned over his shoulder.

De Lancey reached them and grabbed on to Arjuro's robe to stop him, but the priestling viciously pulled away, catching the *provincaro* in the face with his elbow. In an instant, the four guards slammed Arjuro against the wall and Froi heard the crack of the priestling's head against stone.

Froi felt the pounding of blood in his brain chanting at him, replaying the events of the last day. There were too many voices and images in his head. Quintana's face the day before. Gargarin's instructions. Lirah's bitter tirade as he dragged her out of the castle. Those tossed from the balconette, the king's body, the fury of the crowd in the godshouse hall. Suddenly he grabbed De Lancey, snapped the man's wrist, and heard his quick intake of pain. The four guards let go of Arjuro and charged for Froi. And in that confined space where priestlings once prayed and studied and died, he used fists and palms, smashed heads against stone walls, broke bones, bit flesh, and spat it out. *"You're a weapon, Froi. The best we've ever created,"* Trevanion had told him once. And when De Lancey's men were writhing in pain at his feet, Froi's blood cried for more, his breath ragged, his feet dancing around them, wanting them back on their feet. He wanted to do it again.

But Arjuro was there, blocking his path. "Leash it," Arjuro hissed. "Leash it."

Froi couldn't leash it. He didn't know how, and that knowledge made him want to weep. He tried to count. But couldn't remember the right numbers. He hammered a savage fist to his temple over and over again until Arjuro gripped his face between his hands.

"Take a breath."

"I can't remember my bond," Froi whispered hoarsely.

In his head, Froi counted in Lumateran and then Sarnak, but the numbers meant nothing, led to nothing. Arjuro studied his face and then looked down to watch Froi's fingers dance with every number he tried to speak aloud.

"Este, dortis, thirst . . ." Arjuro began counting quietly in Charyn.

Froi's heart fell. All those times, even as far back as three years ago, when he first arrived in Lumatere and they gave him his bond, Froi had used the numbers of the Charyn language without even realizing.

Blood sings to blood, Froi.

Froi closed his eyes and took in a deep breath.

An important rule of the bond was never to break a bone if Lumateran lives are not at risk.

He opened his eyes to see De Lancey nursing his wrist. In the flickering light, he could see Lirah's face.

"They're becoming hysterical in the hall," she said coolly. "They think the street lords have entered."

De Lancey caught one of his guard's eyes and gestured him toward the hall. A moment later, all four men reluctantly limped away.

"Take Lirah's hand, Olivier," Arjuro said quietly. "The steps are steep."

"Yet he's not Olivier," De Lancey said, "are you? The last born from Sebastabol is in the library downstairs with my son, burying the ancient books in case the street lords enter and destroy them." De Lancey's eyes met Froi's. "The real Olivier claims to have spent the last few weeks held captive in the caves outside Sebastabol."

Arjuro's breath was ragged as he looked at Froi, shaking his head with regret. "Bit of truth would have helped."

"You ask him for truth, Arjuro?" De Lancey said. "When you've been interested in no truth but yours."

Arjuro pointed a finger at De Lancey. "And what was your truth?" he said through clenched teeth. "What was Gar's? That my brother didn't murder the oracle? That you didn't send your messenger to betray me? Did you know that the farrier left behind a family, De Lancey? Did you ever give them another thought?"

De Lancey's eyes met Arjuro's, and Froi saw something flare up between them. History was history, he once told the priest-king. Why couldn't it stay in the past? All this hatred between these two men could only mean that once there had been so much love.

"The oracle and the child were already dead. That's Gar's truth!"

Lirah pushed the *provincaro* away with all the fury she could muster. And he winced from the pain, nursing his hand. He couldn't disguise his anger and disgust.

"Oh, we care about children now, do we, whore?" he sneered. "After you tried to murder your own?"

Arjuro grabbed De Lancey's injured wrist and snapped it back into place. De Lancey gasped from the pain.

"Ask the Serker whose child it was Gargarin tossed from that window," Arjuro said. "She should know. It was hers."

"The child belonged to the oracle," De Lancey said. "Born dead. It was what Gar swore to me."

"Yet he told this impostor that the child was smuggled out of the palace," Lirah said, looking at Froi bitterly. "So who are we to believe, De Lancey? A liar or a liar?"

Arjuro stared at Froi, shocked by the words. "When did Gargarin tell you that?" he asked huskily. "When?"

"Today. Before the street lords took him away," Froi said.

"But he told me the babe was born dead," De Lancey argued. "Gargarin swore he was forced to toss a dead child into the *gravina*."

"My son was born with a mighty voice," Lirah said fiercely, a tremble in her words. "And Gargarin tells you both lies. In one breath, a dead child. In the next, a smuggled last born. Do you believe the gods conjured up a spell and made his brother see our worst nightmares?"

"Come," Arjuro said quietly. But he pointed a finger at De Lancey emphatically. "Not you. And bind that wrist."

They left De Lancey standing alone in the dark corridor. Arjuro led Lirah and Froi to the tiny marble steps that spiraled down. But De Lancey was a hard man to lose.

"So whose bastard is this lad, Arjuro?" he called out from the top of the steps. "Yours or Gargarin's?"

Lirah gasped. Froi swung around to look up, almost tumbling down the narrow steps.

"The person I was swiving eighteen years ago hasn't the capacity for childbirth. Curse or no curse," Arjuro said coolly. "Does he, De Lancey?" Arjuro continued down the stairs, refusing to look back. There was a ringing in Froi's ears, and when they reached the landing, his legs buckled under him. Arjuro forced him to sit, resting his back against the wall and pushing his head between his knees.

"Breathe, idiot boy. His words are false. It's pure coincidence." But Froi heard doubt in Arjuro's voice.

"That face can't be pure coincidence, Ari," De Lancey said, suddenly behind them. He reached over Arjuro's shoulder and grabbed Froi's face, but Froi leaped to his feet and shoved them both away.

"Who do I resemble?" Froi hissed. There was silence.

Arjuro looked away.

"Who?"

"The most base of beasts born to this world," Arjuro said sadly. "My father. But I see my father's face in half of Charyn."

Froi sucked in a breath.

"He cannot possibly be Gargarin's son," Lirah said coldly. "I was the only woman he had."

De Lancey gave a short laugh of disbelief. "Don't you think it's strange, Lirah, that you can believe Gargarin is a murderer of babes and oracles, but you can't accept that he preferred another woman?"

"There was no other woman," she spat. She threw a look at Froi. "This one looks like the shit and garbage of this kingdom. Isn't that what they say Abroi is? He could be anyone's trash. Sent by anyone. Probably the Serkers living in the underground city who want their revenge."

The *provincaro* searched Froi's face. "Who sent you?" he demanded. "Was it the Serkers?"

"Does it matter? I didn't kill the king."

"Pity," De Lancey said. "I would have liked you much better if you had."

Arjuro led them to a room laid out with straw cots once used by priestlings. He pushed Lirah toward one.

"Sleep," he said to them, ignoring De Lancey, who stood at the door watching them all. "The sun will rise soon, and it will be another long day."

Froi sat with his back to the others. He felt a hand at his shoulder and shrugged it away viciously.

"Not the time to be sulking," Arjuro said. "What would you expect from me?" he added gently. "A 'Hi-de-ho to you, lad. By the way, you have the face of my demented father, which could only mean that you are either his child or Gargarin's, who also happens to be a killer of women and babes'?"

Froi turned to them. He could see only their outlines in the darkness. Lirah lay with her back to him, her body huddled.

He studied Arjuro closely. "Is there a chance I'm his son?"

That Froi and Arjuro had the same blood was too hard to fathom.

"I don't know," Arjuro said honestly. "The only way I can answer that question is if you tell me the truth. Days ago you informed me that the oracle's child was not tossed into the *gravina*. That my brother murdered Lirah's son instead. Today you tell me he didn't murder the child. That it was smuggled out of the palace. What am I to be told tomorrow? That my brother is dead without me knowing the truth?" Froi saw tears in the man's eyes. "I don't even know your real name, Olivier."

But Froi couldn't tell the whole truth without betraying Lumatere. Did he trust these people enough to do that?

"Do you know a man by the name of Rafuel of Sebastabol?" he asked after a stretch of silence. "He approached . . . my people with a plan."

He saw Arjuro stiffen. Lirah turned slowly from her cot to face them. "I know that name," she said.

"What was the plan?" De Lancey asked from the door.

"That he could get an assassin into the palace to impersonate the last born from Sebastabol."

Froi waited for Arjuro to speak.

"Arjuro?" De Lancey said. "Give him something in return."

"No," Arjuro said. "I'm more interested in what Rafuel of Sebastabol had to say to . . . sorry, what did you say your name was?"

The stare from Arjuro was sharp, and Froi fought back a shiver. He felt as if he were looking at Gargarin.

"I didn't," Froi said.

A hint of a knowing smile appeared on Arjuro's face. "You don't trust me, do you?"

"I don't trust anyone here."

Arjuro looked at him shrewdly, eyebrows raised in contemplation.

"You don't trust anyone *here* in the Citavita? Or anyone *here* in Charyn?"

"Are you saying he's a foreigner?" Lirah asked, studying Froi with confusion.

Froi didn't respond for a moment. "You're not so slow when you're sober, Arjuro."

"He's Lumateran," De Lancey said. "Who else would be training an assassin?"

Froi didn't respond.

"But why would Rafuel of Sebastabol go all the way to Lumatere to find an assassin when he could train one here?" De Lancey continued. "I could have provided him with one or two myself."

"Didn't say I was a Lumateran, and careful, Provincaro, that's the second time you've mentioned the death of the king. You could be accused of treason."

"He can't be a foreigner. He has Serker eyes, and a face from Abroi," Lirah said.

"I disagree," Arjuro said. "In the times when nomads traveled throughout the land, a Sendecanese or Sarnak or even a Yut could be found with Serker eyes."

Arjuro eyed Froi. "Your Charyn is flawless."

"Perhaps I've inherited a sharp mind from my father," he whispered mockingly in Arjuro's ear. "Or perhaps from my uncle. Perhaps I'm gods' touched."

"What else did Rafuel of Sebastabol have to say to your leaders?" De Lancey asked.

"Nothing," Froi said.

The *provincaro* made a sound as if he couldn't believe what he was hearing.

"It's true. He said nothing more to my leaders. But he did make mention of something to me without my leaders knowing."

The others waited.

"But as part of my bond, my captain said I was not to interfere with the matters of another kingdom."

De Lancey gave another humorless laugh.

"They sent you to assassinate the king and that's not interfering?"

Froi felt weary. He wanted more from Arjuro, but the priestling was a man who had been betrayed too many times, and Froi knew he would have to give a whole lot more before Arjuro spoke freely. Two of De Lancey's guards appeared at the door.

"My lord, it's not safe for you here," one said, eyeing Froi.

"Go check on Grij," the *provincaro* said tiredly, and Froi heard the voice of a man concerned for his son. It made him hate everyone even more.

De Lancey's attention was back on Froi.

"Rafuel of Sebastabol made mention of . . . the lost last born of the Citavita," Froi said quietly.

"A myth," Lirah said. "Used to dismiss the importance of Quintana as the last born."

"Not a myth," Arjuro said.

"You can't prove that," De Lancey argued.

"I saw the last born of the Citavita. Held him. Do you need any further proof than that, De Lancey?" Arjuro raged. "Or are we going to have a repeat of eighteen years past? Last time you refused to believe me about the king, an innocent messenger was murdered."

They all stared at Arjuro.

"You held the last born?" Lirah asked.

Arjuro nodded.

"When I escaped from the palace after . . . after taking Gargarin's identity."

"What?" she gasped, stunned.

"It was Gargarin who was imprisoned for eight years," Froi said. "Not Arjuro."

"I took refuge with the only people I trusted in this world. I knew where the priests of Trist were hiding, because they had found a way to send a message to me after my arrest the year before. When I arrived at the caves, they told me the strangest tale. That the night before, they had heard a sound outside and then saw the figure of a young boy fleeing. And at their feet was a filthy basket that smelled of cats with a babe inside. A male. No note. Nothing. They had no idea where he came from."

De Lancey moved away from the door, his eyes wide. Lirah placed a trembling hand to her throat.

"That night, every priest in the cave, whether gifted or not, woke up with the same words on their lips."

"That the last will make the first?" Lirah asked.

Arjuro shook his head. "That if redemption was ever to be possible, a sign would appear in the palace. We had no idea what it meant. We didn't know that at the time Charyn was cursed. All we knew was that the oracle was dead. The priests have always believed that even the gods were divided over this curse. That not one god has claimed it as their own."

"If no god claimed it as their own . . ." De Lancey said.

"Then no god could break it. Perhaps in their realm they've been searching for clues themselves." Arjuro sighed. "All we knew was that whoever left the last born with the priests feared for the child's life."

He turned to Lirah. "Why would the palace have wanted your son dead, Lirah?" he asked. "Was it because the king suspected it wasn't his?"

Lirah made a sound of annoyance. "I was his whore and the whore of anyone he chose to share me with! Why would the king ever have thought it was his child over anyone else?"

"Whose child was he then, Lirah?" De Lancey asked.

"Mine. *Mine.* He belonged to me," Lirah said. "What do you want me to say, De Lancey? I had no idea who the father was."

"Was it Gargarin's?" De Lancey asked again.

"I hardly saw the babe," she said. "And even if I had, do you think I would have seen a resemblance from a newborn? 'Ah yes,'" she mocked. "'Here is the chin of the king's favorite banker or the eyes of his favorite cousin.'"

There was a strained silence. A reminder of what Lirah was forced to be all those years.

"More, Arjuro," De Lancey said. "We need more."

"The priests of Trist asked me that night to name the boy because I was gods' touched and they weren't," Arjuro continued. "A child named by one who is gods' touched is blessed all their lives." Arjuro swallowed. "I knew this babe could not stand out in the world, so I gave him a name with no meaning, from a place with no meaning." Arjuro stole a look at Froi. "I called him Dafar of Abroi. He was smuggled into the kingdom of Sarnak, where the priestlings of Trist had a godshouse despite the Sarnak worship of the goddess. After the random burning down of the Sarnak godshouse four years later, the boy disappeared from our lives."

Froi's breath was caught in his throat.

"I am now sure that the child came from the palace and not the Citavita," Arjuro said.

"A moment ago you said the priests had no idea where he came from!" De Lancey said. "Why would you change your words?"

"Because Olivier the impostor," Arjuro said, pointing to Froi, "has just informed us that my brother claimed to have smuggled a child out of the palace. It could have only been your son, Lirah. Perhaps, without him realizing, it was Gargarin's son. You would not have known that then. But we can only guess it now. Our young impostor's resemblance to my father is quite extraordinary."

Arjuro's eyes met Froi's, and Froi could hardly breathe. *Lirah.* Not cold Lirah, who had despised him from the moment she first laid eyes on him. Not Gargarin.

Froi stumbled to his feet. "I'm not from this place."

Blood sings to blood, Froi.

Lirah's body was rocking, her expression one of horror.

"Lirah?" Arjuro asked. "Who passed your messages to Gargarin when you lived together in the palace? Who was your go-between?"

Lirah couldn't find the words to speak.

"Lirah!"

She shook herself out of her stupor.

"The Sixth Adviser's boy," she said quietly. She stopped, agape, and Froi watched Arjuro nod.

"Rafuel," she gasped. "Little Rafuel, with the cats."

"A sensitive boy," Arjuro said. "Smart, though. He was shouted down daily by his father, by everyone whose path he crossed in the palace. It's how he befriended my brother. He reminded Gargarin of who we once were. And do you want to know something else? In the early days of my imprisonment, when there was trust between my brother and me, Gargarin was my messenger to the priests. He was the only person to have known where they were hiding. Where to keep a babe safe from the palace."

Froi, Lirah, and De Lancey were too dumbfounded to speak.

"I think our Rafuel's been busy these past years searching for the last born." Arjuro's eyes met Froi's. "Did he find you in Sarnak, or have I got it all wrong?"

Froi didn't want to respond. If he said the words aloud, it would all be true and he didn't want it to be.

"I live in Lumatere," he said.

Lirah's shoulders sank. Was it relief or despair? De Lancey shook his head with disappointment, walking away. But Arjuro continued to stare at Froi, as though he were still attempting to work out the puzzle.

"I've not lived in Sarnak for three years," Froi said quietly.

Lirah stared at him, stunned, and De Lancey turned back, hope flaring in his expression. Froi saw a ghost of a smile on Arjuro's face. A nod of satisfaction.

"But what of the babe you did see tossed on the night of the last born?" De Lancey asked. "Who was that if not the daughter of the oracle, or Lirah and Gargarin's son?"

A cry was heard from above, and moments later De Lancey's men appeared at the door.

"They've started the killings again." There was a desperate look of urgency in one of the men's eyes. "It's Gargarin of Abroi, my lord."

Froi shoved through the crowded room and onto the landing.

Across the *gravina,* two men gripped Gargarin, pushing him to his knees. Froi recognized them: Donashe and his companion, who had once stopped Froi on his way from the godshouse to the palace.

Froi knew what they would do next. Hold Gargarin by the legs, but not let go for a moment or two. He could imagine it was torture for those hanging. Blood rushing to their heads, staring down into the abyss. For the women, the indignity of being exposed as their dresses flapped around their faces. The jeering, the laughter, and then at a moment's notice, the street lords would let go.

"We'll pay a ransom. A ransom!" De Lancey shouted across the space, squeezing in beside Froi. "One hundred pieces of gold."

From the palace side of the *gravina,* where they hung off balconettes and battlements, the street lords jeered. "For this bag of broken bones?" Donashe called out.

"Two hundred," another voice called out over Froi's shoulder, trying to get through. The ambassador of Sebastabol.

Lirah was suddenly there beside Froi, her nails biting into his hand. He heard Arjuro's ragged breath beside her.

"We don't make deals," Donashe said. He seemed to have taken leadership of the street lords. "The worthless ones die now. The others get hanged in the main square for the whole Citavita to enjoy."

"He's an architect, you fools," De Lancey shouted.

"Three hundred pieces of gold," the *provincara* of Jidia could be heard saying.

"And where is this gold?" the shorter of the street lords called out.

"From our provinces," De Lancey tried, but Froi heard anguished defeat in the man's voice. "It will take no more than a week to send a messenger and have him return."

Donashe waved him away. "If we can't see the gold now, friend, don't speak another word."

Two of the street lords yanked Gargarin's head back by his hair, and Froi saw a face covered with dried blood and bruises, heard the sobbing around him as those in the godshouse prepared for another day of death. But he saw a ghost of a smile on Gargarin's face. He remembered their conversation in the chamber one night. Gargarin lived on his own terms. He would die the same way. With little fear. Would that be his gift to his brother, Arjuro? To Lirah? To his son? A smile in death?

One of the street lords bent and lifted Gargarin by his feet, holding him head down over the balconette. Everything around Froi sounded strange and so far away. The *provincaro*'s shouting, Arjuro breathing. His pulse pounding.

"A ruby ring!"

Froi hardly recognized the voice as his. All he felt was the sudden weight of the ring in his pocket.

"Belonged to the dead king of Lumatere. The Lumaterans would pay a queen's ransom for it!"

There was a hushed silence around him.

Donashe and the street lords stared at the ring. Despite the space between them, they were close enough to see its worth. Words were nothing to them. How many times had Froi heard that on the streets of Sarnak's capital? "Show us the goods and then we talk."

Froi climbed onto the iron trellis of the godshouse balconette amid gasps and cries from those surrounding him. He leaped onto the protruding granite, his legs trembling. Someone screamed. Froi lost his balance. Found it again. One foot before the other.

He held up the ring and the light from the rising sun caught the stone and Froi thought he had never seen anything so beautiful. It was the ring that had given him a life he could never have imagined. It was all things magnificent about Lumatere.

Donashe stared at the ring. Stared at Froi perched over the *gravina*.

"I'm a thief, friend, and so are you," Froi said. "If you don't recognize the worth in this jewel, then you're nothing but ignorant street scum and there's nothing lordish about you."

Perhaps the silence was only for a moment, but Froi felt as though he was perched on that thin stretch of granite for hours. He wasn't much for praying to the gods, but he prayed all the same.

"Throw it over," Donashe ordered.

Froi knew there was no more bargaining to be had today. He either obeyed the command or watched Gargarin die. He tossed the ring, and the man caught it in his hand, staring at it greedily.

"You get your architect back when I get my three hundred pieces of gold."

They pulled Gargarin up, dropped him to the ground, and kicked him into the chamber. Out on the stone, Froi crouched, straddling it a moment, trying to control the beat of his heart. He slowly turned around and balanced his way back into a standing position. He watched Arjuro shove everyone but De Lancey's men back from the balconette. Froi leaped and gripped hold of its trellis as De Lancey's men reached out to steady him, grabbing him by the hands, clothing, and hair, and dragged him over the wrought iron.

Once on his feet, Froi pushed through the hushed room. Suddenly Lirah was there.

"Who are you?" she asked, her voice hoarse as she gripped his arm.

"I'm Abroi shit and Serker garbage, Lirah," he said, his eyes smarting. "Thank the gods I'm motherless, remember, because any woman would be shamed to call me her son." He pulled free and walked away.

At the end of the hallway, Arjuro sat hunched on the stairs leading down. Froi was forced to climb over him.

"All our young lives, Gargarin and I counted among our blessings the fact that we didn't have to see him in each other's faces, and then you turn up and sometimes I can't bear to look at you, lad."

Froi kept on walking down the steps.

"What name do you go by?" Arjuro asked, his voice ragged.

Gargarin of Abroi was his father. Regardless of who Gargarin smuggled out of the palace, Gargarin was a murderer. That's why Froi was so base and damned. That's why he tried to take Isaboe of Lumatere by force. Because bad blood flowed through his veins. And what Froi despised the most about himself was that he had resented Gargarin and Lirah's indifference. Even without knowing who they were, Froi had wanted something from them. His heart knew first. He longed for Trevanion and for Lord August and even for Perri. They were the men he wanted to have sired him, not Gargarin with his cold stare and awkward ways. Those men made sense with their rules and orders.

"What name do you go by?" Arjuro shouted.

Keep on walking. Don't turn back.

"Olivier!"

"Froi," he shouted back. "My name is Froi. Dafar of Abroi. A nothing name. From a nothing place."

At the bottom of the steps, he took a turn and found himself in the ancient library. Realizing he had taken the wrong exit, Froi turned back to where he had seen a narrow entrance close to the steps. But within moments he was confronted by two lads. Behind him he heard a sound, and another lad came out of the shadows from the library. He knew he was in no danger because the three looked useless. They all wore their hair shoulder-length and one had ridiculous golden curls. Froi would have liked nothing more than to drag them back to Lumatere and throw them in among the Monts.

"You think you can impersonate me and not suffer the consequences?"

Froi sighed. Olivier of Sebastabol. Froi couldn't have looked less like the last born.

"What did I stop you from doing?" Froi asked. "Prancing into the palace and planting the mighty seed of Charyn? Did you honestly believe you would be the one?"

"We had a better purpose, assassin," Golden Curls said. "A different purpose, blast you."

"*Blast you*?" Froi mocked bitterly. "That's the best curse you can come up with?"

A doe-eyed lad stepped forward, his pale, slight fist clenched at Froi's nose.

"If you d-d-did anything to hurt her, I'll k-k-"

"K-k-kill me?" Froi sneered, cruelty in his voice.

Fatigued, he pushed through them. It was too easy to crush these lads. He wanted to go home. There was nothing left for him to do here.

The fist that came out to connect with Froi's jaw was weak in its delivery, and he heard a grunt of pain come from the doe-eyed lad, who rubbed his knuckles.

"We had a plan, a year in the making," Grijio of Paladozza said. "Satch and I had a means to smuggle her out. We knew her life was in danger the moment she came of age with no child."

"We w-w-wanted to save her."

"I would have saved her," Olivier of Sebastabol said. "Perabo of the caves would have saved her. Taken her to Tariq of Lancow, who would have protected her with his life."

Froi's head rang from what he was hearing.

"My father just told me who you are," Grijio said. "Good work done in Charyn, Lumateran," he spat, but there were tears in his eyes. "You go home and tell your people that their assassin did good work in Charyn."

Another fist to his jaw and a boot to his face, and one to his chest. And on his knees, Froi finally understood the truth. That by impersonating Olivier, he had written her death sentence.

He had foiled an attempt by the last borns to set Quintana free.

"Have you got something to tell me, Olivier?"

Froi woke with a start. He had spent the night sleeping by the side of the road that led down to the bridge of the Citavita, joining the throng of people who were desperate to leave. Not even outside the Lumateran gates three years ago, when Finnikin and Isaboe prepared to enter and break the curse, had Froi seen a people so desperate, clutching each other and their possessions. Back then there was at least hope. Here there was desperation.

This is where it begins, he realized. For some it would end in a valley between Lumatere and the province of Alonso. "Why live like a trog at the doorstep of an enemy kingdom?" Lucian had asked on the day Froi left.

Because it was safer than living at home.

He patted the pouch he had hidden in an inside trouser pocket. The night before he had gone back to what he did best. People who were running for their lives were less concerned with their pockets, and the pickings were too easy; he had enough coins in his pouch to prove it. He wondered what would have happened to him if he was still on the streets of the Sarnak capital. Stealing had become too boring. Where would that boredom have led him if Isaboe of Lumatere had not come across him in that square in Sprie?

He shuffled among the crowd and tried to shut out the crying from those who were turned away by another set of cutthroats taking bribes to allow people out of the Citavita. Froi was amazed how swift some men were in plotting a way to take advantage of human despair. He realized that what he despised the most about the street lords and the cutthroats at the gate was that he was looking at himself in another life.

It was on the next morning that he finally reached the bridge. He thought of Trevanion and Perri. Of the tale he had to tell. He thought of Lord August and Lady Abian and the crops and the ideas he had for planting them. He thought of Lucian of the Monts and how he would warn him that what was taking place in the Citavita would bring danger to the valley and Lucian's mountain. He thought of Finnikin and Isaboe and the priest-king and he thought of Tesadora with her Serker eyes. Which made him think of Lirah, and Lirah made him think of Gargarin, and Gargarin made him think of Arjuro. And then all he could think of was her. Princess Indignant. Quintana the ice maiden. Quintana the savage. The abomination. The curse maker. The whore. The last born. The girl who could make rabbits appear on walls.

And before Froi could change his mind, he turned and walked back up to the Citavita, sensing in his deepest core that he would not be returning to Lumatere for some time.

CHAPTER 20

Life in the Citavita each day began with a hanging. One by one, the king's close advisers, physician, banker, and anyone else the street lords found hiding in the king's solar were dragged out into the marketplace, where a crowd would gather around a makeshift hanging gale. The onlookers would jeer and chant and clap with a frenzied glee that had little to do with enjoyment and much to do with malevolence. It had been a week since the events in the palace, and every day Froi held his breath the moment the drawbridge was lowered, wondering who the next victim would be.

Those from the Citavita who weren't part of the vicious crowd or the never-ending stream of people shuffling their way out of the capital stayed hidden in their dwellings, fearful of what it would all mean. "Lad," they'd whisper, their heads suddenly appearing from rooftops. "Lad, what's happening in the marketplace? Will they come for the merchants next?"

During the first days, Froi exchanged his doublet jacket for loose-fitting trousers and a tunic as well as a cap that covered his hair and came close to covering his eyes. But the wool of the tunic itched against his skin, so he stole a flannel undershirt.

Although it was a relief to leave Olivier of Sebastabol behind, something inside of him couldn't help wondering how much he looked like the old Froi. The thief. Street scum.

Most days he saw Lirah and Arjuro in the crowd. Arjuro wore his cape and cowl and reminded Froi of the sketches in the priest-king's books showing the spectre of death who visited a plague-ridden Lumateran village hundreds upon hundreds of years ago and left no one alive. Standing far enough away from Lirah and Arjuro were De Lancey and his men. Froi had discovered through talk around the Citavita that the gold had arrived safely from the provinces and the *provincaro* of Paladozza was waiting for the release of Gargarin before he and his men took their leave.

Apart from his mornings at the hanging gale, Froi spent the rest of his days searching for the man named Perabo, who had once tried to warn Froi about Quintana's fate. In his memory, he saw the scene over and over again. Quintana had stepped toward Perabo, but some sense of duty had made her return to the palace with Froi. Froi wished that Perabo had yanked her out of his arms. He wished that the last borns had been there, all their weak strength combined, holding Froi down so Quintana could escape.

In the second week, the street lords began to hang the king's extended family: cousins, uncles, aunts. Froi watched an entire bloodline disappear from existence as the days passed. As yet, Gargarin had not been released and Quintana had not been hanged, and on a particularly sickening day when the rope half cut off the head of the king's third cousin from Jidia, Froi looked away, and Arjuro caught his eye. The priestling pointed to the road leading down to the bridge before walking away with Lirah.

Froi fought the urge to follow. Despite having to talk himself out of returning to the godshouse each day, he felt a pull toward them. Perhaps he had felt that pull from the first moment he clapped his eyes on these damned people.

Regardless, he trailed Lirah and Arjuro down to a cave house he recognized as the soothsayer's dwelling. The two stopped outside, and Froi knew they were waiting for him.

"Where have you been?" Lirah asked, her voice harsh.

"I don't answer to you or anyone else in this kingdom," he said coldly.

Arjuro entered the cave, and Froi and Lirah followed. It was small, one room only, with stems and saplings hanging from the ceiling and a smothering odor that seemed to be trapped in the cave walls. In the corner was a grubby bedroll, and in the center of the space was a large pot of water in which the soothsayer was stirring a foul-smelling substance among leaves and petals.

He thought of what this wretched woman had done to Quintana year after year, and realized he wanted to hurt her, could easily kill her with his bare hands. But his bond to Trevanion and Perri stopped him. *You kill only those who are a threat to Lumatere, Froi.*

But Lirah of Serker had no such bond. She grabbed the woman by the hair and shoved her head into the pot of water. Froi watched the soothsayer thrash, struggling under Lirah's strong grip. He saw the fury and hatred on Lirah's face.

"Do you like the feel of that?" Lirah said.

"Froi," Arjuro said somewhat calmly. "Stop her, please."

"Why would I want to do that, Arjuro?" Froi said, his heart beating fast at the satisfaction of what he was watching.

"Because I'd like to know a thing or two, and that may not happen if Lirah kills our only source of information."

Froi sighed and stepped forward. He grabbed Lirah's arm

and dragged her back. She struggled against him, and although she had strength, Froi easily overpowered her.

The soothsayer collapsed onto the ground, gasping for air, and Froi couldn't help imagining the child Quintana was, struggling for the same filthy air, year after year.

Arjuro walked toward the woman and stooped, contempt in his expression. When she regained her breathing, the soothsayer struggled to her knees and spat in the priestling's face.

"Oh, the gods' blessed," she mocked viciously. "Aren't those from the godshouse mighty now, Priestling?"

Arjuro wiped the spittle from his face. "These two are here to kill you, and I am here for answers," he said. "So what if we make a deal, old woman? You tell me what I need to know, and I may just spare your life."

"That's not your decision to make," Lirah snapped, struggling to free herself from Froi's hands.

"Answers," Arjuro repeated. "Why did the king order the murder of the male child born to the palace eighteen years ago?"

"No male child was born to the palace," she said.

"On the night of Quintana's birth."

"There was only one babe born that night, and she'll be hanged soon enough."

Froi knew she was lying. The woman hardly made a pretense of it. Her eyes met Froi's, and she inhaled deeply, as if in a rapture.

"And if the king did order the murder of a child," she said, her voice drowsy, "what makes you think he told me?"

Lirah pulled free of Froi's arms and gripped the woman by the throat. "He was frightened to piss without consulting you."

Froi placed an arm around Lirah and pulled her back once more. The soothsayer leaned forward, her face an inch away from Lirah's.

"Spit in my face and I will tear out your tongue," Lirah threatened.

"Oh, there's the Serker savage," the old woman said, closing her eyes and inhaling. It was beginning to sicken Froi. "I smell those of Serker. Waiting. It's what I can do. Smell the dead. And you have the smell of the dead on you, Lirah of Serker. Because you've been there among them."

Froi felt Lirah shudder.

"Do you know what happens each year I lead our abomination to the lake of the half dead? Of course you'd know, Serker whore. You saw them yourself that time you tried to drown the child. The way the dead clambered onto the shores, screeching out their pain. They want to go home, and unless the song is sung to lead them there, they will never have peace and nor will Charyn."

"What is she talking about?" Froi asked.

"Those slaughtered in Serker died voiceless," Arjuro said. "Their names were left unspoken. Only the gods' touched standing on Serker soil can sing them home to their rest."

Froi felt Lirah tremble again. Through all her talk of Serker savages, Froi could sense Lirah grieved for her people.

The old woman inhaled again.

"I used to hear that the wild young priestlings would travel to the marshes to search for the reed of righteousness. They'd crush it, cook it over a small flame, and inhale the scent, and in the euphoria, they would see the gods."

The woman was staring at Arjuro.

"Untrue," the priestling said. Even inside the cave he wore the cowl and gorget, every inch of his body covered except for his face. "It was a game. We were aroused from the vapors. It's why we brought our lovers to the marshes. What was the use of all that arousal if you couldn't share it with the one you loved?"

"But you saw the gods?"

Arjuro refused to speak.

"A priestling once tried to explain it to me," the soothsayer said. "She fainted from merely recalling it."

Still Arjuro didn't respond.

"Even without the pleasures of the flesh, Priestling, was it not beyond anything you had ever experienced?"

After a long moment, Arjuro nodded.

"When I sense the dead, it brings me the same pleasure," she said. "The dead are my reed of righteousness, and when that girl comes into my home, the dead shake this cave with a power beyond reckoning."

Suddenly the soothsayer took Froi's arm, which was still clasped around Lirah. She scraped her tongue against his skin. Froi shuddered and stumbled away.

"Quintana of Charyn seeps from your pores. You'll carry that scent for the rest of your days."

"Come," Arjuro said quietly to Froi and Lirah. "She's of no use to us."

They reached the entrance of the cave, and Froi felt the hot panting breath of the soothsayer at his neck. He felt her hand on his nape, and he spun around and shoved her against the unevenness of the rock.

"Touch me again and I will kill you," he said.

Her breath smelled foul. As if something had died inside her mouth. "Nine months before the births," she said, "the king dreamed that two children would be born to the palace and that the one born first would end his reign. The boy child was born first and was tossed into the *gravina* along with the oracle."

When the soothsayer spoke, there was a whistle to her speech.

"But he made the wrong choice." She looked at Lirah. "The second born, the fruit of his own loins, was an abomination.

Everyone in the palace was frightened of her, running around on all fours like she was some kind of animal. Was she not a savage, Lirah of Serker?"

Lirah looked away.

The soothsayer nodded. "Oh, yes, she was. But everything changed when you decided to dispose of her."

"It was for mercy, you wretch. She begged me."

"And what kind of mercy did she get, Lirah of Serker? Was the little beast who died in your arms the same girl who returned?"

Froi turned, saw the flash of anguish on Lirah's face.

"Her mind came back in pieces," Lirah said.

"Because part of her has no aura," the old woman continued. "Quintana of Charyn returned with the other. A lost spirit collected at the lake of the half dead."

The soothsayer's mouth formed a malevolent smile. "And once they hang that girl, the dead get back their own."

The three of them pushed their way through the crowd camped outside the godshouse entrance. Inside, the number of those taking refuge had tripled, and everywhere he turned, Froi saw sleeping bodies on the stairwell or in any corner they could find. So far the street lords hadn't dared to enter the sacred space, but Froi knew the type well. The godshouse would not be spared.

He followed Lirah and Arjuro beyond the level that housed the Hall of Illumination and onto the rooftop, where Froi was surprised to see a garden. Lirah looked over to where her palace prison tower could be seen. How many times had these two former enemies caught sight of each other tending to their gardens?

No one spoke for a while. The scene with the soothsayer

had unnerved them all, and there were too many unanswered questions.

Arjuro began yanking out his plants, placing those with roots inside a glass bottle, preserving the seeds. Froi recognized a white plant from the priest-king's garden. The yarrow plant was a physician's best friend, according to the priest-king. Zabat had spoken of Arjuro being a physician once, and the herbs and saplings in his garden would have been the tools of Arjuro's trade.

Froi sat beside Lirah. They studied each other, her beautiful eyes confused and full of disbelief, as though wondering how someone as plain as Froi could have come from her loins and Gargarin's seed. He reached over and took her hand, placing a bag of coins in her palm.

"Get out of the Citavita, Lirah," he said quietly. "They've got nothing else to loot, and they'll come here next."

"Where did you get this?" she asked, her voice husky.

"Where do you think? I'm a thief."

She pushed the bag back into his hands. "Then use it to return home, wherever that is. I'm a whore, so I think I can find my own means out."

Arjuro stood, sighing. "When you're both finished trying to frighten each other away with the sordidness of your pasts, can you help me, please?"

Froi and Lirah collected the baskets of bottles and seedlings and followed Arjuro inside.

"Have you heard anything?" Froi asked over their shoulders as he stooped down into the low stairwell.

"Good news or bad news?" Arjuro asked.

"Bad."

"De Lancey has lost contact with the street pigs."

"Good news."

"They've not returned a corpse," Arjuro said flatly.

Arjuro stopped and waited for Lirah to be out of earshot. They watched her disappear into the Hall of Illumination.

"The scribe has accounted for almost everyone," Arjuro said. "They're down to the last few."

"Is there anything . . . ?"

Arjuro shook his head. "None of the *provincari* will risk their lives or their men's lives on her. Even if one or two were willing, they'd be outnumbered. The street pigs have control of the whole Citavita."

"She's their princess," Froi said angrily.

"But not their heir, Froi. At least if she were the curse breaker, she would hold some power, but she's worth nothing. The *provincari* need to secure the kingdom. The only way to do that is to place Tariq of Lascow on the throne."

Froi bristled to hear the words. Too many lives worth nothing.

"You may as well toss yourself into the *gravina* now if you're fool enough to try to save her," Arjuro said.

"I wasn't sent here to save her," he said quietly. "It's not part of my bond."

For the rest of the week, he stood alongside Arjuro and Lirah to watch the hangings. When they were certain that Gargarin and Quintana remained alive for one day more, all three would walk back up to the godshouse, where talk of the street lords entering the sacred space would send those taking refuge into a frenzy. The streets became even more crowded, with most Citavitans now desperate to escape the violence that was rife. Looting had begun. A potter had been killed trying to protect his stall. A stampede at the bridge caused the death of seven others. It was each man or woman out for his or herself.

At the end of the week, it was Aunt Mawfa's turn, and her hanging was hideous beyond imagining. Froi thought of the men he had killed in Lumatere. If he was grateful for anything, it was that most times, he did not see their fear. But here in the Citavita, fear made people beg. Fear was piss running down the legs of those who once stood pompous and proud. Fear was a blood-curdling cry that rang through one's ears for days to come. All he would ever remember about Lady Mawfa's hanging were her little plump legs dangling and how, out of all the deaths, it would have been the one to make Quintana weep.

But he returned day after day, waiting for her to appear. *She is worth nothing,* Arjuro had said. If Froi understood anything, it was that in this world one's worth came from others. He had no worth until he crossed the path of the novice Evanjalin and Finnikin. So he found himself writing his own bond to Quintana of Charyn. Her worth would come from him and Lirah and the idiot last borns. She would not die alone. That would be his bond to her.

And then the day they were dreading came, when there was no one to account for but Quintana and Gargarin. When the street lords dragged them out, Froi had a moment's foolish thought that perhaps he could rescue them, but he was unarmed and there were too many desperate Charynites surrounding him, begging for more blood. He reminded himself, as he had every day since the death of the king, that he had not been sent to this kingdom to rescue a princess. He had been sent to wipe out the royal seed of Charyn, but there had been too many men in this kingdom ready to do that for him.

He was barely able to recognize Quintana, with her blood-stained ugly dress, her filthy face, hair in knots. The crowd cried out for blood. Hers. Froi prayed to whoever was listening that Quintana the ice maiden would be in her head this day. But he knew in an instant it was Princess Indignant. It was the way she wept and fell on her knees, begging, crying out the words,

"I carry the first! I carry the first!" until the street pigs dragged her to her feet by her hair.

Gargarin was trussed, and it had been a savage beating he had received this past week. But Froi knew that Gargarin would be released. De Lancey had paid half the amount of gold only and the street pigs would get the other half when Gargarin was safe. Today, it would be Quintana's day to die.

Without his staff, Gargarin collapsed on the raised floor above them for the umpteenth time. Froi heard Arjuro's broken whisper, "Stay down, my brother. Stay down," and Froi wanted to reach out to him in some sort of comfort. He had realized many times in the past weeks that if anything, Arjuro of Abroi was blood. Without thinking, Froi pushed through the crowd until he was at the platform, his head level with Gargarin, who lay facedown, blood pouring from his nose.

"Are you finished with him?" Froi asked the street lords. The man guarding Gargarin kicked him off the platform viciously and he fell at Froi's feet. In an instant, De Lancey and his guard were there, half carrying Gargarin away.

"Do something," Froi begged the *provincaro*. "Do something for her."

"We've been promised the road out of here, lad," De Lancey whispered. "The best I can do is leave and raise an army to take back the Citavita."

Froi watched two of the street lords drag Quintana to the raised block, and oh, how she fought. To the very last moment she fought, and when the hangman placed the noose around her neck, Froi knew it was Lirah who cried out in a way that tore at him. Froi finally understood what she had tried to do so long ago, in that tub of water. She had tried to take this wretched creature to a better place. To prevent this moment of horror.

And then a bellowing cry rang out. A war cry? Froi swung

around, searching for anything. Any sign. He thought he saw something, but couldn't quite believe it. The last borns? Three of the most useless fighters in existence. He had seen Trevanion teach Vestie of the Flatlands to use a bow, and even she could hit a target, despite the distance. One of them, Grijio of Paladozza perhaps, fell out of a branch overlooking the platform. In the crowd, Olivier of Sebastabol bellowed yet another war cry, while Satch of Desantos tried to jab at the legs of the street lords on the podium.

Arrows went flying in the wrong direction. The idiot, Olivier, was attempting to shoot a mark toward the noose, but he hit the palace wall in the distance instead. From where Froi was trying to get a better look, it seemed as though they were attacking each other. The people of the Citavita began to laugh. Despite the failure of the situation, the street lords reacted, leaping from the podium and shoving their way through the crowd after Satch, who was closest.

And suddenly, in all the absurdity, Froi forgot the orders from his queen. Forgot everything he had been told was right or wrong. Forgot any type of reason. Perri the Savage once told him that moments of opportunity were pure luck; the priest-king claimed that it was the gods sending messages. But both agreed that you took them without question. Whatever it was today, Froi didn't ask, and he took his chance and bolted for the tree that Grijio was attempting to climb, while one of the street lord's gripped his ankle. Froi knocked the street lord's head against the branch, before shoving him away. He scampered up the tree. "Follow," he ordered Grijio. With the last born at his heels, Froi straddled the top branch, grabbing the bow from Grijio's hand. Down in the crowd, he could see Olivier of Paladozza stare up to where he and Grijio sat.

"Bolt," Froi ordered, and Grijio slapped one against his palm, and Froi took aim and fired. "Bolt!" he ordered again.

"Bolt!"

"Bolt!"

"Bolt!"

Froi shot five bolts in quick succession at his targets on the podium. But despite four street lords writhing with pain on the raised platform, the hangman kicked the block from under Quintana's feet and her body began to swing, her hands grabbing at the rope around her neck. Froi cried out, a roar of anguish that came from a place within that he had never acknowledged.

"Olivier!" he bellowed down to the last born in the crowd. "Sword!" Froi leaped from the branch, and flying through the air, he grabbed Quintana's body. As they both swung over the crowd, he reached out to where Olivier held the sword high above his head and Froi grabbed it, stretching the sword in an upward swing to slice at the rope holding Quintana's noose. A moment later, they crashed down into those standing below.

Satch was there before them, pulling both Froi and Quintana to their feet. "Run," he shouted. "R-r-run."

The stuttering last born led, and Froi followed, gripping Quintana's hand, dragging her at times when it seemed she had nothing left inside of her. Grijio caught up as arrows flew past them. The four of them ran through one of the cave houses, climbed up onto a roof, and then crossed the Citavita, leaping from one flat cave to another. Froi had no idea where they were heading, but despite the last borns' inability to fight like warriors, these lads seemed to have purpose. So Froi followed.

Suddenly a hand flew up beneath his feet and Froi was yanked down into a hole through the roof of one of the caves. He crashed down onto the ground of the house alongside Satch. Within seconds, Quintana tumbled in behind them. A moment later, Grijio fell through.

"Quiet," someone whispered, and Froi realized that their breathing was coming out in sobs. He closed his eyes to regain his breath, and when he opened them, he could only see the bottom half of whoever had dragged them into the room. The rest of the man was peering up through the hole in the roof.

"Have y-y-you lost th-th-them?" Satch asked.

The trapdoor was secured in place, and the room was dark. A candle was held toward them and Froi found himself face-to-face with the keeper of the caves.

"Follow," Perabo ordered.

Froi was surprised to see an underground river in the bowels of the city. Perabo led them to one of two small rafts and helped Quintana step onto the first. He then placed a hand on Froi, but it was no hand of assistance. The grip tightened until Froi felt pain. "Did I not tell you to get her out of Charyn?" the man snarled.

"He's n-not Olivier," Satch said.

"He would have known nothing of Tariq's plan to take her out of the Citavita," Grijio added.

"Then who is he?" the keeper asked.

Grijio hesitated in replying. "He's a foreigner. We don't know what his name is."

"Froi," they heard a hoarse voice say behind them.

Froi stumbled toward Quintana, realizing with horror that part of the noose was still around her neck. He removed it, and in the dim light, he could see that her throat was burned from the rope. She was shivering, and he took off his coat and placed it around her.

Perabo gave Froi the oar. "Listen to my instructions. You follow this river until it branches into two. Steer the raft left and travel awhile. When you come to a bend, they will hear you. So wait for two sounds of a rock against rock. Five beats apart. In return, you tap your oar on the roof of the cave. Three taps. Five beats apart. You ask for Tariq of Lascow, heir to the throne of Charyn. You tell them Perabo sent you."

Froi gripped Quintana as the raft swayed from side to side. He looked up at the lads standing beside Perabo. "You'd be safer with us," he said.

"We n-n-need to get back and see if Olivier escaped."

Froi scowled. "You don't have to be nervous, Satch. I'm not going to hurt you!"

He saw a flash of irritation on the last born's face.

"It's a st-st-stutter, idiot. N-n-not fear."

It was a strange path to the hidden compound of Lascow. The roof of the cave was little more than a handspan above their heads, the sides of the raft at times scraping against the wall until Froi was forced to lay the oars aside and push his way down the cave river. There was nothing to be heard, except for the lapping of the water and Quintana's rasping. When they reached a section where the river's current seemed to carry the raft along, Froi stumbled to where Quintana was. He sat down and gathered her in his arms. "Shhh," he whispered. "You're safe. I promise you."

Perabo's instructions were precise. At the bend, Froi heard the sound and waited, and despite the firm grip Quintana had on his arm, he managed to retrieve the oar and tap the cave ceiling three times. A moment later, the pitch-black space was illuminated by a lantern. Froi held Quintana's face to his chest, his eyes blinded by the light.

"We are here for Tariq of Lascow, heir to the throne of Charyn," he said. "Perabo sent us."

The lantern was lowered, revealing the face of a man. He stared from Froi to Quintana and then gave a nod.

CHAPTER 21

Tariq of Lascow was tall for a Charynite. And striking. Froi wasn't expecting tall and striking. For some reason, he wanted Quintana's beloved Tariq to be short and ugly. The heir placed a hand against Quintana's cheek tenderly and then led them down a dank corridor of stone, speckled with a substance that lit their path. They followed him into a large chamber, the floors and walls adorned with beautiful woven carpets of blues and gold and red. There were books and drawings and ochre sticks for writing scattered over the cot that lay on the ground. A mandolin sat in the corner. A small altar was in the center of the room, built upon a piece of rock that extended from the ground. Carved into the rock were symbols Froi had seen in Gargarin's books about the gods. Tariq of the Citavita worshipped Agora, the Charyn goddess of wisdom. A poet, a musician, a peacemaker. Froi wanted to hate him.

Tariq pushed the books and sketches from his cot and took Quintana's hand. "Little cousin, speak. I beg of you," he said as Quintana stared up at Froi. Tariq placed a blanket over her, and she lay down.

"Will you be here when I wake?" she asked Froi, her voice broken.

"Of course," he lied.

Quintana closed her eyes and turned to the wall.

Tariq stood and Froi saw tears in the eyes of the heir. And anger.

"How was it that you didn't get her out in time?" he asked. "We've been waiting for weeks."

"I was careless," Froi said. "For that I'll always be sorry."

Tariq stared but didn't speak. Too much seemed to be going on in his mind, and Froi wondered if the heir of Charyn had to count in his head to control his fury. Or was he just a good man who could walk a path through life without a bond?

"Then forgive yourself now, for we do not need laments of guilt sounding through the air," Tariq finally said.

Froi took one last look at Quintana and fought the urge to reach out a hand to where her throat was red-raw.

"I'll take my leave," he said huskily, walking out of the chamber.

In the light-speckled tunnel, Tariq was on his heels.

"Stay," the heir said. "Eat with us."

It was not an order, but Froi found himself turning back because he realized he had nowhere left to go.

In an adjoining chamber, Tariq introduced Froi to his childhood nurse, a woman named Jurda, who was stunned to hear the story of the escape and rushed to where Quintana lay. Froi watched Quintana as she woke from a half sleep with a hiss and a snarl. He stepped into the room, but Tariq held him back. "Jurda was my nurse in the palace. She is well acquainted with Quintana's . . . ways."

Froi followed Tariq through the nooks and tunnels of the underground village-in-exile of Lascow. They passed women weaving, men working at a kiln. One chamber housed the cattle; another stored the grain. In the kitchen there was chaos and all things familiar. Bread was baking in a large oven, its smoke tunnelling through a hole into the level above. The cook was barking out insults and instructions to a man milking a goat in the corner, while the serving women peeled eggs, giggling among themselves when they saw Froi. Tariq reached over the bad-tempered cook's shoulder and she slapped his hand away, but he took the bread all the same, pecking her quickly on the cheek.

Froi was confused by the language. Although he had picked up a spattering of Charyn, it seemed to sing a different tune.

"What are they saying?" he asked.

"We speak a dialect of the mountains of the north, different from the Turlan mountain folk of the east," Tariq said.

The women continued to speak, looking in their direction. Tariq hid a grin.

"My cousins say that for someone so plain, it's a good thing your build is so pleasing. You have the shoulders of an ox, according to Liona."

"Your cousins are servants?" he asked, his face reddening from the attention.

"This is my family. On my mother's side. Twenty-seven of us in total. We've not dared return home, for we know that if the king found me there, he would not think twice about annihilating all my people on that mountain."

Tariq pointed to a cushion on the ground, and Froi sat. A moment later, a plate of flatbread, gherkins, soft cheese, sliced eggs, and olives was placed before him. Froi waited politely for Tariq to choose first.

"You don't seem the type to follow etiquette," Tariq said.

"I follow a bond that says I grab food after the host," Froi said honestly, staring at the small feast hungrily.

Tariq grinned again. "I have a rule that says whoever is stupid enough not to grab food first deserves to die of starvation."

Froi grinned in response and reached for the cheese.

"Could I ask, sir," Tariq said, after wiping his mouth with the back of his hand, "if you have heard news of Gargarin of Abroi?"

Froi remembered De Lancey's words. That Gargarin had been a mentor to Tariq.

"I'm not a 'sir,'" Froi said, after swallowing the last of the egg. "My name is Froi, and to answer your question, De Lancey of Paladozza paid a ransom and they let Gargarin go. I can't promise his body is in one piece, but he is safe for now."

Tariq sighed with relief. "Is he not the most honorable man you have ever encountered?" he asked.

Froi didn't respond for a moment. "He's a hard man to get to know."

"But once you get to know him, he is hard to forget," Tariq said. "I've never seen so many calf-eyed women in the compound, following him around the year he stayed with us. 'Gargarin, would you like me to rub your twisted bones?'" he mimicked. The cook came to deposit pieces of cooked pig rind on Froi's plate. "'Gargarin,'" Tariq continued, looking up at her, feigning seriousness, "'Would you like me to rub the bone that's not so twisted?'"

Froi laughed. The cook grabbed Tariq's face. "Do you want me to wash this filthy mouth out?" she snapped.

"Even Cousin Jurlista here was not immune to his humble charm." Tariq did a perfect impersonation of Gargarin's awkwardness that not even Arjuro could have matched.

One of the older men sat opposite them. "What news of above?" he asked. "Is it as bad as they are saying?"

"It is very bad," Froi said.

Tariq's expression was pained as he cleared his throat. "Despite my feelings for the king and my father's kin, is it true . . . that they're all dead?"

Froi nodded. "Except Quintana."

"Thank the gods for that. She's my betrothed, you know."

Froi nodded. After a moment, he cleared his throat. "I think it's best that you end the betrothment," he said.

Tariq's eyes narrowed. Froi met the heir's stare.

"And why would you suggest such a thing?"

"Because the people you will rule brayed for her blood," Froi said angrily. "They stood in the marketplace and cheered when a noose was placed around her neck. Why would you subject her to life in the palace after what she has endured? Why would you not want to set her free?"

Tariq looked contrite. "Because we made a vow to each other," he said. "She would break the curse, and I would do everything to bring her to safety."

"Forget the curse," one of Tariq's kinsmen said. "The people of this kingdom will accept you as the rightful heir, but they'll not want to see the face of Charyn's greatest failure alongside you."

"To you, a failure, Gisotte," Tariq said with a gentle reprimand. "To me, a most-beloved betrothed, regardless of our youth at the time we were promised."

"How is it that she escaped the noose?" one of the serving cousins asked from where she was grinding beans.

Froi told the story. He left out the part where the last borns were laughed at, but by the time he was finished, a crowd had gathered around him, stunned.

"You're all heroes," one of the women said, smiling prettily.

Froi felt awkward from all the attention, and Tariq grinned.

"Come," the heir said, jumping to his feet. "Let me show you around."

They left the room amid cries of, "Stay for more."

Tariq laughed as they stooped down into a low damp corridor. "I'll confess to you, we've not seen many outsiders these past three years," he said, "and apart from my correspondence with Grij and Satch, sometimes I feel as though I'm an old man who knows nothing but books and keeping out of harm's way."

"There's not much you need to know about the world," Froi said. "Except how to use a sword and trust very few."

Tariq was silent a moment. "Well, something tells me that both my betrothed and I can trust you."

They reached the end of the tunnel and Froi could see Tariq's eyes blazing with determination. "You must come to the palace with my queen and me. To protect her as you did today. To be her personal guard so I need never worry for her safety."

Froi shook his head, his mouth suddenly dry at the idea of Tariq and Quintana lying side by side, night after night. He looked away, wanting to speak of other things.

"How is it you survive here?" he asked.

"Perabo in the Citavita sends us food. He travels to us once a month. We have a water spring, we have a healer, and we have faith in the gods that Charyn will have a new beginning now that the king is dead."

"Is Perabo's tunnel the only way in?" Froi asked.

Tariq shook his head. "Follow."

Froi followed when his heart told him to leave. But with Tariq, he believed the people of Charyn could find hope. Strangely, he didn't see traces of Finnikin or Lucian in this new king, but a boy he had once met on his travels with Finnikin and Isaboe through Yutlind. Jehr, heir to the throne of Yutlind Sud, had been the first to teach him how to use a bow and arrow. He was a lad of great strength, and Froi saw the same decency of character in Tariq. He needed to believe there was goodness in Charyn after the carnage, so he followed the heir through the underground world of the Citavita and listened to his stories.

They stood at a shaft, and Tariq held out his hand beneath it and Froi did the same.

"Do you feel the air? It's the only other way out of the compound. Gargarin had it built for ventilation and for lowering goods and messages."

"From who? Who do you trust?"

"The people of Lascow have an envoy who lives in the province of Paladozza. He is a passionate advocate of my people and travels to the Citavita each month to bring us news, among other gifts. When Bestiano left the palace with the riders, we received word from our envoy that the *provincaro* of Paladozza pledged an army if we were willing to speak face-to-face."

Froi looked at him, confused.

"Wouldn't the *provincaro* have sent a message through his son Grijio?"

Tariq laughed again. "De Lancey of Paladozza would kill Grij if he knew he was risking his life."

"Well, after today's display, I think the *provincaro* knows everything. Tell me more of Paladozza's promise."

"I agreed to the meeting, and in one week's time, the envoy from the *provincaro* will meet us at the top of this shaft with the promised protection. They will smuggle us out of the Citavita and into the center of Charyn to collect my army. Then we will march back into the Citavita and claim the palace."

Tariq looked around the cave. "And we say good-bye to my underground home."

"A solid home indeed," Froi said, impressed.

"Mostly thanks to Gargarin's plans."

Tariq pointed into another room. "The privy. Gargarin's idea, of course."

"Of course." Froi laughed for the first time in weeks. "He does have his obsessions, doesn't he?"

Froi followed Tariq into a cluster of small caverns.

"The hospital," Tariq said. "Can I introduce you to my cousin?" he asked quietly. "She has had an ailment of the heart for some time now. Nurse says death will take place in the days to come, so we all pray that she will soon be at peace with those who've passed before us."

Her name was Ariel. She would have been a pretty girl. Her cheek dimpled the moment she saw her younger cousin, and she patted her bed for Tariq to sit.

"I have heard the strangest story of a wild rescue in the Citavita," she said, fighting for every breath, looking beyond Tariq to Froi. "I think Cousin Ortense is giddy for our visitor."

She held out a hand and Froi took it.

"And the princess?" she asked.

"She has a strangely strong . . . spirit," Froi said.

"Or two," Tariq added, and he looked at Froi sheepishly. "Did getting used to it take you long?"

Froi shook his head. He realized that nothing about Quintana of Charyn took long to get used to except the idea of leaving her behind.

"Will she visit?" Ariel asked, and Froi heard the tiredness in her voice. "I dreamed of her not so long ago. I told her in my dream that if I had one wish, it would be to die with hope and not with such despair for this kingdom. I told her that I dreamed of entering the other life with a smile to greet them all. 'Good news!' I'd shout. 'Good news for you all.'"

"She'll like that dream," Froi said, a sadness overwhelming him that goodness died when baseness lived.

"We will go collect her, Ariel," Tariq said, on his feet in an instant. "And tonight we will dine, all of us, together here with you, my love."

Tariq seemed to hasten his step out of the room, and Froi watched the heir stop and lean his head against the stone wall. He knew the lad wept for Ariel, and he stood back to give Tariq the time he required to collect himself. Then he followed him through a tunnel to a set of stairs that led them down into another cavern.

Froi felt the cold instantly and realized he was in some sort of crypt. There were two slabs of stone in the middle of the room, one with a body wrapped in white from head to foot.

"It's a Lascow tradition for the dead," Tariq explained. "We lost one of our elders two days past. This is what we will do for Ariel. Wrap her in white linens and call her name out for the gods to receive her. Then we will send her down the underground river and set the raft alight so the gods can see her and lead her spirit toward our people in the Lascow Mountains. Only then can they be sung home to our ancestors."

Froi nodded, touched by the ritual.

"Is that how they do things where you come from?" Tariq asked.

Froi shook his head. "It's important for the Lumaterans to be part of the earth. The earth is the goddess, so by being buried at death, we're returned into her arms."

"Buried?" Tariq shuddered, but then realized what Froi had said. The heir stared, intrigued.

"And what is a Lumateran doing in these parts?" he asked. "I would think you hate us for what was done to your people at the hands of our men."

Froi didn't respond. He cursed himself for the words he had said, but there was something about Tariq that put him at ease.

"When I'm in the palace, Froi, and all is calm in Charyn, my first duty to this land will be to issue an invitation for peace to your queen and her consort," Tariq promised. "The despair of Lumatere is a stain on a Charynite's soul."

"And when that time comes," Froi said, "I will do anything to ensure your safety within my kingdom."

Later, they ate with Quintana and Ariel, and Froi watched the two girls sitting side by side. Quintana had spoken little, her eyes fixed on Froi at every moment. If he stood, she'd stand as well, as though waiting to follow him wherever he went.

Froi watched Ariel take Quintana's hand and Quintana pull away. It made him wince to see how cold she was in their presence, when Ariel wanted comfort in her dying days. But then Quintana bent and whispered into the dying girl's ear, and he saw an expression of pure joy on Ariel's face.

Froi felt Tariq's eyes on him, wary. Suspicious.

"You were staring," Tariq said. "Perhaps at Ariel. She's beautiful, is she not?"

Froi nodded, but Tariq was no fool and he looked toward Quintana.

"She was my first, the princess was," Tariq said. "The breaking of the curse was to begin with us, for we were born in the same year. She's the only girl I've ever lain with. We were frightened beyond anything and had no idea what to do. Do you know who we had to ask?"

"Lirah?" Froi asked.

"No. She was imprisoned, and I was never to meet her." Tariq leaned forward to whisper. "Did you become acquainted with Aunt Mawfa?"

"Yes," Froi said sadly. "Yes, I did."

"I think our Aunt Mawfa was a wildcat in her days," Tariq said. Froi laughed.

"Did she die easily?" Tariq asked quietly.

"Yes," Froi lied, abruptly getting to his feet. Talk of Lady Mawfa and Tariq and Quintana's first time together was making him uneasy.

"I need to go."

Tariq looked dismayed. "Have I offended you in some way?"

Froi looked over to where Quintana was still whispering to Ariel. When he turned back to Tariq, the other lad's expression darkened.

"I can take care of her, you know," Tariq said stiffly. Then his face softened and he grimaced. "We both . . . Quintana and I . . . we both agreed that we would do everything for Charyn. We are fated to be together. *Those born last will make the first.*"

"But Charyn has done little for both of you," Froi said harshly.

"Some of us weren't born for rewards, Froi. We were born for sacrifices."

"I'll not say my good-byes," Froi said, walking away. "It might be best that I leave without ceremony."

"You saved her life," Tariq said to Froi's retreating back. "Charyn may forget that one day, but I won't."

He got as far as the end of the tunnel of speckled light.

"Froi!" he heard her cry. Froi turned to see Tariq gripping her hand and Quintana pulling away.

"Where are you going?" she asked.

He continued his way to the docked raft and began to untie the rope. She reached him.

"Please, Froi. Only you can take care of us," she wept. "Only you."

She held on to him and he tried to push her away gently, tried to get onto the raft, half lifting her back onto the landing.

"Please," she begged. "Please stay and protect us."

"You have an army coming, Quintana. Tariq doesn't need me."

"But we need you, Froi. Not Tariq. We need you."

Froi sighed, pushing her gently away again. "Tariq!" he called out. But she tried to climb on board again, almost toppling into the water, weeping.

"Let us come with you, Froi. Please."

Tariq reached them and tried to remove her from Froi, but Quintana held on fast, sobbing, *"Please, please,"* over and over again.

"Quintana, you'll hurt yourself," Tariq said when she tried to board the raft a third time. "You'll not survive a moment in the capital."

"He'll protect us. He'll make sure nothing happens to us."

She managed to cling to Froi, her arms clasped around him.

"Can we have a moment, Your Majesty?" Froi asked Tariq, his heart hammering hard at what he was about to do. Tariq was hesitant, but then stepped away.

Froi pulled free of Quintana, grabbing both her arms to shake her hard.

"Listen and listen well, Princess," he said through clenched teeth. "I was sent to assassinate you. Do you hear me? By the Lumaterans who despise you. I was sent to snap your neck and put this kingdom and mine out of their misery."

She recoiled, and Froi knew he would take this moment's expression to his death.

Quintana stepped back onto the landing, and her legs buckled. Froi reached to catch her, but Tariq was there, picking her up in his arms.

"Go," Tariq said. "On my word, I promise that I will not let anything happen to her. Go."

CHAPTER 22

The Belegonian ambassador had outstayed his welcome. Finnikin knew it. Everyone in the room, including the ambassador's own scribe and guard, knew it. It had been too long a day, with little compromise. No, the Lumaterans could not send fleece down the river through Belegonia to Yutlind. Belegonia now had a strong market selling their own fleece to wool merchants in Yutlind and Osteria. Did they not have the right during Lumatere's curse to breed their own sheep for such purpose? And no, Lumatere should not expect the Belegonians to buy their ore when the kingdom of Sorel was selling it for half the price. Then there was the subject of Charyn. Belegonian conversation always came back to the subject of Charyn.

"I will repeat this one more time, Your Majesty," the Belegonian ambassador said. "My king is urging you to take up this opportunity. It's what Lumatere has been waiting for."

"Do not presume to tell me what we've been waiting for, sir," Isaboe said sharply.

"The Charynite capital is in anarchy," the Belegonian ambassador said. "The Osterians and Sarnaks have armies in place with our Belegonian soldiers standing by their side, ready to enter at any moment."

"The last I heard, one does not invade merely because another kingdom's capital is in anarchy," Finnikin said from the window overlooking the garden, where he could see Vestie of the Flatlands and Jasmina playing blindman's bluff with Moss, who was guarding them.

He turned back and saw the Belegonians exchange looks. They were going to change tack. He was certain they were going to mention Sorel. They always used that kingdom as a threat in their negotiations. Finnikin tried to catch his wife's eye.

"The Sorellians will take advantage of this," the Belegonian ambassador said.

"You know this for certain, do you?" she asked.

"No, but our spies tell us that Sorel has been in constant discussion with those on Avanosh Island, who have claimed for hundreds of years that the Charyn throne was once theirs. The heir of Avanosh could be what the Charynite people want."

Isaboe looked to Sir Topher. "Why would these people of Avanosh be what the Charynites want?" she asked.

"Because—" the Belegonian ambassador went to answer, but Isaboe held up a hand to stop him. Finnikin was used to the hand. The hand was held up at times when Jasmina tried to argue about what to wear on certain days, and the hand came into play when Finnikin tried to insist that Isaboe had no idea how to win a game of Kings and Queens fairly. His wife's hand was mightier than a sword.

"Because Avanosh is neutral," Sir Topher explained. "During times such as this, a neutral leader will prevent Charyn's *provincari* from going to war with each other if one tries to take the throne."

Isaboe stood and walked to Finnikin, by the window. She leaned against him, so unlike her when they were surrounded by foreigners. He reached out a hand and kneaded her shoulder. As much as he wasn't allowed to say that she looked tired in front of others because *No one walks around saying that men and kings look tired, Finnikin,* he wanted to say the words all the same. *Isaboe, you look tired. Isaboe, you work too hard. Isaboe, you can't solve everyone's problems. Isaboe, you are not responsible for the happiness of every person you meet.*

"Then why not leave the Charynites to be ruled by the Avanosh lot, who will keep their people from going to war?" Finnikin suggested.

The Belegonian ambassador shook his head emphatically.

"If the Avanosh heir ends up in the palace, the kingdom of Sorel will play a role in the running of Charyn," the ambassador said. "We don't want that."

"But you have absolutely no qualms buying Sorellian ore when they are undercutting an ally of yours?" Isaboe asked sharply.

The Belegonian grimaced. "You are misunderstanding the matter, Your Majesty."

"I don't misunderstand matters, sir," she snapped. "I can't afford to misunderstand matters. Each time a queen or king in this land misunderstands a matter, *many* people die. So I would advise you to think carefully of your words."

"Sorel and Charyn have been thorns in our side since the beginning of time," the ambassador said. "Nothing can be worse news than if they unite."

"Not a thorn in your side, Sir Osver," she said, her tone so frigid Finnikin hardly recognized it. "Not a thorn in the side of Belegonia. Perhaps the kingdoms of Osteria and Lumatere and Sarnak, but you share no border with the Charynites. Yet you stand to gain much if they are forced to surrender to these joint armies you have in place."

Finnikin watched his daughter, below, look up from her play, straight to their window. He moved Isaboe aside. If Jasmina saw them now, they would be ending one series of negotiations and entering another. At least they had a chance of winning against the Belegonians, but Jasmina was another matter.

He watched as his father rode into the garden on his stallion. Vestie and Jasmina ran to him with excitement, and Moss lifted them, seating Vestie behind Trevanion and Jasmina in his lap. Trevanion proceeded to canter around the garden while both girls chortled with joy. It made Finnikin smile to see them. Who would ever have thought that Trevanion would be softened by two little girls?

But Finnikin's attention was brought back to the Belegonian ambassador.

"The Charynites murdered your family! The Sorellians imprisoned your captain. The father of your consort. Take this opportunity, Your Highness."

Finnikin could see that Isaboe was speechless with fury at the mention of her family's death.

"Thirteen years ago," he reminded her, "your king and the Charyn king, among others, stepped in and made a decision about who would run this kingdom. Did you see any good coming from that?"

"Regardless of what has taken place in the past, Charyn will be ruled by her own," she said.

"A peasant heir from the mountains of Lascow or a Sorellian puppet from Avanosh?" the ambassador scoffed.

"As opposed to a leader controlled by the strings of Belegonia?" Isaboe asked. "We won't be part of that. Take that back to your king."

When they were finally gone, Isaboe sat back in exhaustion.

"Give me names," she begged Sir Topher, "of men inside

Charyn who are prepared to be king. Fair men. Good men. If there is such a person, then I will be the first to offer them a neighbor's recognition of their right to rule. Better that than a war among every kingdom of this land."

"I'll find out what I can," Sir Topher said, "but from what we know, Tariq of the Lascow Mountains could be our best chance for peace."

Finnikin watched a grimace cross Isaboe's expression. "Did I do the right thing with the Belegonians?" she asked them both. "Or were my emotions ruling me?"

"Nothing wrong with emotions ruling you," Sir Topher said gently. "I think the important thing is to keep our ears open to the events in Charyn. If it's true what they're saying, we need to be cautious. A new king could be a good thing, but Sorel being involved causes me concern."

She looked at Finnikin.

"Would you have made the same decision?" she asked. "That's what I'm asking you, Finnikin."

"What I would have done differently . . ."

She bit her lip, and he knew that look. They were never happier than in the moments when they acknowledged that they would have made the same decision.

". . . is that I would have told the Belegonians what they could do with their plan using different words."

"What words?"

"Shut your ears, Sir Topher," Finnikin said, then spoke the words. He saw a ghost of a smile on her face.

"Ah, my wife likes it when I speak filth," he said, and they all laughed.

Sir Topher excused himself. "We need to prepare for the Fenton lot," he reminded Finnikin.

"The Fenton lot," Finnikin muttered, kissing her a quick good-bye. "I forgot about them."

"I'll walk with you," Isaboe said.

He was quiet as they made their way down to the garden. She spoke to each person they passed. She would ask about a husband's health, comment about the bloom in one's cheek, gently remind another that the hounds needed exercising, marvel at the taste of the grapes served that morning at breakfast. Their people, in turn, would walk away beaming, and sometimes Finnikin wished for the ease Isaboe possessed with the world.

Outside in the garden, they watched Trevanion with Jasmina and Vestie.

"I'm worried about my father," he said. "I think he's beside himself, although he'd rather not admit it. This thing with Beatriss. She's not turned up for the last two meetings with the Flatland Lords and is rarely seen around her village. Lady Abian is out of her mind with worry."

"What's he said?" she asked. "Trevanion?"

"He can't get past Tarah. Each time, she has said Beatriss is resting."

They watched Trevanion hand Jasmina to Moss before dismounting. A moment later, their daughter was hurtling toward them. She'd go to Isaboe first. She always went to her mother first. Lord August had once told Finnikin that there were years when his children were so attached to their mother that he could hardly approach for fear of being cursed by their wails. Finnikin knew those moments well.

With her cheek pressed against Isaboe's shoulder, his daughter stared at him. After a moment, she extended a hand and he pretended to bite at her fingers. Finally she smiled.

Trevanion approached with Vestie clinging to his hand.

"This situation in Charyn makes no sense," his father said quietly.

"Isn't it exactly how we planned?" Isaboe asked.

Trevanion shook his head and looked at the little girls.

Isaboe placed their daughter on the ground. "Can you help Jasmina find a chestnut for Finnikin, Vestie?"

Vestie took Jasmina's hand and went searching.

When the girls were a distance away, Trevanion continued. "They're saying the king's First Adviser, not a nameless assassin, has killed the king."

Finnikin and Isaboe exchanged a look.

"Then where is our nameless assassin?" Finnikin asked, trying to keep the worry out of his voice.

"If he killed the king, he should have been back by now," Isaboe said.

Trevanion nodded, and Finnikin knew his father didn't want to voice their greatest fears.

Isaboe sighed. "You may need to speak to the Charynite up in the mountains again."

"Easier said than done. Lucian sends word that the Monts are making threats against Rafuel of Sebastabol."

"Well, he's going to have to control them," Finnikin said, irritated with the Monts more than Lucian. "He has to be firmer. He can't be one of the lads anymore."

Isaboe turned to Trevanion. "I want you to find out anything you can about what took place in the Charyn capital and keep an eye on the situation with my cousins. If it worsens, send Aldron to take care of it and warn the Monts that if I have to travel up to speak to them, the regret will be theirs."

CHAPTER 23

When Froi arrived back in the capital, the streets were eerily quiet except for the strange autumn winds that had begun to shake the Citavita, whistling a tune that sent a chill through his bones. He found the godshouse ransacked, pages strewn everywhere, straw cots turned upside down, and Arjuro's garden torn up, stomped with the madness of those who no longer believed in anything. He imagined that the street lords had come searching for him and Quintana, and prayed that the others had escaped without harm. He hoped they had at least managed to hide as many of the ancient manuscripts and Arjuro's plants as possible.

He traveled down below, to the bridge of the Citavita, which swayed dangerously from side to side over the *gravina*. Those who had been waiting in line for days were forced to choose between going back to their homes and losing their place, or staying in line, at the mercy of the elements. Froi knew he could easily take the chance and cross now, but something held him back.

A week passed, and the winds continued, managing to tear the sand from the stone of the caves and almost blind those who ventured out to scrounge for food. Even the street lords kept inside, and Froi took his chance each day, wrapping a cloth around his face to search for Lirah and Arjuro.

He didn't dare question what he wanted from Lirah. Was it an acknowledgment that she loved the son she had grieved for so many years? Was it a declaration of love, such as Lady Abian's daily words to her children? If Lady Beatriss could love the child of a man who had violated her, why couldn't Lirah love Froi?

Nevertheless, he scoured the streets and caves for any sign of them, but if there was one thing those of the Citavita knew how to do, it was hide. On a day he was about to give up and chance a crossing on the hazardous bridge, he noticed one of De Lancey of Paladozza's guards duck into a cave house and followed. Once inside, stone steps tunneled down into the ground, and soon enough he heard voices and arguing and tracked the sounds into a hidden inn.

The room was crowded, and Froi recognized more of De Lancey's men and some of those who had taken refuge in the godshouse when the street lords first took control of the palace. At a corner set of benches, he saw De Lancey with his head down, speaking rapidly to the group of men surrounding him. Froi made his way toward the *provincaro* but was intercepted by one of his guards, who clearly recognized him from the attack in the godshouse corridors.

"Leave," the guard said. "We don't need trouble here."

Froi pushed past him, but the man gripped his arm.

"You have a very short memory," Froi warned. "Don't let me remind you of what I can do."

Suddenly De Lancey was between them.

"Come," he said to Froi, holding up a hand to his guard. "I'll take care of this."

"Sir—"

"I said I'll take care of this."

Froi followed De Lancey as he pushed through the crowd and resumed his seat.

"We'll speak later," the *provincaro* told the men at his table, who eyed Froi suspiciously. They walked away, turning at intervals until they left the room.

"What don't they trust more?" Froi asked bitterly. "The fact that they don't know who I am, or the fact that I saved her life and they didn't want it saved?"

De Lancey didn't respond.

"Where's Lirah?" Froi asked, not wasting time.

The *provincaro* shrugged, an effortless movement. "I've not seen her since the day of the hanging."

"And Arjuro?"

"I've not seen him either."

Froi shook his head, giving a humorless laugh. "You've been most helpful, Provincaro," he said as he stood.

"If you ask me where Gargarin is, I can tell you that," the *provincaro* said, his voice silky in its lazy drawl.

Froi stiffened. He wanted to walk away.

"Sit," De Lancey ordered.

"I don't—"

"Now."

Froi sighed and sat, and they eyed each other a moment or two before De Lancey pushed over the carafe of wine.

"I'd prefer food." Froi hoped there wasn't a plea in his voice. Food had been scarce during the week, and he had taken to stealing whatever he could, regardless of who he was taking it from. Those in the Citavita had made it clear that it was each out for his own. De Lancey signaled to one of his men and gave him an instruction before the man walked away.

"We think Lirah and Arjuro are staying at the Crow's Inn, close to the bridge of the Citavita," he told Froi.

"Think?"

"Someone with an abundance of wild hair and clothed in black from head to toe was heard calling one of the street lords a horse arse of gods-like proportions. Could only be him."

Froi closed his eyes a moment, feeling a relief that almost made him faint.

"Are you going to take them with you?" he asked, clearing his voice of its hoarseness.

"No. Should I?" De Lancey asked.

"You'll take Gargarin, but not Arjuro?"

Froi could tell by the narrowing of De Lancey's eyes that he was unimpressed with his tone.

"Well, they're not exactly attached, and Gargarin doesn't owe Arjuro anything," the *provincaro* said coldly.

"But you do."

"Do I?"

Froi bristled. The man was too calm and cool-blooded.

"I would have done the same to Gargarin in that prison cell," Froi said. "If I had seen Gargarin kill the child and the oracle, I would have escaped the exact way Arjuro did."

"So would I," De Lancey said. "I think Gargarin's accepted that, too. But ten years ago, when they released Gargarin from the prison, after they had broken every bone in his body, we searched this kingdom high and low for one of the most brilliant young physicians in Charyn. And Arjuro refused to be found. Gargarin's bones mended twisted."

A plate of pigeon stew was placed before Froi, and he wolfed it down.

"How long since you've eaten, you fool?"

Froi burped and stood. "Not your concern."

De Lancey sighed. “Sometimes I think you and Gri and the lads are a punishment to us all for our wild youth.”

“I’m not one of the lads,” Froi said. “I’m just someone’s bastard, remember?”

There was regret on De Lancey’s face.

“I did not mean for you to find out the way you did.”

Froi shrugged. “You had a dalliance with Arjuro, and you wanted to pick a fight.”

De Lancey gave a bitter laugh. “Dalliance? Is that what he told you?”

“I knew he was lying,” Froi said with a sneer. “As if you would lower yourself. I know your type.”

The *provincaro* was quick. He reached over and gripped Froi by his shirt, bringing him an inch away from his face.

“No,” De Lancey said through clenched teeth. “You don’t. Never presume.”

His guards were at the table in an instant.

“We’ll take him outside, sir.”

The *provincaro* shoved Froi back and waved them away. Froi studied him a moment. He wondered who was telling the truth. Arjuro or De Lancey?

“He lied about the dalliance part,” the *provincaro* said quietly. “We were lovers from when we were sixteen years old until the night of the last born. Nine years. Not quite a dalliance, don’t you agree?” he added bitterly.

“But you betrayed him?”

A flash of regret crossed the other man’s face. “I betrayed many that night. But I believed I was doing the right thing.”

De Lancey poured wine from the carafe. “Do you have trust in your king?”

Froi pushed his mug toward the wine, and De Lancey poured another. “I have a queen, and you have caught me on a mellow day, De Lancey. Because if anyone dared to question my allegiance or trust in my queen and king, I'd take a knife to their throat."

"I trusted my king. I thought Arjuro was mad and in his madness he was risking the life of our beloved oracle. I felt there was no better place to protect her from the Serkers than in the palace. But I was a coward in my plan. It cost an innocent farrier his life, and I realized afterward that the Serkers were not involved."

De Lancey looked up, and Froi followed his gaze to where the three last borns entered the crowded room. Froi watched Grijio speak to one of the guards, who pointed to the *provincaro*.

"Arjuro was your lover, but you had a wife who bore you a son?" Froi accused.

"No," the *provincaro* said. "I've not had a wife. It's far more complicated and tragic than you'd imagine."

"Everything in Charyn seems far more complicated and tragic."

Froi stood, quaffing his wine.

"By the way," Froi said. "It's no business of mine, but I would reconsider asking Tariq to travel into the center of Charyn, regardless of how many men your envoy promises him."

"My envoy?"

Froi saw genuine confusion on the man's face.

"Lad, I have no idea what you're talking about."

The hairs on Froi's arm stood tall as he stared at De Lancey.

"Are you saying you haven't sent an envoy to meet with Tariq of Lascow?"

The last borns arrived to hear Froi's words.

"Who told you that?" De Lancey asked.

"Tariq."

"What?" De Lancey asked.

Froi bolted, shoving through the crowd. He heard the *provincaro* call out Grijio's name and felt someone at his shoulder and knew it was one of the last borns. They clambered up the stairs and out of the cave. Once outside, the wind tore at their skin, but they raced up the Citavita wall, flying over cave tops to reach Perabo's home.

"He'll not let us in," Grijio shouted over the wind. "The rule is that we are never to search him out."

Froi ignored him, fighting the images that came to his mind. *You should never have left her,* he raged to himself.

When they reached the roof of Perabo's cave, Froi grabbed a piece of stone and hammered, shouting out the man's name over and over again, his voice raw. Olivier and Grijio and Satch collapsed beside him, their voices joining in with his, until finally they heard a sound from inside and the trapdoor was lifted, revealing Perabo.

"They've been betrayed," Froi shouted at the man. Perabo ushered them in. Froi leaped down into the room and pushed aside the chest placed over the trapdoor.

"How can you be sure?" Perabo said, crouching down to where Froi pulled at the ring to lift the door.

"They're waiting for De Lancey's envoy."

"And Father sent no envoy!" Grij said.

Perabo grabbed Froi's arm. "Then we do nothing!" he said, anguish in his voice. "That was the plan. That if there's been an ambush, we do nothing."

"You do nothing, Perabo," Froi said, climbing into the narrow cavern below. He landed on his feet and began to run down the tunnel. A moment later, he saw the flicker of light and knew the others had followed. At the place where two rafts were docked, Perabo pointed Grijio toward Froi and handed them a lantern before pushing their raft along. Perabo, Olivier, and Satch took the second raft, and there was a sickening somber silence for too long before someone spoke.

"When?" Grijio whispered as they approached a familiar turn in the underground river. "When did he believe this so-called envoy was to come?"

"He said a week," Froi said. "That was eight days ago."

Froi looked back to the others. "I'll go in first," he said. "I need your sword, Perabo."

"No one goes in unless it's secure."

"Give him your sword, Perabo," Olivier protested. "If they live, the Lumateran has a better chance of getting them out alive."

When they reached the place where they had heard the three beats last time, they waited for the sound. But there was nothing. Perabo tapped the roof of the cave with his oar, but still no one came.

"Gyer," Perabo whispered. *"Gyer."*

Still nothing.

"This is not good," Froi heard Olivier whisper. "This is not good."

Froi stepped out of his raft, and Perabo reached across from the second vessel and handed him the sword with shaking hands.

In the tunnel of speckled light, Froi began to clear his mind of all things that could spell doom and concentrated on what brought hope. He knew that if whoever had infiltrated the compound was smart, they would take Tariq's people hostage and ransom them to the *provincari*. The *provincari* would pay for the heir and his family. Any day now, De Lancey or one of the other *provincari* would get news and deals would be struck and Tariq would be safe. But would Quintana? Would the enemy have recognized her, or would they believe her to be one of the Lascow compound, waiting in exile?

And then he saw the first corpse. Recognized the face of the gatekeeper. What had Perabo called him? Gyer. A small distance away was another corpse, throat slit from ear to ear. Froi's legs almost buckled as he entered Tariq's chamber, where they had first placed Quintana, his heart catching in his throat when he saw that Tariq's nurse lay on the ground, her wounds identical to the men's.

Froi heard a sound and spun around, his sword pressing against the base of Olivier's throat.

"I told you to stay behind," Froi said quietly.

But Olivier could only shake his head.

"We found others," he whispered. "In the kitchen."

It was quick. They had been taken by surprise. The cook still had flour on her hands, the once-giggling cousins were clutching their grinders. Every one of them had the same wound, and Froi's only consolation was that the deaths were quick. He reached over to an egg that had been shelled. Felt it was cold.

"You don't know how smart he is," Grijio said. "He would have found a way to live. He would have."

Doesn't matter how smart you are, Froi wanted to tell them. When you face the end of a sword, it has little to do with smarts.

He walked among the dead. Sometimes he thought he saw her, recognized her dress, and his heart would sink as he crouched to gently turn the body toward him, and then for a moment, all he could feel was relief. Until the next girl and then the next.

Some were still holding hands, as though they had gripped on to each other with fear as the dagger cut the breath out of them. Froi's eyes swelled with a fury of tears. Knew they never had a chance.

He heard a cry of anguish and followed the sound into the tunnel where only a week ago Tariq had stopped to weep for his dying cousin. At the end, where Froi knew there was nothing but steps leading down to the crypt, he saw the others. He couldn't breathe. He could only watch. Olivier crouched down in sorrow. Satch stood with hands to his head, bewildered horror on his face. Grijio was weeping bitterly, his arms clasped around himself, while Perabo's fist pounded at the stone wall until Grijio pulled him away before he could do further damage. When they heard Froi's slow footsteps, they turned, and he saw the faces of men who had lost hope. Not even among the Lumaterans when they had discovered that their heir, Balthazar, was truly dead had he seen such desolation.

Sprawled at the top of the steps was Tariq of Lascow's body. Close by, a girl lay dead. Froi could see by the color of her hair that it was Ariel. He fell to his knees beside Tariq, saw the way one arm lay lifeless against the top step.

"Perhaps they took Quintana," Froi managed to find the words, staring down at the young king who had shown him nothing but kindness. Who had promised nothing but peace.

Perabo shook his head, blood dripping from his fists. "You know better than me, Lumateran. This was a hunting party. No one was to survive. They would have had no idea she was here. They would have killed her not knowing who she was."

"There's another chamber," Olivier said, pointing farther on. "Where the corpses are piled onto each other."

Froi stumbled to his feet. "I need to find her," he said.

There was a trail of blood between the bodies, as though the wretched assassins couldn't allow the two cousins to die side by side. Froi gently dragged Tariq's body closer to Ariel's and turned him on his back.

He heard the swallows of grief around him as he reached out

to close the young king's eyes. He couldn't help noticing that although Tariq was cut from ear to ear, much the same as everyone else, the assassins had also hacked at the inside of his arm, as though with a blunt sword.

Froi had been taught that dead men sometimes spoke louder than those who breathed. He searched the space around them for a sign, and saw it there, close to Ariel's body. A small decorative dagger, sharp enough to slice paper and do little else. Had Tariq tried to fight the assassins with a letter opener? And if so, why cut his arm so crudely? Suddenly Froi's eyes were drawn to the wound on Ariel's throat. Crudely hacked, much the same as Tariq's arm, but unlike the precise wound at the heir's throat.

"What is it, Froi?" Grijio asked.

Froi shook his head, unable to speak. He needed to think. Had Tariq's visit to his cousin's deathbed been interrupted by the assassins and had they tried to escape together? Had Tariq tried to fight them with the only weapon he had, which was then used against him? Yet the wound to his throat was delivered by the sharpest of weapons.

"We need to find her corpse," Perabo said, his voice rough in its sorrow. "And then we get out of here. There's nothing we can do."

"Come, Froi," Grijio said. "We've seen enough."

The last born glanced at the two bodies one more time.

"She was a beauty," Grijio said softly. "I knew her before her illness. She had the brightest eyes I'd ever seen."

Froi had to agree about the beauty. Despite Ariel's ghastly pallor, she looked peaceful, almost a hint of a smile on her face. But then a strange thought struck him.

"Her eyes are closed," he said. "Perabo, stop!" Froi called out to the keeper of the caves, who had already begun to walk away.

"What are you saying?" Grijio asked.

"Every body we've passed has had eyes that are wide open in death. Except for Ariel's."

He reached a shaky hand to touch the girl's face and froze. The others were back alongside him. Froi grabbed Perabo's hand, placing it on Ariel's face.

He watched the man flinch. "She's been dead for at least a day or two. The stiffness has already entered her bones!"

"Why would they slit her throat if she was already dead?" Olivier demanded.

"Fro," Satch said urgently, his voice a gasp.

"It's Froi."

"There!"

They looked back to the step where Satch pointed and where Tariq's hand had first rested when they found him. And they saw the letters F—R—O written in blood. Froi studied Tariq's hand. A finger was stained with blood.

"He cut himself to bleed," Froi said urgently, looking around for something else. Anything. "He hacked himself with the paper dagger so he could write those letters, but he was interrupted, and even after they slit his throat, he dragged himself from here to there," he said, pointing to the trail of blood.

"So he could finish your name?" Olivier asked.

Tariq would have known that nothing would keep Froi away the moment he heard Quintana's life was in danger. The young king was speaking to him beyond death.

"Why hack at Ariel's throat?" Froi asked the others, needing them to think with him.

"He wanted them to believe she was already dead," Perabo said. "That one of their own had already come across her."

"Because then"—Olivier's eyes blazed with excitement—"then they wouldn't go near her body!"

"Because they'd realize she had died much earlier and he

didn't want them to know that," Grijio suggested. "But it doesn't make sense. Why?"

"Sagra!"

Froi flew down the steps, the others following. Tariq hadn't dragged himself to the steps to complete Froi's name. He had done so to point him in the direction of the crypt.

"Quintana!"

"Be as smart as you were kind, Tariq," Grijio prayed.

Froi burst into the crypt where two bodies wrapped in white linen were lying on a slab of stone. He began to tear at the cloth around the face of the smaller of the two.

"Stop!" Olivier said, grabbing Froi's shoulder to pull him away.

"You'll offend the gods!" Grijio shouted.

Froi threw the last born aside, desperate to get back to the gauze-covered body. He tore at the fabric around the mouth, trying to find a beginning or an end. The moment they heard the sound of a gasp beneath, the others were around him tearing at the bindings until the face was free. Froi grabbed Quintana to him, fighting back a sob as her breath returned.

"Tariq?" she whispered hoarsely. "Where are you, Tariq?"

He helped her to the steps, his own heart pounding as hard as hers.

"You're going to keep your eyes shut, Quintana. Do you understand?" he said as they stumbled up the steps. He wanted nothing more than to protect her from the sight that would meet them at the top. He covered her eyes with a hand, but she tried to pull free, struggling against Froi viciously.

"Don't look, Your Highness," Grijio pleaded as they reached the top of the steps.

She shook her head, clawing at Froi's hand. "I want to see. I need to see. *Tariq,*" she shouted.

Froi dragged her away and they struggled over the slippery surface of the bloodied ground around the bodies of the two cousins.

"Perabo will keep us safe until we can travel to where De Lancey of Paladozza is staying," Froi said in an attempt to comfort her. "The *provincaro* and Grijio will be the first to leave the Citavita when the bridge is open, and you'll go with them."

And it was only when Froi almost lost balance that Quintana finally broke free and turned back to where Tariq's body lay with Ariel's.

"Close your eyes, Quintana!" Froi begged.

But she sank onto her knees, taking Tariq's and Ariel's lifeless hands in hers and pressing them to her face. And she wept a pitiful cry from a place in her spirit so hopeless that Froi thought she'd will her own death.

Perabo placed a gentle hand on her arm.

"It's not safe here, Your Highness. We must go."

But she refused to move, and the keeper of the caves picked her up in the crook of his arm and dragged her away. Froi knew that he would remember her screams for days and years to come. Despite their pleas that she close her eyes, she looked into the face of every one of the Lascow dead and spoke their names out loud, until the gods took mercy on them all and broke her voice and she could speak no more.

Grijio, Olivier, and Satch stayed for the first two days, but Grijio was desperate to return to his father.

"He'll tear himself apart with worry," the last born said. "I will speak on Quintana's behalf and pray that he'll give her sanctuary."

They looked over to where she lay on the bed, facing the wall.

"And you?" Olivier asked Froi.

"I'll return home."

"Then at least travel with us part of the way," Grijio said.

Froi shook his head. "My weapons are hidden in a cave near the bottom of the *gravina*. They're all I own."

Grijio nodded and held out a hand. Froi shook it. He turned to Olivier.

"Were you treated well in captivity?"

Olivier was silent a moment. Then he nodded.

"I'm going to join Lascow's army," Olivier said. "I know they are gathering one for Tariq."

"B-b-but you don't know how to fight," Satch said.

"The days of keeping the last borns weak and safe are over," Olivier said fiercely. "I'm going to be the best fighter they've ever seen."

Froi held out his hand to Olivier, and the last born shook it firmly. Then Satch's.

"If Gr-Gr-Grij's father does not t-t-take her to P-P-Paladozza, I'll speak to my people in Desantos."

"If not, keep her safe, Froi," Grijio said solemnly.

He missed them the moment they left, and the days that followed were long. Froi spent his time playing silent card games with Perabo and listening to the wind howl. It was a sound he had not heard before, and at times he felt as though the gods were wailing with fury. Perabo said more than once that it was as though they were heralding the end of time.

Quintana's silence was the most frightening. It had been four weeks since the king's death and she had experienced more during that time than another would in an entire life.

"Where will you take her?" Perabo asked quietly one night.

Froi had no idea how to answer the question.

"I need to find Arjuro of Abroi first. And Lirah of Serker. I think they're both staying at an inn near the bridge. I need to get them all out of the Citavita."

Perabo looked down to where Quintana lay.

"I don't care what you've done to save her," he said bitterly. "I would have had her halfway across this kingdom if not for your deceit."

Days later, when the winds finally died, Froi shook her out of her stupor and helped her up.

Without a word, Perabo went to a basket beneath his cot, pulled out some clothes, and handed them to Froi. Froi helped Quintana dress in the man's garments. He grabbed the knotted mass of her hair and stuffed it inside his cap. He took the coat Perabo held out and placed it around her, fastening it all the way to her bruised throat.

"Head down," Froi ordered gently.

Perabo stood on a stool and pushed the stone away from the ceiling. When he gave the signal and stood aside, Froi lifted himself out, holding a hand down to Quintana. She grasped it. Froi pulled her out of the cave house, and not letting go of her hand, he led her across the roofs of the caves.

When they reached the center of the Citavita, he felt her shudder, saw the hanging gale perched high on its platform. The moment the winds had died, it seemed as though every Citavitan was determined to leave. Froi had never seen so many people in the one place, shoving their way through to the road that led down toward the bridge. He placed an arm around Quintana, holding her close to him, tenderly pressing a kiss to her capped head. They were jostled, elbows shoving against them, their bodies wedged in the crowd. And then Quintana looked up at him, and Froi would remember that look for a long time to come. Betrayal. Hurt. Sadness.

And before he knew it, before he could stop her, Quintana let go of his hand, and suddenly the crowd swallowed her. He went to shout her name but knew that it would alert those around him to discover who was in their midst. He shoved his way through the crowd, trying to catch a glimpse of her, but everyone looked the same in their grays and their browns, and he wished for the awful pink dress so he could find her, protect her. But the crowd surged forward, down the Citavita walls, and Quintana disappeared with it, leaving an emptiness inside Froi that he could barely comprehend.

He went searching for Lirah at the inn by the bridge but found only Arjuro.

Arjuro ushered him into the minuscule chamber. It was almost as if they were charging for broom closets these days.

"Is it true? About Tariq of Lascow?" Arjuro asked, his voice ragged with emotion.

Froi nodded. "Where's Lirah?"

"Next door."

Froi left the room and knocked on the adjacent door, but there was no answer.

"Lirah," he whispered, not wanting anyone to make the link between their guest and Lirah, the king's Serker whore.

"It's Froi," he said. "I need to speak to you."

But there was no answer.

"She's not there."

Froi spun around to see Gargarin leaning on the banister, holding his staff in one hand and a crutch under his other arm. His face was so drawn that it made Froi want to look away.

"What do you mean she's not here?"

"She's left. Gone. Don't ask me where."

Froi was stunned. "Gone?" he asked. "I need to speak to her. Gone where?"

"I said I don't know. According to the innkeeper, she left not even an hour ago. For all I know, she's probably halfway across the bridge by now."

"No," Froi said, pushing past Gargarin. "It's too crowded. She would never have gotten across this last hour."

Froi ran down the stairs and outside, to where the stream of people passed the entrance of the inn. He tried to push through toward the bridge but was shoved back.

"Wait your turn," a man shouted.

Froi was desperate. He looked around and up to the roof. The stone of the inn was too flat to climb, so he pushed his way back inside and took the steps, two at a time. Gargarin was still there, and Froi ignored him, grabbing a stool to stand on and reaching up to where there was a ceiling hatch. He shoved the stone away and climbed onto the roof, where he spent the rest of the day searching the crowd below for any sign of Lirah. He could see the queue all the way up the Citavita wall to the palace, but he was determined not to move until every last one of them passed him by. Arjuro joined him and they sat in silence, and then they heard Gargarin struggling through the hatch to join them. After hearing him suffer for some time, Arjuro stood and walked to the opening and dragged Gargarin up through the hole.

"They're idiots for leaving," Froi said, pointing to the people below, when Gargarin was settled beside them. "Do they think it's any better out there?"

Neither of the brothers spoke. Froi leaped to his feet when he thought he saw a woman with Lirah's rich long hair, but sat down again when he realized he was mistaken.

"They're leaving," Gargarin said, "because they know it will be a bloodbath."

"With the street lords?"

Gargarin shook his head.

"If there is one thing a king and heir is able to do, it is to create agreement across the kingdom that the right person is on the throne, no matter how bad their blood might be. We no longer have that ugly luxury. So mark my words. Bestiano will return. He'll come at a time when the people of the Citavita will be desperate for stability and peace. He'll take up residence in the palace, kill a street lord or two for show. But then the *provincari* will send their armies. The *provincari* will never abide Bestiano or another *provincaro* on the throne. So a battle will be fought here," he said, pointing to the people. "In their blood."

"Nice to see that you are still a regular prophet of doom," Arjuro muttered.

"Nice to see that you didn't heed my instruction to cross the bridge with the Paladozza people!" Gargarin snapped.

"Maybe Lirah did," Froi said. "Travel with De Lancey, I mean."

Gargarin shook his head. "I was there to see the Paladozza compound off."

"And why didn't you go with the mighty De Lancey?" Arjuro asked.

"Because I had unfinished business."

"Of course," Arjuro said. "You decided to stay around so the street lords could finish off their business with you? Because from what I can see, there's still an arm or bone in your body that they didn't break!"

A head appeared through the hole in the roof, and Froi recognized the innkeeper's wife.

"We're shuttin', so come inside, Priestling, and tell your friends to pay for a room or go elsewhere," she said.

"Did the woman in the fourth room leave a message?" Froi asked her. "Say where she was going?"

"She didn't need to say where she was going. Out of the Citavita, that's where she was going."

She disappeared inside.

Gargarin struggled to his feet and looked down at Froi. "Join the line tonight and get out of this kingdom by morning."

"I'm not going anywhere!"

"Until when?" Gargarin snapped. "Until Lirah comes back and leaves you a message? She's gone. She's been a prisoner on this godsforsaken rock since she was thirteen, Olivier. She's not coming back."

"Froi," he shouted. "My name is Froi."

He leaped to his feet, wanting to hurt Gargarin for not even getting that right. "And I'm not pining for Lirah. You are. I just wanted to see her face so I could tell her that I hate her!" Froi grabbed Gargarin by the coarse cloth of his tunic. "I had a life with people who I would die for! You've all ruined everything. I despise you," he spat.

"You're supposed to despise him," Arjuro muttered. "He's your father."

"Shut up!" both Froi and Gargarin shouted.

The innkeeper's wife appeared again. "Out," she hissed. "I want you out."

Scowling darkly, the three of them made their way to the opening. Froi grudgingly shoved Gargarin down, holding him by the back of his undershirt until Gargarin's feet touched the ground inside. Froi followed, and the innkeeper's wife stood before them, a broom in her hand.

"The priestling can stay only because I don't want another curse befalling this house," she continued in her furious tone. "But you two, go. That beautiful woman and her precious boy must be grateful to be halfway across this land rather than putting up with any of you."

The three of them exchanged looks as the innkeeper's wife walked away. "What boy?" Froi asked.

"Out," she ordered over her shoulder.

Arjuro went to follow, a question on his lips, but Froi dragged him back, waiting for the woman to be out of earshot. Suddenly, he understood the truth.

"We dressed Quintana in Perabo's clothes," he said quietly. "So she would be mistaken for a lad." His eyes met Gargarin's. "She came to Lirah, and now they're both somewhere out there."

Gargarin's eyes were cold.

"A good thing. It's best we all go our separate ways. There's nothing left for us here. Nothing left for you."

Froi nodded, bitterness in his heart.

"You've made your thoughts clear, *Father,*" he spat.

Gargarin flinched.

"You have no place here, Dafar of Abroi," he said. "It's time for you to return to your people."

Part Three

Quintana

CHAPTER 24

Six weeks after Froi arrived in the capital to kill the king of Charyn, he crossed the bridge that would mark his journey home to Lumatere. As he turned back to look just once, the Citavita seemed ghostly in the morning mist, half concealing the strange cluster of rocks with their secret worlds beneath. He couldn't help but think what would happen to Perabo and all the cave dwellers who had intrigued Quintana that day they spent together. Or those in the castle who were too unimportant to be counted on the death list. Did the cook and the servants and the farriers survive? Did the street lords take their bloody revenge on the soothsayer, aligned to the king for so long? How long would the soulless cutthroats control the lives of all those innocent people? He had heard news that one of the street lords had run off with the ransom of three hundred pieces of gold and the ruby ring, leaving his companions with not a penny. Froi had learned early in life that there was no honor among thieves, and judging from the thirst for blood of those who had murdered the palace dwellers, he could only imagine the fate of the traitorous thief when his former companions caught up with him.

Before Froi on the bridge were the last of those who had decided to leave the capital, including Gargarin and Arjuro. Arjuro kept a distance between himself and his brother, and Froi easily caught up with the priestling.

"Where will you go?" he asked Arjuro quietly. Gargarin had made it abundantly clear that he was going to join De Lancey in Paladozza and that Arjuro and Froi were not invited.

"Osteria is said to be beautiful at this time of the year."

Froi knew the priestling was lying.

The bridge ended and the crowd traveled north on the road that ran alongside the edge of the *gravina*. Most of the day, the people were silent, and Froi knew their bodies were hunched under the weight of knowing that they were leaving their home and had nowhere to go. He couldn't help turning to look back, time and time again, until the rock of the Citavita was a blur.

They reached the three roads that crossed in Upper Charyn, and most took the path east to Sebastabol or Paladozza. A handful continued on the road north that would lead them to the provinces of Jidia or Desantos. Froi's path was back down the wall of the *gravina* to collect his weapons.

When the last of the Citavitans had disappeared, Froi still waited with Gargarin and Arjuro. Perhaps a part of him was waiting for something more.

But Gargarin's stare was cold. "You deserve all the calamities of this world and the next if you ever return to this cesspit of a kingdom," he said, before leaving in the direction of the crowd and not looking back once.

"Thank you for your time," Froi shouted after him. "It's put to rest some idiotic romantic notions!"

Gargarin didn't stop, nor did he turn around.

"Bastard!" Froi shouted. "Curse the day you were both born," he shouted at Arjuro as well.

"Someone's already beaten you to that one, whelp," the priestling said, taking the road south.

He was going home. Home, he thought for the tenth time that day, traveling down the mountain of rock. Home, where foreign blood had become family to him and where men were strong and virile, not all twisted and broken without a clue of how to defend themselves, or reeking of ale or wine or whatever it was that helped Arjuro endure a day. Home, where no one judged him. Not even the queen, who had every reason in the world to judge him. Lumatere was everything Froi wanted to be, while Charyn was a reminder of everything he despised about himself. That unwanted pathetic street urchin who had begged for food, the surly boy who had sung his song for the rich street pigs of Sarnak and allowed himself to endure so much depravity just to survive. *Weak boy. Stupid, useless boy.* Froi wanted to kill that boy he had been. If not for Lumatere, he would be nothing and have no one.

Except it was only when Froi had come to Charyn that he realized there had been nights in Lumatere when he felt loneliness beyond imagining. Not once had he felt its intensity here in Charyn. *Because you were busy in Charyn. You had too much to do.* But he knew he was fooling himself. And now, under this full moon, on his way back to his beloved home, Froi felt the ache of loneliness return. But he fought back the feeling, making plans for the morning instead. He would retrieve his weapons, and then he'd travel to the province of Jidia and pick up a horse. He'd ride two days, he told himself, not even stopping for rest. The sooner he returned to Lumatere, the better for him. He knew the excitement would return the moment he left the outer region of Alonso. There, Lucian's mountains would appear in the distance and Froi would understand what it meant to be home.

After a moment or two of lying down and staring at the stars, he allowed thoughts of Quintana to enter his head. No matter how hard he tried to fight it, she seemed to be there all the time. Usually she was asking a question of him in her indignant tone. Sometimes he would feel her cold stare of annoyance. Other times the savage would growl low in his ear, a sound from a place so primitive that it thrilled him each time.

He closed his eyes and tried to sleep, but then he heard a sound. Not just of the nocturnal world, but something human. A humming. He had seen the last of those from the Citavita head east and knew it couldn't possibly be any of them. Twigs crackled and he stood, listening before following the sound and then his nose. The strong smell of roasting meat—a gamey smell, hare perhaps—permeated the air.

Up ahead was a small incline off the main path. Froi climbed toward it. He heard a soft song being sung, a prayerlike warble so beautiful in pitch that it made him stop a moment. For, despite all the horror he had endured on the streets of the Sarnak capital, because he knew how to carry a tune, the sound of this song made him want to weep from the pure beauty of it. He climbed farther up and looked over the incline, into a cave where he saw a man hunched over the small fire.

Arjuro.

"I was told that the Osterian border lay south," Froi called out.

Arjuro jerked in surprise, but after a moment, the priestling went back to stoking the fire, not even bothering to turn.

"This is south," Arjuro said, pointing to where he sat. "South of that cave. South of that rock."

"You're a fool not to have gone, Arjuro."

"Then come and join me, Abroi's youngest fool."

Froi couldn't help smiling.

He sat before the fire, and Arjuro held out a morsel. Not hare, but some kind of rodent.

"I heard Gargarin tell you to pack some food," Froi said, trying to keep Gargarin's reprimanding tone out of his voice.

Arjuro feigned a moment's thought, his fingers at his chin for emphasis. "Hmm, what was I doing when he told me that? Ah, yes, I think I was too busy ignoring him."

Perhaps Froi's strangest sadness this day was that the brothers weren't traveling together.

"What are you doing here, Arjuro? You can't stay hidden at the bottom of the *gravina*. There's nothing here."

"Just the way I prefer it," Arjuro said. "This last month of sharing everyone's breathing space and stench has driven me quite mad."

Froi saw the truth on Arjuro's face. He had no place to go. Suddenly he was overwhelmed by fierce emotion for this bitter man. *Blood sings to blood.* Rafuel's words were never so true.

There was silence for a time as they ate, the fire illuminating the remoteness out here in a world that seemed forsaken by all. Froi found himself clearing his throat.

"Well . . . I have connections," he said. "In Lumatere."

"And you're telling me this why?" Arjuro asked.

Froi felt foolish, but he spoke the words anyway. "I can take you home with me. The queen may grant you sanctuary because you're the last of the priestlings. I heard them say it once. That the first people they'd allow into Lumatere were those who were the last of their kind."

Arjuro studied him in the flickering firelight, and Froi had to look away. It was all too intense for him. It wasn't like the moments of disappointment and reprimand or approval from Trevanion and Perri. They kept emotion out of their stares. Arjuro didn't.

"Well, first, I'm not quite the last of my kind," Arjuro said. "There are many hidden priests and priestesses in Charyn, mostly in the mountains outside Sebastabol. Second, you can't take me home as though I'm some kind of puppy, and third, I'd rather live on rodents for the rest of my life than live in Lumatere."

"Well, that's rude," Froi said. "I'll not offer again. And I meant that you're the last of the priestlings, not priests."

"Another irritating fact," Arjuro said. "I'll be forty-three in the spring. Do you know how demoralizing it is to still be called a priestling?"

Froi tried not to smile but couldn't help himself. There was silence again, but he was getting used to it. Back in Lumatere, Froi was the instigator of silence. Here, he was the one who always seemed to end it.

"The song you were singing? What was it?"

Arjuro looked up again, his expression somber.

"It's the song of the dead. If it's sung by the gods' touched, sometimes the soul of one who is lost may be able to return home."

"Home?"

"Wherever they came from. When a Charynite dies, their people call their name out loud for the gods to hear and then the gods allow the souls to enter a sphere within the city or province. So the living and dead live side by side. But if their names are not called out loud, the gods have no idea where they are and the souls are lost."

"That's what the soothsayer said," Froi said. "About the ghosts of Serker."

Arjuro nodded. "Their names were never called out. They never will be, because too many of them died and no one has a record of all the names. Serker was razed to the ground."

"Who were you singing to?"

"I can feel restless spirits in these parts."

Arjuro began to sing the song of the dead again, and his voice was so deep and pure that Froi could imagine the beauty of him as a young priestling, charming the world, loved by the handsome De Lancey, spoiled by the oracle, adored by his brother. In his song, he sang names that sounded strangely familiar, and when Froi heard the name Mawfa, he knew that the priestling had memorized every one of those tossed from the palace balconette or hanged at the gale.

"Can you not sing for Tariq?" Froi asked quietly, after the song was sung.

Arjuro shook his head. "Tariq belongs to Lascow. He doesn't want to be kept in the Citavita. He wants to return to his mountains."

Froi shivered at the thought that if he was to die and they called out his name, he would have no idea where his spirit would belong.

"What is your plan, Arjuro?" he asked. "The truth this time."

Arjuro shrugged. "First I'll find out what that fool brother of mine is up to, and then I'll probably head to the Sebastabol mountains."

Froi was confused, but that was nothing new when it came to Arjuro.

"What's Gargarin got to do with anything now?" he asked, trying to keep the curiosity out of his voice.

"Do you honestly believe he's gone to Paladozza?"

Froi nodded, surprised by the words.

"Despite our years apart, I can pick my brother's lies in an instant."

"Then where is he?" Froi asked.

"Is that excitement I hear in your voice?"

"No," Froi snapped, but his heart was beating hard. "Go on."

"Very rude to speak with your mouth full."

"Hmm, pity my family wasn't around to sit me down and teach me how to behave properly."

Something flashed in Arjuro's eyes. He reached into his pack and retrieved a bottle, holding it up in the light from the fire.

"Mead, not wine, but it will have to do."

Arjuro took a swig and handed the bottle to Froi.

"Where is he?" Froi asked quietly, despising himself for wanting to know.

"He could still be struggling down this *gravina*," Arjuro said. "I traveled after you and didn't come across him. He probably stayed a while in Upper Charyn, deliberating. He likes to deliberate, my brother does. When we were boys, he'd spend hours and days deliberating about whether it was safe to escape from my father."

A rare flash of pain crossed Arjuro's face at the memory.

"And in the palace prison, I can assure you he deliberated for eight years."

Arjuro's eyes met Froi's. "As we speak, he'll be deliberating about whether he should have explained that he ordered his son home to Lumatere because he wanted him safe, or whether his son will despise him for the rest of his days if the words remained unspoken."

His son. Froi had never been anyone's son, although at times he had sensed a father in Perri. Even Lord August, after a good day's work, would gather his sons and Froi together in thanks. Something inside Froi's gut twisted at Arjuro's words. *Oh, you fool, Froi. You've always wanted to be someone's son.*

Arjuro smiled sadly. "He's probably wondering about whether it's better to trust his instincts."

"What do you think his instincts are telling him?"

Arjuro shrugged. "Does it matter? I'm going to follow his example, Dafar."

Froi shuddered at the sound of that name.

"I'm going to tell you to go home to Lumatere and not look back," Arjuro said gently.

Froi held a hand out for the bottle, took another swig. "I've only come this way for my weapons."

"Good."

Froi nodded, handing the bottle back to the priestling. "But do you want to hear what *my* instincts are telling me right now?" He didn't wait for Arjuro's response. "My instincts tell me that Lirah took Quintana to the only place that has ever been safe to her and that Gargarin is searching for them. He needs absolution. That's what I've discovered about him these past few weeks. You see, Gargarin returned to the Citavita to tell you and Lirah the truth and then to kill the king. He failed at all three."

Froi's instincts were good. He could tell. Arjuro stopped mid-swig.

"He's heading toward the cave you both claim as yours," Froi continued, almost cheerfully. He liked being right. "The one where you hid the oracle and where I first saw Gargarin's scowling face. Where he took Lirah and you took De Lancey once upon a time when life was joyful."

Arjuro gave nothing away.

Froi continued. "Lirah mentioned the cave. You mentioned it. In between getting his bones broken and being imprisoned, Gargarin mopes in the cave. De Lancey fantasizes about the cave." Froi shook his head mockingly. "If those frescoes could talk, they would blush from what they've seen the brothers of Abroi get up to in that cave."

Arjuro was silent, but after a moment, Froi saw his mouth twitch.

"Still shocks me that you're not as stupid as you look, runt."

* * *

Rain fell throughout the night, making their journey down the *gravina* even more difficult than when Froi had climbed it weeks before with Gargarin. Arjuro cursed and grumbled for most of the time, and if Froi didn't know every Charynite curse word when he set out that day, his companion had introduced him to most by late afternoon.

When rain came pelting down again, they crawled into the closest cave, its ceiling too low to stand. Arjuro sat for most of the night at the entrance of the tiny space, brooding.

"My brother's an idiot," he said, refusing to lie down. "He's probably dead at the bottom of the *gravina,* stacked on top of the rest of those bodies they tossed down."

Later, Froi was awakened by the sounds of voices, but then he heard nothing and thought he had imagined it.

"What are the chances of someone other than Gargarin being down here?" he asked Arjuro in the dark, knowing the priestling was awake.

"Apart from Lirah and the girl, probably none. This isn't exactly the fastest way to the rest of the kingdom. People only come down here to catch trout and I don't think anyone in Charyn feels like fishing at the moment."

The world was silent again and it was at such times that Froi missed Quintana most. Missed the solace he felt as they lay beside one another. He fell asleep thinking of their last night together in the palace, when her legs had wrapped around him and he had heard the cry in her voice as she buckled against him. *"Again,"* she had whispered. *"Again."*

He woke to a sound and realized he had groaned aloud.

"Think of an ice-water bath," Arjuro mocked from where he sat. "It always kills any desire in me."

* * *

Early the next morning, they heard the sound of shuffling along the path outside the cave.

Arjuro made a strange birdlike sound, and Froi could have sworn that there was excitement on the priestling's face.

"You don't speak to him for eighteen years, and you still share a whistle?" Froi whispered.

"Nothing wrong with a whistle."

Froi chuckled. "You would like Finnikin of Lumatere. He has a passion for whistles. One for his wife. One for his hound. One for his daughter. One for his father. And then there's the one for when he's merely enjoying the day."

A moment later, they heard the birdsong returned.

Froi crawled out of the cave. Gargarin was sitting low behind a rock ahead of them, as though trying to avoid being seen by someone farther down. Gargarin turned, held a finger to his lips, and beckoned Froi over, not even questioning what he was doing there. Gargarin pointed down into the gully. Froi saw the cave where he had hidden his weapons, marked by the image of the fan bird. But farther down, where the stream passed Gargarin's cave, he saw horses.

Froi pointed up and quietly climbed to a higher rock. From there, he saw the palace riders instantly. At least ten of them had set up camp downstream from Gargarin's cave.

"Not good," he said when he climbed down. "They're here for something, and I don't think it's us."

"Have you seen Lirah and the girl?" Arjuro asked, joining them.

Gargarin shook his head. "But I saw two men watch our cave for some time."

Gargarin said the "our" unconsciously. "Then your man arrived, Froi."

"My man?" Froi asked, confused.

"That whining idiot Zabat."

"With palace riders? Bestiano's? You're wrong."

"Not wrong at all," Gargarin retorted, as though he were never wrong. "First Dorcas entered with two riders. Then another rider arrived with Zabat. Zabat entered and I've not seen the three inside since."

"Zabat," Froi whispered again, trying to understand what Rafuel's messenger was up to. "With Bestiano's men?"

He thought a moment. He needed to get his short sword and daggers, and then he would work out a way to speak to Zabat. "Follow me."

Ensuring that the path was safe, they moved quickly down toward the rock marked with the fan bird. Froi lay on his stomach and squeezed his way to the rim of the cave. He felt around in the darkness, but there was nothing there.

"My weapons," he called out to them softly. "Someone's taken them!"

He searched again, his hands patting every nook and cranny. Frustrated, he began to worm his way out.

"Well, at least you have the sword the keeper of the caves gave you," Arjuro said.

When he was out of the cave, Froi looked up at Arjuro with annoyance.

"This?" Froi snapped, clutching at the scabbard. "This is just a . . . a stick with a blade. Not a sword. Perri had my short sword and daggers made for me. With *Froi* engraved on them all."

"Well it's a good thing they're lost because *Froi*'s not exactly a name," Gargarin said. "It's just a sound those imbeciles came up with."

"Yes, you'd think the Sarnaks would be able to say a word with more than one beat by now," Arjuro mused.

"This coming from the idiot who named me *Nothing*," Froi snapped, jumping to his feet. "My weapons are missing," he hissed.

"We heard you the first time," Gargarin said. "And that stick with a blade is going to have to do for the time being, because I doubt very much that Zabat and Bestiano's men are meeting in our cave for an Arjuro–De Lancey inspired dalliance."

"You can't be sure Lirah and the girl are in there," Arjuro said.

Gargarin didn't respond, but his brow was creased as if trying to work out a riddle. After a moment, Arjuro asked, "What?"

"Why would Bestiano kill the king now of all times? What does he want from the princess?"

"What he's always wanted from her," Froi said bitterly. "He believes she's the vessel. She produces the heir and he can walk straight back into the palace with power."

"Then why didn't he take her with him when he left the palace? If he planned to kill the king, why didn't he plan to take the one he believed to be the vessel when she was right there in front of him?"

Froi shrugged, and Arjuro waited for Gargarin's explanation.

"I think he was taken by surprise," Gargarin said. "I think someone else killed the king and Quintana was a witness to it all. Locked in that strange mad head is the truth."

"But how did Bestiano know she would be here?" Froi asked.

"The same way he knew where to find Tariq. He has spies," Gargarin said, a pained expression crossing his face, and Froi knew he was thinking of the slain heir. Perhaps Tariq was the son Gargarin always wanted.

"Let's presume that his men are secretly watching the flow of people coming over that bridge and there she is with Lirah. Not recognizable to the rest of Charyn, but certainly to the king's riders, who saw her every day. So they follow her down here."

Froi went back into the rock to search for his weapons a third time. If he was to release Quintana and Lirah, he would need them. Gargarin grabbed him by the scruff of his neck.

"The weapons aren't there!" Gargarin snapped. "Do you think they'll appear like magic?"

"Then I'll have to go in and speak to the riders unarmed. They won't kill me—"

"Of course they will."

"They won't," Froi argued. "I'm Lumateran. The last thing they want is for the Lumaterans to invade."

Arjuro made a scoffing sound. "You think Lumatere will invade because of you? Are you that important?"

Froi looked away. "Isaboe would invade if you kidnapped a servant, let alone a friend."

"Isaboe? We're on first-name terms with the queen of Lumatere, are we?" Gargarin asked.

Froi found himself bristling. "What? Do you think I'm some cutthroat for hire who they found hanging around the palace walls with the words 'I want to kill a Charynite king' tattooed on my arse?"

"No, but I didn't expect you to live in the palace guardhouse."

"I don't. I live in the Flatlands with a family that has given me a home these past three years. Lord Augie is a—"

"August of the Flatlands?" Gargarin stared with disbelief. "The ambassador to Belegonia?"

"So he knows the queen and he lives with nobility," Arjuro said, bored. "Should we be impressed?"

"And I'm presuming you were taught to speak Charyn by the holy man?" Gargarin continued the interrogation.

Arjuro stared. Suddenly he seemed to care. "The priest-king? As in the blessed Barakah of Lumatere?"

"He doesn't enjoy titles these days," Froi said quietly. Suddenly the brothers seemed strange and slightly defensive. Gargarin closed his eyes for a moment, and Froi couldn't tell what he was thinking.

"Go. Home," Gargarin said tiredly. "Just go. You don't belong here. You belong there. You can play with nobility in the Flatlands and continue your lessons with the holy man. But don't stay here and waste your life."

"I want my weapons back," Froi lied, "and I know Zabat is the one who took them. I'm going to ask for them politely."

"How can you possibly think that's a sound idea?" Gargarin asked with frustration.

"I'm a foreigner, Gargarin. Zabat and Dorcas know that. The last thing they or Bestiano want is to instigate a war against Lumatere."

"If Zabat knows so much about what you're doing in Charyn, he can have you arrested for conspiracy to kill the king, which will acquit Bestiano and allow them all to return to the capital," Arjuro said.

"Arrested by who?" Froi argued. "No one's in charge except for those savages in the Citavita. If Zabat is working for Bestiano, they won't have the power to arrest anyone just yet. They're fugitives themselves."

"Then it's better that I go," Gargarin said.

Arjuro was looking from one to the other. "You're both idiots," he said angrily. "I suggest the three of us get out of this death pit before it's swarming with Bestiano's riders."

"I said I'm going." Froi pushed past Gargarin. Gargarin grabbed him by his tunic.

"Do you honestly think you can release the women and escape that cave with five of them surrounding you and no weapon? Because I can assure you that the guard standing outside will not allow you to enter with that sword, regardless of how worthless you think it is."

"If they know I'm Lumateran, they will not kill me," Froi hissed, wondering if Gargarin was hard of hearing or plain stupid. "They will ransom me instead. Your life as a Charynite, on the other hand, is worth much less and you know it."

"I say we walk away," Arjuro repeated. "You, you, and me," he said, pointing to all three of them. "She's not worth your lives. Neither of them is. The whole of Charyn will agree with me."

"Do you know what my captain and his second-in-charge have told me over and over again?" Froi asked.

"Not interested," Arjuro said.

"That if there is no means to an end, then buy time," Froi continued. "Each moment you buy provides you with more of an opportunity. Someone makes a mistake. Some distraction occurs. The scenario changes."

"Yes, from two corpses to three," Gargarin said.

"Well, I could always go," Arjuro said. "They're not going to kill the last priestling."

Gargarin stared at his brother as though noticing him for the first time. "Why aren't you on the road to Osteria?"

"Because I'd like to die of natural causes and not of boredom, brother," Arjuro responded.

Froi won the argument and made his way toward the stream to Gargarin's cave. When he was within shouting distance, he stepped out of the clearing, both arms extended wide. The two palace riders stood to attention, and Froi watched one disappear to alert those inside.

A moment later, Froi found himself lying flat on the hard earth while his whole person was checked for weapons.

"Tell Zabat I want to speak to him. Tell him it's Froi of Lumatere. He'll know me better as Olivier of Sebastabol."

He was dragged to his feet and pushed toward the cave. At the entrance, he was checked again and then dragged inside.

He noticed the walls first. Painted with grand images of the gods, strong and mighty.

On a filthy cot in the corner sat Quintana and Lirah. When Lirah saw him, she closed her eyes with what seemed bitter despair. Quintana's eyes flashed with what he could only understand as some kind of victory.

Dorcas's expression revealed nothing except slight irritation, which was nothing new when he was looking at Froi.

"Tell your guard to stay," Zabat ordered Dorcas.

"Zabat?" Froi asked, pretending hurt. "Do you not trust me?"

Dorcas ignored them both and looked back toward the guard. "Did you disarm him?"

"He wasn't armed, sir."

Zabat's expression was disbelieving. "Search him again. Be careful. He'll go for your weapon."

Froi held out his arms impassively as he was thoroughly searched for a second time, his eyes never leaving those of Rafuel's traitorous messenger.

"I'm praying for your sake that you haven't betrayed your brothers in the valley, Zabat," he said.

"And why is that?"

"Because I'll have to kill you. It's part of my bond."

Zabat had the good sense to look nervous.

"A smart man chooses the side with more might, but if it's any consolation, we all work for the good of Charyn," he said.

The fool looked to Dorcas and the two guards, pleased with his words. They ignored him.

"Leave," Dorcas ordered Froi. "Take Lirah of Serker with

you. We have no quarrel with Lumatere, if it is true that's where you're from. Tell your people to keep out of our affairs."

"Why can't I take her with me, Dorcas?" Froi said, pointing to Quintana. "She's worthless."

"My orders are to return the princess to Bestiano. It is imperative that she explains the truth of the curse after all these years of deceit, so the true last-born girls of Charyn can do what they were born to do. It is the role of the riders to keep Charyn secure."

Dorcas spoke as if he were reciting the original order he had been given.

"Was it your sword that killed Tariq of Lascow?" Froi asked. "Did you follow the order to kill him? Kill all those innocent people in his compound?"

"If I was there, I would have followed orders," Dorcas said. "But I was sent here. Regardless, I am comforted by the idea that Bestiano brought to justice those who were responsible for planning the murder of our king. The kills were said to be quick and clean."

"You weren't there because you're nothing to them, Dorcas," Froi said forcefully. "You've been assigned to run after a useless princess. You weren't there because Bestiano and his riders don't want you to know the truth. That according to the *provincari,* Bestiano killed the king."

"The *provincari* have their own reasons to lie," Dorcas snapped, and for once Froi saw his uncertainty.

"The riders murdered the rightful heir, Dorcas," he continued. "The only man who could bring justice to Charyn. And you would have done the same because you're a fool who doesn't know how to do anything but follow orders."

"Bonds? Orders? What's the difference?" Zabat interrupted. "Your orders are the same, Lumateran."

"In any case," Dorcas snapped. "Bestiano's fight is not with foreigners. It is with the men who planned the murder. So I ask you again to leave and take Lirah of Serker with you. We're not the street lords. We have no intention of slaughtering without reason."

"How will the seed be planted?" Quintana asked coldly from the cot.

Everyone turned to stare.

"So the true last-born girls of Charyn can do what they were born to do?" she repeated his words. "Who will fight to be the sire? Will it be Bestiano? Will the riders gather up the girls for him, Dorcas? Will you be reduced to that? Will you kill the fathers who fight to keep their daughters safe?"

Dorcas looked away, uncomfortable.

"Are you envious, Reginita?" Zabat spat out the words. "Isn't that what you call yourself? Are you envious because your father did not fight for your safety?"

She shook her head. "Just dismayed that the lie we told these years past was futile."

Zabat's smile was of unpleasant satisfaction.

"So here is the truth. Was I not always right when no one else would believe me? The *reginita,* she claimed to be. The little queen." He looked at Froi. "How many years did we waste listening to her tell the people that she was the only one among the last borns who could break the curse?"

Froi looked at Quintana. He didn't know what to believe.

"Nothing in the curse said that I would give birth to the firstborn," she said, her voice cool. "Just that it would be the *last* who would do so. But I made sure my father gave a royal decree that only the *reginita* and a last-born male would break the curse. Myself and Tariq, my betrothed, the rightful heir. Anyone else who dared try would be defying the gods. My father was forced to believe me. The king had offended the gods in two kingdoms by then, and no one feared them more than he did."

"Why would you tell such a lie?" Dorcas asked.

"Why do you think, Dorcas?" she said sadly. "Because I grew up in the palace and had come to understand the baseness of a man's heart. They branded the last-born girls on our thirteenth day of weeping. Tariq and I knew what that meant. My mother, Lirah, was sold in her thirteenth year. Do you honestly think the branding was for any other reason but to destroy the bodies and spirits of young girls destined to produce the first?"

Zabat's expression was ugly.

"You made up a story to win your father's attention. Because he despised his abomination," Zabat said.

Lirah stood and glared at Zabat, who took a step back. She indicated Froi with a toss of her head. "He will kill you, fool. Mark my words. I saw him maim four of De Lancey's men in the godshouse in the blink of an eye."

The second rider was nervous, staring from the women to Froi. Dorcas looked at Froi uneasily, a film of perspiration on his brow.

"Search him again," he said.

"Let him go." Quintana sighed, dismissing Froi with a wave of her hand. "He's no threat to you or Bestiano. He was sent to end my life, not yours or my father's. That is the truth. He admitted it to me himself."

She stood, and the riders stepped toward her. Fear was in the room. Even in Quintana's eyes. Froi saw it there, combined with fury, and it was directed his way.

"But I want to speak to him first," she said. "To say that although you've betrayed me, Lumateran, I want you to know that those gifts you left me in that little treasure chest with the fan bird etched in its stone are ones that I will always carry in my heart."

Froi fought hard to conceal every thought that ran through

his mind. Every emotion. The thrill and satisfaction that came with the knowledge of what she was trying to tell him.

He looked at Dorcas. He needed to buy time.

"This is not my fight," he said after a pause.

Dorcas nodded, pleased. Relieved.

"Good to hear. Don't ever let me see you in these parts again, Lumateran."

Froi turned to walk away and then stopped.

"Can I . . . ?" Froi looked down, pretending awkwardness. "Can I bid her farewell?" He leaned close to Dorcas. "I did share her bed," he whispered, "and I did lose a bit of my heart to her. Or to one of those who live inside of her, anyway."

Dorcas stared from Froi to Quintana and nodded. "Make it quick."

Froi joined her where she stood beside the cot. He took her hands and felt where she had concealed the daggers he'd buried in the cave. He was impressed with the way the scabbards were perfectly placed.

"Did I ever call you useless?" he asked softly.

"Three times," she said, her tone sour.

"Three times, you say?"

"Yes, we tend to count the amount of times we're called useless by one person. Bestiano made mention of it thirty-seven times."

"My, my, you do have a good memory for details."

She nodded. "And I do believe you referred to me as worthless moments ago."

He rubbed her palm intimately and then placed his hands on both her shoulders, feeling the scabbard across her shoulder.

"Their measurement of worth, Princess. Not mine."

He leaned forward to press a kiss to her mouth. Regardless of the circumstances, she still moved her face slightly so his lips touched her cheek instead.

"You've lost that privilege," she said coolly.

"Pity."

Froi yanked the two daggers from her sleeve and hurled one at Zabat, catching him between the eyes, the other at the second rider's thigh as he kicked the man's sword from his hand and spun Quintana around to retrieve the short sword at her shoulders. He pushed her behind him, smashing Dorcas across the temple with the handle of the sword just as Lirah scrambled for a dagger. The third guard entered the cave, weapon raised, hesitating one moment too long as he stared at the body of the dead man and at Dorcas struggling to his feet. In an instant, Lirah had a sword pointed at the back of the man's neck and Froi put a foot on Dorcas's chest.

"I'm going to regret not killing you," Froi said, looking down at him, "but it's not in my bond to take your life."

"And it was in your bond to take his?" Dorcas gasped, pointing to Zabat's body.

"Zabat has brought war to the edge of my kingdom. My bond is to destroy anyone who is a threat to Lumatere."

Satisfied that the three riders were tied up securely, Froi stepped outside to where Quintana and Lirah stood. He whistled softly and listened for the whistle in return. They heard it and he followed the sound along the stream and up a path. Arjuro's head suddenly appeared behind a twisted knot of shrubbery that concealed a low narrow entrance to a cave. Froi gently pushed Lirah before him, then turned, only to see Quintana running.

From him.

Enraged, he tore after her, catching her on an incline, causing them both to tumble to the ground. He heard voices and held a hand over her mouth as they tried to control their ragged breaths. He knew by the sound of the footsteps that there were two others circling.

"Go check on Dorcas," he heard the rider closest to them say.

A caterpillar found its way across the rider's boot, and Froi watched Quintana's finger reach out and softly brush its texture as if she'd never seen anything so strange before. Froi knew the moment she felt its sting, her eyes wide with shock. Forgetting his anger for a moment, he gripped her finger in his fist to soften the pain. When the riders walked away and they heard the last of their footsteps, Froi grabbed her hand and dragged her into the cave where the others hid.

When he was satisfied that the cave entrance was concealed by the shrubs and they were safe for the time being, he turned to where she sat huddled against the wall, her arms clasped around her knees, eyes fixed on Froi's as if he were some fiend rather than the one who had saved her life.

"You could have got us killed," he whispered with anger. "All of us. You never run from me again. Do you hear?"

Lirah crouched beside Quintana. "Try to sleep," she murmured, but Quintana shook her head and whispered in Lirah's ear, her eyes never leaving Froi's the whole time.

"No," Lirah said patiently, "I think you're both safe for now."

Through the night, Froi lay awake, listening for every snap of a twig or voice outside. He could see the outline of Quintana sitting up, felt her eyes boring into him. In the morning, when a little light entered the cave, he found her seated exactly as she had been the night before, her eyes fixed on where he was.

"I'm going to catch us something to eat," he muttered, and before the others could argue against it, he was gone.

CHAPTER 25

That day, the base of the *gravina* swarmed with more riders. Although it seemed dangerous to catch a hare and risk the Charynites following the scent of it roasting, Froi caught two all the same, figuring that they'd just have to eat them raw if they were hungry enough.

"They know we're here," he whispered to the others when he returned. "Their numbers seem to have doubled overnight."

"Perhaps they're just passing through on their way to Jidia," Arjuro said.

"They're here to stay," Froi said flatly. "And so are we until they're gone."

"I've found something." Gargarin's voice came from the back of the cave, and Froi followed, squeezing into the nook beside him.

Gargarin took Froi's hand in the dark and pressed it around a small opening in the stone.

"It could end the moment you crawl in, but it's worth a try."

"These caves are supposed to lead to the steps of Jidia, sir." Quintana's voice was suddenly there at his shoulders.

"The steps of Jidia are a myth," Gargarin said.

Froi poked his head inside the space, relieved for once that he wasn't the size of a Lumateran River man. He climbed in and began to crawl.

"Don't go too far," he heard Gargarin order, and the words echoed over and over again.

He didn't have to. The tunnel led to another cave that was darker by far, but it was a safer place for them to hide.

In their new home, Arjuro built a small fire. Quintana had returned to her indignant self, except when Froi dared to look at her, which produced a savage snarl.

"Lirah mentioned that you managed to smuggle the assassin out of the palace all those years ago, Sir Gargarin," she said at one point during the night when they were trying to get some sleep. "Rather than toss him into the *gravina* with my first mother, the oracle."

It took Froi a moment to realize he was the assassin she was referring to. There was an uneasy silence at the bluntness of her words.

"Who was it?" Arjuro asked Gargarin, when no one spoke. "The babe who died that day?"

"Later," Gargarin muttered from his bedroll, turning away.

"Now," Arjuro said. "It's been too long. I need the truth. So does Lirah."

"Now you need the truth?" Gargarin said bitterly. "Later, I said." He stole a look at Quintana.

"Are you waiting for us to sleep before you speak of it, Sir Gargarin?" she asked indignantly. "Because we can't, you know. Sleep, that is. Not with the assassin here, threatening us and the little king."

"Us? The little king?" Froi said, looking at the others with disbelief. "Are you all hearing this?"

Lirah closed her eyes as though she had heard it one too many times.

"The Princess claims . . . believes," she corrected herself, "that she carries the first."

Quintana made a clicking sound of annoyance with her tongue. "I explained to you, Lirah. I'm actually the queen of Charyn. I was wed to King Tariq in his compound before they slaughtered him. When one is wed to the king, she is given the title of queen regardless of how powerless she remains. I do love a title."

There was another uncomfortable silence. This time her attention was on Gargarin.

"Is it true you murdered my first mother, the oracle?" she persisted.

Answer her, Froi wanted to shout. So they didn't have to hear her guileless voice speak of death and carnage.

When it was clear that there would be no sleep for any of them, Gargarin sat up.

"I was handed a child that night said to have been birthed by the oracle," he said.

"It was the king who placed him in my arms. Told me that the babe would bring Charyn to its knees if he lived. That if I loved my king and believed in the gods, I would do as instructed. First, I was to toss the babe over the balconette into the *gravina* and then dispose of his dead mother in the same way. Better the people of the Citavita believe that the oracle plunged to her own death than know she was defiled by the Serkers and died giving birth to an abomination."

Froi could hardly breathe.

"Of course we know now that the oracle and the priestlings were not attacked by the Serkers." Gargarin shook his head with bitterness. "To this day, I'll never truly know what I would have done if fate had not stepped in."

He looked at Lirah. "You were my fate, Lirah. First, because of your screams. I thought you were birthing your child, but now I know you were waking up with the oracle's daughter in your arms instead of the son you had seen. Your pain penetrated those walls, and while the king and his guards left the chamber, I found myself alone with the child I was ordered to kill. Not a minute had passed when I heard a sound from the bed where the dead oracle lay beneath the sheet. Dead from childbirth. Unbeknownst to the king and his men, between her thighs lay a second girl whose first breath had been her last."

Froi saw a flash of pain cross his face.

"There were three babes born in the palace that night. Lirah's son and the oracle's twin daughters."

Quintana rocked back and forth. Lirah was too stunned to offer her comfort, and Arjuro looked so ill that Froi thought he'd throw up at any moment.

"And as fate would have it again, strange lonely Rafuel came searching for one lost kitten to add to the litter in his basket. So I took my chance and placed the living child among them. Into the hands of an eight-year-old boy who had never known love except for those damned cats. Then I carried the oracle and her dead child to the balconette and I gave the child a name. To my shame, I had no idea what the oracle's name was. All I prayed for was that you managed to call out her name to the gods, Arjuro, from where they had shackled you on the opposite balconette to watch. So that her spirit could find her child at the lake of the half dead and take them both home."

Arjuro shook his head. "Oracles didn't have names. To call an oracle by her name would make her human, and we were never to see her as human."

So the oracle queen and her dead child were to be separated for eternity.

Quintana's face was transformed into an expression of sadness beyond belief. She shook her head. Froi couldn't speak, could hardly breathe from knowing how close he had come to death the day he was born.

"What did you name her?" Lirah asked. "The dead babe?"

"Regina," Gargarin said quietly. "The babe was the daughter of the oracle queen, so I felt she deserved the name of royalty."

Froi heard Arjuro's sharp intake of breath. The priestling's eyes were fixed on Quintana with a mixture of horror and intrigue.

"You were born first," Arjuro said quietly.

"My son was born first," Lirah said. Froi noticed that both Lirah and Gargarin spoke about their son as though it were someone other than himself.

"But not *to* the palace," Arjuro continued. "He may have been born *in* the palace, but not to it. The only children fathered by the king belonged to the oracle, the woman he violated the night he and his men slaughtered the priestlings and blamed it on the Serkers."

Arjuro's eyes were still fastened on Quintana.

"Two children would be born to the palace," he said. "And the one born first would end his reign."

Froi recognized the soothsayer's words. The king's dream.

"How did you kill him?" Arjuro asked Quintana quietly.

Froi saw Gargarin's and Lirah's confusion and felt his own. But Quintana seemed to know exactly what the priestling was asking, for she neither argued nor feigned innocence.

"The *provincari* said that the guard searched you thoroughly," Arjuro continued.

"Arjuro?" Gargarin barked. "What are you saying?"

They waited and waited. But Arjuro refused to respond.

"The assassin taught us how to kill a man in five seconds," Quintana said. "And the circumstances demanded that I did."

"Sagra!" Froi said, stunned.

"Where did you conceal the dagger?" Arjuro asked. He stood and walked to where she sat upright against the wall and crouched before her. "Where?"

She leaned forward whispering, "I don't want Lirah to hear this, blessed Arjuro."

"Why not?" he whispered back, fascinated.

"It will upset her. We don't want to upset Lirah. I believe that the last time Lirah became upset, her Serker blood helped curse the kingdom."

"Arjuro will tell me anyway, Quintana," Lirah said.

They waited, Arjuro still before Quintana. She looked past him to Lirah.

"There's little that can upset me now. You know that," Lirah prodded, but Froi could see she was lying. Lirah seemed frightened of what she was about to hear.

"We never had a dagger," Quintana said. "But we knew where Bestiano kept his hidden."

"How?" Gargarin asked.

"Because when he came into my room those nights he would always remove the dagger before . . . but he would leave the scabbard. He never took it off. Never."

There were tears in her eyes. "*Never*. And it chafed my skin each time and I'd say, *'Bestiano, it hurts.'*"

Quintana stared back at the only mother she had ever known, and Froi saw on Lirah's face a look of fierce anguish. It spoke of heartbreak and guilt and rage, and Lirah shook her head, not wanting to believe, tears spilling down her cheeks. Her consolation for this strange daughter all these years was that the last-born males hadn't hurt her or taken her by force. But she had never imagined the king's adviser would believe he could father the first.

"I insisted on the guards searching Bestiano, knowing they

wouldn't. He saw the king most days, so why search him now? But the damage was done because I'd put doubts in the heads of the *provincari* who were witness to it all.

"And so I walked into my father's chamber, shut the door, and to Bestiano I did what the assassin told me to do. Render a man useless with a knee between the legs. And then I grabbed his dagger from its scabbard and I walked to my father and I plunged it into his side."

Froi saw the vicious little teeth clench in victory as she remembered the moment. "'That is for my mother!' I said, and then I twisted the blade. 'And that is for Lirah of Serker.' Then, in the third second, I cut him from ear to ear. 'And that is for the people of Charyn!' Only then did I cry bloody murder. 'Bestiano has killed my father!'"

They all stared at her, speechless. Quintana gripped Arjuro's hand.

"My mother is lost, blessed Arjuro, never to be reunited with her daughters," she said. "The only place she'll find us will be in our dreams."

Arjuro pressed her hand to his lips. If there was one person he had adored in this world apart from his brother and De Lancey, it was the oracle.

"If it's the last thing I do in this mortal world, Your Highness," he said, his voice ragged, "I will find her spirit and call her home."

Quintana leaned forward, her lips close to the priestling's ear. "If the assassin comes near us or the little king, will you help me cut out his heart, blessed Arjuro?"

Arjuro turned to meet Froi's eyes. "Yes, I think I'd have to."

The next day, Froi returned from his surveillance to find Arjuro and Gargarin waiting for him in the outer cave. Today it had been too dangerous to venture close to the stream, and he had to be satisfied with berries as his pickings.

"She believes she's with child and that you've been sent to kill the heir to Charyn," Gargarin said tiredly.

"Yes, we've already established that," Froi said. "Are you telling me you believe her?"

"I don't know what to believe, except that the most useless girl in Charyn has managed to do something that most men have failed at, including the both of us. So I'm going to have to be less skeptical about her ramblings in the future."

Froi couldn't believe what he was hearing. He turned to Arjuro.

"So now you think she's the answer to Charyn's dreams as well?"

Arjuro shrugged. "There's nothing like a bit of patricide and regicide to convince me of someone's worth."

"I don't care what any of you think," Froi muttered, preparing to crawl into the inner cave, "because the way I see it, when we get out of here, I'm taking her to the cloister of Lagrami in Sendecane. They'll take care of her there for the rest of her life."

Gargarin gripped Froi's arm gently.

"We thought it best if you sleep in a separate place until we work out her state of mind. Lirah says—"

"Lirah?" Froi said bitterly. "Lirah would like me in a separate place? She weeps for her boy all her life, but the moment she's faced with me as a son, it's all too disappointing, isn't it?"

Arjuro made a sound of annoyance.

"That's not what she said at all," Gargarin said. "Quintana is not of sound mind at the moment, Froi. Anyone can see that."

Froi shoved him away and crawled into their cave.

Sitting up against the wall as she had since they arrived, Quintana stared up at him, her eyes swollen from the fatigue of keeping them open.

"Tell her to sleep," he ordered Lirah.

Lirah stood and walked toward him.

"She claims you will kill her and the child if she dares to sleep," Lirah said quietly. "It's why she ran from you both times before."

"Her delusion about this child will get her killed, Lirah. Speak to her."

Lirah shook her head. "I pledged to take her somewhere safe. When she came to me that day in the inn and told me you were in Charyn to assassinate her, she was inconsolable. Not just about the carnage in Tariq's compound, but over fear of what you would do. 'He'll kill the little king,' she cried, 'and Charyn will be cursed for eternity.'"

There was anguish in Lirah's eyes. "I owe her this and regardless of whether I believe she is imagining this child, I need to be with her."

"Why is she so certain?" Froi asked.

"She claims the gods wrote it all over you. She is mad beyond reasoning, and we did this to her. I did. The king. You. The whole of Charyn. We created that," she said, pointing to where Quintana stared from her corner.

Froi pushed past Lirah toward Quintana, but her savage hiss of fury and ragged breaths of fear filled the cave. Froi felt himself being dragged back by Arjuro and Gargarin while Lirah went to Quintana, murmuring words in the mad girl's ears.

"Tell her to sleep, Lirah," Froi begged, pulling away from the others.

But the sound of Froi's voice was Quintana's undoing and she cried out hoarsely, "Please, Lirah. Please, I'm begging you. Make him leave."

Lirah turned, and Froi saw it in her eyes. She wanted him

gone as well. Shaking free of Arjuro's arms he walked away and crawled back into the outer cave.

He spent the week playing cat and mouse with Bestiano's riders, watching them search the larger caves each morning. Some days Froi made sure he left a false trail, which had them whispering with feverish excitement. Most days he returned with food and placed it in the tunnel between the outer and inner cave for the others to eat.

They came to the outer cave often, except for Quintana, but Froi barely spoke.

"We can't stay here," Gargarin said a week after Froi had been banished from Quintana's presence.

Froi practiced some weapon drills, ignoring him.

"Either we find a way out past their camp or give her up to Bestiano's men," Arjuro said.

Froi stumbled a moment, his short sword falling from his hand.

"If they believe she is with child, it buys her time," Arjuro said. "What did you say about buying time? Each moment provides . . . blah, blah, blah."

If Froi chose to speak to them, he'd say it was a bad idea. And what would Bestiano and the riders do after they discovered Quintana had been telling lies when her belly failed to swell. But he didn't choose to speak, and soon they left.

Later, Lirah came to visit.

"Gargarin says you're sulking," she said coolly. "And Quintana's still not sleeping, so perhaps you should return and sit in a corner away from her."

"I don't sit in corners, Lirah."

"This is not helping anyone."

"Is there food in her belly?" he snapped, pointing a finger to her face. "In all your bellies? If not, get out of my cave!"

With a hand, she shoved him back. "You listen to me, you little Serker savage—"

"*Your* Serker savage, Lirah," he mocked viciously, stepping closer. "His."

She shoved him again and he felt fury in the push. "You were sent to assassinate her, Froi. What do you expect? Regardless of everything, *everything*," she spat, "Quintana was placed in my care, and for so long I was the only one she trusted when cowards tried to kill her time and time again. Do you want to know the first time it happened? Have you ever seen a four-year-old child retch over and over again, trying to purge herself of the poison they put in her food, begging me to stop the pain?"

He thought of all those times Quintana tried to eat from his plate and from the plates of those around her.

"I would never have done it," he argued.

"Why not? It's part of that wretched bond of yours to those revenge-seeking Lumaterans. It's the code you live by. Why would I think any different?"

Because you're my mother, he wanted to shout.

"I stay here," he said, turning his back to her. "Go back to your cave and don't bother me again."

Arjuro accompanied him outside one day, regardless of whether Froi wanted the company or not. The stream was the best source of food, but it was guarded day and night, all the way to the northern wall of the *gravina*. After a good bout of rain the day before, Froi watched one of the riders collect a bounty of fish and eel, placing them in a sack that writhed with life.

"If you could get that stash, it would last us days," Arjuro whispered from where they hid in a small ditch behind a cluster of reeds.

They waited for most of the morning, and when the rider was satisfied with his catch, he picked up the sack and walked away, disappearing into the copse of poplar trees that led to the Charynites' camp.

"Stay here, and whatever you do, don't move until I return," Froi ordered.

He followed the rider, leaping across stepping stones to avoid using the dirt track, which could easily alert the others to him. The Charynite stopped soon after and placed the sack on the ground, standing against a tree to relieve himself. Perri always said that there was an advantage in attacking a man with his pants down. Most men went to protect their private parts before anything else, and if a pursuer was to give chase, it would also take a moment for the victim to pull up his trousers. So Froi came up from behind and knocked the man across the temple with the handle of his short sword before grabbing the sack of writhing fish and eels, and then he bolted.

"He's here!" he heard the rider bellow. *"This way."*

At the stream where Arjuro was hidden, Froi forced the sack into the priestling's hands.

"Run!" Froi hissed. "I'll lead them away."

Without waiting for Arjuro's response, Froi raced back the way he had come and found himself face-to-face with the first of the riders. He leaped up and gripped the tree limb above, one boot each pounding in both men's faces. He jumped back onto the ground and took the path that circled the riders' camp, knowing it would draw them away from Arjuro and their cave.

He reached the wall of the *gravina* heading north and saw the tunnel through the thick stone that he had traveled through Zabat on their journey to meet Gargarin. It would take him to the road leading him to Alonso and then Lumatere. *Home,* he thought. *Home*. And the fury he had felt in the caves toward Quintana and Lirah and Gargarin and Arjuro, and the knowledge that they would be left with a small bounty of food, steered him to take the path home.

Without looking back.

CHAPTER 26

Aldron arrived one morning with instructions from the palace. Although Lucian knew he had the full support of his cousin Isaboe, it still shamed him that he could not restore order among his people. There had been a week of hostility on the mountain, and he had begun to wonder if it was best to send Yata down to the palace to keep her safe from the bitter words and simmering unrest.

"If you're here to guard the prisoner, Aldron, we'll help you," Jory said, strutting to where Aldron was dismounting outside Lucian's cottage. Everyone knew Trevanion and the Guard were keeping an eye on Jory, and he was the envy of most Mont lads his age. Usually he would receive a friendly cuff to his chin from one of the Guard in response to his remarks. Except for today.

"I'm not here to guard the prisoner," Aldron said coldly. "I'm here to protect him."

Aldron's order was to take the Charynite down to the valley and shackle him to a tree on the Lumateran side of the stream. It was a safer option than keeping him up on the mountain.

Later that day, Lucian and Aldron escorted the prisoner through the crowd that had gathered outside. Tension was rife, and under the watchful gaze of most of the Monts, even Aldron looked uneasy. "What's going on here, Lucian?" he asked quietly.

"The Monts being Monts."

From where he sat, on a horse tethered to Lucian's, Rafuel of Sebastabol caught his eye.

"You honestly don't think they're going to ride down that mountain and come for me," he said. Lucian repeated his words to Aldron.

"Tell him I have orders to keep him alive," Aldron said. "So if my orders are to keep him alive, he stays alive."

Lucian translated.

"And if his orders are to kill me?" Rafuel asked.

"Rest assured that you'll be dead before you have time to give it a second thought," Lucian said.

When they reached the valley, there was no one to be seen on their side of the stream. Lucian climbed up the oak that shaded the camp and saw Tesadora and her girls chatting with Phaedra and Cora in the vegetable plot that the Mont boys had once destroyed. *Chatting*. Lucian had noticed that ever since Lady Beatriss had sent down the clay cooking pot, his wife and her people had become friendlier to one another, but *chatting* to Tesadora and the novices was something new, and Lucian was determined to put an end to it.

Aldron pitched the tent beside a tree and per Trevanion's instructions, he shackled Rafuel securely. Tesadora and the girls walked over, and Aldron asked for the chronicle Tesadora held. He leafed through it.

"Two hundred and forty-seven of them?" he asked. "There are more Charynites in the valley than Monts on the mountain."

"We would have more Monts on the mountain if you two would return to your homes," Lucian told his cousins Constance and Sandrine, who had been living in the valley for two weeks now with Tesadora. They gave Lucian a look that would curdle milk and he thought it best not to say another word to them.

"Is the queen going to set him free?" Sandrine asked, studying their Charynite prisoner carefully. "They are a puny lot, aren't they?"

"Despite it all, they are quite pleasing to the eye," Constance added. Tesadora gave them both a scathing look.

"Yes, well it's a pity you weren't introduced to some of the Charynite soldiers during our ten-year imprisonment," she said, her tone acid. "I doubt any of the girls were cooing at how pleasing to the eye the enemy was when they were forced into their beds."

The girls looked away, horrified and ashamed. "We meant no offense, Tesadora," Sandrine said.

Tesadora gave the Mont girls a meaningful look, flicking her eyes toward Japhra before picking up the pots and walking away toward the stream. Lucian looked over to where Japhra was staring at Rafuel. Lucian knew little of her story except that she had been dragged to the palace by the impostor king when she was twelve. Years later, Lady Beatriss had managed to smuggle her out of the palace and they traveled for days across Lumatere until they reached Tesadora and her hidden cloister at the Sendecane border. The girl was said to be damaged, but she had a fierce attachment to Tesadora and a talent for healing more powerful than Lucian had ever seen. When her eyes looked past Lucian to their prisoner, he noticed that Rafuel was returning her gaze, and suddenly a rage came over Lucian. The rule was never to forget who the enemy was, and there had been times these past weeks when Lucian had forgotten. But not today. He grabbed Rafuel by his hair, pulling his head back. "You don't look at our women," he hissed. "You don't talk to them. You don't touch them. Is that clear?"

Rafuel didn't respond, and Lucian saw sorrow in his expression.

"Lucian. Aldron."

Tesadora came running out from the trees that concealed the other side of the stream.

"Riders," she said when she reached them. "Coming from the direction of Alonso."

Lucian and Aldron crept toward the stream, the waterberry tree keeping them hidden. Across the stream, Lucian could see the cave dwellers standing, ten or so horsemen riding toward them.

"King's men?" Tesadora asked.

Aldron shook his head. "From how we hear it through the Belegonians, there is no king of Charyn."

"No king?" Lucian asked. "When?"

"Perhaps a week or two ago."

"Where's Froi, then?" he demanded. "If he succeeded, he should be home by now."

Aldron shook his head. "There's too much uncertainty about who actually assassinated the king. Some are saying he died at the hands of his First Adviser."

Lucian turned back to where Rafuel was chained to the tree and crept beside him.

"Your king is dead, Rafuel. Approaching now are men with no uniforms, but they ride with great authority."

Hope blazed in Rafuel's eyes. He leaped to his feet before collapsing under the weight of the chains. He strained to look through the trees across the stream.

"Perhaps Zabat has returned with Froi," Rafuel said. "Unshackle me and I can see for myself."

Lucian looked at the shackles and then at the prisoner.

"If you run, Charynite, I will kill you," he warned, reluctantly unlocking the chains. "If I don't kill you, which is highly unlikely, then Aldron will kill you. Aldron is the queen's bodyguard, so you can imagine his aim is almost as good as mine."

The moment the chains were off, both Lucian and Rafuel wormed their way to the stream, beside Tesadora and Aldron, who had crept closer to see what lay through the reeds.

"I never doubted the lad would succeed," Rafuel said with a chuckle.

"From the way we hear it, the king's First Man was the assassin," Lucian said.

Rafuel turned to him in disbelief. "You mean the king's adviser, Bestiano? It doesn't make sense."

"So who's in charge if the king is dead?" Tesadora asked Rafuel in Charyn.

Lucian noticed that her language skills had improved since the Charynites had first arrived.

"The son of the king's first cousin," Rafuel said. "Tariq. His father died of a mysterious illness in the palace three years ago, and Tariq's mother's people managed to have the lad smuggled out. If he sits on the throne, the priests will be happy, the *provincari* will be happy, and Charyn will be happy. Royal blood without the insanity. Nothing like it to make a Charynite dance with joy."

"One can understand why," Lucian murmured.

"But it has been foretold that the last will make the first and the Princess Quintana will produce a male child by the time she comes of age to be both a curse breaker and heir. All we will need is an honorable man, unaligned to the provinces, to act as regent to the boy until he comes of age. If that does not come to pass, we will be happy for Tariq to take the throne and for the priests to come out of hiding and find a better way to break the curse than turning our women into whores."

"But if a son comes from the princess, wouldn't your people despise his tainted blood?" Lucian asked.

Rafuel turned to Tesadora. "What do you believe? That one is born evil or raised evil?"

"Why ask me?" she snapped.

Rafuel shrugged. "Because you seem the type to have an opinion about such things."

She looked away. "No child is born evil," she said quietly.

"And I'm presuming that you and your men know exactly who the honorable regent to the heir will be?" Lucian asked.

Rafuel nodded, grinning, trying to make himself comfortable. "We do indeed. He has a fiercely smart mind and is the fairest of men. All he needs is convincing that his place is in the palace."

"And does this paragon of virtue have a name?" Lucian asked.

"He exists. That's all you need to know."

Rafuel nudged Lucian, and the idiot Charynite's good humor was contagious. "Be reassured, Mont, tonight you travel to the capital with our lad."

"Our lad?" Lucian asked. "Froi's ours, Charynite."

But Lucian grinned all the same and even Tesadora seemed happy at the news. He hadn't realized how much he missed Froi's visits up to the mountain. The boy had worked harder than any other these past three years, perhaps because he had the strongest wish for the queen's goodwill. Lucian imagined Isaboe and Finnikin's joy as Froi rode into the palace village. Trevanion and Perri and the rest of the Guard would drag him away to find out what they could about the death of the Charynite king, but Lucian knew that deep down everyone would be relieved that Froi was returning home unharmed.

"There are my lads," Rafuel said, excitement in his voice. The seven men stood huddled together.

"I can't see Froi with the riders," Tesadora said as the

horsemen came closer. She snaked through the reeds, within a breath of the stream.

"Come back, Tesadora," Aldron whispered.

The closer the horsemen rode, the more silent the valley dwellers became. From his vantage point, Lucian could see it in the way Kasabian and Cora and Rafuel's men and everyone else stood, their bodies rigid.

"Do you recognize any of the riders, Rafuel?" Lucian whispered.

Rafuel did not respond. Closer and closer came the men, and Lucian feared they'd cross the stream. The order was that if any Charynite other than Phaedra crossed the stream, the Monts would see it as an attack on Lumatere.

"Rafuel?" Tesadora whispered.

The prisoner's silence made Lucian uncomfortable. He could see by the expression on Rafuel's face that he recognized no one among the newcomers.

There were twelve men in total. They dismounted, and in the eerie silence that followed, Lucian watched them shove through the camp dwellers.

"They're searching for someone," Lucian whispered.

Rafuel shook his head slowly. "I don't recognize them, but they're certainly not palace riders, so we have nothing to fear."

"Then who could they be?" Lucian asked.

Rafuel shrugged. "The priests have spies in places that I don't even know. We had one or two inside Lumatere for the first year."

"What?"

"Rest assured," Rafuel said, "the hidden priests of Charyn and the army they have built for Tariq will never be a threat to you." But his voice had lost its humor. It was laced with fear.

Rafuel's eyes fixed on the horsemen as they began to surround his men.

"Oh, gods," Rafuel said, his voice anguished.

"What?" Lucian asked.

"They're here for my lads."

Aldron motioned them to silence. They watched as the leader of the horsemen paced the path before the camp dwellers, the sword in his hand pointed back at Rafuel's men.

"We're searching for a man named Rafuel of Sebastabol," he called out. "The leader of the seven traitors who planned the murder of our king."

Rafuel was muttering. Praying. From where Lucian lay, he could see that Rafuel's men were doing the same while the camp dwellers stared at the seven men, confused. Rafuel's lads had only made themselves known these last weeks. Tesadora had said there was talk among them all that a Charynite had taken a dagger to Japhra, but the camp dwellers had no idea who and they especially never suspected he belonged to the quiet seven, who were all scholars and kept to themselves.

"I repeat, we're searching for Rafuel of Sebastabol." The voice of the horseman was coarse and ugly, and its threat chilled Lucian to the bone.

The man's hand suddenly snaked out into the crowd and grabbed Kasabian by the neck, shoved him down to his knees, and stood behind him with a sword across his throat. Cora cried out.

"Stay back, Cora. Stay back," Kasabian instructed his sister.

Lucian elbowed Aldron, staring at him helplessly. Aldron shook his head bitterly. "This is not our fight, Lucian," he whispered.

"They're going to kill an innocent man," Lucian said.

"This is not our fight, I say."

Rafuel suddenly stumbled to his feet.

"I'm Rafuel of Sebastabol."

Yet it wasn't Rafuel's voice that rang out, but one from across the stream. Both Aldron and Lucian dragged Rafuel down before he could be seen.

"No," Rafuel whispered in horror. "No, Rothen."

Lucian discovered later that the young man was a scholar from the province of Paladozza. He was of Rafuel's age, with a dark trimmed beard and a shaggy head of dark curls. Lucian had watched him speak to Phaedra this last week. Instead of cowering, she had been animated. It had angered Lucian for some reason. The leader of the horsemen looked back to where Rothen stood with his hand raised. Kasabian was shoved aside as the leader walked back to Rafuel's seven men and grabbed Rothen, dragging him to the stream, forcing him to his knees.

"If you are to arrest us for treason," they heard another of Rafuel's men say with great urgency, "then you try us in a court of Charyn law, by the seneschal of the Citavita. That's the law."

The leader of the horsemen stared back at the speaker. Everyone watched in terrified silence.

"And who are you?" the horseman asked pleasantly.

"My name is Asher of Nebia," the man said, and Lucian could hear the tremble of fear in his voice.

The leader shoved Rothen away and walked toward Asher of Nebia.

Lucian heard Rafuel's sigh of relief.

"Smart man, Asher," Rafuel whispered.

"Asher of Nebia," the horseman said. "My name is Donashe of the Citavita, and let me tell you this, friend. There is no seneschal of the Citavita. The Citavita is dead. The king is dead. So when my men and I came across the king's riders pledging to pay ten pieces of gold for the body of every traitor responsible, then that's the only law I care to follow. And if they promised me twice that amount for the head of Rafuel of Sebastabol, then who am I to say no?"

In an instant, he grabbed Asher by the hood of his robe and dragged him to the stream amid the screams and shouts from those around them. With both hands, Donashe of the Citavita forced Asher's head into the stream while the scholar's body thrashed violently.

Lucian heard a cry behind him and turned back to the novices and the Mont girls, who were clutching each other in terror.

"Up the mountain," he hissed to them. "*Now*. No horses. Run and don't let them see you!"

When he turned back, Asher's body lay still in the stream. Donashe of the Citavita stepped back and held up a finger.

"One," the Charynite announced. "According to our source, there are six more led by Rafuel of Sebastabol."

Rafuel tried to raise himself again, struggling as Aldron pinned him down, and Lucian kept a hand to his mouth.

"You'll get us all killed," Lucian whispered. "Our women, too. Is that what you want?"

Only then did Rafuel stop, and when both Aldron and Lucian were certain their prisoner would not try to surrender himself again, they let go of their hold and continued their blood-chilling vigil.

Lucian could see Kasabian through the reeds, and he knew from the quick flicker of his gaze across the stream that Kasabian could see them. Although not the oldest of the camp dwellers, the man was a quiet leader of sorts and had made a point of becoming acquainted with all the camp dwellers. Lucian's heart sank. Did the man expect him to act on their behalf or stay hidden?

"So let me ask again." Donashe's voice rang across the valley camp. "Where is Rafuel of Sebastabol?"

"I am Rafuel of Sebastabol," Rothen said. "Take me and get

your gold. The rest of these men are priestlings. Not traitors. These people are landless. They care not for the politics of their kingdom. They want a scrap of dirt to call their own!"

Donashe of the Citavita grabbed Rothen's face and stared at it long and hard. "I think you're lying, friend. You're not fair enough to be from Sebastabol. I think you're hiding your leader somewhere in this camp."

"There were eight of us," Rothen said. "One took a dagger to a Lumateran woman's throat and was banished by the leader of their Monts. His name was Rothen, and he's halfway to Desantos by now."

Donashe shoved Rothen away and grabbed another one of the men, slight in build and the youngest by far.

"Faroux of Paladozza," Rafuel choked out hoarsely as the Charynite horsemen sliced the lad from ear to ear. "Let me stop this, Lucian. *Please*. I beg of you."

It took Aldron and Tesadora's help to hold Rafuel down. For one so slight, he fought like a demon, weeping with silent despair. Lucian had seen his father die before his eyes, but he couldn't think of anything worse than seeing Finnikin or Froi or his Mont cousins being slaughtered while he stood and did nothing.

Later, when he tried to explain it to his *yata*, he spoke of the fear he saw in the eyes of those young men who knew that death was upon them. Fighting a battle to the death seemed a natural way for a warrior to die. It was the way Lucian's own father had died. But waiting for death? Knowing the inevitable? That day innocent men died in front of Lucian's eyes. They died savagely. Some were cut down with a dagger to the gut, others with a blade to the throat. Each time, Donashe of the Citavita asked for the leader. And each time, Rothen swore he was Rafuel of Sebastabol.

"Where is Rafuel of Sebastabol?" Donashe asked when the sixth man lay dying at his feet. Rothen dropped to his knees, holding his companion in his arms.

"Forsake me, you bastard gods," he prayed, *"but do not forsake beloved Charyn!"* He was cut down within moments.

Beside Lucian, Rafuel wept quietly. "I need to call out their names to the gods. I need to call out their names."

"Open your mouth and they will kill you next, fool," Lucian said quietly.

Lucian caught Aldron's eye, and he could see that the Queen's guard was shaken by what they had witnessed. Death was death. That it had taken place this close to the Lumateran border would set the kingdom on edge.

"Rafuel?" Tesadora whispered. "What in the name of Sagrami are they doing?" Her expression was a mask of horror and sadness. Lucian watched two of Donashe's men line the seven bodies up across the edge of the stream.

But it was what the other horsemen were doing that sent an icy finger down Lucian's spine. Screams were heard as the youngest of the women were dragged to where Donashe stood, then forced to their knees, side by side. Each girl was searched for the sign on the napes of their necks. The sign of the last born, Rafuel explained.

When Donashe failed to find what he was searching for, the girls were pushed away and Lucian heard cries of relief. Until the next girls were pulled from the arms of crying mothers and helpless fathers.

"They're searching for last-born women," Rafuel whispered, his voice broken. "Which can only mean that Quintana of Charyn is dead."

Tesadora gripped Lucian's arm. "We have to do something."

Suddenly Rafuel caught his breath, his eyes meeting Lucian's.

"What?" Lucian asked.

"Phaedra!" Rafuel whispered hoarsely.

"She'll know to keep her head down," Lucian said.

"No, you don't understand. They're looking for last borns, Lucian. Phaedra is the only last born in this valley. Most other last-born girls are in hiding. Their fathers and mothers knew this day of weeping would come."

Lucian stared across the stream, searching for Phaedra among the camp dwellers. "Why would Sol of Alonso not have hidden his daughter?" he asked.

"He did," Rafuel said. "He made a pact with an enemy leader eighteen years ago to protect his daughter from this very moment. He sent her to Lumatere."

Phaedra watched from where she knelt beside Florenza of Nebia. As a last born, she had known that this day would come, and had always told herself she'd be brave. Perhaps it was the wish of the gods for her to be taken by the men of the palace to create the first. But after what she had witnessed this day, she could not imagine the gods sanctioning such cruelty and horror.

Her only reprieve was that no girl in this valley had the mark of the last born. Phaedra had checked them all herself. No girl but her, and here she was on her knees, five women away from whatever it was that Quintana of Charyn had been called on to do for all these years. *The last will make the first*. What if there was nothing left of the spirit of the last to give to the first?

The men were almost upon her when the leader of the horsemen looked up across the stream. Phaedra could only see Kasabian and Cora from where she knelt, and on a day when she didn't think hope existed, she saw it in their eyes.

"Introduce yourself, stranger," the leader of the horsemen ordered.

"I'm no stranger," her Mont husband said, astride his horse. "I'm Lucian of the Monts, the custodian of this valley. State your business here, Charynite."

She hadn't realized until that moment that she had always enjoyed the sound of her Mont husband's voice. It was strong and gruff, and it spoke with little nonsense and a good deal of substance.

"Regardless of whose valley it is, these people are ours and we do as we're ordered," Donashe said.

"Ordered by whom?" Lucian asked. "The palace?"

The man hesitated.

"State your purpose, Charynite. Is this palace business?" Lucian demanded, pointing to where Phaedra and the others knelt. "Are these girls palace business?"

"We're searching for our last borns—"

"Last borns?"

"We've come from the Citavita, friend," the man said, trying to keep a civil tone. "These are uneasy times in Charyn. We're collecting any last born to ensure their safety."

Lucian nodded, watching the man closely.

"Wise of you, Charynite. I would do the same to protect the young women of my kingdom. I invite you to take any last born you can find. But you have the wife of a Mont leader, who also happens to be cousin of the Lumateran queen, there before you."

Lucian clenched his teeth. "On. Her. Knees."

The Charynite stared at him with disbelief.

"Your wife?"

Lucian pointed down to where Phaedra knelt.

"Why would your wife be a Charynite in the valley, Mont?"

Lucian trotted his horse around the horseman to where Phaedra knelt and held out a hand.

"The first step to peace between Lumatere and the closest

province of Charyn was the betrothment of myself and the *provincaro* of Alonso's daughter."

Phaedra raised herself onto trembling feet.

Donashe stared at them both. "Why would you allow your wife out of your sight, Mont?"

Lucian bent and grasped Phaedra's arm, dragging her onto the horse.

"She claims that the blood of her people in the valley sing to her each day, and if I don't allow her to come down the mountain, she gives me grief." Lucian placed his arms around Phaedra. "Let us say that I'm a very indulgent man and my Little Sparrow is most convincing."

With that, Lucian steered the horse toward the stream.

"Then we look forward to speaking to your Little Sparrow tomorrow," the horseman called out, "about the well-being of her people."

Phaedra cried out at the threat in those words. She looked back to where the camp dwellers stood.

"That was a warning, Luci-en. About what he is going to do to these people."

"Not your concern," he said.

"It is my concern," she cried. "I'm a *provincaro*'s daughter. It is our duty that we protect those not born with our privilege."

They didn't speak for most of the journey up the mountain, but his grip around her was tight and she felt the tremble in his body.

"I saw it all," he said, as if he could no longer contain it. "I saw it all and did nothing."

What would his father have done?

The first person Lucian could see when he reached his village on the mountain was Rafuel, crouched in the dirt with his head in his hands, weeping. The Charynite was surrounded by Tesadora and Aldron and Tesadora's girls. The Monts who had been there to see the prisoner off were here to see him return. They watched in tense silence.

Lucian could tell that they had been told of the day's events, for they all seemed shaken. He lowered Phaedra to the ground and a moment later Yata was there with a blanket around the girl.

"I sent one of the lads to the palace," Yata said. "Let's hope the Guard will arrive tomorrow with instructions."

"What happened, Lucian?" his cousin Yael asked.

"Are we at war?" another called out.

"I don't understand," Alda said. "What are those Charyn riders doing in the valley, Lucian?"

He looked at Rafuel and then Aldron. "I think it's safer for him to be back in the cell."

Aldron shook his head. "He'll just find a way to smash his head apart against the stone wall."

No one knew what to say about the Charynite. He was weeping, chanting the names of his lads over and over again.

"I don't understand," Jory said, staring down at Rafuel. "Tell him to stop."

But Lucian understood. He grabbed Jory and dragged him to the younger lads who followed Jory day in and day out.

"See these seven, Jory," he asked, fury in his voice. "Well, imagine you were on one side of the stream hiding, while on the other side of the stream someone slaughtered your lads and cousins, right in front of you. And there was nothing you could do, Jory, because we were holding you down to stop you from being slain yourself."

Lucian then grabbed Phaedra.

"Lucian!" Yata warned.

"And see this woman, Jory," he said, turning Phaedra around

gently and revealing the strange lettering on her neck. "This woman is just like our queen. Marked as a slave to do things we don't want to imagine happening to our own."

Lucian pulled Jory toward Phaedra. "Treat her as you would beloved Isaboe, Jory. Follow her everywhere she goes. Down the valley and across the stream. Everywhere. And if any man touches her, Mont or Charynite, you put a sword through his heart. Do you hear me?"

Jory stared at Lucian and then at his father. His father nodded.

"Take your *pardu*'s sword," Yael said quietly.

Lucian looked around, searching for the older lads.

"I want one of you in every tree in that valley. Not concealed. I want those animals to see us. I want them to know that if they dare slaughter *anyone* on our land, they die."

And then he walked to Rafuel and gripped him by the arm. Lucian pulled him to his feet and took the Charynite to his home.

That's what Saro of the Monts would have done.

CHAPTER 27

In a mostly deserted village outside Jidia, Froi broke into a stable. He needed a horse, and this dusty village of sunken empty wheel ruts and a wind that cried out its grief seemed his only option. Despite what these people had possibly endured, Froi's necessity was greater, and he felt little remorse at what he was about to take from them. That, in itself, brought him relief. He had become too soft in the palace and needed to find the ruthless warrior inside that Trevanion and Perri marveled at.

"You're probably best not doing that," he heard a voice behind him say. Froi hoped that the man wasn't holding a weapon. He was desperate to get home, and a man with a gentle voice was going to get in his way.

He turned to see a couple standing at the entrance of the barn. They were perhaps in their middle years, but it was hard to tell. Reed thin from the sorrow of life, they leaned against each other as though nothing else could hold them up but the other.

"It will get you no farther than half a day's ride away," the man continued. "He's an old thing, Acacia is. Belonged to our boy and refuses to die."

Froi sighed. Why did everyone in Charyn seem to have a story in their eyes? And when had he started caring?

"Have you come from the Citavita?" the man asked.

"No," Froi lied. "From Alonso."

Both the man and woman studied him cautiously. "We watched you arrive, lad. You came from the south, not the north."

Don't let me hurt you, old man. Don't let me hurt you both.

He knew he could easily fight these people and win. If he wanted the horse, he could take the horse. He had the power, regardless of who owned the stable. Power was everything. Until he realized that law belonged to the street thugs who had brought him up on the streets of Sarnak's capital. Not Trevanion. Power, the captain had told him, meant nothing whether in someone's home or their village or their kingdom or their palace. Respect and honor meant everything.

"Can I beg of you a place to sleep in your stable, then?" Froi asked. "And a plate of food? I'm good for a day's work, and if your second field isn't weeded soon, you'll have planted for nothing."

So Froi worked alongside the man and woman all day. They were a quiet couple, and like many of those Froi had met in Charyn, there was a sadness in their whole beings that was years in the making. It was in the way they walked and toiled. It was in their silence, and it was in their words. They grew barley and broad beans and cabbage. Not to trade, but to survive. The soil was poor from little rain, much the same as the rest of the kingdom outside the walls of the provinces. There was no future for them out here. Froi wondered what had happened to the rest of the villagers. He counted eight cottages in total but could see that it had been quite some time since they were lived in.

The man, named Hamlyn, asked him about his family, but Froi didn't respond.

He could have lied to himself and said that he had thought little of Quintana, Lirah, Arjuro, and Gargarin these past few days, but he didn't. He had thought of the four of them every moment. But he was too close to home for regrets, and he owed them nothing.

That night, he waited on the porch for his food but none came until Hamlyn stepped outside with an expression of irritation on his face.

"We are hungry, lad. We can't wait much longer for you," Hamlyn said before disappearing inside.

Froi entered the small cottage and looked around. It was plain and as clean as could be found in a place so dry and dusty. There was one bed at the end of the room. Outside he had noticed the woodfire oven, but inside was a large pot, from which Hamlyn's wife dished out a bowl of barley soup. When Froi saw the plate set for him at their table, he felt shame. Who was he to deserve their hospitality after what he had planned to do? Hamlyn's wife placed a large chunk of bread at the side of his plate, but none beside hers or Hamlyn's.

"Life on a farm is hard enough," Froi said after a slurp, dividing his bread into three and placing a piece by both their plates. "Why stay here and not inside the walls of Jidia?"

Hamlyn's wife looked up for a moment, and then she went back to her soup.

When neither responded, Froi asked about news from the capital.

"There's confusion," Hamlyn said. "We had visitors ride through here seven days past. Their stories differed. Some claimed that one of the *provincari* planned the murder of the king and that Bestiano is our only hope. Another believed it was the hidden priests who managed to get an assassin inside. One or two of them whispered that Bestiano had killed the king and that his riders are occupying the base of the *gravina* and raising an army from Nebia."

"And what are your thoughts?" Froi asked.

Hamlyn shrugged. "We have nothing left of worth for a king's army," he said bitterly.

Later, Hamlyn's wife gave Froi a blanket, and Hamlyn accompanied him to the stable.

"I found it easy to break inside here," Froi said quietly when Hamlyn handed him the lantern. "Tomorrow I'll secure some of these old planks."

Hamlyn nodded. Froi couldn't help but notice how large the stable was. How empty it was except for Acacia. Hamlyn caught the question in his eye.

"I worked with horses," he said. He smiled at the memory. "Some would say that once I was the best in the outer reaches of the province. In the days before they put the walls around Jidia, men would travel for days to purchase a good horse from me."

Hamlyn held out a handful of oats to Acacia, and Froi watched the old horse nuzzle against its owner.

"Thirteen years ago, the king's riders came through this land, and they took our horses," he said quietly. "And they took our sons. They took all the lads. Mine was of your age."

"Took him to the palace?" Froi asked.

"No," Hamlyn said. "They needed an army to support the new king of Lumatere."

Froi fought hard to hide his shock.

"For ten years we wondered what happened to him inside those walls," Hamlyn continued, as though he had waited a lifetime to speak. "When the Lumateran curse lifted, we waited for him. One or two of our neighbors' sons returned. The Lumaterans had released them, but the lads came back broken. They had shame in their eyes."

Froi couldn't speak. How much despair had this man's son created in Lumatere? Worse still, had he died at Froi's hands?

"And then we began to hear the stories. Of what the Lumaterans claimed our sons did during those ten years."

Not claims, Froi wanted to shout. What the impostor king's army did to the Lumaterans was more than claims.

"It keeps us awake at night," Hamlyn said. "What did a boy who was brought up with such kindness and love do to those people?"

Froi finally looked at Hamlyn.

"You thought I was your son returning?"

Hamlyn gave a painful smile. "Foolish thoughts. He'd have reached his thirtieth year by now." He closed his eyes a moment, as though to recover himself. "But I dreamed of him two nights past. And in my dreams he told me a lad would arrive with the words of our gods written all over him."

Froi flinched to hear Quintana's words spoken by another.

"The only thing written over me are my wrongdoings, Hamlyn," he said.

Froi tossed and turned half the night, but then he slept and dreamed, and when he woke, he couldn't remember the dream. He could only remember its force. He convinced himself that he only dreamed because of Hamlyn's words the night before. But the dream teased him all day, as though it were going to reveal itself any moment. All day he hacked at the earth with frustration alongside Hamlyn and his silent wife, trying to recall even a sliver of what had gone through his mind while he slept.

When Hamlyn's wife walked toward the well, Hamlyn watched her, wiping the sweat from his brow.

"It's her way to be quiet and gentle," he said, and Froi heard love in the man's voice. "Long ago, she claimed to have lost her purpose."

"Because your son was gone?"

Hamlyn shook his head. "No. Long before that." They both watched her lower a pail into the well.

"Arna was the midwife for all of Jidia, as well as our village."

A horse handler with no horses and a midwife in a barren kingdom.

"She can be spirited at times. When she carried our son in her belly, she slept with a dagger, I tell you. A she-wolf, she was. She would have sliced open any man who was a threat to her boy."

And here in this infertile field with two broken people, Froi remembered his dream.

Hamlyn's wife, Arna, returned and gave a bowl of water to each of them, and Froi drank thirstily.

"I need to travel to the Citavita," he said, wiping his mouth with the back of his hand.

"Not a good idea," Hamlyn said.

"I need to be with my family," he said quietly. "They are hiding in the caves at the base of the *gravina*."

"Why would they be hiding in the same place as the king's riders?" Hamlyn asked.

"For reasons that could get you killed if you knew the truth."

The next morning, Froi woke to find Hamlyn and his wife standing before him. He had dreamed again. This time it was of Arna, a she-wolf guarding her young. Except the teeth and snarl were those of Quintana. Arna crouched and handed him a pack, and he smelled fresh bread and cheese and smoked meats. Hamlyn gave him a map.

"Have you heard of the stairs to Jidia?" Hamlyn asked.

"They say there's no such thing," Froi said.

"Who says?" Hamlyn said with a smile.

Froi dressed quickly and placed the food and map in his pack. He looked at Arna, then placed his arms around her, and she held on tight as though she held the son who would never return and he held the mother Lirah would never be to him.

"You're hiding something, Froi," Hamlyn said, handing him a crossbow with the letter *J* etched into the wood.

"Everyone is hiding something, Hamlyn," Froi said. He shook the man's hand. It was a Charynite's gesture. "But it's best you do not know what it is."

He walked away but turned back once.

"What was the name of your son?" he asked, his finger tracing the groove in the weapon they had given him.

"John," the man said. "John, son of Hamlyn and Arna of Charyn."

CHAPTER 28

Froi had been on his own now for the better part of the day, traveling through a labyrinth of caves as he followed Hamlyn's map, which was peppered with a series of twists and turns and strange markings. He marveled each time he came face-to-face with a matching symbol carved into a crevice or the image of a bison scratched onto the ground, its hump pointing him in the direction of the people he needed to be with. Hamlyn had explained that the underground caves were built thousands upon thousands of years ago, when those of Sendecane had taken on the worship of the goddess Lagrami. They had been persecuted by their godless king and escaped across two kingdoms to hide in Charyn, preferring to burrow their way into the earth rather than give up their faith. In later years, their descendants settled aboveground in the kingdoms of Charyn, Lumatere, and Sarnak. The Rock people of Lumatere were fair in skin and gold of hair, much like Grijio of Paladozza and Hamlyn and Arna of Jidia. Froi had grown up among those in the Sarnak capital with the same coloring. Had they come from the same Sendecanese who had hidden in these caves in the past? Was it why Finnikin's people settled themselves on a rock and not the Flatlands or

Mountains? He thought of Quintana, who looked different from everyone Froi had come across. She was every color of Charyn stone. Flecks of browns and grays and golds.

Outside the caves and back at the base of the *gravina,* Froi couldn't help but marvel at how it had taken him half the time to travel back to where he had begun his journey. He wondered what else the caves could offer those who were desperate not to be found. He waited until early morning to make his way to the others, praying they would still be there. He was more than half a mile upstream and could see only three of Bestiano's riders. He figured they would have had no clue about where he was this last week. Perhaps they had become lazy. But not too lazy. They wanted Quintana. Bestiano wanted her. She was his only way back into the palace and to power. Bestiano's capture of the king's true assassin, the king's own treacherous daughter, would bring him some kind of credibility among some of the *provincari.* Despite everything that had taken place between them, Froi was her only chance of survival. If Quintana, Gargarin, Arjuro, and Lirah had left the cave or been caught by the riders, Froi would search for them and not return to Lumatere until he knew they were safe.

Later that morning, he crept through the entrance of their cave. When he was satisfied that the branches and bracken were back in place, he turned, only to see Lirah wielding Gargarin's staff at his head. Froi ducked, and something flashed in her eyes. Was it relief that he wasn't a rider? Or relief that he had returned?

"You got lost, did you?" she asked coldly.

They stared at each other for a long time, and Froi felt the anger return.

"Not what you wanted, am I, Lirah?" he spat out. "Not what you dreamed of?"

"I never wanted and I never dreamed," she said quietly, taking the pack from his hand. "So don't presume you know what passes through my head."

She walked away but turned when he didn't follow.

"I think it frightens her more when you're not around than when you are," she said. "Come."

There were no hugs or tears on Froi's return. Only hostility. Quintana was cold, and Arjuro plain grunting rude. Gargarin refused to look at him, his head bent over his wretched sketches of water troughs and whatnot. In the center of their cave, Froi emptied his pack. He saw their eyes widen when the bread and cheese and bacon appeared before them, and he wondered how long it had been since they last ate.

"You think we'll forgive you, just like that," Arjuro said, keeping his distance.

Froi retrieved a bottle of mead from his pack. "As I don't believe I did anything that requires forgiveness, I'll merely hand this over for you to swill in silence."

"You've been gone six days," Gargarin shouted, finally looking up and throwing his pages across the cave. "Six days! We thought you were dead!"

Froi was surprised by his outburst. Lirah merely picked up the scattered papers, shuffling them together. Quintana was staring at the food. She looked pale and drawn, the dark circles under her eyes even more pronounced.

"Eat," Froi ordered. But still she refused to step closer.

"Who gave you all this?" Lirah asked, kneeling beside Froi, pages in hand.

"A couple on a farm beyond the *gravina*," he said, breaking some bread and placing a piece of cheese inside. He held it up to Quintana, who gazed at it hungrily. When she refused to take it, he bit into it, chewed, swallowed, and held it out to her again. This time she took it.

"I tried to steal a horse and they let me stay a night or two." He looked at them, nodding. "Good, honest people. They treated me like they would a son," he added, his tone emphasizing the last part.

Arjuro took a swig of the mead, wiping his mouth with satisfaction. "Who would have guessed? He's a needy little thing, isn't he?"

For a long time there was only the sound of chewing and grunting. Froi watched them all, a strange sort of peace coming over him.

"I know how to get to Jidia without the riders seeing us."

Everyone stopped chewing and stared.

"The steps of Jidia," he said.

Gargarin shook his head with disbelief.

"It's a myth."

Froi waved the map in front of his face.

"Not according to this map. We're going to have to take a chance and leave here. The cave is half a mile downstream. If we travel in the dark, in the early hours of the morning, we should be safe."

"I say it's a mistake," Gargarin said. "We could be following a trail that does not exist and end up creating a prison for ourselves in those caves. Starving to death at that."

"Always the optimist," Arjuro muttered.

Later, Froi and the others lay, trying to sleep. All except for Quintana, who still sat upright, fighting to stay awake.

"I dreamed," Quintana said. "Two nights past."

While the others murmured their acknowledgment, as though they had become used to her ramblings, Froi's heart began to hammer in his chest.

"I dream between sleep and wakefulness," Quintana continued indignantly.

"I, for one, would like to have the opportunity to sleep now, so I can dream," Arjuro said, drowsy from the mead.

Gargarin made a sound in agreement, but Froi kept his eyes on Quintana, the light from the flames making her look ghostly, even fragile.

"What did you dream about?" he asked, and he couldn't keep the gruffness from his voice.

Quintana held up a thumb and two fingers, a question in her eyes. It was the identical gesture Lirah had captured and painted on the wall of her prison all those years ago.

Froi crawled out of his bedroll and picked up Gargarin's quill and papers. He tried to get closer to her, but she hissed like the cats he had seen on the streets of the Sarnak capital, protecting their litter from the daggers of hungry men.

"Froi," Lirah warned from her bedroll.

Froi began to draw. "I dreamed of this," he said when he finished the sketch, holding it up. "I dreamed . . ."

He felt his face warming up.

Suddenly the others were wide awake and looking his way.

"You dreamed what?" Gargarin asked "What have you drawn there?"

Froi held it up over the light of the fire.

"I dreamed she was drawing these letters on my body," he mumbled.

He felt four sets of eyes on him, three sets looking at him questioningly. "Didn't you say nothing intimate took place between you two?" Gargarin asked suspiciously.

"Didn't say that at all," Froi said, on the defensive. "What makes you think something did take place between us?"

Arjuro made a rude sound. "It's in your voice, you little snake."

Lirah was looking at Quintana as suspiciously as Gargarin had looked at Froi. "I thought you said he pleaded illness and lack of interest each time," she said.

"Well, he did," Quintana said indignantly. "But on the final night, he was up for swiving and I was reassured once again that the gods had sent him to break the curse."

"We don't use that word, Princess," Gargarin said politely.

"I use it all the time," Arjuro said. "One of my favorite words, actually."

Froi didn't think there'd be any sleep tonight, judging from the idiotic conversation.

"What made you so sure he was sent to break the curse, Quintana?" Lirah asked patiently. "Why not the other last borns?"

"It's written all over him. Have I not said that over and over again, Lirah?" Quintana asked, annoyed.

Froi shuddered. There were too many signs to ignore now. Hamlyn's dream of his son. Quintana's strange words. Rafuel's excitement that day in his prison.

When no one had spoken for a while, he turned to them, giving up the pretense of anyone getting sleep.

"The man whose farm I worked dreamed that his son warned him about someone coming their way with the words of the gods written all over him."

Now he truly had everyone's attention. Gargarin stood and walked to where Lirah was studying Froi's sketch.

"What is it?" Froi asked.

"You've never seen this?" Lirah asked, surprised.

He shook his head, frightened by their scrutiny. Lirah looked at Quintana. "Can we show him?" she asked with a gruff gentleness.

Quintana studied Froi a moment or two before gathering her hair in her fist and turning to reveal her neck. The sign of the last-born girls. Identical to the lettering he had sketched on the parchment. In his dream, she had painted the [illegible] word on his back with strokes that had made his skin feel alive. He had awoken, aroused. Had some kind of sorcery helped her creep into his dream as Isaboe was able to do with Vestie of the Flatlands?

"What does it mean?" Froi asked, his throat feeling as if he had swallowed sand.

Gargarin was studying his face. "It means that perhaps something good came out of Abroi after all," he said quietly.

Froi was shaken awake. In an instant, his hand snaked out and caught the throat of whoever loomed over him. When he saw Gargarin's pale face, he let go, shoving him away. "I could have killed you, idiot!"

"What is it?" Arjuro murmured from his bedroll.

"Come with me," Gargarin said. "Both of you."

Froi looked over to where Quintana sat watching them, the lids of her eyes heavy with fatigue.

Gargarin led Froi and Arjuro to the small entrance and began to crawl through the tunnel into the first cave. They followed him out into the dark.

"The sun is about to rise," Gargarin whispered. "Humor me. Please."

Gargarin's eyes flashed with a fervor that Froi hadn't seen in them before. There was too much strangeness in the air, and he wanted to run from it all. He wanted to follow bonds and plow land. Not believe in a grieving father's dream and a mad girl's ranting.

"Those who are gods' blessed can read the words of the gods when the sun appears." Gargarin said. "It's why Arjuro wakes early and why he sat on the godshouse balcony each morning. He was waiting for a sign to appear on the palace walls."

Arjuro looked away, a bitter expression on his face.

"But perhaps you've been looking in the wrong place, Arjuro. On the night Froi was left with them, the priests of Trist dreamed that the words of a prophecy would appear in the palace. True? I never believed that. I thought they'd appear in any one of the thousands of caves in Charyn, and when I was released, I searched for years and years."

Arjuro's eyes finally met his brother's.

"You should have gone to Paladozza," he said sadly. "At least De Lancey would have given you an easy life."

"Some men aren't born for an easy life, Arjuro. And I'm not out here for regrets and what-ifs."

"Then what are we doing out here?" Arjuro asked.

"Remember the readings of Carapasio?"

"Who?" Froi asked.

"A first-century gossip," Arjuro said. "He bored us to death with his ramblings about life a thousand years ago. I had to read them as part of my godshouse education when I was sixteen."

"He means I read them for him and recited them to the priests who thought I was Arjuro," Gargarin said.

Arjuro looked sheepish. "But I did end up reading them later."

"Where were the words of the gods first written in Charyn?" Gargarin asked his brother.

Arjuro was confused for a moment. "Why do you ask—"

Arjuro stopped, some kind of realization on his face.

"What?" Froi asked, now looking from Arjuro to Gargarin. "Can one of you explain instead of doing that frightening nodding thing where you look too alike?"

"The gods wrote their words on the body of the first oracle. She had pitched her tent, drawing crowds from all over the Citavita with her ability to foretell the future. She had no past and no name, but written all over her were the names of provinces and the rules for living and dying. It's how they find the oracle each generation. An oracle dies, and soon after, a young girl arrives on the doorstep of the godshouse after traveling for days and weeks. No family. No past. Sent by the gods, they say. Except for these last eighteen years."

"And you believe that?" Froi asked.

"Get undressed, Froi," Gargarin said.

"No!" he said, horrified. It was freezing, and if the riders came across them, he'd be unarmed.

The sun began to appear in the sky, and Gargarin snapped his fingers impatiently. Froi grunted, annoyed.

"Trust me," Gargarin hissed.

Froi removed his clothing, grumbling.

"Be careful," Gargarin said, and Froi realized he was speaking to Arjuro. "Don't look straightaway, Ari. Remember what it would do to your eyes when we were children."

Froi had no idea what he was speaking about. He tried to twist his body so he could look over his shoulder to his back. But he saw nothing.

"What's there?" Froi asked, half believing that perhaps words would magically appear. Gargarin forced him still, cold hands on his shoulders. Froi waited, felt the moment the sun entered the cave, welcomed the way the light crept in, caressed his arm, his shoulder, and then all over his body. And still he waited, wanting to believe, not realizing how desperate he was to.

Then he heard the sound. Of pure unadulterated pain. Froi swung around, and Arjuro was bent over, palms to his eyes, writhing in agony. Gargarin was beside him in an instant, but Arjuro pushed him away.

"I can do it. I can do it."

"What's happened?" Froi asked.

"Turn. Turn," Arjuro whispered hoarsely, his eyes weeping blood. Froi shook his head again.

"Turn, I say."

Froi swung around, his heart hammering, sweat pouring from a body that seemed on fire, and still he heard the gasps coming from Arjuro.

"He's in pain," Froi argued. "This isn't right."

"If I speak it aloud, are you still able to write it down?" Arjuro asked Gargarin, his voice broken.

Gargarin was staring at Froi, stunned. It was as though he were seeing him for the first time. "Stay still," Gargarin said, almost reverently. "Speak it, Arjuro. We will decipher it together later."

Arjuro spoke, and Froi heard words from a strange tongue. Not of Sarnak or Lumatere or Charyn. A tongue, not quite human, spoken from a voice so torn that it made him sick to think of the pain. Gargarin scribbled down his words with twisted fingers, sometimes asking Arjuro to repeat a word.

When Arjuro was finished, Froi dressed quickly while Gargarin pulled Arjuro to his feet, trying to hold his brother up with his own feeble body. Froi pushed him gently out of the way, placing Arjuro's arm around his shoulder.

A startled Lirah was on her feet the moment they entered their nook.

"What happened?" she asked, helping Froi lay Arjuro down. His eyes were red raw and still weeping blood.

Gargarin tipped the mead into the cloth of his shirt and wiped Arjuro's face clean and Froi saw tears in the priestling's eyes.

"I thought they had forsaken me," Arjuro whispered.

And Froi could see that Arjuro was crying with joy.

For the next two days, Gargarin and Arjuro sat with their heads together, scribbling, arguing, writing. Froi was used to their silence together, but not this. There were times when he saw the power of the brothers combined and understood what it was that made them so desired in the godshouse and the palace. He came to understand the difference between the gods' blessed and a smart man. His uncle was one. His father the other.

Later that night, Gargarin shook him awake. "We've got to remove her from danger," he whispered. "I don't know what she is . . . what you both are, but if I'm going to believe anything in this damned life of mine, it's that the gods sent you to cure this wretched kingdom."

Froi sat up and retrieved the map from his pack.

"Then we do this my way," he said. "We take the steps to Jidia."

Early the next morning, before the sun rose, they left their hiding place and traveled upstream to the cave that would lead them to Jidia. As they passed the camp of riders, Froi could see two on guard. He made a signal toward the others, and they stayed low behind two fallen logs while Froi stealthily climbed the closest tree. Once up high, he shot three bolts from the crossbow into undergrowth on the other side of the stream. Alerted to the sound, the two riders made their way across the water. The moment the men were out of sight, Froi leaped down and led the others away.

Inside the caves, they traveled for most of the day, Froi forced to stop time and time again, searching for the next instruction on the map. When he stopped for the umpteenth time, Arjuro took the map from his hands and studied it a moment before handing it back and leading the way. At first Froi was irritated. There were no secret symbols or ancient words that needed to be deciphered. But then he realized Arjuro had an extraordinary ability to recall what he had studied only once. The priestling never looked at the map again.

"Don't ask me to explain it," Gargarin said quietly. The cave had narrowed, and they were now walking one behind the other.

"Perhaps it comes with being gods' blessed," Gargarin said. "When we were younger, he could read a book and memorize every page, regardless of its size."

"Then why did you sit for Arjuro's exam when he would have had a better chance of remembering every detail?" Froi asked.

"The gods' blessed might have genius," Gargarin said, "but that doesn't stop them from being lazy."

In front of him, Quintana stumbled. With no sleep, little food, and fatigue beyond anything he had seen in her yet, she had trudged most of the day.

"Not long now," Lirah reassured her, despite the fact that they had no idea how long it would be.

"I can carry you," Froi said quietly.

He heard a low growl come from Quintana.

"I think that means no," Arjuro said.

There were one thousand, three hundred, and twenty-three steps to Jidia. They were narrow and steep, with nothing but dents in the stone, molded by shoulders pressed into the smothering walls over thousands of years. Arjuro's oil lamp extinguished, and it was pure darkness, the type of darkness to conjure up evil. On the steps of Jidia, there was no place to root. No space above their heads. No room for one foot to stand alongside another. No end in sight. Three years training to be the most powerful warrior in the kingdom and nothing had prepared Froi for this.

But it was Arjuro who stopped, trapping all of them behind him. His breath was ragged. Not the sound of weariness but of being choked of air, because hideous memories could swallow a man whole. And suddenly Froi was trapped someplace else. In a past so painful. A hand pressing his head down into the folds of a filthy straw mattress. He wanted to fight whoever it was. Had always tried, but he wasn't strong enough. *Because he's just a boy and he's so small and when he grows up, he'll learn how to fight and he'll learn how to kill, but for now he just wants to breathe!*

"Blessed Arjuro, I'm very tired," Quintana said indignantly, with only the sound of their ragged gasps surrounding them. Froi thought he would beat the others out of the way, if only he could move and breathe. So he counted in every language he knew, took gulps of air that was still and stale, attempted everything he could to crush the thoughts that ran through his head. That he would die on these steps. He'd die, because he was weak and pathetic and too scrawny to protect anyone, let alone himself. He was nothing.

"Arjuro!"

Lirah's voice was loud and firm. On Froi's shoulder, he felt a gentle hand. Gargarin's. As though he knew that it was not only Arjuro who was suffering in this darkness.

"You're not there, Arjuro," Lirah said. "You're here. Where he can't hurt you. You're safe!"

And all Froi could feel was Gargarin's hand and all he could hear was Arjuro's breath begin to even and all he could see was

Lirah two steps before him. Lirah, who knew Gargarin's worst nightmares and in knowing his, she knew Arjuro's.

You're not there, Froi. You're here. You're safe.

And they continued to climb.

The steps to Jidia didn't quite lead to Jidia. They led to another cave, where they chose to rest for the night. Gargarin lay out the last of the twigs and reeds, and they huddled around the meager fire, sharing what was left of their bread crust and cheese rind. It was some time before anyone spoke.

Later, Gargarin and Arjuro sat apart from the others, deciphering the words from the gods. Gargarin would show Arjuro the parchment, and most times Arjuro would disagree.

"I think that's the language of the godshouse of Ariadinay and this comes from the godshouse of Trist," Arjuro said, pointing to the words. "Different gods trying to break the curse."

Quintana would look up from where her head lay on Lirah's lap. Tonight she was pure Aunt Mawfa. Froi could have sworn he saw her place the back of her hand across her brow.

"Why don't they just ask me, Lirah?" she asked. "I can tell them what it says."

"Because they're idiots," Lirah replied.

Arjuro scribbled down more words and showed Gargarin, who shook his head. They had been secretive in their work, and Froi knew that they would reveal little until they were confident.

"You're wrong," Gargarin said.

Froi sighed. It meant another exchange. The last had almost resulted in a slapping sort of fight over parchment and quill that was horrifying. Froi tried not to imagine the humiliation of Trevanion and Perri witnessing it.

"Who's gods' blessed?" Arjuro snapped. "You or me?"

"Oh, that is stooping low," Gargarin retorted. "Being able to read the words written by the gods themselves means nothing if you haven't studied the different interpretations. If you hadn't wasted most of your youth inhaling the reed of retribution and swiving De Lancey, you'd probably know a thing or two today."

"I'm quite intrigued by the reed of retribution," Froi murmured from his bedroll.

"It made them both stupid," Lirah said. "They loved nothing more than stripping naked and reciting very bad poetry with an adoring De Lancey looking on."

Arjuro and Gargarin exchanged stares of such incredulity that it almost had Froi laughing. Even Quintana lifted herself to see their reaction.

"Artesimist? Bad poetry?" Arjuro asked.

"You're a disgrace to Serker, Lirah," Gargarin muttered. "Artesimist was the greatest poet of all time."

It was hours later when Froi sensed that they were finished. It was in their hushed whispering and stolen glances at Quintana. Their expressions were slightly manic and strangely euphoric, despite the day's harrowing journey.

Quintana watched them watch her, and all three waited for another to speak.

"What is it you want to know?" she finally asked.

"What you saw written?"

"On the assassin?" she asked.

Gargarin glanced over at Froi, a ghost of a smile on his face. Froi bit back his anger.

"You've worked it all out?" she asked.

Gargarin nodded. "Well, not just me, of course. Arjuro helped."

"Then why do you ask what I see written on the assassin's back when Arjuro has witnessed the words himself?"

Gargarin was silent.

"Ah," she said, nodding, "You're testing me. You want to hear it from me first, in case you think I'm influenced by your words."

"Perhaps we're testing ourselves," Arjuro said. Even after a day or two, his eyes were bloodshot and swollen from having read the words of the gods in their purest form.

Quintana tilted her head, studying Arjuro's face.

"It doesn't hurt so much to read if you go like this," she explained, squinting fiercely. Froi heard Arjuro chuckle.

"Wish I had been told that long ago," he said.

This time it was Quintana who was silent.

"What did you see written, Princess?" Gargarin asked again.

She looked up at Lirah, who nodded with encouragement.

"The one who reigns must die

At the hands of she born last,

And the last will make the first

When the bastard twins are one,

And blessed be the newborn king,

For Charyn will be barren no more."

Arjuro and Gargarin let out ragged breaths in unison. Gargarin placed his head in his hands.

"I didn't know you were bastard twins," Froi said, confused.

"We're not," Arjuro said. "You are."

"What?" Froi was on his feet, staring at Quintana, horrified. "We're twins?"

"Calm yourself," Arjuro said condescendingly. "The princess is the bastard child of the oracle and the king. You're the bastard child of these two. Born almost at the same moment in the same palace."

Froi was still confused. "I don't understand what it means by 'when the bastard twins are one.'"

"And if you don't understand it, fool, I'm not explaining it to you," Arjuro said.

"Joined," Gargarin explained instead. "*Joined*," he added, for emphasis.

"Oh," Froi said, his face flaming again. "You mean when we . . ."

"Swived," Quintana said. "I do remember the exact moment when we became one, because I—"

"No need for detail, Quintana," Lirah said. "Remember what I told you. If you talk of such things, you'll only be judged by strangers."

The atmosphere in the cave changed the moment Quintana did. Her stare toward Lirah was bitter. Froi could see that the others were uncomfortable with this Quintana. They liked the indignant princess, and she knew it.

"We're judged by strangers now, Lirah," Quintana said coldly.

Arjuro moved closer to her. "May I?" he asked. She nodded, and he sat before her. "Do you know where she is?" he asked quietly.

He was speaking of his beloved oracle.

"When I was a child, I told Lirah that I knew a way to see my mother and for Lirah to see her beloved boy waiting for us in the lake of the half dead. So I ordered Lirah to cut our wrists in the tub."

"Gods," Gargarin muttered. Lirah looked away, the memory so painful.

"But Lirah saw nothing and came back half mad, so they placed her in the tower."

"And you?" Arjuro asked, hopeful. "You saw the oracle?"

Quintana looked up at him and shook her head.

"No. She never reached the other side. Sir Gargarin told us

that he didn't know her name, so how could she find her way?"

Her eyes stayed on Arjuro. "But we sensed a part of her across the *gravina,* blessed Arjuro."

"Is that why you wanted to throw yourself in?" Arjuro asked. "So you could be with her?"

"Throw ourselves in?" she asked, astonished. "Why would you think such a thing? We wanted to enter the godshouse. We sensed our mother's happiness there. Her scent. Her voice. It's where she dreamed, and those dreams still hovered in the air. We tried over and over again to speak to you about allowing us in, but you didn't seem to hear us. Sometimes, we'd try to get as close as possible to the godshouse across the *gravina,* but we were afraid to leap."

Arjuro looked down, shamed.

"But when I visited the lake of the half dead that time with Lirah, we did return with a spirit. I didn't realize who that was until you told us the story of our day of weeping, Sir Gargarin."

She didn't speak, and they all waited, desperate for more answers.

"Princess?" Gargarin prodded gently.

Froi recognized it clearly. There was talk in her head. He recognized it in the way her face twitched and flinched. She mouthed words, but they heard nothing.

Lirah reached out a hand to touch Quintana's mouth.

"Don't let this kingdom turn you into a voiceless fool, brave girl," she said. "Speak."

Quintana's eyes refused to meet any of theirs. Was it her madness that she was trying to conceal?

"One of us returned," she whispered, "with the spirit of the sister who died."

Froi saw his own confusion reflected on Gargarin's and Lirah's faces. But not Arjuro's.

"Which of you is Quintana, and which one is the sister?" the priestling asked.

She shook her head.

"I don't know anymore," she said. "I don't know who I am without her, and she doesn't know who she is without me. We don't know who came first. All we know is that we share . . . we share . . ." She leaned forward to whisper. "We share the one who may have cursed the kingdom. Lirah says they called us the little savage in the years before she drowned us and that everyone approved of who came back from the dead, because we were tamed."

Arjuro was entranced with the story. "Go on," he said, with a reverence Froi had never imagined he would possess for anyone, let alone the daughter of a hated king.

Quintana thought for a moment. "We came back with the words I wrote on the chamber wall. That the last will make the first. And I waited all these years for the one to plant the seed and sire the curse breaker and future king." Her eyes met Froi's over Arjuro's shoulder. "He arrived in the form of an assassin from an enemy kingdom. When I woke up that next morning after he had planted the seed, I knew that the king had to die."

Let her be a madwoman, Froi prayed. *Let her be mad.*

"Do you honestly think that I would bring a child into that palace after everything my father allowed to happen to me?"

"Smart girl, my love," Lirah said.

"I tried to tell the street lords in the Citavita that day of the hanging. But no one would believe me. Except for Tariq and the people of Lascow. It was his idea that we wed. He said it would protect my son's right to the throne even more."

She looked up at Gargarin. "I'm the queen of Charyn, sir. A powerless queen except for what I carry in my belly. In less than seven months time, I'll give birth to the little king. Tariq said you, sir, are to be my son's First Adviser. Until then, he's mine to protect, and whatever part I took in cursing Charyn at my birth will not compare to what I'll do if anyone attempts to destroy me before then."

She directed those words at Froi with venomous certainty.

He couldn't think, and he needed to count because Froi's bond to Lumatere was that he'd destroy anything that was a threat to his kingdom. She was a threat. The child she carried was a threat. His child. His seed.

In an instant, he shoved the others aside and was there before her, dagger in hand.

"Use it!" he hissed, grabbing her hand and closing it around the handle of the dagger. He pressed the blade against his throat. "If I'm a threat, use it the way I taught you."

"Froi?" Gargarin barked. Lirah and Arjuro tried to drag him away, but he shoved free of them, a wild animal.

"Do it," he whispered hoarsely, his face close to Quintana's. "Do it if you fear me!"

She bared her teeth, pressing the blade against his throat, a flicker of victory in her eyes.

"Froi! Enough," Lirah cried. "She'll do it. You know she will."

Both Froi and Quintana pressed harder until he felt the skin tear, the blood trickle. *"Do it!"*

At that moment, she looked so destroyed that Froi wanted to put her out of her misery and slice his own throat. He had done this to her.

She broke, dropped the dagger, and pushed him with all her might, but Froi held her as she struggled against him, a wild cat in his arms, her hoarse screams muffled against him. He kept his arms trapped around her, his mouth to her ear.

"You will not fear me," he said, speaking his bond to her. It was the only bond that would count from now on. "If I tell you to run, you run. If I tell you to hide, you hide. If I tell you to kill, you kill."

And then the fight left Quintana and Froi carried her to his bedroll near the fire, where they wrapped her in blankets, all of them, with hands that trembled with truth.

The last will make the first.

Froi lay against her, and Quintana's body heaved with fatigue and fear and a desperate need to protect what lay inside of her. She was Hamlyn's wife Arna, a she-wolf who wanted to protect her babe. His arms were a band around her as she faced away from him, but after a while, he heard the evenness of her breathing and prayed that she slept. Instead, she reached behind and took his hand, holding it up to the dwindling light of the fire, playing with his fingers. On the wall he saw the shape of a rabbit, and he pressed his chin against her shoulder as they watched their fingers dance across the contours of the cave.

And for hours and hours she slept, but no one else could. After so many years of living in a barren kingdom, they could hardly comprehend what this news would bring. Every sound seemed a threat to Quintana. A threat to Charyn.

"Everything changes," Gargarin said quietly. "Everything."

And when she woke more than a day later, the crazed stare of sleeplessness removed from her eyes, Froi watched her. Waited to see who they would be facing. But the eyes weren't cold and they weren't savage, so he sighed with relief.

"You call me Froi. Not assassin. Do you hear?"

She nodded.

"You may call me Quintana."

CHAPTER 29

The province of Jidia was situated above a deep underground spring with waters said to be warmed by the breath of the sun god thousands of years ago. The spring drew those from all corners of Charyn for the cures it promised and the cleansing it provided. The province also boasted the most amount of rainfall, with fields rich and fertile. Protected by a high stone wall, it had thwarted most attempts by the palace over the centuries to become the kingdom's capital.

"Arjuro spent a year here studying the water's healing power," Gargarin said as they approached the two guards at the province gates.

It was always Gargarin who spoke of Arjuro's gifts as a physician and healer, while Arjuro made rude sounds.

"No interest to me these days," the priestling muttered.

"Then why did you grow your herbs and plants on the godshouse roof?" Lirah asked tartly.

"And save the seedlings?" Froi added, remembering their last days in the Citavita, when they had retrieved plant roots and seeds that Arjuro later hid in a cavern at the base of the godshouse.

Arjuro muttered some more. These past days of travel through the caves, Froi had begun to notice that Arjuro's hands shook at times. Some days he was so bad-tempered it was unbearable. Gargarin usually bore the brunt of his anger and made things worse by being oblivious to Arjuro's moods. Froi knew the priestling craved the brew that had been a companion to him all these years. He had seen how vicious a man could become without it.

Their plan for Jidia was simple. Too simple, in Froi's eyes. Gargarin would ask for an audience with Provincara Orlanda and request province protection on the queen's behalf. Despite its simplicity, Froi did not protest. They were all looking forward to sleeping in proper cots and filling their bellies with whatever the province had to offer.

"The *provincara*'s kitchen speciality is a lamb stew that is second to none," Gargarin said.

"And if she refuses to see us?" Lirah asked.

"The *provincara* will see us for certain, Lirah," Quintana said. "She fawned all over Sir Gargarin in the palace."

"She fawned all over Bestiano equally and most probably succeeded in finding a place in his bed that night, so caution is required," Gargarin said in his usual practical tone.

"Fawned?" Arjuro asked.

"Like this, Brother Arjuro," Quintana said, pressing her chest against him. Through her perfect mimicry, she reminded Froi exactly of the *provincara*. She was back to being Princess Indignant. A relief after days with the cold Quintana, who, despite their truce, couldn't resist a snarl or two any time he came near. He had refused to sleep anywhere but by her side, dagger in his hand at all times. Most nights he wanted to reach out and touch her, wanted to speak the words that no one had dared to speak. That what grew inside of her belonged to him. He had no idea what that meant. All he knew was that he would kill to protect Quintana and she would kill to protect the child.

At the gates, two guards asked for their papers.

"We've come from the Citavita. Not much time to collect things like that," Gargarin said. "We'll be waiting at the godshouse baths. Could you send a message to the *provincara* to find us there? Tell her it's Gargarin of Abroi who asks."

The guard shook his head. "The *provincara* is a busy woman," he said dismissively. "And you don't enter without papers."

The second guard approached and whispered into the first man's ear. Both looked at Quintana, who stared back at them. Froi stiffened, stepped beside her. He didn't want to imagine what would happen if Quintana began to make savage mewing sounds when the guard or any other stepped too close. Both guards studied Froi, and he unclenched the fist at his side. Gargarin's instruction had been to keep out of trouble's way and not draw attention. The second guard continued to stare, but then he nodded.

"The godshouse baths," the man acknowledged. "The *provincara* will send for you there."

At first Froi thought Gargarin had made a mistake and led them into the *provincara*'s compound and not a godshouse. He had never seen a more opulent place of worship. His experience had been Arjuro's home or the priest-king's cottage. But here in Jidia, the godshouse was almost the size of a Flatland village. Outside there were gardens, olive groves, and an amphitheater that could easily seat thousands. Inside there were steam rooms and baths and chambers with private altars where wealthy Jidians would make sacrifices to the goddess of the elements. In Lumatere, sacrifices to the goddess were never of animal flesh and blood, but here in Charyn, flames and animal flesh were the perfect beacon for the gods. It was why they burned their dead and refused to bury them in the ground. So the gods could follow the light and song to take a spirit home.

In the foyer, minstrels played while attendants rushed around with linens and floral-scented soap, serving teas and sweet cakes. In the alcoves, Froi could see lively discussions between patrons while others played board games or disappeared into the rooms that housed the sacred baths.

In one of the nooks, where they waited for the *provincara* to make her appearance, Gargarin spoke about the springs. Froi pretended not to listen, and Quintana walked away, to look in the different rooms. Lirah listened, though. Froi thought of her prison with its books and her drawings. Who would Lirah have been if they hadn't sold her to the palace at the age of thirteen? Perhaps not a rich man's wife, but certainly the wife of a smart man. Gargarin sketched her a diagram, his twisted hands precise, and Froi had his first glimpse of how things would have been between the two of them. Lirah liked facts, and Gargarin enjoyed explaining them. For this time alone, they seemed to forget their troubled history. Despite his pretense, Froi learned how rainwater fell on the hills outside the province walls hundreds of years ago.

"It seeped through the stone thousands of feet beneath us, where natural heat raised the temperature and the heated water rose to the surface crevices and cracks, and then up through the stone," Gargarin explained. Any talk of water excited Gargarin.

"De Lancey brought me here when I was released from the Citavita," he continued. "Soaking in that water, it was as though I died and went to the heavens."

"Did he make believe you were me?" Arjuro sneered.

There was a strained silence.

"You're speaking out of line, brother," Gargarin warned quietly.

"Are we not copies of each other? It would matter little to those who take us as lovers."

"It would have mattered to me," Lirah said. Any truce between the two had disappeared during Arjuro's mood of the last days.

"I wouldn't have thought any lover in your bed made a difference to you, Lirah."

Lirah stared at him with hatred in her eyes. "Not my bed. Never my bed. I don't own one, priestling. I've not owned one all my life."

"You would never have told us apart in those days, I tell you," Arjuro said. "You could have shared my bed and not known the difference, Lirah."

"Enough," Gargarin said, and Froi saw fury. "We no longer live in those days. You and I don't have the same bruises and broken bones, Arjuro. They are all mine."

There was much left unsaid in Gargarin's words. *All mine but meant for you,* Froi imagined him saying.

Arjuro walked toward one of the smaller shrine rooms.

"You cannot present yourself to the gods in that state with such a stench," Gargarin called out after him.

Arjuro dismissed him with a wave of his hand. "No soak can cleanse the filth from our hearts and minds, can it, Gargarin?"

There were no more lessons after that. Just a strained silence until a godshouse guardian approached and led Quintana and Lirah to the women's baths and Gargarin and Froi to those of the men. Froi was cautious. Quintana hadn't been out of his sight since his return to the caves, and he trusted her with no one. More than anything, the godshouse guardians seemed more like the *provincara*'s Guard.

"She'll be safe enough," Gargarin said. "It's a sacred place, and if there is one thing the Jidians won't do, it's sacrifice the peace they have enjoyed here for centuries."

Froi paid his coin and followed Gargarin into the bathhouse. It was hazy with steam, its walls carpeted with moss and ferns. Gargarin stepped into the hot water, and Froi followed, shocked at the state of Gargarin's body, his rib cage and shoulder blades protruding. Faded bruises from his beating at the hands of the street lords adorned his back and chest. Froi saw the strange twist in his arm where two bones had poorly mended years before.

Settling beside him, Froi couldn't help comparing himself to this man who was his father. Even in good health there would have been little resemblance between them.

"Those from Serker resembled bull terriers," Gargarin said, turning to Froi as if he could read his mind.

Froi looked away. "How come Lirah doesn't?"

"Because when the gods made Lirah, they broke the mold."

Gargarin closed his eyes, surrendering to the water.

"If the water is so comforting, why not settle in Jidia?" Froi asked.

Gargarin opened one eye. "Orlanda likes to own those who answer to her, body and soul. It would tire me out."

Froi found himself grinning, and Gargarin flinched. Could Froi not even own his gestures without reminding the brothers of their barbaric father?

Suddenly there was a shout and a commotion and a scream or two. Gargarin and Froi exchanged a look.

"You don't think—?"

"Whore!"

Froi quickly clambered out of the water and grabbed a cloth from an attendant, wrapping it around his waist before slipping and sliding across the wet floor toward the female bathhouse.

Screams of outrage accompanied his entry, and he stepped back outside, waiting. By the time Gargarin caught up, trying to secure his cloth, Lirah was being dragged out by a guard with Quintana in tow. Both were still fully dressed. Behind them, Froi recognized Provincara Orlanda hissing with fury and being fussed over by her attendants. When she saw Gargarin, she instantly regained her composure.

"Gargarin, dear friend," she managed to say through gritted teeth.

"Orlanda." Gargarin stared from Lirah to Quintana. "Has there been an issue?"

"There's been issue, indeed," Orlanda seethed. "Follow."

Lirah shrugged free of the guard viciously, and they followed the *provincara* and Gargarin to a small private praying room.

The *provincara* dismissed her guard and attendant and closed the door behind them.

"There is a stable beside the inn, close to the wall gates. You would have passed it on your way here. It's where you are to shelter for the night."

"A stable?" Gargarin questioned. "Orlanda, I'm traveling with Quintana of Charyn."

"And why would I not know that?" she continued, almost spitting out the words. "I will not have her sanctioned by my house."

Arjuro was shoved into the room by another set of attendants, cursing at the top of his voice.

"We warned her, Sir Gargarin," Quintana said. "Twice. Three times."

Orlanda stared at Quintana with contempt. She pointed to a doorway behind the altar. "That will lead you to the town square. Make sure you're discreet and travel straight to the stable. In my own time I will call for you."

The *provincara* walked out.

"Dressed like this?" Froi called out, looking down at his cloth. "I want my weapons!"

Moments later, unfamiliar clothing was thrown into the room.

"Why would we want to draw attention to ourselves?" Gargarin demanded of Lirah. "What happened to being discreet?"

"It was the *provincara,* Sir Gargarin," Quintana said, turning the other way as the men dressed. Froi waited for Lirah to turn. He wasn't usually so bashful about presenting a bare body to the world, but this was Lirah. She humored him and looked away while Quintana continued to explain.

"She took us to a private room and said she wanted us gone from her sight. *'From my province,'*" she shrilled, mimicking the *provincara*'s outrage.

Froi pulled on a pair of trousers that were small and uncomfortable. He would need to return later to retrieve all their goods.

"I tried to be very polite, sir, but the moment I stepped forward, she pushed me away and spoke words that we won't repeat, will we, Lirah?"

Lirah repeated the words all the same. Even Arjuro flinched.

Gargarin ushered them all toward the doorway that would take them through a passage to the town square. "And I warned her, sir. Three times I warned her, not to press such a fist against me as she shoved."

"And?" Gargarin asked, leading them through the darkness.

"Well, I didn't have a choice but to try to choke the life from her," Quintana explained. "Three times I warned her."

Froi was furious. "Are you both fools?"

"I'm going to have to agree," Gargarin said, seething. "Fools."

"Three warnings?" Froi asked with disbelief. "*Three?* There are to be *no* warnings. If someone touches you again, Quintana, you grab the first thing you can and hurl it at them."

"No. Not exactly what I would suggest," Gargarin said. "It would help if this kingdom didn't see us as a family of savages."

There was silence after that. It was too strange a word for Gargarin to use. *Family.*

It was after midnight that they heard a sound outside the stable door. Froi retrieved his sword and wordlessly instructed the others to stand back.

"Gargarin," he heard a female voice whisper. Froi looked at Gargarin, who nodded.

"Orlanda?"

The door was pushed open, and the *provincara* entered. Beside her were two guards, their eyes searching the room before she ushered them out and shut the door.

"Orlanda, you cannot keep the queen of Charyn in a stable outside the protection of your home," Gargarin said.

"She fancies herself as the queen now, does she?" Orlanda said. "First the princess, then the *reginita,* and now she's the queen."

"She was wed to the heir, Tariq, before Bestiano's men slaughtered him and his entire compound."

Orlanda stared at Quintana. "Why would that fool boy do such a thing?" she asked, not questioning Gargarin's belief that it was Bestiano's men.

"Because in Tariq's eyes it was the only way to protect Quintana. And her child."

The truth was certainly the last thing Froi expected to hear from Gargarin.

The *provincara*'s laugh was bitter and furious. "Gargarin. I've never taken you for a fool. Are we still to believe this lying spawn of a whore?"

Froi watched Gargarin's face, but there was no reaction to

the slur toward Lirah or her description of Quintana. Froi hated his weakness. Trevanion would have smashed a man in the face for such words. Perri would have had him limping.

"Then don't take me for a fool, Orlanda. Take me for the smart man you know me to be and ask yourself why I would believe a story unless I know it to be true."

"I want to see her belly," the *provincara* said, grabbing Quintana by the arm. Although Froi could see no change in Quintana, when he had lain beside her the night before, he had felt the swell in her body.

"If she touches her, I will bite off every one of her fingers," Lirah warned.

Orlanda slapped Lirah hard across the face.

Quintana pushed between them, grabbed the *provincara*'s hand, and placed it under her shift. Froi watched the woman's eyes widen, saw the disbelief and then the flare of hope.

"You can't stay here," she said, her voice hushed. "I can't protect her."

"Bestiano has only fifty or so riders," Gargarin argued. "You have enough in your army to fight them!"

Orlanda shook her head, unable to tear her eyes from Quintana. "Have you not heard, Gargarin? Bestiano is in Nebia. He has secured the confidence of the *provincaro* and has the entire Nebian army at his disposal."

"What?"

Even Lirah and Arjuro were stunned by the news.

"And if they enter my province demanding I hand the princess to them, I cannot sacrifice my people for her."

"You're going to allow another province to align themselves with a man who wants the palace?" Gargarin asked.

"What choice do I have?" she cried. "Do I need to remind you of Serker? Ask anything from me but this."

Gargarin took time to think, and Froi saw a determination in his expression. "When the time comes, I want your army. I want it combined with armies from Paladozza and Sebastabol and Alonso and Desantos."

She nodded, almost relieved to know she would be rid of them. "There's a plague in Desantos. You don't want an army from them."

"But you'll pledge yours."

"Yes. But you need to go. They will know you're here. Those in the godshouse baths who spy for the palace and now for Bestiano saw you and will already be sending word. When the *provincaro* of Nebia and Bestiano come to my gates, I will tell them the truth. That I will not be embroiled in this matter of Quintana of Charyn and that I sent you away. When the time comes and you ask for an army of men, I will honor my pledge to you."

Gargarin nodded. "We'll leave in the morning and we'll need horses."

The *provincara* glanced at Quintana one more time.

"Thank the gods this babe belongs to Tariq of Lascow and not one of the province lads. That would be all we need," she said bitterly. "One province believing they had the seed to break the curse."

She went to leave.

"Orlanda," Gargarin said. "An apology."

She turned and smiled tiredly, but with gratitude. "Not required, dear Gargarin. For old times' sake, I'll forgive you."

"No. An apology to the queen and to her mother."

There was that tone again. The one that demanded so much without him having to raise his voice.

"And who are you to demand an apology on her behalf?" she asked, hurt in her voice.

"It doesn't matter who I am," he said evenly. "But I would hate to have to tell my king in years to come that I stood by and heard words spoken against his mother and his *shalama* and did nothing."

The apology was not quick in coming, but the woman was no fool.

"My apologies, Your Highness," Orlanda said.

"Majesty," Quintana corrected.

"My apologies, Your Majesty." The *provincara* turned to Lirah. "My apologies." She turned back to Gargarin. "My guard at the gate recognized her. Both of them. It's well known throughout the land that the king refused to allow his daughter and whore . . . his daughter and her mother," she corrected herself, "to cut their hair. I'd be careful if I were you. If all is true, we do not want her dead before she births the curse breaker."

But we don't care if she dies after. The words she left unsaid were clear.

After she was gone, there was silence for a while.

"How big is this army?" Froi asked them.

"Big." They all spoke at once.

"If you combine the armies of the other provinces, you can fight them," Froi said.

"They're not Charyn's only problem," Gargarin said tiredly. "The moment the kingdom begins to war with itself, those surrounding us will surely invade. Belegonia and Lumatere have been waiting for the perfect moment."

"Lumatere will not invade."

"They'd be fools not to, and I've never taken your queen and her consort for fools," Gargarin said tiredly. His eyes met Lirah's.

"Cut her hair," he ordered. "She'll be recognized in an instant by anyone who's been to the palace and by anyone who's heard of how long and strange it is."

Quintana started, horrified. "My hair? But Sir Gargarin . . ."

Gargarin walked away to one of the few stalls that didn't accommodate a cow or pig or horse. Quintana followed. "I can cover it with Froi's cap," she cried. "No one will suspect, Sir Gargarin. No one."

"This is not up for discussion. Lirah will cut your hair, and we will travel to Paladozza and try very, *very* hard to keep you alive. You were recognized within seconds in a province that can switch its allegiance at a whim."

Quintana wept. "My father said it was the only thing that was beautiful about me."

"He lied, Your Majesty!"

Cruelty always seemed to stop Quintana's tears. Froi's cruelty had stopped them in Tariq's caves when he told her why he was sent to Charyn. Gargarin's words stemmed them now. Froi knew it was the indignant one who wept and the ice queen who knew how to endure the cruelty. He watched it all play out on her expression until Lirah took her hand and, sending Gargarin a scathing look, led Quintana away.

Froi joined Gargarin where he sat on the bale of hay, studying the maps.

"When do we leave?" Froi asked.

"Early. I want us to get to Paladozza through this mountain pass that becomes a thoroughfare for cattle and goods by midmorning. Then it's a day or two across flatlands."

"And then what?" Arjuro asked, from the stall beside them. "Are we going to travel from province to province, begging them for sanction?"

"De Lancey will take her. He will be pleased with Orlanda's pledge of her men, and he'll organize the rest. If De Lancey succeeds, Quintana will return to the Citavita with a Guard made up of the united provinces and there may be some hope for Charyn yet."

"The *provincara* pledged the men to you, Gargarin," Arjuro argued. "Not De Lancey. Not to another province."

"And what do you propose I do?" Gargarin asked. "March into the Citavita as the captain of the future King's Guard? Do I look the part?"

"Captains don't make the plans," Froi said quietly. "They carry them out. In the absence of a king, a First Man makes all the plans."

"I'm no First Adviser," Gargarin corrected. "I'm just one who doesn't have to be gods' blessed to predict what will happen.

"And what is that?" Froi asked. Arjuro came around to their stall, waiting for Gargarin's response.

"Quintana of Charyn lives only until she births the first," Arjuro said bluntly when Gargarin didn't respond. "It will be the first who is returned to the Citavita, and whoever has him in their possession will rule as regent until the king comes of age. Let us hope that it is not Bestiano for the sake of the child and let us hope it is not a *provincaro* for the sake of the whole kingdom."

"And if it's a girl child?" Froi asked.

"You pray to every god you trust, Froi, that this child is not a girl," Gargarin said. "Because she may end the curse, but they still need a king to rule. This is not Lumatere. They will break Quintana, producing another and then another until it's a male, and if that does not happen, then they will begin on her daughter when she's of age. Do not underestimate Charyn's desire for the heir to come from royal blood, regardless of how they feel about the dead king."

Froi shuddered. "What do you mean she'll live only until she births the first?" he asked.

"If I were Bestiano and I knew the truth, I'd have her tried for the murder of a king. The people of Charyn would accept the ruling. Why care what happens to the princess if they have the heir and curse breaker?"

"And how will they rid themselves of Quintana the last?" Froi spat out the words. "Will they ensure that she dies in childbirth? Will they have some ambitious boy from the dregs of Charyn toss her from the window of a palace to please his master? Wouldn't want her there as a reminder of Charyn's curse, would you?"

Gargarin had proven himself to be a man who rarely lost his temper, but Froi could tell by his clenched fists that he had pushed him to the edge.

"If you do nothing to protect her, I'll take her away."

"Is that a threat?" Gargarin asked.

"No, a promise," Froi said. "You try to stop me, Gargarin. Just try. I'll break every bone in your body. You know I will. I'll take her to Sarnak or even to Sendecane, where no one ever need know who she once was."

"But do you know who will stop you, Froi?" Gargarin said. "She will. Allow her the dignity of being able to save her kingdom."

"Dignity," Froi spat. "You're a coldhearted dog. You tell her there's nothing beautiful about her and you call that dignity."

Gargarin stared up at him coldly. "If that is the way you chose to interpret my words, then there is nothing I can do to change the way you think."

Gargarin walked away. Arjuro was silent, but suddenly he flinched with surprise.

Froi turned to see Lirah, her hair hacked short, her stare toward Gargarin defiant. If anything, her furious work had made her more breathtaking. She was all face, all eyes of a storm, and Froi could not believe he was born from one so beautiful.

Gargarin stared at her coldly, shaking his head with bitter amusement. "I'm not the enemy, Lirah. Save your fury for when we confront Bestiano."

Gargarin pushed past her to the back of the stall, where Quintana sat on the ground with her head in her hands. Her hair was not as short as Lirah's. It rested at her chin, and she resembled one of the pages from the palace of Lumatere.

Froi watched Gargarin sit on the bale of hay before her, clearly uncomfortable. After a while he reached out to lift her chin, but she resisted and kept her eyes cast to the ground.

"It would have been feasible for the gods and oracle to choose another vessel to carry the first, but they chose you, Your Highness. Do you know why?"

Froi winced. He would have begun with an apology. Even he knew that. "No stories or explanations," Finnikin had once told him. "When it comes to women, straight into an apology and you will find the rest of your life bearable." Although Finnikin and Isaboe spent much of their time arguing, Froi still believed it to be sound advice.

Quintana was silent. Froi wondered if she had heard the question.

"Because I'm the king's daughter," she answered after a while. "That's why the gods chose me. Because the royal bloodline is everything. It began with the gods."

"True, but why not Tariq? He was still of royal blood."

"But they did choose Tariq."

"No, Quintana. They didn't. You know that. They chose you and they chose Froi, not Tariq." He glanced at Froi. "I can't say why they chose Froi. I know little of him, despite everything. But I think they chose you because they were watching and saw that not once in this cursed and wretched life of yours have you lost hope or complained."

The *reginita* looked up, indignant. "Oh, I complain all the time, Sir Gargarin. All the time. They must not have been listening close enough," she said, "Once or twice I even threw a rock at one of the frescoes on the palace walls placed there by the gods. *'Who cares if you can draw?'* I shouted. *'Send us some hope.'*"

Gargarin sighed. "But they did send us hope."

She shook her head.

"Do you remember those days they had me chained to your father's desk, believing me to be Arjuro? At first I wanted to hate you. When I believed you to be Lirah's child, I knew in an instant that you were the king's and not mine. You have one or two of his features. But I surprised myself. I lived for those moments when you came into the room with your wonder at the world. 'Good morning, Arjuro,' you would say to me, and although it wasn't my name, and although I was chained to a desk like an animal, you made me feel human."

She raised her eyes, almost shyly. Froi liked the way Quintana's strange face was framed by the hacked length of hair.

"And if someone asked me to paint a picture of joy and hope, I would have painted you. In my eyes, *that* is beauty. Not what your father had to say about your hair."

"You're only saying that to make us feel better."

Gargarin was amused by the idea. "No, not really. I have no idea how to go around making people feel better. Ask Arjuro. He always said I had the ability to walk into a room and make everyone feel instantly worse. And to be honest, I found your hair quite annoying. Too much of it, everywhere. You look much more handsome now."

"But we don't want to look handsome," she cried. "We want to look beautiful."

She touched her hair with regret. Gargarin looked at Froi and then back to Quintana.

"Did you know that the queen of Lumatere's head was bare when Froi first met her?"

Why did he do this? Froi wondered. Make Froi hate him one moment and then change his mind an instant later.

Quintana sat up, suddenly interested.

"Less hair than Lirah's?" she asked, looking over Gargarin's shoulder at Froi.

"Much less," Froi said.

"She must have looked absolutely ridiculous."

"Thankfully I'm drawn to *absolutely* ridiculous-looking girls," Froi said, sitting beside Gargarin before her. He saw a flash in her eyes. Their irises were tinged with yellow today. He had lost count of how many times their color had changed.

"Lirah said my father would never let her cut her hair and that it was just a different type of shackle. Isn't that strange, Sir Gargarin? That her beauty was her downfall and my plainness is mine."

"You're just fishing for compliments," Froi said, annoyed.

"You said I was plain," she said, pursing her lips. "I heard you on the balconette."

"Princess—"

"Queen," she corrected.

He leaned forward, his mouth close to her ear.

"Quintana," he said instead. "You haven't been plain since I saw those teeth."

Later, Froi made sure the stables were secure and walked back into the godshouse baths the way they had come through the underground passage.

Inside there was no one, and Froi went into the room where they had undressed and found their clothing. He retrieved his dagger and short sword and placed the pack on his back. In the adjoining bath chamber, he heard a sound and walked to the door. Torches illuminated the space, giving it a ghostly hue in this light. From where he stood, he was surprised to see Arjuro in the water, his bony body even paler than Gargarin's.

Froi approached and was about to call his name when he saw the true horror of what Arjuro's long black robes concealed. The priestling's back was a mess of puckered white flesh. It was as if someone had torn strips from every part of him. Worse was what lay scorched across Arjuro's pale shoulders.

It was the Charyn word for *traitor*.

CHAPTER 30

"Lady Beatriss," Beatriss heard Tarah say gently from the door of her chamber. "Lady Beatriss, you have a guest."

Tarah came to the bed and removed the blanket from around Beatriss and began laying out some clothing.

"Tell them I'm not myself today, Tarah," Beatriss murmured.

It was what Tarah had told anyone who came to the house for the past week.

"But Lady Beatriss, it's the queen."

Beatriss did the best she could to look presentable, but nothing could be done about her limp hair and dull complexion. Tarah had chosen her favorite calico dress, but these days she resembled a scarecrow in it.

Beatriss was even more shamed to see the queen sitting in her kitchen.

"Come into the solar, my queen," she said quietly. "My apologies that I was not here to meet you at the door."

The queen embraced her, pressing a kiss to her cheek, and dismissed the idea of another room with the wave of a hand. "And when did you stop calling me Isaboe?"

Outside her kitchen window, Beatriss could see the Queen's Guard, scattered to ensure Isaboe's safety. Those who knew the land were running their fingers through dry dirt, shaking their heads.

"I can only stay awhile," Isaboe said. "I have to get back to feed Jasmina."

"Perhaps a mug of buttermilk and honey," Beatriss said, making herself busy. "It's Vestie's favorite when the weather becomes cooler. I'm afraid it will be a short autumn, and next thing you know, we'll all be confined indoors because of the cold."

Despite her ridiculous chatter about weather and her refusal to look at the queen, Beatriss felt the younger girl's eyes on her. When it was difficult to ignore her any longer, she turned to face Isaboe.

"Why do you look at me in such a way?" she asked huskily.

"Because I'm worried for you, Beatriss," Isaboe said, not one to play with words. "So is Abian, but she says you won't see her. And we don't want to write to Tesadora. You'll only end up living in that cursed valley, like every other woman or girl who comes in contact with her."

They both managed a smile. "I miss her," Beatriss said, searching for the sweets she had hidden from Vestie. "It's an ache I feel. Who would have thought that Tesadora and I would form such a friendship?"

She placed the mug and sweets before the queen and sat opposite, fighting to keep back the tears. "She gave me purpose."

Isaboe gripped both her hands. "You'll always have purpose, Beatriss."

"It shames me to think highly of those days . . . those awful, *awful* days," Beatriss said, tears biting her eyes. "But . . . in the last five years of the curse, I knew who I was for the first time in my life. Not the daughter of a Flatland lord or even the woman loved by the captain of the Guard. I was Beatriss of the Flatlands."

The tears did fall, and Beatriss despised her weakness.

"My people are scattered and miserable, Isaboe. I've failed them. I've failed everyone I love."

The queen stood and led Beatriss to the window, pointing outside to the dead field.

"*That* is not failure, Beatriss. *That* is something beyond your control. Beyond any of our control. That land will not yield, and it's not because of anything you did or didn't do. Perhaps it will never yield, but you cannot stay here in ruin, waiting for that day."

Beatriss shook her head. "I can't leave this place, Isaboe. *I can't.*"

"Why?" Isaboe asked, frustration in her voice. "For pride?"

Pride? Beatriss's pride was long gone. It was smothered by the smugness in the expressions of the Flatland lords. It was shattered by the disappointment in Trevanion's eyes.

"My daughter is buried here," she said quietly, pained to say the words. "Down by the river. I can't leave her spirit alone. I feel her every day, Isaboe. I can't leave her behind."

Beatriss saw a wince of regret in Isaboe's eyes. In exile, the queen had taken the name of Beatriss and Trevanion's first child to keep herself safe. *Evanjalin* had been the name of Trevanion's mother, and Beatriss knew that each time the queen or Finnikin passed through Sennington, they visited the babe's grave. She also knew that Trevanion didn't.

"Forgive me, Beatriss. I beg of you. Idiot that I am," Isaboe said.

"Nothing to forgive."

Isaboe returned to the table, nursing her buttermilk. Once again, Beatriss felt the dark eyes studying her.

"Can I tell you of an idea I have?" the queen said. "I keep

Finnikin awake with ideas, you know. I've been thinking of the tales Rafuel of Sebastabol has told Finnikin about Charyn during his interrogation up in the mountains. Even my idiot cousin Lucian is captivated. Our neighbors had schools of philosophy and art and studied the books of the Ancients. It wasn't only Charyn. Belegonia is a place of learning too. The stories Celie comes back with fill Finnikin and me with envy. We can't begin to think of the way they see us. Backwater cousins."

"We're no such thing," Beatriss said firmly. "Our healers are gifted, taught by Tesadora. They've kept the fever out of this kingdom these past years, and we lose fewer women to birthing now than any other time."

Isaboe shook her head. "But their talents are wasted. I can understand why Japhra followed Tesadora to the valley. It's what you said, Beatriss. It's all about purpose. And look at the priest-king. He manages to see the smartest of our kingdom in his overgrown garden. And for what? Where does a learned man or woman go in Lumatere? To quarry stone? To milk a cow?"

Isaboe looked around the sun-drenched room.

"This place, Beatriss," she said, "this house could be a place of learning. Could you imagine the spirit of the first Evanjalin soaring here?"

Beatriss was stunned by what the queen was suggesting.

"The priest-king's shrine house has gold and they'll pay you well, and I know Augie has said many times he'd buy your southern paddock and we could sell your north paddock to whoever runs Fenton. Your villagers will be taken care of between Sayles and Fenton. Tarah and Samuel, of course, will come with you to the palace to live with us."

"The palace?"

Isaboe nodded emphatically, traces of a smile on her face.

"I'm selfish, Beatriss," she said. "I have a room of men to

help me rule a kingdom, but I need good women to help me raise my children."

A look passed between them. "You're with child," Beatriss said, reaching out to clutch Isaboe's hand.

Isaboe nodded, biting her lip and looking toward the entrance before leaning forward.

"I need help with Jasmina, Beatriss," Isaboe whispered. "Just between you and me, my beloved daughter is the worst-behaved child in Lumatere."

Beatriss laughed.

"No, it's true," Isaboe said. "No one will admit it because they think I'll have them imprisoned or beheaded or whatnot, but Jasmina's tantrums can be heard from the Rock."

"You try to do it all, beloved," Beatriss said. "You can't."

"My mother did," Isaboe said. "She raised five children and helped my father run this kingdom."

Beatriss scoffed gently at the words. "Isaboe, I was there as a companion for your sisters. No one loved the dear queen as I did, but she had help. A lot of help. Your *yata* was with her every second week, as were your aunts. Get those Mont girls off the mountain and into the palace. Some of them are stifled up there. Why do you think they're down in the valley with Tesadora? They would be a delight to have around. And dare I say it, perhaps it's time to remove Jasmina from the breast."

The young queen seemed stricken at the thought.

"You will not lose your bond with her, Isaboe."

Beatriss looked at the queen tenderly. "When Vestie was born, I couldn't feed her. Tesadora found one of the River girls who had just birthed a babe, and later we fed Vestie goat's milk. Can you ever deny the bond I have with my child?"

The queen didn't respond, but Beatriss could see the tears threatening to fall and so she embraced her.

"I was supposed to come here for you," Isaboe said. "Yet you're my strength today, Beatriss."

"Then let's be strength for each other."

There was a knock at the door. Isaboe quickly wiped her eyes and stood, smoothing down her dress. Tarah was there with one of the Guard to take Isaboe back to the palace.

"Will you accompany me home this afternoon?" the queen said. "I'd enjoy more time to talk."

When they reached the palace, Finnikin was arriving on horseback with Sir Topher. Beatriss watched as he kissed his queen and then whispered in her ear.

"Yes, she knows," Isaboe said as Finnikin turned to embrace Beatriss.

"Isaboe's convinced it's a boy with the same certainty that she was convinced Jasmina was a girl," he said to Beatriss.

"Oh, my beloveds," Beatriss said, cupping a hand to both their faces.

"Mercy," Finnikin said, grinning from ear to ear. "We're going to have a bed full of children, and I'll have to holler out to my wife, 'Hello there! It's been a long time since we last spoke!'"

Isaboe laughed. It had been some time since Beatriss had seen the two so relaxed.

"And she doesn't bleed for nine whole months," Finnikin said.

When the queen bled, she walked the sleep of all of Lumatere, and when she walked the sleep, she shared with Finnikin the fears and worries of their people. Vestie walked the sleep with her, and Beatriss remembered how carefree her daughter had been during the time when Isaboe carried Jasmina. The thought lifted her spirits even more.

* * *

Beatriss spent the rest of the afternoon in the main village at the toy-maker's cottage, wanting to buy something special for Vestie. She had decided with Isaboe that it was time for her daughter to come home.

As she walked out of the cottage, she bumped into Genova, the wife of Makli. They ignored each other, and with her head down, Beatriss made her way to the bakery.

"Lady Beatriss," Genova called out.

Beatriss stopped and turned back to the woman.

"I'm sorry about my husband's behavior," the woman said. "I can't speak for my boy because he's a child, but according to Kie, your daughter told him he had the face of a witch's wart, which gave great offense."

Beatriss had heard the term come from Vestie's mouth once or twice. Her daughter had spent too much time with Tesadora, who loved nothing better than teaching Vestie new insults each time they saw each other.

"It's hard for Makli, and that's not to excuse his words at all, but we were in the camp with Lord Selric and his family. In Charyn. It was very fast, the way the plague took them." The woman looked away.

Beatriss walked to her, reaching out a hand to Genova's arm for comfort.

"The children went first and then his wife. The goddess was cruel in that way, for it should never be in that order."

Beatriss nodded.

"One of the last things Lord Selric asked Makli was to ensure that Fenton stayed alive and united. Yet here we are with half of us gone, and in these past three years, no one has dared purchase the village, which is ridiculous, really. Could you imagine Lord Selric preferring that Fenton go to ruin rather than someone else raising it to its glory? I think Makli believes that he failed his lord, and he thinks those of you who were trapped inside don't understand the pain of those in exile."

Genova had a singsong way of speaking, cool and practical.

"The man I love suffered greatly in exile," Beatriss said. "So strong is his pain that it drives us apart. I understand what you went through more than you can imagine."

Genova nodded curtly. "My husband's a good man. He's too proud to say he regrets his words to you, so I'll say it for him."

"And I will speak to Vestie about the witch's wart."

When she returned to Sennington with Vestie by her side, Beatriss looked out at her land and thought of the priest-king and his school and of Tarah and Samuel and Makli and his family and Lord Selric. Two villages, both half of what they once were. But the queen was right. This land was dead, and she and Vestie could not continue dying with it. But could she live in the palace? So close to Trevanion and the memories of what took place there, both the good and the awful? Perhaps she'd be better off in the main village. Some said she had a gift with a needle and thread, and she had a good eye for fabrics. Isaboe had expressed that they were poor country cousins in more ways than one, especially in their dress. "When I see the Belegonians come with their finery and even those tedious Osterians with their fashions, I feel as if they return home and tell others of our dowdiness," the queen had told her on their journey home. But would Beatriss feel stifled in the palace village without the Flatlands surrounding her?

Traveling toward them was the priest-king on his donkey and cart, and suddenly Beatriss found herself smiling as Vestie ran toward him, zigzagging from side to side, her arms outstretched as if they were the wings of a bird. Isaboe had said that the priest-king would come visit the moment he got word of Beatriss's acknowledgment of his offer.

Sennington would be a place of learning, guided by a man who had journeyed step by step with their cursed people and managed to find his way again. Beatriss watched as Vestie reached him, and she already felt the spirit of the first Evanjalin soaring alongside them.

CHAPTER 31

Their plans were changed the next morning by Quintana.

"We go over the mountains," she said. "The dying man of Turla is waiting."

The others exchanged a look. When the cold Quintana spoke, there was an uneasiness in them all, even Lirah, who knew her best.

"I say we choose another time for that, Your Highness," Gargarin said in a firm but polite voice. "It will add at least a few days' ride to our journey if we take the mountains to Paladozza and not the underground pass."

"There will be no other time," she said dismissively, looking at Arjuro. "Are you ready, priestling? I have a sense that the gods are leading us there for a reason."

She walked away toward the three horses they had been given, and Froi knew the decision was final.

"I like it better when I'm blessed Arjuro," Arjuro muttered.

With great patience, Gargarin put away the map he had studied all night.

"Let's all agree that we're going to try to get out of Turla with no marriage contracts, no broken bones, and no body parts sacrificed to the gods," he said.

He poked a finger at Froi's shoulder. "And you're going to have to control any need to prove yourself as a man."

"I've never had to prove my worth as a man to people I don't care for."

Gargarin sighed. "Then you've not met a Turlan."

Lirah easily mounted one of the horses, and Froi followed suit, directing it to where Quintana stood. But she wordlessly chose to travel with Lirah, and Froi saw no reason to get on the wrong side of both women today.

"You're going to have to ride with me," he told Gargarin.

"If you're one of those reckless fools with a need for speed, I will travel with Arjuro."

Arjuro's horse had already taken off with little control from its rider, so Gargarin had no other choice but to clumsily climb onto the horse.

"How does our path differ from your plans yesterday?" Froi asked, grabbing Gargarin by the sleeve of his coarse undershirt to secure him on the horse.

"We go over the mountain and not under. It's about a day's ride to the peak."

"You need to hold on tighter," Froi ordered as Lirah and Quintana galloped past them.

"Why?"

"Because I'm one of those reckless fools with a need for speed."

Halfway up the Turlan mountains, Froi knew they were being watched. He pulled at the reins and stopped their horse, looking around at rock, wild tufts of dull brown grass, and little else. Someone who knew how to stay concealed was out there, and Froi was not taking chances. He steered his horse to Quintana and Lirah's, circling them.

"If I say bolt, you head down the mountain," he said quietly to Lirah, who was holding the reins. "Regardless of what she says," he added, his eyes meeting Quintana's.

Arjuro rode up beside them. "This is a mistake," Arjuro said. "There's something strange here, and that's not the coward in me speaking. It's the gods' blessed."

"Which is exactly why we're here, Priestling," Quintana said.

Gargarin made a sound of displeasure. "They've not come down this mountain to speak for themselves for more years than I can remember, Your Majesty," he said. "So they're going to be suspicious of anyone traveling through their land."

"Find me someone in Charyn who is not suspicious," she said. "Come. We're wasting time."

Later that afternoon, they came across a lone cottage, and a hound accompanied them for a stretch before turning back. Froi could see that the peak of the mountain was at least another day's ride and that they would have to stop soon to set up camp. The autumn days were short, and he didn't want them traveling in the dark. Soon after, however, they reached a village, and from where they sat astride their horses, Froi could see views of Jidia below. Depending on the Turlan numbers, any army that chose to ride up that mountain didn't stand a chance.

In an instant, they were joined by one man after another—from cottages, stables, and farther up the mountain—and as Froi had suspected, some of the men had followed them from the mountain below. They were accompanied by their goats and cattle, and even a family of ducks decided to join in. But no women. Froi cared little for the way they stared at Lirah and Quintana. Although there was no trace of the malevolence seen in the Citavitan street lords, the Turlans were ripe with a barely suppressed spirit that unnerved Froi. They were called mountain goats by the rest of the kingdom, and in his entire existence, Froi had never seen men with so much hair sprouting from heads, faces, arms, chests. They were solid, unlike most Charyn men he had come across.

When they dismounted, Gargarin led Froi and the others to what looked like an outdoor ale house. The younger Turlans shoved at Froi as he passed them.

"They're just playing with you," Gargarin said quietly. "Do not react."

"I was never one for playing with others," Froi snarled.

His anger seemed to excite the Turlan lads even more.

A man clothed in calf hide and a fleeced coat approached, his hair long and coarse and fair.

"We're on our way to Paladozza and hoped to beg a place to stay for the night," Gargarin said. Froi was impressed by the lack of fear in his voice and his very practical aim of securing accommodations for them all.

Before another word was spoken, the man walked to Arjuro and backhanded him across the face. Arjuro toppled to the ground, and Froi charged for the Turlan. Instantly, two others grabbed both his arms. Gargarin was at his brother's side, fury in his expression.

"We come in peace and you greet us like the enemy!" he shouted.

The man spoke a strange dialect, and Froi watched Gargarin shake his head in confusion. Arjuro tried to lift himself from the ground.

"We have no one you want," Quintana said. She turned to Gargarin. "That's what he said. 'We have no one you want.'"

Arjuro sat up, wiping blood from his mouth.

"We are searching for the dying man of Turla," Quintana announced coldly.

The man stared, as if noticing her for the first time. He walked toward her and roughly grabbed Quintana's face in his hand. She snarled and bit his hand, and Froi struggled against those holding him back.

"Why travel over the mountain when you can take the pass?" The man spoke in Charyn. He seemed to be the authority in the village. Perhaps even the mountain. His question was directed at Gargarin.

"The girl dreams of the dying man of Turla. That's all we can tell you," Gargarin said with honesty. "My brother is the last priestling of the Citavita godshouse and a physician. It may be that he has a purpose here."

The Turlan leader continued to study Quintana's face. "Is she a last born?" he asked warily. There was silence until Quintana nodded. There was regret on the Turlan's face, and he shook his head.

"We will not protect her, so don't even ask," he said. "We have enough of our own to protect." He stood before Arjuro, who was still on the ground.

"My name is Ariston, and I'm leader of this village," he said. "The first time I saw the dying man of Turla, I was a boy. That was forty-five years ago, and the one thing I remember him shouting was not to trust the men in black robes, for they will take your children." The Turlan's eyes were hard. "We may not have children to speak of, Priest, but if you bring harm to any of my people, I will choke you by the hood of your robe."

Arjuro stared. "The priests would never take a child."

"Are you calling me a liar?" Ariston asked.

"No," Arjuro said. "I'm saying you're mistaken." He looked at Quintana. "Now more than ever, I need to meet this dying man to know the truth."

Ariston of Turla studied them all. "The dying man lives on

the other side of the mountain, half a day's ride from here. I'll lead you there myself soon enough." He turned his attention back to Gargarin. "Your name."

"Gargarin of Abroi."

There was a snicker. One of the Turlans made a sheep sound at the word Abroi. Froi started counting. The moment they let him go, he was going to have to hurt someone.

"And your women?" Lirah asked tersely. "Are they not here to greet us?"

Ariston appraised her with satisfaction.

"At this time each year, the women travel up the mountain before they make a sacrifice to the goddess of winter to protect us through the cold months. They cleanse their spirits, for the goddess will not accept their gifts if they smell of the stench of man."

"A wise goddess indeed," Lirah said. "You have no reason to hold back our lad, so let go of him now."

Ariston gave a signal to his men to let go of Froi.

"Tomorrow we hunt the wild boar to prepare a feast for the women. Your lad there looks strong. It's a privilege that we allow him to join us."

"Joust!" one called out. Another stepped forward to shove Froi back. Another thumped at his own chest twice.

"Our younger men have felt a need to relieve the tension." Ariston laughed.

"Our lad isn't one for fighting," Gargarin said in a dismissive tone.

"Who are you trying to fool, Gargarin of Abroi? Your lad came up this mountain with a fight in his spirit and an eye out for danger."

There was a shrewd, questioning look on Ariston's face. They may have been mountain goats, but they were no fools.

"We might want to keep him for ourselves."

* * *

They weren't quite savage, Froi thought the next day. Just untamed. As though up in these mountains they had become one with the wild. They were coarse, and quick with a bow, and he managed to please them by taking part in the hunt and contributing at least one arrow to the boar they caught. But for all their fierceness and skill, they were vain. Froi had seen peacocks once, and the men of Turla resembled them in the way they strutted. Sometimes, back in Lumatere, Finnikin would imitate the way the Mont lads walked. He'd take off his shirt and pound at his chest, and he'd walk in the same way they had seen birds walk in Yutlind. The queen and Froi would laugh at the sight of his lanky milk-white body. But the Monts had nothing on these men.

Display followed display of their might, yet they never tired of competing or showing off. A joust. Sword challenges. Target practice. Races of speed. Races of endurance. Every sentence spoken between them was a challenge.

That night there was a feast, but still no women. The ale was plentiful, and that made Arjuro happy, at least.

After dinner was wrestling, just in case the men of Turla had not had enough of an opportunity to show their skills and attributes. They had an annoying habit of finding any opportunity to walk around Quintana and Lirah with bare chests and their trousers worn low. Rings pierced their bodies in places that made Froi wince at the thought of the pain inflicted. Lirah did nothing more than roll her eyes with irritation, but Quintana seemed strangely relaxed with the Turlans in a way Froi hadn't seen before. Then one of the younger men decided to carry over a litter of pups to her, and Froi thought Quintana the Indignant was back when she allowed the dogs to lick her face. He'd prefer

Quintana the Indignant to appear right about now. She was an innocent when it came to men. This Quintana understood desire. She had proven it that night they were together. And now, in the way she allowed the Turlan lads to stand so close.

"It's a primitive bond," Arjuro explained. "They're mad. She's mad. Don't try to compete."

"Why would I possibly want to do that?" Froi snapped, eyeing the way her face lit up each time a Turlan spoke to her, young or old. He could see from gestures that one was explaining the rules of wrestling to her, which was ridiculous because there were no rules at all. The young Turlan even dared to place an arm around her shoulders as he pointed at what was taking place in the match. Froi wanted nothing more than to pull the ring on the man's chest through the flesh and cause as much pain as was humanly possible.

After what seemed like an hour of men in bare chests rolling around in dirt, a stocky lad with an abundance of hair came to stand before Froi. He waved two hands toward himself in an invitation to fight.

"A friendly wrestle, perhaps?" Ariston called out from where he sat beside Gargarin.

Gargarin waved the offer away on Froi's behalf.

"Our lad is bashful," he said.

The Turlan who sat beside Quintana heard the words and whispered something in her ear. Froi saw her lip curl in amusement.

He leaped to his feet and removed his shirt.

"The thing is," Arjuro said, rubbing the ointment on Froi's bruised body later that night in the cooper's cottage the five of them shared. "I probably would have stayed down the tenth time the human bear had your head between his thighs."

"Did you not hear me call out to stay down that last time?" Lirah said.

"He's never been one to listen," Gargarin muttered, sitting opposite Lirah at the table, scribbling in his journal. "Deserves all the pain."

Froi closed his eyes, wincing. "I would so appreciate it if everyone refrained from expressing an opinion."

When he opened his eyes again, he felt the force of Quintana's stare.

"There's no shame in losing against the Turlans," she said.

"I didn't lose," he said just as Arjuro finished. Froi got to his feet, really wanting desperately to stay calm. "And you would have known that if you had watched instead of playing with those yappy dogs at the exact moment I snatched victory!"

Quintana's stare continued, but she refrained from speaking.

"And I'll have you know that not once have I lost a fight this year against anyone from the Lumateran Queen's Guard!" he added, sitting next to Lirah, who was trying to remove blood from the trousers he had worn in the wrestle.

"You said they were forty years in age, Froi," Quintana said, irritated. "Can you honestly compare the Turlan lads to the old?"

Arjuro made a rude sound. Even Gargarin looked up from his writing, slightly wounded by her words.

"The younger men would like us both to join them for tale-telling time," she said.

"Wonderful idea," Arjuro said. "Perhaps you can join them, and they can pierce both your bodies with blunt instruments and leave us old and decrepit alone to get some rest."

Quintana turned her stare to Arjuro. After a moment, she smiled. "You're very funny, Priestling. The funniest man we know."

Arjuro was wary of her mood. "What?" he asked. "Funnier than Bestiano? Because I hear he is hilarious."

This time she laughed and then Lirah joined in, and Froi couldn't help laughing himself, although it caused him pain. He caught Gargarin's stare.

Quintana reached out and touched Lirah's mouth and then Froi's.

"When you laugh, you look like your boy, Lirah."

Princess Indignant was back the next morning as they prepared to leave. She spent her time skipping after the hound pups, looking up at Gargarin longingly.

"Are they not the most beautiful pups you've ever seen, Gargarin? It's as if the gods are begging us to take—"

"No," Gargarin said firmly.

Ariston joined them on horseback, and Froi had a feeling it was more about keeping an eye on them than the need to help.

"We missed your women last night, Ariston," Gargarin said smoothly. "Is the goddess of winter keeping them from you?"

"The cleansing takes time," Ariston replied.

Gargarin and Ariston spoke among themselves most of the way up the mountain. From what Froi could hear, it was mostly about produce and irrigation, and it wasn't hard to see that both men were impressed with each other, despite their lack of trust and the very little they had in common.

Froi and the others were quiet for the rest of the way, and he could see that Arjuro was curious about this strange visit to the dying man. No matter how much Arjuro had tried for the last two nights, he had not uncovered the reason for Ariston's warning against the godshouse priests. Froi wondered what had taken place forty-five years ago on an isolated mountain peak to warrant such an accusation.

As Ariston had promised, it was half a day's ride, and Quintana slept against Froi's back most of the way.

"Why is she always tired?" he asked Lirah.

"Because she's making a baby," Lirah said quietly to prevent Ariston from hearing. "In the first few months, when I was carrying mine, I was weary to the bone."

Froi noticed that she said "carrying mine," not "carrying you." Lirah and Gargarin still had not acknowledged him as theirs, and he realized that he wanted more from them than they were willing to give. But they seemed broken people who were not good with words, so he kept his silence.

When they reached a small hut close to the peak of the mountain, Ariston helped Quintana dismount, and once again he grabbed her face, this time more gently, to study her. Lirah exchanged a look with Gargarin, and he shook his head to silence any question from her lips. Although it seemed unlikely that Ariston had ever traveled to the Citavita and seen Quintana before, the Turlan was strangely suspicious of her.

A woman stepped out of the cottage, having heard the horses. She was perhaps sixty in age, her face long and thin. She seemed guarded, until she saw Ariston and greeted him with a nod. But then she noticed Arjuro and her expression changed to hostility.

"Why bring a godshouse priest to my father's house, Ariston?"

"Because I believe these people have a story to tell," he replied.

Arjuro stared at the woman as if he were seeing an apparition.

"What is it you see in me?" she asked angrily.

Arjuro looked beyond her into the open doorway of the cottage.

"I truly feel I can vouch that they mean no harm, Hesta," Ariston said. "I'm curious myself."

The woman, Hesta, walked away and entered the house. Froi

and the others looked at Ariston for guidance. He nodded, and they followed her inside to where a weathered man lay on a cot. Skin and bones, he seemed, with gnarled hands that Quintana reached out to trace with an inquisitive finger.

"He's the oldest man I've ever seen," she said indignantly.

The woman stared at her in amazement.

"Who are you?" Hesta of Turla asked her abruptly.

"R-Regina," Quintana said, but she was an awful liar, because she looked at Gargarin for approval. Froi made a point of rehearsing her with a different name. Not Quintana. Not Reginita. Not anything that would have strangers connecting her to the palace.

"I've dreamed of the dying man of Turla," Quintana said. "Do you call on my dreams, old man?" she asked loudly. Gargarin winced. This was certainly one of the moments where they needed the decorum of the other Quintana.

The old man stared at her through milky eyes tinged with blue. He beckoned her with one of his gnarled hands, and she leaned forward for him to speak against her ear.

"Your whiskers are tickling," she said.

The man chuckled, and Hesta softened.

"My father has been dying for almost nineteen years, yet he refuses to be taken."

"But he seems in so much pain," Arjuro said, lifting the man into a sitting position so he could breathe easier.

"Why would he share his dreams with our girl?" Gargarin asked.

"You need to tell me who she is before I answer that question," the woman said firmly, but Froi could see fierce emotion in her eyes as she stared between her father and Quintana.

"Is he gods' touched?" Arjuro asked.

Hesta shuddered. "I've not heard those words for many

years now. He refused to say them out loud after the godshouse priests came."

They waited and she sighed. "Yes, he is, and I am too, but not enough to make us special." She looked down at her father tenderly. "He was good with his herd. The perfect shepherd."

After too long a bout of silence, Hesta shivered. "You're frightening me."

Gargarin bowed his apology. "My name is Gargarin, and this is my brother, Arjuro; Lirah; and . . . our young ones," Gargarin said. "We have no idea why we are here except our girl has dreamed of your father all her life."

"He wants to die," Quintana announced. "But he's waiting for the spirit of another. That's what he tells me in the dream. He's looking for his lost lamb."

Hesta studied Quintana warily. "Why you?" she asked.

Quintana looked at Gargarin, who sighed, not knowing how much to divulge.

"Let's just say she isn't who she seems."

"Can she not speak for herself? She seems simple."

"I'm like you and your father," Quintana said. "A bit of a gift but not enough to make me special."

There was silence from the others, made uncomfortable by Quintana's frank words.

The woman noticed her father's hand hovering above his blankets and gripped it.

"What can you tell them, Hesta, that may make sense?" Ariston asked.

She shook her head, confused. "What is there to tell?"

Froi walked away in frustration. They were talking in circles and wasting time. Hesta seemed nervous at his movement.

"You've come from the Citavita, haven't you?" she asked

bitterly. "What could we possibly have left for you after all these years?"

"Hesta?" Arjuro said, as though asking her permission to use her name. She nodded. "Can you tell us the story of the priests coming to take away the children?"

She shook her head. "Not the children. One child. A gifted child, beyond anything conceivable. If it was to rain in four days' time, she would say the words, 'In four days time it will rain.' If a man she did not know in a village half a day's ride away was to die soon, she would say it long before the man would die. People came from all over the mountain to hear their future spoken by this child.

"When she was thirteen, the godshouse priests came to see us and asked her questions all the day long, when she only wished to play with her lambs. Oh, the songs she'd sing to bring them home," Hesta said, closing her eyes. "I can still hear them in my sleep."

"What happened to her?" Lirah asked, shivering.

Hesta's eyes were far away, and the dying man held one of her hands.

"They stole her. In the dead of night, the priests stole her. We never saw her again."

Arjuro held a palm to his brow as though he could not quite believe what he was hearing.

"In years to come, they may have covered her face when she walked among the people, but I knew who she was."

Arjuro let out a ragged breath.

"Arjuro?" Gargarin asked.

"The oracle queen was a Turlan mountain girl?" Arjuro said, looking at Hesta for confirmation. "Stolen from her people?"

There was a hushed silence among the others.

Arjuro reached out and touched the woman's face.

"You have some of her features," he said with a gentle smile. "I lived with her in the godshouse of the Citavita. I was a young lad, and she was a fair bit older, but we shared a . . . strange humor. They said I was her favorite."

He pointed to a chair beside the dying man's bed, and she nodded. Arjuro sat.

"I never really quite believed that the oracles were demigods who found their way to the Citavita godshouse," Arjuro said.

"But most people do," Gargarin said. "They need to believe it."

"The last thing they'll want to hear is that she came from the backwaters of Turla," Ariston said, his face pale at what had just been revealed.

"Who were you to her?" Hesta asked Arjuro.

"A priestling. Those of us who were gods' touched lived at the godshouse from when we were sixteen to twenty-five. After that, we could go as we please, live the way we wanted, but during those years, we lived and breathed for the godshouse. We were the voice of the oracle, really. She rarely ventured outside the godshouse walls, and when I think of it now, perhaps she was as much a prisoner to the Citavita as . . ."

Arjuro looked at Lirah. As much a prisoner to the godshouse as Lirah was to the palace. Two young girls taken from their homes at the same age. One to be the king's whore, the other to be oracle to a people.

"As far as we priestlings were concerned, she had always been there. We thought she was ancient, of course. The hubris of the young who think that everyone else is too old or too young." He smiled. "Old and decrepit, and she would have been younger than my brother and I are now."

Arjuro took the old man's hand.

"If what you fear is that she was controlled by the priests who took her, then I will reassure you that the oracle allowed no one, man or woman, to tell her how to think or what to say. Regardless of how she was placed in the godshouse, she had power. We loved nothing more than watching the older priests travel from the provinces and get a serving from her tongue. More than anything, she could not be bought. She could not be convinced to lie. The gift of foretelling, she would say, was not meant to bring on war and nurture greed. It was meant to guide."

Froi could see that Hesta was touched by Arjuro's fierce respect for her sister.

"And the events in the godshouse all those years ago?" she asked. "The carnage?"

"All true, I'm afraid," Arjuro said sadly.

"And she took her life all those months later?"

Arjuro looked at Gargarin.

"No," Gargarin said. "I was with her at her death. She died . . ." he swallowed hard. "She died in childbirth."

Hesta was shocked to hear the words.

"How can that be?" Hesta asked.

"It was . . . nine months after the attack on the godshouse," Arjuro said.

Hesta wept, understanding the truth.

"By who?" she asked, her voice broken. "Was it the Serkers?"

No one spoke for a moment.

"By my father, the king," Quintana said, her voice quiet. "When Lirah and I went searching for my mother's spirit that one time in the lake of the half dead, it was not to be found. But there was another. A second child born dead, who had somehow become separated from our mother, the oracle, in spirit.

Hesta stared at her, stunned. "Your mother?"

A look passed between the two of them, and Hesta shivered.

"She was just the oracle queen to us," Arjuro said. "Blessed, we would call her. At their deaths, Gargarin gave the babe a name. Perhaps it was for that reason Regina of Turla made it to the lake of the half dead to wait for her mother's spirit. But her mother's name was never known, and so the oracle has been lost, except in the dreams of her father and her daughter."

Hesta's eyes were still fixed on Quintana.

"Solange," she said. "My sister's name was Solange."

Quintana looked down at the old man. "He cannot bear the idea of being separated from his daughter in both life and death. He needs to take the spirit of Solange with him, and somehow she sent me to him because he wants to die."

She turned to Arjuro. "Can you do that for him, Arjuro? Now that you know her name. Can you call her spirit home after all these years?"

Arjuro nodded solemnly.

"Leave us," Quintana said to Froi and the others. "I need to speak to my Turlan kin."

Outside, Ariston took a ragged breath.

"Our women are hidden," he said after a while. "Ever since the talk of calamity in the Citavita, we've kept them protected. We long suspected that the oracle came from Turla. If the priests found an oracle among us long ago, then the palace will find a girl to produce the first now. The last thing we wanted were madmen riding into our villages and taking our last borns."

"Do you know what the lettering means, Ariston?" Gargarin asked.

The Turlan shook his head. "We've always believed the mark of the lastborn to be a message from the gods."

"It's not godspeak," Arjuro said. "But it is certainly a message of some sort."

Ariston looked back into the cottage.

"I thought it strange that the girl had some of the features of our Turlan women," he said. "But the despised king's daughter? We are lowly enough in this kingdom without Charynites claiming that the curse maker belongs to us."

"You're never to speak of it," Gargarin said sharply. "Do you hear me? The mystique of the oracle stays as it is. As far as this kingdom is concerned, the oracle was not from Turla and she did not birth the king's child. If a king is born to us in years to come, ignorant men could use that against him."

Ariston nodded, looking back at the old man's cottage.

"Will you come down from this mountain, Ariston?" Gargarin asked. "To fight for Charyn when the time comes?"

Ariston shook his head. "We're Turlans, not Charynites. We fight for no one, only to protect ourselves."

"How can you say that?" Froi shouted angrily. "You practice all day long to be the best, but you can't fight for your people. In Lumatere, no one is prouder of being a Lumateran than a Mont. Why can't you be both?"

"You're a Lumateran?" Ariston asked, surprised.

"Does it matter?" Froi asked.

"Do you know what we say to each other every day, Lumateran?" Ariston asked. "'Remember Serker.' Annihilated by Charynites. They had no one on their side but each other. Mark my words: you will find no province who will fight for Charyn. You don't have to be a mountain goat to know that."

"Would you fight for a king, Ariston?" Gargarin persisted. "For the curse breaker? Would you fight so that your last-born girls need not fear the mark on the back of their necks?"

"I would fight to the death to protect my people on this mountain," Ariston said, glancing at Froi. "You know, they say that the Lumaterans will strike when we least expect it, out of revenge for Charyn's part in their cursed ten years."

Froi shook his head. "They would never attack the innocent."

"Where do you hail from in Lumatere?" he asked suspiciously.

"I was found in exile," Froi said, having no reason to lie to Ariston. "I belong to all of them."

Ariston glanced at the others, as though not knowing what to believe.

"I mean no offense, Gargarin of Abroi, but the sooner you and your companions get off my mountain, the safer I'll feel for my people."

They camped that night under a full moon and a sky crowded with stars that made Froi forget that there was an old man waiting to die and remember that there was a kingdom dying to live.

Quintana hadn't spoken a word since she walked out of the cottage with Hesta. She merely rested her head in Lirah's lap.

"I think it will be soon," she whispered.

And soon it was. Hesta came outside to feed them goat stew, and when she returned to the cottage, the old man had died without her there.

"By his side all these years," she said, weeping, "yet he died alone."

Arjuro stood to follow her and sing his song, calling the spirit of the oracle and her father.

"Arjuro," Quintana said, sitting up. "You must call hers as well."

He nodded. "The oracle queen?"

"No," she said firmly. "Regina of Turla. You need to return her spirit to where it belongs."

Lirah froze. Froi leaped to his feet, shaking his head. "Quintana, what are you saying?"

Gargarin and Arjuro stared at her in anguish.

"We cannot protect this child if we are not whole," Quintana said.

"Arjuro, don't do it!" Lirah said.

"There's nothing wrong with two people living inside of you," Froi said. "You said it yourself. That I have more than one. We all do." He turned to Arjuro. "Sing the old man and the oracle home, Arjuro, and let's leave this place and take the princess to the safety of Paladozza."

But Quintana's eyes stayed on Arjuro. "If you loved my mother, blessed Arjuro, you'll do it. You'll do it for these people. Solange of Turla deserves to be with the spirit of her dead child and perhaps only then can she guide the little king into this world."

Arjuro's eyes filled with tears, shaking his head.

"They crave each other, Arjuro. Mother and daughter. It's why we wanted to enter the godshouse all those times, remember?"

"These gifts are curses," Arjuro cried. "Curses."

Later that night, Froi heard Arjuro's voice waver across the mountain, and under the light of the moon, he saw Gargarin's wonder at the beauty of his song. Close by, Lirah held Quintana in her arms, waiting for Arjuro to sing the name they were dreading to hear.

"Solange of Turla, Argus of Turla, and Regina of Turla."

At the sound of her name, Quintana's cry was hoarse and full of a grief so profound. "Lirah," she cried. "Lirah, I'm dying inside. I'm dying inside without her. Tell him to stop."

Part of Quintana had left this world and Froi knew that part of him was gone as well.

CHAPTER 32

For two days, they rode in silence. Quintana had spoken only once on the morning after the old man's death. She had taken Hesta of Turla's hand in hers.

"You spent your life tending to the dying, kinswoman Hesta," she said. "When my son is born, I'll call for you to come help me take care of the living."

She rode the first day with Lirah, whose own sadness seemed fierce, and there were few words spoken for most of their journey down the mountain.

It was a relief to reach the flat plains of Charyn after the back-breaking days on the steep narrow mountain track. Although there was little to see except brown tufts of grass haphazardly appearing from time to time between the rough and broken earth, Froi could tell that their mood had lifted.

"This is the worst hit area for lack of rain," Gargarin told him. "It's one of the reasons Paladozza is a jewel for those traveling from the capital to the east."

That night, they came across a camp of nomads and exchanged a few copper coins for a meal of sugar beets and barley soup, and a tent to share.

"I'll ride with her tomorrow," Arjuro said as they watched Lirah coax Quintana into eating something. She had curled herself up inside the tent from the moment they had arrived and still had not spoken.

Froi walked to where Lirah was feeding the horses. He reached out toward one of the animals, who tossed its mane, its nostrils flaring.

"My captain is a great lover of horses," he told her. "For his birthday last year, the king and queen found a mighty horse like this after sending the Guard out to search the kingdom high and low."

"The Serker breed is the greatest in the land," Lirah said. "When those from the palace ravaged the province, they kept the horses, and they took them to Lumatere five years later." She pressed her nose against the animal.

"Gargarin once told me the ancient tale of a winged horse sent by the gods to Charyn," she said. "As it fell to earth, its wings were clipped by the branches of a tree in Serker, but its might and beauty stayed. I'd been looking for a reason to love Serker all my life, and there it was with that story."

"You must have been appreciative," Froi said.

"Yes, so appreciative I let him into my bed."

Froi looked back toward the tent, where Gargarin stood watching. He felt awkward listening to any story about Gargarin and Lirah, but he was more frightened by Lirah's silence than her words.

"How did you cross each other's paths in the palace?" he asked.

She stared across the open space, a restlessness to her.

"He liked to please the king," she said quietly. "I was the reward."

"You were Gargarin's whore?" Froi asked flatly.

She sighed. "It's a bit more complicated than that."

"Whenever Gargarin says those words, it means the end of a conversation," he said. Her eyes met his, and then he saw a ghost of a smile on her face.

"He was shamed by the king's offer. 'We can sit and talk,' he told me the first time. I knew the stories of his priestling brother and suspected that Gargarin preferred the company of men in the same way. I told him there was nothing to speak of. I had lived in the palace since I was thirteen, and before that I lived in savage Serker. The only thing I cared to remember from life in Serker was that I loved horses. It was my one indulgence in the palace. Gargarin, as you can probably tell by his riding, didn't care for horses, and that ended our conversation the first night."

She stroked the horse's mane, looking across the plain once more.

"Do you want me to race you?" Froi asked. Lirah was used to a cell and a small garden. He should have known she would crave space. Her eyes, usually so cold and condemning, flashed with excitement, and they both mounted their horses. Lirah was off before he could give the command. She was a good rider, better than him, despite her years of imprisonment. Froi hadn't been on a horse until three years ago, when he met Finnikin and Isaboe on their travels. It was Trevanion who had taught him to ride well, although he and Perri had conceded that Froi was not a natural on a horse. But it was in Froi to be fearless and reckless, so he took more chances with speed and caught up with Lirah.

"The next time Gargarin pleased the king, I was given a history of Serker," she continued, her usual bitter expression replaced with a glow. "He loved to explain things, and in my twenty years of living, no one had ever treated me as anything but a possession. The time after that, he read to me. The times after that, he began to teach me to read. By winter, I could read and write, and by the summer, I knew I was in love with him."

Lirah looked back to where Gargarin still stood in the distance, watching.

"Yet he had not laid a hand on me."

Froi shook his head with disbelief. "Only Gargarin."

She smiled. "Yes, only him. So I seduced him," she said quietly. "All those years a whore, but I had never wanted to seduce a man until then."

She looked at him with a wolfish expression. "Do you know how I did it?"

"Is it going to make me blush?"

"No." She laughed. It transformed her face for a moment, and Froi loved nothing more than knowing he could make Lirah laugh.

"I recited love poetry written by the water god when he was courting the earth goddess. The man had taught me to read, so I rewarded him with words of passion."

Froi waited, wanting more. "What did he do then?"

"He pleased the king every opportunity he could."

Froi couldn't help laughing.

"And we spent that year with Arjuro and De Lancey. They hated me. I hated them. Gargarin loved us all. We all loved Gargarin, and those three lads felt as if nothing evil would ever touch their lives."

The sadness was back there on her face.

"Then the slaughter in the godshouse happened and everything changed. Arjuro was arrested, and Gargarin was inconsolable. Mark my words, he will never ever love anyone as much as his brother, despite everything."

There was no envy in her voice, only regret.

"Gargarin was desperate to find a way to have Arjuro set free and began making plans to take us all to Lumatere."

"Lumatere?" Froi said, surprised.

She nodded. "He said they had good rainfall."

They both exchanged a look and laughed.

"You can imagine what type of strange man he'll be as he grows old," she said.

They made their way back to the nomad camp, and already Froi felt as if he was losing Lirah back to her cold spirit.

"Did Gargarin believe it was his child you carried?" he asked.

"I think he hoped," she said. "But didn't care. It's strange to meet a man who doesn't judge."

She looked at Froi, the hard expression back on her face.

"In light of all our truths, do you wonder how I could imagine that he was a murderer of a blessed woman and a babe?"

"I think the proof was there," Froi said with honesty.

"I knew how much he wanted Arjuro free," she said bitterly. "I knew how much he wanted to take me away from the palace. I thought he sold his soul for it all."

They reached the camp. Gargarin limped toward them.

"Even with his body straight, I can't imagine him standing out," Froi said quietly. "Why love him and not a man with more command?"

She stroked the horse's mane.

"Don't ever underestimate him. He's the most powerful man you'll ever know."

Froi approached Quintana, who was sitting up with her hands wrapped around her knees.

"You're going to have to ride with me now that we're a day

away from Paladozza," he said. "If we have to bolt for our lives, I'm the only one who can protect you."

She nodded, and then her eyes met Froi's. His heart missed a beat. He felt a grief so deep. And a desire so fierce. Up until this moment, he had not known who the true Quintana was. Who they had lost when Arjuro sang his song for Regina of Turla. But now the relief in seeing her cold savage eyes made him feel guilty beyond reckoning.

He helped Quintana mount first, and then he settled himself behind her, his arms cautious around her waist. He could tell that her belly had grown, and he settled his hand flat against it, heard the bloodcurdling snarl in an instant. But Froi refused to remove his hands.

"I pledged that I would never do anything to hurt him," he said. "Or you."

It was some time before her body relaxed against his.

"Does it hurt to have him growing inside?" he asked quietly.

She shook her head, and he could see the nape of her neck.

He traced a finger along the lettering there, but she shrugged him away with a growl. He remembered what the soothsayer had said about the little savage born to the palace. Without the indignant Reginita calming her, Quintana could not control her fury.

"Tell me more about this," he said, his thumb gently caressing the mark. If he was going to protect her, he needed to know everything that made her who she was.

"My father had the female last borns branded," she said. "His men went from province to province, village to village."

"Why?"

"He said to protect them, but we . . . I feared for them. Have you seen Lirah's branding? In Serker, one was branded with the name of one's owner."

He wanted to ask her so much more but couldn't find the words without sounding like an idiot.

"Where did you go?" he asked, his voice husky. He saw her stiffen again. "Where did you go when the *reginita* was the one who presented herself? Where did she go when you did?"

"We went nowhere," she said. "We would never have left each other alone. If I left her alone, she'd say strange things. If she left me alone, I'd do bad things. So we made a pact. To always be with each other."

"What bad things would you do?" he asked.

She didn't respond.

"Did you kill the king or did she?"

Still nothing. He wanted her to acknowledge that it was she who had bed him the night they gave themselves to each other. That his broken spirit and hers had created rather than destroyed something for the first time in their wretched lives.

But there was no more talk from her that day.

They saw Paladozza from a distance, and in the early evening light, it seemed a magical place of strangely shaped stones and flickering lanterns. Froi glanced at Gargarin and Arjuro, who were sharing the same mount. It was the first time the brothers were returning together to the home that had brought hope into their lives as children.

As was the case with the Citavita and Jidia, there was little beauty outside the province, but a promise of so much from afar. Unlike Jidia, Paladozza had no wall to guard it and, stranger still, no army except for a small troupe of soldiers and bodyguards who protected the *provincaro* and his family and kept order among the people.

"De Lancey's great-grandfather wrote that there was something about a stone wall that invited invasion," Gargarin said, "and something about an army that threatened war to its neighbors."

"De Lancey's great-grandfather was an idiot," Froi said bluntly.

"The thing about Paladozza is that it has too much to offer. Art, music, enjoyment of life. Why would the palace want to ruin that by invasion when they are guaranteed a portion of the revenue?" Arjuro said.

"You ask such a question at a time like this?" Froi said in disbelief. "Do you honestly think Bestiano and the army of Nebia are talking each other out of invading Paladozza because they love art and music? Wouldn't they invade Paladozza instead and enjoy what it has to offer by force?"

"You don't know the people of Paladozza," Gargarin said. "They would never cooperate with an invader."

"So we just ride in?" Froi asked. "No papers. No explanation?"

"None at all."

Froi stared into the distance, shaking his head with resignation.

"I suppose before the five days of the unspeakable, Lumatere was such a place. Anyone could come and go to enjoy what it had to offer."

Arjuro spluttered. "I can't believe you're comparing Lumatere with Paladozza."

Froi counted to ten. Arjuro was truly beginning to irritate him.

"I take great offense at your insult to my kingdom," Froi said, trying to keep his tone even.

"It's not your kingdom, you little Serker shit from Abroi! Charyn is."

"Sagra," he muttered. Quintana twisted around on the horse, her face so close.

"You're easy to rile, Lumateran," she said.

And there it was. He was no longer referred to as the assassin, so Lumateran would have to do. And he realized that despite the fact that he wanted to toss Arjuro from his mount and give a sermon on all things wondrous about Lumatere; despite his wish to attempt a mock raid on Paladozza to prove how stupid they truly were; despite wanting to lecture them on the appreciation Isaboe and Finnikin had for all things artistic, what Froi wanted to do above all else was kiss Quintana.

"Little Serker shit, we're speaking to you," Arjuro called out. *"Sagra!"*

Quintana turned again and he saw the ghost of a smile on her face as he counted to ten, his mouth clenched with fury.

"I resent that you persist in labeling him a Serker shit and not a shit from Abroi," Lirah said coolly.

"Thought you didn't care about Serker, Lirah," Arjuro mocked.

She shot him a malicious smile.

"You know what I think, Arjuro?" she said. "I think you have suddenly come to life because De Lancey is beyond those poplar trees and you will always be a panting boy when it comes to Paladozza's handsome *provincaro*."

Arjuro was furiously silent after that.

Gargarin did what Gargarin did best and sighed. "I'm begging you all to allow me at least one night's rest in Paladozza before De Lancey has us forcibly removed."

Froi fell in love. He didn't want to. Not with a Charyn city. But he did because people didn't stand around in Paladozza and stare suspiciously; they sat around and spoke to each other and laughed. Because at the entrance to the city, they had a town square called the *vicinata* where the people of Paladozza would take a stroll at night or watch performances or set up market stalls where merchants sold sweet tea and pastries and let Froi and Quintana taste at least five before handing over a coin. Because it was the first time he saw Lirah animated with a stranger as she spoke to an artist about his paintings. Because Gargarin and Arjuro had their heads together over books in a stand. Because for once in Froi's life, everything felt in place.

Similar to the Citavita, the road that ran alongside the entrance to the city was steep, but not as narrow. Unlike the Citavita, the stalls that lined the road were not selling goods for survival, but trinkets and beautifully crafted daggers and swords and fabrics full of color. When they reached the top, where the *provincaro*'s residence was built, there was a small piazza where soft-furred hounds were for sale. Close by, a fountain belched out water with great force.

Froi kept an eye on Quintana, who seemed to gravitate toward the hound, her eyes begging Gargarin for one of their young.

"No!" Gargarin said.

Who would have thought that their savage cat was soft for puppies?

It made Froi smile, despite the fact that arrows had been pointed at him from the moment they arrived. Gargarin stood beside him, looking straight up to where a group of De Lancey's men were hiding.

"You were mocking me," Froi said.

"Not quite." Gargarin chuckled. "One doesn't exactly have to have a wall surrounding them to be a firm believer in protection. The city is trained to go to ground within minutes of an army approaching. They've had drills ever since I can remember."

Froi was irritated.

"So how observant are you?" Gargarin asked.

"Very. It's what I'm trained to be." Froi paused and looked around before exchanging a glance with Gargarin. "Four behind the first rock shrine we passed, and two on the rooftops of the house with red gables. Another two on the balconette of the inn with the image of the boar on the front. They make as though they are playing cards, but they throw down their hand too quickly." He turned and pointed up to a grand house above the piazza. "Most are up there, at every level and every window. Probably De Lancey's residence. There are at least six in this square."

Gargarin nodded. His expression showed appreciation.

A moment later, Froi was flat on his face with four of De Lancey's guards searching him.

"It seems they still haven't gotten over the incident in the godshouse hallway," Arjuro said, crouching to his level. Quintana was there as well.

The guards dragged Froi to his feet and wordlessly removed his short sword from its scabbard on his back and the daggers from his sleeves.

"What did you do to them in the godshouse hallway?" Quintana asked. The guards didn't seem interested in the others, and Froi knew this was personal.

"He showed them a thing or two about hand-to-hand combat," Lirah said. "Just before he stood on the piece of granite over the *gravina* and bargained for Gargarin's life. While they stood around looking stupid." She was angry. "He's bleeding, you fools."

"Bargained with what?" Quintana asked.

"A ruby ring given to him by his queen," Arjuro said as De Lancey's men shoved Froi forward toward a narrow path that led them to an even higher level of the city.

"Your queen gave you a ruby ring?" he heard Quintana ask coldly.

Froi grabbed her hand and gently placed her between himself and one of the guards. She twisted away, almost breaking his fingers. De Lancey's men allowed her to step away.

"You're leaving her unprotected, you fools," Froi said. He shoved away from them and grabbed Quintana roughly by the wrist, pulling her back into the confines of his protection.

"Now you can pretend you have some control over this situation," he told the men pleasantly, only too aware that the true danger lay in Quintana's fury.

"Is that what she bribed you with to assassinate me?" she asked, trying to pull away. This time the guards had the good sense to keep her close.

"I thought we were finished with the talk of assassination," Froi said, his voice weary.

"Is she your lover?" she demanded.

They reached a gate and walked into a courtyard with more guards. Surrounding them was a cluster of pristine white dwellings. De Lancey came out onto the balcony of the largest dwelling, holding a lantern in his hand. He stared down at them with irritated dismay.

Grijio's head appeared beside his father's. Then they both disappeared and it was a few minutes before they walked out into the courtyard. As usual, De Lancey was impeccably dressed, in loose white trousers and a cambric shirt. De Lancey embraced Gargarin and barely acknowledged the rest except for Quintana. His eyes went straight to her belly.

"Is it true?" he asked gently.

"True indeed," Gargarin said.

Grijio let out a breath that he seemed to have been holding.

Gargarin grabbed two of De Lancey's men by the back of

their necks and forced them to face Froi. "He protects the princess and you protect him. Does that sound like an order?"

There was nothing sinister about the mood between the *provincaro* and his men, and they walked away.

"My swords!" Froi called out. One of the guards returned his weapons, taking a moment to study the craftsmanship of the short sword.

"I'll let you play with it if you're nice," Froi mocked.

It was tense after the guards left. Grijio dared to break the silence, but he chose the wrong person to address.

"How long has it been, sir, since you returned to Paladozza?" he asked Arjuro politely.

"Nineteen years."

"Why so long, sir?"

"Because the memory of a farrier whose head was sliced clean from his body kept me away," he snarled.

Froi saw De Lancey freeze and Grijio flinch. A look of great pain and remorse passed between father and son. Had they spoken of the part De Lancey played in an innocent man's death?

"Come inside," De Lancey muttered to Gargarin. "I don't want to kill him in front of my people. They're not used to the sight of blood."

They followed De Lancey and Grijio up a flight of stairs that took them into a hall, overwhelming in its beauty. Frescoes of every creation story Froi had ever heard from this land and those of the lands said to be across the great oceans adorned the wall. He even recognized that of Lumatere's, a luminous goddess emerging from the earth.

De Lancey took them to a dining room where a long table was set up for three.

"Another five places, Jatta," he called out.

There was silent awkwardness again, and Grijio held out a hand to Quintana.

"Would you like to see the songbirds I once wrote to you about?" he asked.

She hesitated, looking around the room, squinting.

"Perhaps you can bring the cage in here, Grij?" De Lancey said.

"You'll love them," Grijio promised, running out of the room.

De Lancey removed five glasses from a tray. "My son—"

"His son," Arjuro mocked under his breath.

De Lancey stared at him, decanter in hand.

"And what is that supposed to mean?" De Lancey asked.

Gargarin stood and limped toward the *provincaro*. "Perhaps I should take over here, De Lancey."

"No. I want to know what he meant by that," De Lancey said.

Froi stared at Arjuro. He looked so strange and out of place with his dark robes in this pristine room.

"Your boy out there?" Arjuro shook his head with disbelief. "You disappoint me, De Lancey. We always mocked those fools of men who needed young flesh beneath their body to make them feel powerful."

Gargarin removed the decanter of wine from De Lancey's hand.

"How dare you? My son—"

"*Your son*? You have no son," Arjuro shouted. "Why the pretense? Eighteen years ago, you had no bride. Yet you have a young lover—"

Gargarin wasn't quick enough to save the glasses. De Lancey dived across the table and grabbed Arjuro around the throat just as the glass hit the ground and shattered. It took Froi and De Lancey's men and even Lirah and Jatta, the serving woman, to pull them apart.

Grijio raced in holding a cage of lovebirds, only to see his father being held back.

"What did he say to rile you so?" Grijio asked his father, putting the cage aside.

De Lancey adjusted his clothing and was full of decorum once more.

"He accused De Lancey of taking you as a lover," Quintana said calmly.

In some way, there was little difference between this Quintana and the indignant *reginita*. They both had the habit of not recognizing when to refrain from speaking.

Grijio snorted with laughter at the idea. A young woman hurried into the room, her blond curls bouncing around her face, her eyes wide with curiosity.

"What happened?" she asked. "I heard shouting and . . ." She saw the glass on the ground and looked at De Lancey for an explanation. Froi noticed that in contrast to the richness of De Lancey's complexion, his children were fair and blue-eyed.

"Arjuro accused Father of taking me as a lover and Father took great offense and leaped across the table to strangle Arjuro."

The girl was as stunned as Grijio.

"You mean, the priestling's here and nobody told me?"

She looked around, searching the table. Grijio pointed to Arjuro.

The girl shuddered. "All these years I've been expecting a demigod. A less decrepit version of Gargarin."

"My daughter, Tippideaux," De Lancey said dryly. She noticed Gargarin.

"Welcome back, sir."

"Thank you, Tippideaux," Gargarin managed politely, looking somewhat insulted by her image of Arjuro.

Tippideaux eyed Lirah next with a question hanging in the air.

"Lirah of Serker," her brother said, blushing the moment he looked at Lirah.

"The king's Serker whore?" Tippideaux asked, her curls bouncing as she turned to De Lancey for confirmation, as if it could not possibly be true. "What a strange night this is, Father."

"Lirah of Serker," her father corrected, looking wary as Tippideaux's eyes found Quintana.

Everyone in the room except for the two girls seemed to wince at the thought of what would take place next.

"Quintana of Charyn," Grijio introduced, sending his sister a warning look.

Tippideaux was aghast and held up a hand as if to shield herself from the sight of Quintana. If she weren't so awful in her honesty, Froi would have laughed.

"What a ridiculous way to wear one's hair," she said, horrified. She cast a look down Quintana's form. "And that dress does not suit your figure, Your Highness."

Grijio cleared his voice. "She's . . ." He leaned over and whispered in his sister's ear.

Finally they had a moment's reprieve.

Tippideaux of Paladozza fainted.

Later, Froi sat with Gargarin and De Lancey in a large reading room. The walls were stacked high with books, and the floor was covered by a thick rug that enabled them to lounge on cushions for comfort.

"This could cause hysteria," De Lancey said. "We could have women fainting all over Charyn."

"But Tippideaux—"

"Doesn't faint," De Lancey interrupted. "Tippideaux causes people to faint."

"What are your thoughts?" Gargarin asked.

"The princess can't stay here, Gargarin. I have no way of protecting her."

"You have no way of protecting your people, you mean," Froi snapped. "Like you had no intention of bargaining for her life in the Citavita."

"No," De Lancey said, anger lacing his words. "I have no way of protecting her. My people know what to do in an invasion. We go to ground, and believe me when I say we can live underground for as long as it takes. But if they come in the dead of the night to take her, there will be nothing I can do."

Froi looked away in disgust, but he felt De Lancey's stare piercing into him.

"Your boy needs to learn manners," the *provincaro* said. "He has little respect."

"Only for those who deserve it," Froi said.

"Wonderful. An Arjuro in the making," De Lancey muttered.

One of his people came in to serve sweet wine and dried apricots. Gargarin waited for the man to go.

"Where would you suggest, then?"

"Sebastabol," the *provincaro* replied. "They have the ocean on one side and a wall on the other. It's impossible to invade. And apart from the fact that the *provincaro* is still furious about the kidnapping of Olivier, I think we can convince him to offer the princess sanctuary."

"How discreet are your guards and servants?" Froi asked.

"They've been with me a long time. My guards are the sons of my father's guards, and my servants raised me and my children."

"Then speak to them tonight and tell them they must not reveal who your guests are," Froi said.

De Lancey nodded. "But Gargarin and Arjuro could be

recognized in the city. Bestiano's men will certainly know they're traveling with the princess."

"We'll stay indoors." Gargarin looked up at the books, a ghost of a smile on his face. "There's enough here to keep me happy."

Froi found Quintana, Grijio, Tippideaux, and Arjuro in one of the hallways, leaning on a massive window ledge, looking outside. He squeezed in beside Quintana and she stiffened. It seemed a long time since the discussion of the ruby ring, and he knew he would have to work hard for her trust.

Down below was Paladozza in all its nighttime splendor. It was a province of flickering torches, and there was a beauty in the way they danced that soothed him.

Arjuro pointed down to one of the rooftops, where an altar was lit by a single flame.

"I lived at the godshouse school there," he said quietly. "And every night, Gargarin and De Lancey would be at this window and we'd wave good night to each other. I couldn't bear the idea of going to bed without doing that."

There was silence for a moment.

"I wish you'd forgive my father, Priestling," Tippideaux said. "I think then he'd forgive himself and get on with his life."

Arjuro grunted.

"We forgave him," Grijio said quietly. "Why can't you?"

"And what did he do to you?" Arjuro asked bitterly, turning to them both. "Betray you? Make you feel ashamed of him."

"When my mother was carrying me in her belly and Tippideaux was two years old, De Lancey paid my father two silver pieces to run a message for him. A message he was frightened to send in person."

The last born studied Arjuro. "And I think you know the rest."

Arjuro closed his eyes as the truth registered. "You're the farrier's children?"

Tippideaux nodded. "Our mother died giving birth to Grij," she explained. "Father always tells us that what began for him in guilt has become the joy in his life."

Arjuro looked pained. He turned and walked away. Froi wanted to follow. He suspected that the days to come would break the priestling.

"Princess," De Lancey suddenly called out from the other room.

"Yes," Quintana and Tippideaux called back in unison, before staring at each other with horror.

After an awkward silence, Tippideaux linked her arm with Quintana's.

"We're going to have to do something about the way you dress, Your Highness. And your hair. I can't be seen walking around my father's province with someone looking so strange. I'm well known for my good taste."

She led Quintana away.

"And an important rule for you to remember," Froi heard her say. "In my father's house there's room for only one princess."

Grijio felt it best that they gave Quintana and Tippideaux time on their own, so Froi sat with him on the roof of Grijio's chamber and swapped stories of their journey from the Citavita. They both agreed that Froi's had been the more incident-filled. Later, they joined the girls in Quintana's chamber and Froi chose an adjoining servant's quarters to sleep in.

"We can accommodate you in a bigger room of your own," Grijio said, looking distastefully around the small space where a cot lay on the ground against the wall.

Froi shook his head. "It's best that I stay close to her."

They both looked back into the chamber where Tippideaux was attempting to remove snags from Quintana's hair. Quintana, in turn, had her nails dug deep into Tippideaux's arm, and Froi could see she had already drawn blood. There was a look of great satisfaction on her face.

Both Froi and Grijio sighed.

"At least Olivier of Paladozza will be visiting in the next few days. He is fun to be around. Tippideaux giggles shamelessly in his presence, so she might not be so pedantic about keeping Her Highness . . . tidy."

"Strange days ahead," Froi said.

"Indeed."

When the others left, Quintana looked up to where Froi stood at the entrance that divided their rooms.

He pointed to her hair. "It looks . . . neat."

"If I had known my hair would be such a concern to this kingdom I would have cut it bare like your beloved queen long ago."

Froi counted to ten.

"She didn't give me the ring as a bribe to assassinate you," he said, trying not to clench his teeth, because it was part of his bond not to. Teeth clenching, Trevanion explained, was a hostile act.

"It was Zabat who gave the order. And I'm not sure whether you've noticed, but I had every opportunity to carry it out and didn't."

"Then why would she give you a ring?" she demanded.

"Why would you care?" he demanded in response.

How could she look so different from the Quintana he met in the palace? Not because of the hair, but because of her expression and her manner and the anger that permeated every part of her being.

"Did the queen of Lumatere ask you to bed me as a means to find a way into my father's chamber?" she demanded, her tone so cold.

"Do you want to know the truth?" he said. "Because I doubt you'll believe anything I say tonight."

"Do you want to know my truth?" she cried. "That they called me Quintana the whore for so long and I never felt like one until now!"

Froi felt like a proper fiend.

"Quintana—"

"Get. Out."

He stepped up onto the roof above their compound only to find that he wasn't alone. Arjuro was there, nursing a bottle. Froi saw a naked love in the priestling's eyes as he stared out into the distance to the mountains of rocks with wind holes carved out of the stone. Tonight they flickered with the flames of campfires built to keep their occupants warm.

"They're called the fairy lights of Paladozza," Arjuro said.

This wasn't just another kingdom; it was another world.

A song was sung across the landscape, and it made Froi's skin tingle in its purity. It reminded him of the pleasure he felt every time the priest-king sang the Song of Lumatere, yet he could not remember the words. But here in Paladozza, in the enemy kingdom of Charyn, a song sung once became a tune he walked to.

"Heard every word," Arjuro said quietly, looking at him. "Between you and Quintana. You're falling in love with her. Don't."

"You're an idiot, Arjuro," Froi said, irritated. "And you're drunk, as usual."

"Not that much of an idiot and not that drunk. It's why you had to prove yourself to the Turlans."

Froi got to his feet, but Arjuro grabbed the cuff of his trousers and dragged him down to sit again.

"If she births this child and they allow her to live, the best plan is that the *provincari* allow her to stay in the palace to raise the little king herself. She will be wed to one chosen by the *provincari,* and it won't be you, Froi. It won't be the son of the king's Serker whore. It won't be the Lumateran exile who has found himself in these parts. Charyn won't care who the father of the child is, as long as there is a child. But they will care who brings up the future king. And it won't be the grandson of a pig farmer from Abroi."

Froi looked away, but Arjuro grabbed his face between his hands. "You are better than anything my brother and I could have imagined," he said fiercely. "Better than anything Lirah of Serker dreamed of in her boy. Walk away from Quintana, Froi. For her sake and yours. Fall in love with another girl and be a king in your own home."

CHAPTER 33

From the carnage in the valley came some kind of order in the mountains for Lucian. Despite the fact that Phaedra chose to continue her work among the camp dwellers, Lucian insisted that she live with the Monts and travel down to her people with Jory as her personal guard. On the first day after the slaughter, Lucian rode down with them to see how the cave dwellers were faring. He found the Charynites silent and grieving, frightened by the stories coming out of the Citavita. There was also rumor of plague in the north.

"It's just talk," Kasabian said as they watched one of the cutthroats steer a cart of bodies toward the road to Alonso. "Every once in a while they bring up the plague to frighten us, as though there's not enough in this kingdom to do that."

"Well, it's working," Harker said. He was the husband of Jorja and the father of Florenza, who had escaped through the sewers.

Lucian noticed that Harker and Kasabian and even Cora treated him differently today, as though compared to those who had savagely cut down Rafuel's men, Lucian had lost his place at the top of their list of enemies.

"Where do you think they're taking the bodies?" Lucian asked, looking up to where the leader of the cutthroats emerged from one of the caves. The man held up a hand of acknowledgment, walking toward them as though Lucian was an old friend.

"Who is this Rafuel of Sebastabol?" Kasabian whispered to Lucian. "I don't remember there ever being any other than the seven."

"They've . . . they'd," Cora corrected herself, "always kept private, those lads did."

The leader reached them, extending a hand to Lucian.

"We didn't get a chance to introduce ourselves yesterday. My name is Donashe of the Citavita," he said, an easy manner to his voice so unlike the deadness in his eyes. Lucian ignored the hand. When Donashe of the Citavita saw the Mont archers in the trees, he shook his head with regret.

"You insult us, Mont. We are no threat to you and your people. Why would we risk a battle with Lumatere?"

"I will remind you of this one more time," Lucian said coldly. "You had my wife and the women of this camp on their knees. You killed seven defenseless men."

Lucian watched as Phaedra approached. He sent her away with a toss of his head, wanting her nowhere near these men.

"Apart from your wife," Donashe said, "we have the right to do what we want with our people."

"And if any harm against your people or mine is committed on Lumateran land," Lucian said, "then I have the right to do what I want with you."

Each night on the mountain, Lucian and Phaedra sat around Lucian's table, speaking of the day's events. Rafuel, Tesadora, Jory, and Yael would join them.

"Today," Phaedra said, pouring a hot brew into their mugs from over their shoulders, "they separated the men and the women."

"Never a good sign," Tesadora said flatly.

"In each cave there are at least five or six people, although these numbers will swell because of the new arrivals from the Citavita," Phaedra continued.

She had a gift for switching between the two languages with ease although it was less necessary now that Rafuel's Lumateran had improved.

"Are they really palace riders?" Yael asked.

"No," she said. "They're said to be street lords from the Citavita."

"Gods," Rafuel muttered. Lucian watched the Charynite make room for Phaedra to sit.

"Street lords are obviously not men of title in your eyes," Lucian said to the Charynite.

"Only titled with the words *thug* and *brigand,*" Rafuel said bitterly. "The gods only know what state the Citavita is in."

Tesadora paled, and Lucian knew she was thinking of Froi. They had not heard a word from him since he left at the end of summer, and with the slaughter in the valley suggesting a traitor among Rafuel's contacts, they were beginning to fear for their lad's life.

"Do you have an idea why these men have chosen to stay in the valley?" Lucian asked Phaedra.

She nodded. "I think someone from the palace has told them to be his eyes and ears out here in the west and that they'll be rewarded for any information they can find. Their leader, Donashe, was betrayed by one of his men in the Citavita. He trusts no one and has allegiance only to those in power who will pay him well."

"Blessed Sagrami," Tesadora muttered.

"I have an idea," Phaedra said, looking at Rafuel, as though he was in charge and not Lucian.

"About having another spy in the camp with me."

"You're not a spy," Lucian pointed out.

She looked up at him, almost vexed. "I'm overhearing conversations and retelling them back to you," she said. "In Charyn, that's called spying, Luci-en."

"Yes, Luci-en," Tesadora mocked. "I believe it goes by the same name in Lumatere."

"Don't even suggest that Tesadora and the girls come down with you," Lucian said. "Isaboe and Finnikin have forbidden it."

"Yes, well, forbidding always works on me," Tesadora murmured.

"Go on with your idea," Rafuel instructed Phaedra. Lucian bristled.

"I heard Donashe complaining that they cannot get any of our men to assist them with keeping order," she continued. "His men may be armed, but there are too few of them, and sooner or later, there'll be too many of us."

"How can they possibly believe any of your men would act as guards against their own people?" Yael asked.

"With you Monts in the trees, they know they can't use force," Phaedra said. "What they need is for a newcomer to arrive and put up his hand for the work."

"A Mont spy," Jory said excitedly.

"Monts speak Charyn like fools, Jor-ee," she said. "Not possible."

Phaedra pointed to Rafuel. "He would be perfect."

Rafuel was the only one who thought it was a good idea.

"They don't know who I am," the Charynite argued. "No one does. The other valley dwellers would not have seen me with . . ." He swallowed hard. "With my lads," he said huskily.

"Let me befriend the murdering bastards. Find out the truth of what's going on in the Citavita and the rest of Charyn. Then, when I have their trust, I can escape. Perhaps try to get to Sebastabol. Find out the fate of your assassin."

"No," Lucian said.

"What am I doing here?" Rafuel asked, rage and grief in his eyes. "Nothing. Your lad Froi is out there, who knows where, and I'm hiding on your mountain while they're slaughtering the finest minds in Charyn!"

"It's not my decision to make," Lucian said. "I'll take it to the queen and Finnikin."

Rafuel shoved back his chair and left the cottage. Lucian knew exactly where the Charynite was heading, as though he was a guest and not a prisoner. He spoke of it with Tesadora later as they stood outside after the others had left.

"Talk to Japhra, Tesadora," he said. "Her sharing his bed is madness."

"I can't stop her any more than you can. She was sharing his bed long before now. Even before he took a knife to her throat."

She secured the shawl around her shoulders, staring out into the darkness. Lucian had underestimated how hard she had taken the death of the Charynites. She'd been quiet these last days, more fragile. He had no idea what to do with a fragile Tesadora. He was even thinking of sending for Perri, but Lucian knew the guard was escorting Lady Celie to Belegonia, where she would spend time in the royal court.

"It doesn't make sense," he persisted. "Japhra and Rafuel."

"Why should it make sense, Lucian?" Tesadora argued, irritated.

"Because Japhra was dragged out of her home and violated by his people."

"By one of our people," she said fiercely. "The impostor king was half Lumateran. I think we all forget that sometimes."

"But why choose a filthy Charynite?"

Tesadora looked over his shoulder, and he knew that Phaedra stood there at his cottage door.

"Good night," Tesadora said, walking toward Yata's home.

Inside, Phaedra was preparing her bed.

"You still speak of us as if we're animals," she said quietly.

"You were listening to a conversation that had nothing to do with you," he said, his voice cool, placing more logs on the fire.

"I'm one of those filthy Charynites," she said. "In what way has it nothing to do with me?"

Later, they lay in the dark, Lucian in his bed and Phaedra on her cot on the floor. He wanted to speak. Perhaps tell her that of course he didn't see her as a filthy Charynite.

"Japhra told me," she said quietly, as though she had waited half the night to speak. "That Rafuel is the first person — the first man she's encountered who doesn't see her as broken. He sees her as gifted. In Charyn we call the gifted ones gods' blessed. Lumaterans seem frightened by the gods' touched, but Rafuel is in awe of her."

Lucian was beginning to get used to hearing Phaedra's small observations at night. Whether Lumateran or Charynite, people revealed things to her that they told no other. More than anything, he realized that he liked her voice in the dark. It made him feel less lonely. Only last night he had spoken to her about life in exile and had found himself recalling memories cast aside since his father's death.

And then there was cousin Jory, who was experiencing a bout of puppy love for Phaedra that irritated Lucian.

"Off home now, Jory," Lucian said for the fourth night in a row when everyone else had left.

"We're still talking, Phaedra and I," Jory said. "Don't let us keep you up, Lucian."

"Go," Lucian ordered. "Home."

Jory rolled his eyes. "We'll talk tomorrow, Phaedra," he said.

Lucian shut the door behind the lad. "If he's annoying you, tell him so," he said gruffly.

"He's very sweet," she said, standing to push aside the table where her bed was to be laid out. Lucian ushered her away and placed the table against the wall.

"Without a word from me the other day, I heard him make his apologies to Cora and some of the other women about his past behavior." Phaedra laughed. "Except he decided to actually use the word for the body part he exposed, which I think horrified the women even more."

"What was the word?" he asked.

She whispered it and he laughed, wincing.

"The idiot. They're a bit raw, our lads."

One night when Perri was in the mountains, Phaedra came home from the valley, flushed with excitement.

"I overheard a story today," she told Lucian and the others. "About the events that took place in the Citavita after the king was murdered."

"Was this Donashe in the capital then?" Rafuel asked, his hands clenched. Lucian had noticed that the Charynite spent his day brooding with fury, wanting nothing more than to kill the men who slaughtered his lads.

"Indeed he was there. They say he was one of the leaders of the street lords who stormed the palace," Phaedra said.

"Who does he answer to?" Cousin Rafuel asked. But Lucian could think only of Froi.

"Have they seen our lad?" he demanded.

"And the princess?" Rafuel said.

"Let her finish the story," Tesadora snapped at them all, nodding to Phaedra to continue.

"It's hard to believe any of them," Phaedra said, "but those closest to the king were hanged one by one each day in front of the Citavitans. On the last day, the princess Quintana was dragged out to the podium. A noose was placed around her neck and the princess's body did indeed swing."

Tesadora shuddered. After watching her mother burn at the stake, Lucian imagined that any public execution horrified her, regardless of whether it was the enemy or not. Rafuel buried his head in his hands.

"But listen," Phaedra continued. "They say a barrage of arrows flew from one of the trees above, maiming the street lords who stood guard. Then a lad charged through the air, capturing Quintana's body and freeing it from its noose."

Phaedra stared around at them all, a feverish excitement in her eyes. "Both the princess and her rescuer have not been seen since."

"Froi!" they all spoke at once and then laughed when they realized they had.

"But why would Froi waste his time saving the life of someone whose father he was sent to assassinate?" Lucian asked.

"I think most people were trapped inside the Citavita after the street lords took over," Phaedra explained.

Perri was not convinced. "I know the lad. It would have to be something powerful to trap him there."

"Or someone," Tesadora said with a sigh. "They must have

formed a bond. Our idiot boy and the princess. What's he gotten himself into?"

Perri shook his head. "Not possible. Froi has a bond to his queen."

Rafuel made a rude sound of amusement. Lucian didn't like his expression.

"Deep down," the Charynite said, looking at Perri and speaking Charyn slowly, "you don't honestly believe Lumateran blood runs through his veins, do you?"

Phaedra translated his words nervously to Perri.

"I understood exactly what he said." Perri's tone was ice-cold and deadly.

"Did you really believe that I traveled through five provinces and failed to find a Charynite lad capable of impersonating a last born and killing a king?" Rafuel asked.

Perri leaned forward, his face less than an inch away from Rafuel's.

"I'm not going to have to kill you, am I, Charynite?" he asked quietly. "Because I'll do it in a heartbeat, regardless of who sits at this table."

"What is the truth, Charynite?" Yael asked. "What is it you know?"

"Froi wasn't impersonating a last born," Rafuel said.

Lucian was confused now, and he could see the others were as well. Except for Phaedra. He saw the realization on her face.

"He is a last born," she said, stunned.

"Not just one," Rafuel said. "He's the very last of them—I'm sure of it. He could easily be the one to break the curse."

"You believe all that talk," Lucian scoffed, "about lasts and firsts? It's the talk of a mad princess."

"As I've said before, I believe it in the same way you believed that your queen could walk the sleep of her people trapped inside your kingdom," Rafuel said.

"How did you find him?" Tesadora asked.

Rafuel had the good sense not to look away when speaking to her.

"I knew that the last born was smuggled into Sarnak as a child. I knew his name was Dafar."

"But here we are in Lumatere," Perri said. "And our lad's name is Froi."

"It's all fate, and hunches," Rafuel said. "I was a soldier, you see. Forced into the army. Placed at—what did you call it, Mont, that day three years ago when my lieutenant took your people hostage at the Osterian border? The arse-end of the land."

Perri was quick, his hand around the Charynite's neck.

"Let him speak!" Tesadora shouted, peeling Perri's fingers from where they gripped Rafuel.

"You were on the Charyn border when we rescued Froi from the barracks there?" Lucian demanded, but the answer was on Rafuel's face. Worse still, Lucian remembered the comfort of that day, the knowledge that his father was walking down that Osterian hill to save the exiles. A week later, his father was dead.

In an instant, his fist connected with Rafuel's face and the Charynite was on the ground. Lucian grabbed his father's sword hidden against the leg of the table and swung it above his head, ready to strike. He felt Phaedra's trembling arms around him, holding him back. "Please Luci-en. Please," she begged, weeping.

"Lucian," Yael said quietly.

Phaedra's hand pressed against the thump of his heartbeat. A small hand, but strong.

"I fell into the hole they dug into the ground," Lucian said, "where our people would have been buried. Forgotten. Do you remember, Perri? You and Trevanion helped Finnikin drag me out that night."

Lucian's eyes bore into Rafuel's. The Charynite's mouth was bleeding.

"You were going to slaughter our people," Lucian said. "You were one of them."

"Perhaps," Rafuel replied. "Perhaps I would have followed orders. Perhaps I would have walked away and caught an arrow in my back for deserting my post. I'll never know. You all turned up, and I thought the gods were smiling in the favor of good men for once."

Lucian could still feel Phaedra's trembling arms around him. He remembered what she had witnessed days before in the valley. He lowered the sword.

Rafuel sat up, wiping the blood from his mouth.

"Our squad leader at first believed your lad was the lost heir of Lumatere," Rafuel said. "Because of the ruby ring and the words he was shouting. Our men beat him up enough to discover that he was no one but a Sarnak thief named Froi."

Rafuel looked at Tesadora.

"A thief with strange un-Sarnak eyes and a very un-Sarnak name that reminded me too much of Dafar of Abroi, the last born of Charyn, known only to the priests and those who smuggled him out of danger on the first day of weeping eighteen years ago."

"But you did nothing when they beat him," Perri said. "We found him black and blue and tied up like a dog in your barracks."

"There was nothing I could do," Rafuel said. "But I swore on my life that he'd be rescued that night. Do you Lumaterans honestly believe it would have been that easy to enter the barracks undetected?" There was a certain look of victory in Rafuel's eyes. "You got him out of there alive because I allowed it to happen. You killed two men on guard and our squad leader because I let it happen. And when I wrote to the priests of Trist afterward, they allowed you to have Dafar of Abroi for all of these years because we hadn't found his purpose yet. We knew he'd be safer with you."

Perri stared down at the Charynite. "You have no idea what you've done, confusing that boy's bond," he said. "If his corpse is returned to us because of the danger you've put him in, I will slice you from ear to ear."

Rafuel gave a rueful smile.

"Do you expect me to have regrets?" he asked. "When it's you Lumaterans who speak an unwritten law that makes the most sense to me."

"And what is that, Charynite?" Tesadora asked.

"What needs to be done."

CHAPTER 34

Olivier of Sebastabol arrived a week later, riding into the courtyard of the *provincaro*'s compound with a flourish that Froi had failed to capture during his time in the palace impersonating the last born.

"How can someone travel three days and still be in good cheer?" Grijio asked, laughing up at his friend. Olivier dismounted, and Tippideaux was picked up off the ground and swung three times, giggling with delight. She and Olivier could have passed as siblings with their wide blue eyes, but there was a way Tippideaux flirted with Olivier that told Froi she wanted more than a brother's affection from Sebastabol's last born.

While the Sebastabol guards gathered Olivier's belongings from one of the pack horses and disappeared inside the compound, the last born hesitantly held out a hand to Froi, who willingly shook it.

"What is the news?" Grijio asked as they walked inside, noticing the envelope in Olivier's hand.

"We've heard that Bestiano has a large army camped outside Nebia," Tippideaux said. "Tell us it's not true, Olivier."

"Perhaps Bestiano is not so bad for Charyn at the moment," Olivier said. "I sense a more potent enemy at our gates."

He glanced at Froi questioningly as they crossed into the visitor's quarters.

"Then who is the enemy if not Bestiano?" Froi asked coldly, not liking the implication of his look.

"The moment Charyn falls into civil war, the surrounding kingdoms will invade as retribution for Lumatere," Olivier said. "The Belegonian army has gathered outside their borders with Osteria and Lumatere, and waits for word from both kingdoms to join them."

Tippideaux paled, and her brother placed an arm around her, sending a warning glance to Olivier, but the last born of Sebastabol was oblivious.

"Most of the people I've come across in my travels through Charyn are going underground, fearful of rape and pillage," he continued. "The Lumaterans will exact their revenge."

Froi grabbed Olivier by his vest, slamming him against the wall. "You dare to say such a thing, Charynite? No Lumateran soldier would take a woman by force."

Grijio pulled Froi away from Olivier, and an uneasy silence settled around them.

"But will the Lumaterans invade, Froi?" Grijio asked quietly.

Froi had come to respect this even-tempered lad. "I'm not privy to the business of my kingdom," he said honestly, "but invading Charyn was never part of the plan."

Froi bent to pick up Olivier's cap and handed it to the last born. Olivier took it, a solemn expression on his face.

"Pray that you know your queen and her consort well, Lumateran," Olivier said. "A war between our two kingdoms is the last thing we all want."

* * *

In the drawing room of the guest compound, Olivier was reintroduced to Quintana. His eyes roamed around the room surreptitiously before returning to her stomach.

Tippideaux patted Quintana's dress around the waist, proudly. Froi saw Quintana's lips curl. He had taught her a counting exercise the night before so she could control her savage rage when provoked. Froi could tell today that Quintana made it only as far as the number four before twisting Tippideaux's fingers away.

"I shaped an outfit to disguise her belly," Tippideaux continued, as though nothing had happened. "She'll be showing soon, and we don't want to draw attention to her. It's all in the paneling, you know." She looked at the others for approval. "Because of my gift with the needle, I'm called on frequently by the fatter women in Paladozza to design their outfits."

Quintana had developed an impassive stare that she reserved solely for Tippideaux. During the last week, Grijio and Froi had taken bets on who of the two girls would look away first. Secretly, Froi was dying to see them both in hand-to-hand combat with a bit of hair-pulling thrown in.

"You look much better than the last time I saw you, Your Highness," Olivier said cheerfully.

"Well, I suppose it was because I had a noose around my neck then, and they're always so unattractive," she replied bitingly.

There was a strained silence, and then Olivier had the good grace to grin.

"Then it's true that you do have a sense of humor," he said, placing an arm around both girls. Quintana stiffened, and Olivier had the sense to let go.

"I arrived at the same time as a troupe of actors, and their costumes and props looked a treat. What say you all that we go down to the *vicinata* and watch the greatest show in the land? That's what it said on their caravan," Olivier said.

Olivier's good cheer was contagious, and they spent the day browsing through the stalls of the *vicinata,* talking to the merchants, snacking on corn sticks, looking through the armory. Froi noticed that Quintana was drawn to colorful things, and he watched her glance through the stalls where rolls of brightly hued cloth and carpets adorned the space. Olivier dragged Froi and Grijio to the window of an ale house, known to be the most disreputable in town.

"We'll steal away and come here one of these nights without your father's men knowing, Grij," Olivier said. "It will be wild."

Later, they stood in the crowd watching the actors perform and Froi's sides ached from the laughter. He heard Quintana's laughter, and it was not the endearing snorts of the *reginita,* but a sweet sound to his ears all the same. He managed to push closer to the front and place her before him, his chin leaning on her head, his arms around her to protect her against the jostling of the crowd.

The troupe was made up of five men who each played a number of characters. They covered everything from a witless fool's amorous adventures to the comic feud between two neighbors over a pig named Herbert.

A few moments into another skit, Froi knew there was something wrong.

"Let us go," Tippideaux said, urgently grabbing Quintana's arm. "My father said not to be late for dinner."

"Can we not wait for the next to finish?" Quintana asked.

"Let us go now!" Tippideaux pulled her away, and when Froi saw one of the troupe actors place a straw-colored broomstick of hair on his head, Froi understood Tippideaux's persistence. Another actor wore a crown, and what they did onstage was lewd. The crowd laughed at their bawdy antics, and Froi wished he was with the indignant *reginita.* She would not have understood what she saw, but Quintana did and he could see the tears of rage and hurt in her eyes. He saw the shudder of her body.

Don't let her think of Bestiano, he prayed to the most merciful of the gods, if one existed in Quintana's life.

Few words were spoken on their walk back to De Lancey's compound other than Quintana's ragged breathing and mutterings. But then her mutters became words. Numbers.

And then the numbers became grunts and she was weeping with fury, tearing at her hair. This was Quintana without Reginita to calm her down. All rage with little reason.

"We need to do something," Grijio said as one or two of De Lancey's neighbors emerged from their homes to see what the commotion was about. "If they suspect who she is . . ."

By now Quintana was shouting the words, pounding at her head with her palm. Froi grabbed hold of her, but she slipped out of his hands and onto the ground, crawling into a crevice in a wall, pressing herself into it as though she wanted to disappear inside the stone. He knelt, taking her face between his hands.

"It doesn't go away if I count," she said, sobbing. "Nothing goes away."

"Then we'll find something else," he said gently, and placed his lips against her ear. "Think of her," he whispered. "What would she say to you? Think of the *reginita*."

And he watched as the fight left her body and only then did he look up at the others and see the horror and the sorrow in their expressions. Here was the mother of their heir. Their curse breaker. Did Charyn stand a chance?

"Do they think I'm that hideous?" Quintana finally asked in a broken voice. Her words made Froi's heart twist even more. "Do they think I would have done such things with my father?"

The others chorused their *no* emphatically.

"Father has probably mentioned that I'm a genius at writing plays myself," Tippideaux said. "Well, when I have the time, I will pen the true story of Quintana of Charyn." She gave Quintana a determined nod. "And of her beautiful and faithful friend, Tippideaux of Paladozza."

Tippideaux held a hand out to her. Quintana studied it. Froi feared she would bite the fingers off to the bone.

"Will Quintana of Charyn be beautiful in your play?" she asked quietly.

Tippideaux thought for a moment.

Just say yes, Tippideaux.

"She'll be strangely intriguing," Tippideaux said, her eyes far away. "With a touch of mystery and savagery that will bewitch only the bold and courageous among us."

Froi and the lads held their breath.

After what seemed an eternity, Quintana took Tippideaux's hand.

He spent each morning on the roof with Lirah, watching the sunrise. Most times it was to observe if Bestiano's riders were heading for Paladozza. Despite there being no province walls, the land outside to the south was flat and Nebia's powerful army would be seen from miles away.

In Paladozza a peculiar world of color existed on the roofs of people's houses. Unlike Lumatere, with its lush greens and golds, here the strange landscape of stone cones and cave houses was colored in shades of light pink and soft brown and white. Once upon a time, stone had been stone to Froi. In Paladozza it had a beauty he was beginning to love.

One morning, De Lancey joined them and they sat appreciating the view.

"They say a volcano erupted thousands upon thousands of

years ago," De Lancey explained. "And the ash and rainwater made that stone. It's called tufa." He pointed to one stone house and then another. "That one is made of lava and that one out of sandstone. It's why they differ in color."

Lirah shivered, and Froi shared his blanket with her, placing it around them. They sat shoulder to shoulder in silence awhile.

"Where's Gar?" De Lancey asked Lirah.

"Sleeping," she said, getting to her feet and yawning. "Planning armies. Building water meadows. Writing letters."

She tapped Froi on the head. "Gargarin said you write down ideas faster than anyone he knows. Make yourself useful today."

She disappeared down the steps into the house.

"It's a good thing that Lirah and Gargarin are on speaking terms," Froi said. "For the sake of everyone."

De Lancey gave a short laugh. "I think they're doing more than speaking, Froi."

Froi could hardly comprehend the idea of Lirah with Gargarin. Perhaps when they were young, but not now. De Lancey surely had it wrong.

"Will the brothers travel home to Abroi?" Froi asked.

"Abroi?" De Lancey said with disgust. "Abroi is a swamp of ignorance, and you don't want Arjuro anywhere near that madman father of theirs. This is their home. And it's the home of anyone who belongs to them. You and Lirah included."

"I have a home," Froi said.

"But does it speak to you in the same way Paladozza does?"

Froi turned to him, exasperated. "Speak? Sing? What is it with you Charynites?"

De Lancey stared at him shrewdly. "Do you honestly think that the queen of Lumatere followed a map home? She followed a song. Does Lumatere sing to you, Dafar?"

They were interrupted by the sound of horse hooves clattering on the courtyard stone, and they stood to see who it was.

"At this time of the morning, it could only be a messenger," De Lancey said, a worried expression on his face. "Go find Gargarin."

Froi knocked on Gargarin's door and entered. In a corner, Lirah was tying a brightly colored braid of rope around the hips of her simple gown. Gargarin was at a desk, placing a wax seal on a letter. Only then did it occur to Froi that Lirah and Gargarin were sharing a chamber. He felt an anger beyond reckoning. Was he the last to know? Was Froi merely an insignificant part of their past, one they could easily overlook? Especially now that they were thinking of no one but themselves. He hated them both: Lirah for being stupid enough to believe Gargarin cared about anything, and Gargarin because it was easy to hate Gargarin, the weak and useless cripple.

"De Lancey wants you in the main hall," he snapped before walking out.

Grijio and Olivier arrived at the same time as Gargarin, all waiting to hear the news.

"A letter from the *provincaro* of Sebastabol on behalf of the ambassador of the principality of Avanosh," De Lancey said.

"Where's Avanosh?" Froi asked. He tried to recall whether the priest-king or Rafuel had mentioned it.

"It's a small island," Grijio explained. "Off the coast of Sebastabol in the Ocean of Skuldenore."

"Closer to the border with Sorel than to Paladozza," Olivier said. "Those of Avanosh are the greatest bellyachers about who has the right to the throne based on an incident hundreds of years ago. In the past, they've sought the support of Sorel to secure the throne of Charyn."

"Do they have the right?" Froi asked.

Gargarin shook his head. "Not anymore. But they are of royal blood dating back to the Ancients, and they are considered Charynites."

"Then what do they want?" Lirah asked.

De Lancey turned back to the letter.

"According to the *provincaro* of Sebastabol, Feliciano of Avanosh is the perfect candidate to be the queen's consort. A titled duke, unaligned."

Froi stared from De Lancey to Gargarin, stunned. A consort for Quintana?

"The *provincaro* says that we need stability within our kingdom and the only way to achieve that is to appoint a neutral consort," De Lancey said. "We also need to keep Belegonia and Lumatere from invading, and what better way than to have a consort with strong ties to a powerful neighbor like Sorel?"

"Gods," Gargarin muttered.

"That's not all," De Lancey said. "The Avanosh entourage is a week's ride from us as we speak."

CHAPTER 35

Phaedra was pleased that the queen of Lumatere had released Rafuel to the valley as a spy. Pleased, and somewhat flattered, because it was Phaedra's plan they chose to follow, detail by detail. Rafuel would be escorted by the Monts downstream, and at a safe enough distance, he would cross and join Charynite exiles traveling toward the valley from Alonso. Rafuel was to ensure that he impressed the camp leaders and was to find out more about what was taking place in the Citavita and the rest of the kingdom.

A week later, Rafuel and Donashe entered the cave where Phaedra was tending to a dying man from the valley. She felt their eyes on her as she kneaded the old man's tired bones, but she refused to acknowledge them and continued her work. The old man had said he liked her voice, so Phaedra told him stories passed down to her in Alonso. She thought it sad and strangely wrong that her voice could be the last he heard in this world. When she was satisfied that the man slept, she stood to face Donashe.

"I demand that his wife be moved into this cave with him," she said, trying to keep her voice strong and determined.

"Who is she to demand?" Rafuel asked coldly. It was as though Phaedra were facing a stranger and not the Rafuel she had come to know.

"She's the wife of the Mont leader," Donashe said, his eyes glancing at Jory, who was instantly at Phaedra's side.

Rafuel whispered something in Donashe's ear, and both men laughed. Phaedra's face reddened with humiliation. She would have liked to demand to know what had been said, but instead she pointed back to the old man.

"He's dying. Where is your compassion?"

Donashe seemed irritated by her pleas, but he agreed to let the man's wife share the cave. Phaedra watched the camp leader place an arm around Rafuel's shoulder as they walked away. "To be a good camp leader, you have to let them think they've won a few rounds, Matteo."

"Our Matteo was convincing," Phaedra said to Jory a little uneasily as they rode home that day.

"Too convincing," Jory muttered.

Phaedra continued to stay with Lucian on the mountain. It had always seemed strange to her that for one who led the Monts, Lucian kept his dwelling small. Yata, on the other hand, lived in what the Lumaterans referred to as the royal residence. It had many rooms and had once accommodated the whole of the queen's family when she was a child and spent the holy days in the mountains. It was secure and perfect for when the queen and her consort and child came to stay. Lucian's cottage had two rooms. When Phaedra lived here as his wife, she had shared his bed, or a corner of it anyway. Now she slept on a cot near the fire.

* * *

Some mornings she'd wake and his bed would be empty, and she'd wonder which of the Mont girls he lay with. On one such morning, a man named Orly came knocking about a missing bull and she found herself traipsing through the mountain, searching for the animal. When they dragged Orly's bull back to his stable, Phaedra noticed that the cow shed had been left open, and pointed it out to him.

"Didn't understand a word you said," he said. "You should learn how to speak proper like."

"I said," Phaedra repeated slowly, "that the door of your cow shed is open."

He stared back at the shed. "The cow belongs to my wife," he said, irritated. "Fool of a woman."

She saw his wife standing on the porch, watching them both, and with a wave of her frozen hand, Phaedra walked away, feeling cold and miserable.

When she arrived back at the cottage, it was still empty. The fire had died down, and the room was cold. Try as she might, Phaedra couldn't start it up again, and she felt as useless as when she lived here as his wife. Lucian arrived soon after, grunting with displeasure at how cold the room was.

"You couldn't have made some porridge, I suppose?" he snapped.

She watched him grab a bowl of cold stew she had left from the night before.

"Your *shalamar* sent it over yesterday," she said, not having anything else to say.

"Yata," he corrected, wolfing down his food. She noticed that when he was tired and cold and hungry he had the worst temper.

"We say *shalamar,*" she said.

"Well, that's a ridiculous word, and we say *yata,*" he said firmly, the discussion finished as far as he was concerned.

"And the word for *shalamon*?" she persisted.

He refused to respond.

"That's our word for grandfather," she said.

"Pardu," he muttered. "Are you happy now?"

"A strange word."

"Not so strange at all," he said.

"And you know better, do you?" she asked, feeling her temper rise despite the fact that she had never been known as one with a temper.

"Well, I'm not the one unable to say simple words," he said.

"Well, actually, you are," she said, sitting opposite him.

"Me?" he asked, putting down his spoon and finally giving her his attention.

"You say 'Phedra,' and my name is Phaedra."

"I do not. I say Phaedra," he insisted.

"To your ears it sounds like Phaedra; to a Charynite it sounds like Phedra."

"I'll call you whatever I like," he muttered.

"Of course you will. You're the king of the mountain. Why wouldn't you do as you please?"

She stood up and searched for her shawl, preferring to be anywhere else.

"King of the mountain?" he shouted. "I've just spent a night birthing a foal. I'm frozen to the bone, my food is cold, and it seems as if my wife has been bitten by a viper."

"I'm not your wife," she cried. "I'm just a fool Charynite girl you sent back, ridiculed by your people with not so much as a thank-you for traipsing half the morning looking for that wretched bull."

Lucian sighed. "Orly was here? You should have sent him away."

"Yes, that would have made me more well liked than I already am."

He looked at her hands clutching her shawl, and then he sighed again, stood up, and left the cottage. A little while later, he returned with four small logs.

"Come here," he said gruffly, and he showed her how to build a fire and light it. "This cold will only get worse, and you can't go around freezing half to death."

That day in the valley she felt Rafuel's eyes on her as he whispered to Donashe and pointed her way. Later, when she was at the stream with some of the other camp dwellers, Rafuel approached.

"You," he snapped, pointing to Phaedra. "I want a word. There's a set of rules you need to follow."

Kasabian and Harker stood, and Phaedra saw them turn to Jory.

"Don't let her out of your sight," Harker snapped. Both men were less than forgiving of Jory and his Mont cousins' nightly excursions into their camp weeks ago. Jory had responded in turn by choosing to charm the Charynite women. "They don't even know how to fight," he muttered once to Phaedra about the men. "So who am I to care what they think of me?" But she could tell that deep down the lad was desperate for their approval.

Phaedra waved their concerns away and followed Rafuel along the stream, with Jory trailing behind.

"They are aligned to no one," Rafuel said quietly. "They're scum who are traveling through the provinces searching for last-born women after Quintana of Charyn's failure at the coming of her age. On the road between the Citavita and Sebastabol, these men were stopped by the king's riders, or I should say, Bestiano of Nebia's men. They were told that in the valley at the foot of the Lumateran mountains, a group of landless Charynites were camped and that among them were seven rebels led by Rafuel of Sebastabol. They knew this information because Bestiano's men had apprehended a spy, who I believe was Zabat.

"Never," Rafuel said, grabbing Jory by the ear to bring him closer and to give the impression that he was reprimanding the Mont, "trust a whiner from Nebia."

"Matteo!" Donashe called out. Rafuel and Phaedra turned, and the man shook his head. "Don't touch the Mont. We can't have trouble."

Jory pushed him away but hid a smile all the same. "Yes, don't touch the Mont, Matteo," he mocked.

"Do you think they're spying on Lumatere?" Phaedra asked. "Or are they truly after you?"

"These men are cutthroat opportunists. They have purpose. They think, much like Matteo of Jidia, that if they do the right thing, they will be rewarded in the new Charyn. Perhaps be appointed palace riders. Here in the valley is the closest they can come to proving themselves. This land we stand on may be Lumatere's, but they see the people as theirs to do with as they will. It's all about power, Phaedra. Always about power and who grabs it first."

"Then tell your people to leave," Jory said. "They'd be idiots to stay. No one's keeping them imprisoned."

Rafuel stared at Jory as if he could not believe what he was hearing. "Do you not understand, Mont? These people have nowhere else to go. They will endure anything for the slightest chance that your queen will let them into Lumatere."

Most nights, the Monts came to Lucian with all sorts of favors and complaints. As Phaedra fell asleep that night, she heard the slur of tiredness in Lucian's voice and knew that if she were his proper wife, she'd order them all home. The next morning, she heard Orly call out for his bull again and this time she hurried to the door before the man came knocking.

"He's sleeping," she said firmly.

Orly tried to look over her shoulder.

"Then, wake him up."

"Why, when I was able to help yesterday?" she said briskly, grabbing her shawl. "Let's go. We're wasting time."

This time Orly's wife, Lotte, was with them. Her cow had managed to escape as well.

"I hope wherever they are, they're together," Lotte said.

"Who?" Phaedra asked.

"Why, Bert and Gert. Who do you think, idiot girl?"

Later, when they found the bull and cow in two separate fields, Phaedra saw Orly's relief and Lotte's sadness.

"It's your people," Orly snapped at Phaedra as he placed a plank across the stable door. "Coming up this mountain and making mischief."

Phaedra walked away, but made it only as far as the stone hedge of their land before returning, walking straight into their cottage, where husband and wife were warming their hands over the fire.

"First, I'm not an idiot girl," she said firmly, "so don't call me one again, and second, my people don't have the strength for mischief. The only thing they have the strength for is breathing. And another thing. If a bull went missing every morning among the people of my province, neighbors would help each other. Where are your people now, Orly of the Monts? What kind of place is this if the only help you can find is from an idiot girl who belongs to your enemy?"

Phaedra turned and walked straight into Lucian, who stood at the entrance of Orly's cottage, staring at the three of them, a bear of a man in his coat of fleece and his fierce dark eyes. No one spoke, and he stepped aside. Phaedra bristled at the silent order. Her Mont husband wanted her out of his sight.

When she reached the stone hedge for the second time that morning, Lucian was there beside her. "Now let me do the counting," he said, and suddenly she felt the weight of his fleece on her shoulders and a comfort beyond imagining, because it was his gruff voice that warmed her as much as his coat. "First, these are the mountains, Phaedra. People freeze in winter up here, so you don't leave the cottage in all hours of the morning wearing a shawl to protect you from the cold. Understood?"

She could smell the bread wafting out from the baker's cottage. The Monts were finally beginning to awaken, the start of another miserable day for Phaedra.

"Second, Orly's bull is my problem, not yours. Understood?"

Phaedra didn't respond.

"And third, you'll have to forgive my people. They are still grieving their leader."

She stopped and looked up at him. "Their leader is living," she said firmly. "He's standing in front of me, and the only person on this mountain who is not acknowledging him these days is the leader himself."

Phaedra saw Lucian's fury first, and then she saw his eyes water. Was it from the cold bite of the morning air or something else?

"I'll never be as good as him," he said. "They know that. We all know that."

She shook her head. "Speak the truth, Lucian."

"What truth?" he asked angrily.

"You don't want him here because of the mistakes you think you're making. You want him here because you loved him and he's gone and you can't say those words out loud."

He stared down at her, but Phaedra refused to look away. And then he moved closer, his lips close to her ear as though he was afraid the mountain itself would hear his words.

"Sometimes . . . I miss him so much, I can barely breathe."

* * *

He joined them in the valley later that day, and Phaedra took him for a tour of the caves. He was polite and attentive to all he met, including Kasabian and Harker, who she felt Lucian was trying hard to impress after Jory's reports about how cold and unforgiving the men of the valley were to Mont lads. Phaedra could tell her Mont husband liked Kasabian best. Kasabian reminded Phaedra of her own father, and he was gentle in a way that his sister, Cora, wasn't. But Cora was trustworthy and worked hard. Both were good people who Phaedra believed had much to offer Lumatere if they were ever allowed to enter.

After a brief, terse conversation with Donashe and his camp leaders, Phaedra took Lucian to Cora's cave. There was always tension in that dwelling because Cora disliked Florenza and Jorja. She believed they had airs and graces despite their journey and referred to them as the Ladies of the Sewer. There was a lazy girl named Ginny, who Cora called Lady Lazy Muck. Cora had a name for everyone.

"I want to be placed with my brother," she snapped.

"You know they'll never allow that, Cora," Phaedra said patiently.

There was a new woman in the cave. An older woman who came from the north and never stopped speaking. Yet no one understood a word she spoke.

"Dialect," Phaedra explained to Lucian.

"Her mouth never stops," Cora muttered.

The woman from the north spoke to Lucian, and Phaedra wanted to giggle, watching him nod seriously. "Hmm, yes," he would say every once in a while.

Outside, he stared at Phaedra, slightly stunned.

"If you ever take me into that cave again, I'll lock you up with my great-aunts, Yata's sisters!"

"You would not enjoy that, Phaedra," Jory piped up as they walked back to the Lumateran side of the stream.

"Rafuel said the same about that cave," Phaedra said, laughing. "He calls it the cave of she-devils. The women hate him most of all."

"They don't hate me," Jory boasted. "I can charm Angry Cora. She says she hates idiots and everyone she meets is an idiot."

When they reached the stream, Lucian grabbed Phaedra around the waist, lifting her over the water so her feet wouldn't get wet. She had seen him do the same thing with his Mont cousins and Tesadora. Phaedra's face flamed when he did it for her, so absently.

"You're a good spy too," Lucian said to her. "Except spies usually have more important subjects than women named Lady Lazy Muck and Angry Cora and the Ladies of the Sewer."

She found herself laughing again, and he looked at her strangely.

"You don't do that enough," he said quietly.

It was strange what Phaedra became used to living among the Monts. She liked their directness and lack of pretense. She liked the way they worshipped in the open at shrines that could be planted at the side of the road wherever someone pleased, rather than godshouses that were built thousands upon thousands of years ago. She liked having her hair braided by Yata, who once took Phaedra's face in her hand.

"I had granddaughters with eyes as pretty as yours once," the old woman said sadly, and Phaedra knew she was speaking of the queen's sisters, who were slain in the palace all those years ago.

What Phaedra didn't like was their food. It was very plain, and it lacked taste.

Finnikin of Lumatere, his father, and Perri the Savage were visiting one night with Tesadora, and the consort noticed Phaedra's lack of appetite.

"Best food I ever had was in Yutlind," he said.

"The best food in the land is in Paladozza," Phaedra insisted.

"You've been there?" he asked with excitement.

She nodded. "The *provincaro* invited my father during one of Charyn's very brief moments of peace between the *provincari*. He is very handsome, De Lancey of Paladozza is."

"Then why didn't your father marry you to him?" Lucian asked sharply.

"Because he's old. Nearing at least forty-five years."

The captain and Perri looked up, mid-mouthful, and exchanged looks. Tesadora laughed at their reaction.

"Regardless, Provincaro De Lancey loves the company of women, but not in his bed," Phaedra said.

"Ahhh," they all said, intrigued.

It was late in the night when everyone left. The consort and the captain were staying in Yata's home with Perri and Tesadora.

"They asked quite some questions tonight," Lucian said from his bed. "I never know what they're up to."

"Should the valley dwellers be worried?" she asked.

"No, but I get a sense that my cousin Isaboe wants to travel down the mountain again, so perhaps Trevanion and Perri are ensuring it is safe for her."

"If they won't allow Tesadora among Donashe and his men, I can't imagine them permitting the queen."

Lucian gave a short laugh. "The queen doesn't wait for permission."

Phaedra thought about it. "It would mean so much to the valley dwellers if she visited, especially with the child. That precious girl would lift their spirits for days and days."

"Try having Jasmina for days and days and she'll lift your temper," he said with a laugh. "She's a minx, that one."

"Sometimes I imagine Charyn children in the valley," she said. "Wouldn't that change everything? Closer to Lumatere, I wonder if the children would feel a stronger kinship to it."

"Will you ever feel that?" he asked quietly.

"Never. Regardless of where I live, I will always know I'm a Charynite. Even with the shame of our past, I've never wanted to be anything else, and I pray to the gods that one day I will love the person who sits on our throne as much as you all love your queen and her consort."

And that was how Phaedra became part of two worlds. Up in the mountains, if it wasn't the Queen's Guard who wanted to speak to her, it was the ladies of the Flatlands who were keen to send her seeds for the valley's vegetable patches. She met the queen's First Man one night when he wanted to see the census she had been chronicling. Sir Topher, the most distinguished man she'd ever met apart from De Lancey of Paladozza, wanted the names of those who were landless first and promised to take their names back to the queen. Perhaps soon the first of the valley dwellers would be given permission to enter Lumatere.

Down in the valley, more people arrived and there was talk of a plague in the northern province, causing fear to flare up among the people again. From her cot on the ground, Phaedra spoke to Lucian about her memories of the plague from years past. She became used to the strange conversations where she spoke Charynite and he responded in Lumateran, except now it was done out of convenience rather than spite. And it was on those nights that she imagined that she loved him, and it shamed her that he did not love her in return. He was the only man she had lain with, and she hadn't enjoyed the experience. But it was this Lucian that she had learned to love.

Despite his wishes, Phaedra still found herself some mornings searching with Orly and Lotte for Bert. Lotte had made Phaedra gloves fashioned out of cowhide that kept her fingers from freezing. After their search each time, Phaedra would sip tea with Lotte while Orly built a shrine in the paddock, thanking the goddess that Bert was returned to them once again.

"He'll run out of room for shrines," Phaedra said as they watched him from the window of the cottage.

"Perhaps if Bert mated Gert, there'd be peace on the mountain," Lotte said quietly.

Phaedra looked at her. After a moment, she smiled and then she laughed. Lotte was surprised at first, and then she laughed with her.

"Oh, Lotte. What have you been up to all this time?"

"Do you promise not to get angry?" she asked Lucian as they traveled down the mountain that morning. Jory was riding ahead.

"I never make promises I can't keep," he said.

She sighed. How many times had she heard those words from her father?

"Luci-en, I think Lotte has been letting the bull out of its pen. It's why no one has been caught yet or confessed. Orly won't let Gert breed with Bert, and his wife has been hoping that if both animals are free to wander, they'll find each other."

Lucian turned in the saddle to look at her, stunned, and then he shook his head and laughed.

"I have the smartest wife in Lumatere and Charyn combined."

CHAPTER 36

The talk of a consort made Froi tense. It made Quintana tense. She called him *fool* more often. He called her a cold-hearted cat. If she wandered away from his protection in the *vicinata,* he would snap at her. If she walked away and Froi didn't follow, she'd accuse him of placing her life in danger. If she removed her clothing in front of him at night, as though he were some eunuch, his words would be cruel. If she told him to turn the other way or go to his quarters while she undressed, he'd remind her that there was no part of her body he was yet to see. In the palace when Princess Indignant had been about, she would break the tension between them. He realized that the desire between Quintana and Froi had always been there and that Reginita had balanced it with her innocence.

"Bed the girl," Olivier said with exasperation. "Put us out of our misery."

And then there was the matter between Arjuro and De Lancey. Froi feared what the friction would lead to and wished that Gargarin would intervene, but now more than ever, the gulf between the brothers was wide and the hurt too deep.

"What do you think they're talking about?" Grijio asked one

morning as they peered out of the grand window of the hallway into De Lancey's private garden. Tippideaux was squeezed in between them.

"Whatever it is, it's making Arjuro angry," Froi said.

"He's not choking your father, is he, Grij?" Olivier asked.

"Gods. You don't think they're kissing, do you?"

"That's a shove."

"Looks like an embrace from here."

All agreed the next moment was a shove.

"How appalling!" Tippideaux said. "I think the priestling just punched Father in the mouth. Where are the guards?"

They heard a sound behind them, and all four were reluctant to move away but turned to Quintana.

"I'm looking for Lirah," she said coolly. "What are you doing up there?"

"We're spying on Father and Arjuro," Grijio said, making room for her. "Care to join us?"

"Don't be so rude. Get down, all of you."

"That's definitely kissing," Olivier said with authority, having turned back to the window.

Quintana pushed herself in beside Froi, shoving Tippideaux to the side. She had never been able to resist the drama Arjuro brought into their lives, whether it was on the balconette of the palace or here in De Lancey's compound.

"Did you see the way she did that as if she owns this window?" Tippideaux sniffed.

Quintana stood on tiptoes beside them. Froi hoisted her up around her legs. She placed her arm around his shoulders for support.

They all watched the two below for a while. For a long while, actually, and Froi heard Tippideaux sigh because it was romantic in a strange way. Froi wanted them to keep on watching because if he turned his head a fraction, it would be buried in Quintana's neck, an area of her body he had ignored all those nights they shared a bed. She looked down at him, and he dared not look away. She was all twitches and gold-speckled brown eyes today.

"I caught Gargarin and Lirah kissing in such a way one morning," she said. "As if they wanted to consume the soul of the other."

The mention of Lirah and Gargarin infuriated Froi, and he let her go abruptly and walked away.

He spent the rest of the day in the library, penning a letter to Finnikin and Isaboe. If there was ever a chance of getting something to them, it could be from Paladozza. Gargarin entered later, and Froi stood to gather his pages, wordlessly leaving Gargarin's quill on the desk where he found it.

"Keep it. I have another," Gargarin said. "I've not seen you all these days, Froi. Stay so we can talk."

"About rainfall?" Froi said sarcastically. "And garderobes?"

Gargarin gave him one of his piercing stares. "Ah, so we're in that type of a mood."

"Not in any mood at all." Froi shrugged nonchalantly, walking to the door.

"We need to build her an army," Gargarin said.

Froi stopped.

"This business with the Avanosh people disturbs me," Gargarin continued. "The last thing we want is Sorel running our country through a puppet consort."

"Knowing Sorel, they probably will," Froi said.

Gargarin looked bemused. "You're an expert on Sorel, are you?"

Froi walked back to where Gargarin had laid out a map on the desk, then watched as he marked the provinces they could trust. There weren't many.

"Let's just say I was a guest in Sorel," Froi said. "A guest of one of their slave traders."

Gargarin's hand froze.

"The slave traders of Sorel?" Gargarin asked, his eyes registering the horror of what Froi was saying. The stories of the traders and the fate of their victims were well known across the land.

Froi shrugged again and looked away.

"Don't tell Lirah," Gargarin said quietly.

Froi shook his head, not believing what he was hearing. "Wouldn't want to upset Lirah with my sordid past."

Gargarin hissed with frustration. "Froi, what has gotten into you? Be angry at me, but don't shut her out. If she doesn't know how to speak the right words with you, it's because she doesn't know what you want from her."

"But she knows what you want from her, doesn't she, Gargarin?" Froi spat.

Arjuro walked into the room, putting an end to the discussion. Froi could see that the priestling's body was tense with fury as he reached Gargarin and examined his map.

"So where to next?" Arjuro demanded to know.

Gargarin didn't respond but rolled up the chart quietly.

"You're in a hurry, are you?" Arjuro asked. "To walk away?"

The brothers' eyes were fixed on each other with bitter regret. At that moment, they could not have looked more different.

"You think I don't see it every time you look at me?" Arjuro asked. "The contempt."

"Not contempt, brother. Just sadness," Gargarin said, limping away from both Froi and Arjuro.

Arjuro grabbed Gargarin and threw him to the wall. "Say the words," Arjuro hissed. "Say you despise me for what I allowed to happen to you, because I see fury in your eyes, despite your soft tone."

Froi stepped between them, a hand to both their chests. Gargarin shoved them both from him.

"I don't despise you for what you allowed to happen to me," Gargarin said through clenched teeth. "I despise you because when I was released, you refused to be found and I needed you more than anything in my life. Not to mend my broken bones, Arjuro. I needed my brother to mend my broken spirit."

The next day, Arjuro was not to be found. His belongings were gone and no message was left. De Lancey sent his men to search, and Froi waited the whole day in the courtyard for them to return. The moment the guards arrived, De Lancey and Gargarin came down the steps, desperate for answers. But Arjuro had become a ghost.

"What about the godshouse?" Froi asked. "He'd wave to you and Gargarin every night when he was at school there."

"It was the first place we looked," one of the guards said.

Gargarin looked defeated and limped away. De Lancey followed.

"Did you know that someone stripped the flesh from his back and branded the word *traitor* across his shoulder blades?" Froi called out.

Both Gargarin and De Lancey looked back, anguish in their expressions. Froi nodded. "I saw him one night in the godshouse baths of Jidia. I think it's why he keeps himself covered up."

"We will find him," De Lancey said.

Gargarin shook his head. "No. We won't. If there is someone who knows how to disappear without a trace, it's my brother."

Apart from searching for Arjuro, Froi spent the days awaiting Feliciano of Avanosh's arrival and avoiding Quintana, Lirah, and Gargarin. Most times he was in the company of Grijio and

Olivier. Grijio knew of a cave with a long straight tunnel where Froi could teach them to hit a target with an arrow.

"It was my secret place for target practice when we planned to save Quintana," Grijio explained. "I'd leave a bow and a quiver of arrows there so the guards would not see me walking out of the compound holding a weapon. If they knew, they would have told my father for certain."

"Did you . . . ever actually hit a target?" Froi asked politely.

Grijio grinned. "No. Not once. My eyes are not good. They never have been."

The cave tunnel was long indeed, and Froi set up a target and gave his first lesson.

"You'll never get it this far back," Olivier said, straining to see where the target was in the dark of the cave.

"A wager?" Froi asked, steadying his hand, one eye closed. The lads loved a wager.

"One piece of silver a hit," Olivier offered.

Froi succeeded first go and held out his hand, laughing.

Then the others tried. Grijio was all thumbs and fingers while Olivier seemed a natural, although it was a while before he hit the perfect target.

When they weren't practicing hitting targets, they would sit on the roof of Grijio's secret cave overlooking the province and answering a string of Olivier's theoretical questions.

"What if you were given a choice between being the captain of the Guard or the king's First Adviser? Which would you choose?"

"King's First Adviser," Grijio said. "Or ambassador, at least."

"Captain, of course," Froi said.

Olivier thought of his own question. "I don't enjoy taking charge, so I'd be hopeless at both. But I'm good on a mount, and if I knew how to fight, I'd be honored to be a royal rider."

They continued their quizzing as they walked home. Grijio hollered a "Hello there" to everyone he passed.

"What if you had to choose between the most beautiful girl in the land, who was stupid, and the ugliest girl in the land, who was smart?" Olivier asked, running out of intelligent things to ask.

"Why can't there be one in between?" Grijio asked, dismayed. He sighed, thinking. "The problem with being a last-born male is that there aren't many women to pick from," he said. "I'd like her to be as smart as I am. Someone who doesn't just place worth on the build of a man or his ability to fight."

"That's very smart of you, Grij. Because your build and ability to fight are not your strong points," Olivier said.

Froi laughed and, on Grijio's behalf, jabbed Olivier with the arrow he was holding.

"One who knows the languages of the other kingdoms," Grijio continued. "Who doesn't believe the world ends at our borders. One who is kind." He looked at the others pensively. "We don't have enough kindness in this land."

"You're describing the queen of Lumatere," Froi said.

"Is she as beautiful as they say?" Olivier asked.

"She is indeed."

"Is your queen what you are searching for in a woman, Froi?" Grijio asked.

Froi thought for a moment. "I never imagined I was looking for something in a woman. But if I did, I'd have to judge her by the way I felt lying beside her before I went to sleep at night and how I felt in the morning waking up to her."

"Oh, too profound, my friend," Olivier mocked. "Much too profound."

When Froi arrived in the compound, he found Quintana in the courtyard. She had taken a liking to the pups there. When she

spoke to them, he heard the *reginita's* indignant voice and for a moment, he thought she had returned. But Quintana had learned that pups and people reacted better to the sound of her sister's voice than her own.

"They like it if you do this," Froi said, his voice husky as he tickled the belly of one. She tried herself and laughed at her pup's antics.

"Do you have one back home?" she asked.

"No, but Finn and Isaboe do. A massive hound. Finn calls her the bitch of Lumatere."

Quintana smiled a moment. "Finn and Isaboe," she said quietly, her eyes meeting his. "They seem so real when you name them."

He followed her into De Lancey's courtyard and up a passageway, a shortcut to their quarters. As she walked before him, he couldn't help reaching out and touching the exposed place at the back of her neck. She stopped but didn't turn. And it was as if she were waiting for something. Before he could stop himself, his arm snaked out to pull her toward him, his tongue tracing the writing at her nape. She shuddered in his arms.

When she turned to face him, Froi's mouth was on hers. His hand crawled up the skirt of her dress, his fingers finding their mark gently. *Be gentle, Froi,* he hummed to himself and the Serker inside of him shouted for more, but he took only what she would offer. He felt her hand find its way to the band of his trousers and he groaned aloud, trying to swallow the sound with their mouths.

But then she was gone, pushing him away.

"Why?" he asked, anguish in his voice.

She walked away, but he followed, a shaky hand to her shoulder. A servant came down the passageway toward them, and Froi turned, needing to conceal his arousal. Quintana took the chance to escape up the stairs.

By the time he reached the chamber where she lay on the bed, he was furious. He walked into his quarters and slammed the door, kicking it once, twice. He turned the key in the lock, fearful of where this rage would go. Always fearful. He wondered when he would ever trust that his anger was just anger and not a desire to hurt another, or a reminder of his past misdeeds. The bruised look in Quintana's eyes would also serve as a prompter. Each time he saw it, Froi would be reminded that the brutal actions of men were designed to break the spirits of the others. It was what he had tried to do in a Sorellian barn with Isaboe of Lumatere. Although a voice inside had chanted to stop that night, Froi would never know if he would have. And he wanted to know. He wanted to say the words, "I would not have gone through with it." But he'd never know, and that was his punishment. That, and being in love with a girl whose spirit had been broken by men like Froi.

Later, when dinner was called, he stepped outside his room to where she still lay on her bed with her back to him. He walked stonily past her to the door, but her voice stopped him leaving.

"Because I remembered your words," she said quietly. "I remembered that you liked me least. You said it in my palace chamber. 'Have one of the others wake me, for I like you least.'"

She turned to face him and brushed tears fiercely from her face. "Sometimes when I see what's left of Quintana of Charyn through my own eyes, I think I can learn to love her. But when I see her through your eyes, I despise her."

If she saw Quintana of Charyn through Froi's eyes, he knew she'd see a part of himself.

"Come," he said huskily, holding out a hand. "You need to eat."

CHAPTER 37

The day came when the Avanosh party arrived. Froi, Grijio, Olivier, and Tippideaux stood at the window watching the entourage ride into the courtyard. There were twelve of them, dressed in bright silks and carrying banners representing the ocean god.

The moment the youngest of the party dismounted, Froi and the others snorted with laughter.

"What is he wearing?" Tippideaux gasped.

"Could they be any tighter?" Grijio said.

"Where would you hide a weapon with such stockings?" Froi said.

"I can tell you where it looks like he's hiding a weapon from here," Olivier responded.

They watched De Lancey greet Feliciano of Avanosh and his people with a shake of a hand to each male and a kiss to the hand of each woman. Feliciano presented De Lancey with a small box, and Froi and the others watched De Lancey open it.

"Father's very unimpressed," Tippideaux said. "I can tell by his shoulders."

* * *

Dinner that night was a tedious affair, with Gargarin noticeably absent and the introductions going for far too long. There was handshaking and more handshaking, and boisterous laughter from the Avanosh uncle and aunt that had no substance. Froi had heard enough empty laughter in his lifetime not to trust it.

Feliciano was a handsome young man who constantly looked at his uncle before he spoke. He was seated beside Quintana, who in turn was polite and restrained.

"You are the light of our lives; you know that, don't you?" Feliciano said to her. "I've heard such words all across Charyn. The birth of your child is a gift only deserving of you."

Olivier made a sound of disbelief and stole a look at Froi, making a motion as if he was going to be ill.

"Thank you, Feliciano," she said politely, reaching over to take a piece of pheasant from his plate.

"They spoke of the insanity of your hair, but not once did they mention a sweet face and pretty eyes."

More looks between Froi and the others.

Tippideaux whispered her intense dislike of the whole situation to Froi and the lads. "When a woman has not received much flattery in her life, she will be seduced."

"It's Quintana," Froi murmured in reply, watching the idiot Feliciano flick a piece of hair from his eyes. "She'll never be taken in by charm and lies."

De Lancey introduced his children first and then Olivier of Sebastabol and Froi of Lumatere.

"A Lumateran in these parts?" the Avanosh uncle said. "From what part of Lumatere?"

"I was found in exile, sir," Froi said.

"You speak Charyn like a nobleman."

"It's not that hard to do anything like a Charyn nobleman," Froi responded, eyeing Feliciano.

"And your purpose in Paladozza?" the uncle continued.

"I travel with the princess, sir. I'm good with a dagger and a short sword and serve as her personal guard."

"Well, I don't believe your services will be required anymore," the uncle said. "We have our own guards, and we're hoping to take the Light of Charyn back to the island with us. No better place to protect a mother and her unborn child than an island."

"We haven't spoken about the princess leaving us, my lord," De Lancey said.

The uncle removed an envelope from his pocket. "We've traveled for some time, De Lancey, and have obtained the signatures from every *provincaro* apart from yourself, Nebia, and our unfortunately plague-ridden Desantos friends. The *provincari* of Charyn have approved the marriage of my nephew and the queen."

"Three of the *provincari,*" De Lancey corrected. He stared across the table. "If I could be so bold as to ask to see the document, my lord."

The envelope was passed down the table, and Froi wanted to tear it to pieces when it reached his hands. Olivier, instead, dropped it in his soup, apologizing profusely while the uncle forced another smile. The document reached De Lancey, who studied it awhile and then nodded.

"Well, that is that, then," De Lancey said quietly, looking at Quintana.

The uncle from Avanosh searched around the table. "And we were told Gargarin of Abroi was a visitor, De Lancey, yet he's nowhere to be seen."

Lirah placed down her fork. "He was feeling sick to the stomach tonight, my lord."

The man stared at her, uncomfortable.

"Lirah of Serker," she said. "Do you remember me? The king introduced us," she added, her words weighted with hatred. The uncle from Avanosh didn't respond.

Meanwhile Feliciano's cousin Abria seemed to have taken a liking to De Lancey, her hand constantly at his sleeve.

"Someone should tell Abria that your father hasn't been intimate with certain parts of a woman's body since his mother birthed him," Olivier whispered.

"Hush, Olivier," Tippideaux said, giggling.

After dinner when they all got up, Froi moved around the table to reach Quintana, but Feliciano was closer and there before him.

"If you would join me in my compound, Your Highness," Feliciano said. "My servants can have your items removed from your current room. My uncle will set a guard at every entrance of our residence."

"The protection of the queen lies with me," Froi said, leading Quintana away with a firm grip on her arm.

Tippideaux met them by the door.

"Aren't they hideous?" she said, yanking at a piece of Quintana's hair as though willing it to grow longer. "Froi said you would never believe the charm and lies," Tippideaux continued. "You deserve better than that."

"Lies?" Quintana asked, looking at Froi. "And what part was the lie? The sweet face or the pretty eyes?"

"That's not what I meant," he said, feeling the need to choke the life out of Tippideaux.

The very annoying Feliciano was back between them, holding out a hand to her.

"My uncle insists that you enjoy our hospitality, Your Highness."

Quintana caught Froi's eyes and he shook his head, but he

know the damage was already done. He watched her place her arm on Feliciano's sleeve.

Froi and the others stood beside De Lancey, watching the Avanosh party walk out of the dining room.

"What on earth did they give you in the box, Father?" Tippideaux asked. "When they arrived?"

"Sand," he said. "From their island. Sand. As if we don't have enough sand in our stone here."

Froi's mood was flat, his mind not able to get around Quintana and her consort alone in their residence. So later that night when Olivier suggested stealing out into the city below with a promise of ale, women, and good conversation, Froi readily agreed.

They found themselves in the bawdiest ale house in Paladozza, according to Grijio, who looked worried. He was recognized instantly as the son of the *provincaro*, and they were offered ale all night, although the offer always came with the words, "Perhaps a favor from your father, young Grijio."

But the ale did nothing to alter Froi's mood.

"You're in love with her?" Grijio said quietly.

Froi didn't respond.

"I don't mean to give offense, Froi," Olivier said, "but she's not an easy person to like. One doesn't always warm to her."

"There's more to her," Froi said, not denying either of them. He wanted to explain it, hoping they'd understand.

"Until three years ago, I couldn't read and write, I couldn't ride a horse or shoot an arrow and didn't know the difference between a turnip seed and grain. The men who have taught me everything back home, they often say to me, 'Froi, what if all your talents were left undiscovered?'"

He looked up at them. "It's the same with her. Imagine who she would be if we unleashed her onto the world. I think she would rip the breath from all of us."

Froi drank more that night than he had ever drunk in his life. Drinking was forbidden by the Guard in Lumatere unless off duty, and even then it had to be in moderation. But Froi was sick of bonds. Sick of moderation. Sick of having to hold back.

The next morning, however, Froi wished he had held back. With little memory of what they had done the night before, all three of them were summoned to the *provincaro*'s library.

De Lancey was there to remind them of everything, fury in his expression.

"Exposing yourselves? To the locals?"

Froi vaguely remembered that part.

"Drunk? Singing bawdy songs about the gods of other kingdoms? Pissing in the prized gardens of Lady Orsa?"

Grijio looked shamefaced. Olivier pretended to. Froi's head was spinning too hard for anything to make sense.

"The Avanosh puppets think this is a province of debauchery!"

Grijio looked up. "You've never cared what people say about us, Father. About the way we live."

"But the rule has always been to conduct yourself with dignity, Grij. To have respect for others so you can demand respect back. There was nothing, nothing dignified about your behavior last night, or those women."

Women? Why didn't Froi remember women? How could he not remember women?

"What women?" he asked Olivier as they walked out.

"They want to meet us tonight," Olivier whispered. "Are you in, Grij? Froi?"

"They are so much older," Grijio said. "What do you think they'll want from us?"

At the entrance to the courtyard, they bumped into Feliciano of the Red Tights, as Olivier insisted on calling him. Froi had a hazy memory of strands of a song they penned for Red Tights the night before at the inn. Words to suggest that Feliciano's trousers resembled a sock and Froi was sure that the word describing Feliciano himself rhymed with sock.

"My betrothed and I would appreciate less noise when you arrive home," the heir to Avanosh said pompously. "It woke us last night."

Feliciano was pinned to the wall before Froi could count out his bond, a hand to the other lad's throat. Olivier and Grijio pulled Froi away before his fist could connect.

The moment he could escape, Feliciano scampered down the stairs. Froi pulled free of the others and walked back to his chamber. The image of Quintana and that idiot together last night, today, and forever, made him want to kill someone.

Suddenly Lirah was at the top of the steps, her hand on his arm to stop him.

"Where have you been for sunrise these last days, Froi?" Lirah's voice was always blunt, emotionless. "Gargarin says you're not yourself."

"Gargarin doesn't know who I am," he snapped, "so how could he possible know I'm not myself?"

"Well, he would like you to come visit," she said, her voice calm. "He needs to speak to you urgently. This business with Avanosh is a worry."

"I'm not his messenger boy," Froi said. "He has you for that. A good deal for him, indeed," he added spitefully. "He gets to bed you, and you run errands for him."

She stared at him, a flash of anger and hurt in her eyes. She nodded, as though comprehending his words. "Well, there it is," she said. "There's the Serker male. Can only express pain through bitter words." She let her hand drop and walked away.

Froi took a deep breath and turned back down the steps again. He was in the mood to find Feliciano again and tell him exactly what he thought of him. But outside in the courtyard, he could only find Olivier and Grijio.

"Tonight," he said. "If you're up to it again, I'm in."

CHAPTER 38

No matter how hard they tried, Froi and the lads were unable to lose De Lancey's guards that night. The three had to settle for drinking in the ale house under close watch.

"I can't believe that if I take a woman tonight, my guard will probably stand at the foot of the bed and give instruction," Grijio said, forlorn. "I need to get out of Paladozza."

Olivier laughed. "And there are those who would die to live here. Our lad," Olivier explained to Froi, "is frightened that the princess will be the only girl he'll ever have lain with."

"We didn't actually lie with each other," Grijio said. "She made me leave the moment it was over, and believe me, it was over in the blink of an eye. She was very particular about not sharing her bed. Wasn't she, Froi?"

Froi looked from one to the other. "What impression have I given either of you that I want to hear or discuss anything about the princess and last borns and consorts?" he said, anger lacing his words. He was fighting with all his might not to think of Quintana and that idiot Feliciano.

Olivier called for another round of drinks, and the subject

of Quintana was finished with. But after a pint or two, Olivier leaned forward and ushered them toward him.

"I don't trust the Avanosh lot. Why would the *provincaro* of Sebastabol not have sent that note through me?"

"The seal was there. My father saw it," Grijio said.

"I still don't trust them."

Froi studied the last born. "What are you thinking, Olivier?"

Olivier looked over their shoulders to where Froi knew De Lancey's guards were standing watch.

"We do what you and I and Satch and Tariq set out to do in the Citavita, Grij," Olivier said. "We save Quintana." His eyes caught Froi's, and he winked. "We give her a chance to unleash herself onto the world."

Froi stared at him.

"When?"

"This is going too fast, lads," Grijio said.

"Not fast enough," Olivier responded. "Yesterday they met. Today betrothed. Tomorrow she'll be gone and we will not be able to protect her.

"Maybe Avanosh is the safest place for her," Grijio said, regret in his voice.

Froi would never believe that to be true.

"Maybe," Olivier said. "But maybe they're under orders from Sorel and one day we will be part of that heinous kingdom of prison mines and slavery."

Froi was on his feet. He could hardly breathe at the thought of his son and Quintana in Sorel with no one to protect them. Olivier grabbed him by the sleeve and yanked him back down.

"You can take Quintana through one of the caves that lead up to the central hills," Olivier whispered. "I can lead you, Froi. I know the way."

"Then I'll come too," Grijio said.

"No, you need to stay here, Grij," Olivier insisted. "To give them false leads. They need to think we've traveled south or east."

"Just say . . ." Grijio began, looking at Froi cautiously.

"Just say what?" Froi demanded.

"Just say Quintana may not believe she needs saving?" Grijio said. "I saw her with Feliciano today, and she seemed charmed, alarmingly so."

Froi had noticed too. Quintana was a tamer person in the presence of the Avanosh lot.

Olivier sat up straight, and suddenly a grin appeared on his face.

"We'll speak of this again later," he said. "The women are approaching."

A moment later, Froi felt a hand run through his hair and then he saw a pretty face and lips painted red.

"This one is mine," she said, pulling him to his feet. He looked into her eyes, warm and laughing eyes, but not those he wanted to be looking into. Not the face. Not the body with the round belly and strange scars. Not Quintana.

"I'm bonded to two women," he blurted out because it was the ale speaking and Froi was coming to realize that he was very stupid under the influence of ale.

"Well, aren't we the intriguing one?" she whispered in his ear.

Back in Quintana's room, he saw the empty bed for the second night in a row. He stared at it a moment, fury clenching his hands. He locked her door, wanting to throw away the key, to stop himself from tearing through De Lancey's compound and finding that idiot from Avanosh. He didn't want to count to ten and remember his bond. He wanted to feel the anger, and with every image that came to his head, Froi's rage grew and grew.

Later he heard the doorknob rattle, and he grabbed his dagger and leaped to his feet. But whoever it was knocked, and he opened the door to see Quintana standing in the hallway, dressed in her nightgown, trying to peer over his shoulder. He stepped in front to block her way.

"What are you looking for?" he asked coldly.

"Who are you hiding back there?" she asked, trying to push past him until he felt the pounding of her heart against his own chest and the sound of her breathing against his ear.

"What makes you think I'm hiding anyone?"

And when he saw her mouth curl into a snarl, his blood began to beat into a frenzy of excitement and he matched her heartbeat, breath by breath. She stepped to his side, trying to get into the room, and he blocked her again and again and again until she clenched her fists and pounded his shoulder.

"Did you bring a woman back here?"

"Did you share his bed?"

Suddenly Olivier and Grijio and Lirah and Tippideaux appeared in the hallway.

"Answer me," she shouted.

"Answer me!"

"You're drunk!"

"Did you let him touch you?"

Quintana cried with fury. "You dare to accuse me of such a thing when you come back to my room with the smell of a woman on your stinking body."

"Did you let him swive you?"

She threw herself at him, and it took both Olivier and Grijio to hold her back.

Froi snarled and clenched his fist.

"Do it. Do it!" she cried until Lirah came between them, grabbing both their hands.

"Enough," Lirah said calmly, and she held them both to her. Quintana was sobbing, "I don't understand this, Lirah. I don't understand," and Froi wanted to sob the same words.

"Because matters of the heart are not there to be understood, brave girl," Lirah said as Tippideaux led them away, fussing like a mother hen.

The lads stared toward where the women disappeared and then exchanged looks.

"I must say I found that . . . quite exciting," Olivier said.

Grijio nodded. "Feel my pulse."

Later, Froi lay in his cot on the ground, hating her. Hating. First opportunity he got, he wasn't going to take her through the cave with Olivier. He was going to go on his own and travel back to Lumatere and he was going to ask for a Flatland girl's hand in marriage and live on a pocket of land for the rest of his life and never leave Lumatere again. No. A River girl. He'd marry a River girl because they were wilder, but still not savage one moment and ice-cold and vicious the next.

He heard a sound at his door and sat up, and he saw her there in the shadows, holding a candle and staring down at him.

"I took no woman," he said, forgetting every vow he had just made never to speak to her again. "Allowed no woman to touch me."

"The guard said the women were like flies on you all."

"But I was thinking of another and I couldn't bear their touch."

And he saw it in her eyes. *Still.* The belief that there could be someone other than herself. *You,* he wanted to shout. You. No one but you. *Stupid, stupid girl.*

And when she didn't leave his door, Froi pulled back the blankets and shuffled over to the wall. He held out a hand, and he saw in her expression that she wrestled with the savage inside of her, but Froi's hand stayed outstretched. She would never trust easily. Never. But he would make it his bond to ensure that one day she would trust him without hesitation.

And then she was lying there beside him.

"My feet were cold in their part of the compound," she muttered.

"Well, we can't have that, can we?" he said, warming them against his and tucking the blanket over her body.

"I heard the Avanosh aunt say, 'She should grow her hair to hide that pointy chin and pointy nose.'"

"If I see that pointy chin and nose hidden, I'll have to hurt someone."

"You're supposed to say I don't have a pointy chin or pointy nose," she said, somewhat dryly.

"But you do," he said. "And you also have pointy eyes," he added as he kissed both lids, "and a pointy mouth," he teased, pressing his lips against hers, "and a pointy tongue." His body covered hers as he held her face in his hands and captured her mouth, the silk warmness of her tongue matching his, stroke by stroke. Then he felt the sharp nip of her teeth as his mouth dared to leave hers, traveling toward her throat, fleetingly tracing the scars from the noose. "And a pointy, pointy heart," he murmured, feeling the powerful beat that her enemies had tried to crush from the moment she was born. One hand cupped her breast as his other hand lifted the folds of her nightdress and drew her closer.

"Does the queen of Lumatere have all those things?" she asked quietly.

Froi didn't want to talk about the queen of Lumatere. He didn't want to talk about anything. His need for Quintana was fierce. It had been a long time since that last night in the palace.

He fumbled at the drawstring of his trousers, loosening them, then taking her hand and pressing it against him. Still, she stared with a question in her eyes. Froi knew she wanted more from him and although he ached for her, he fought hard to control his desire. Counted to ten in every language he knew. Counted to ten again. And again. Until his breathing was less ragged and his hand linked with hers. Finally he sighed and placed his arm around her, drawing her close.

"The queen of Lumatere complains constantly of her nose. 'Too big,' she says. Finnikin just shrugs and says, 'What would I do with a queen who has a little nose?'"

Quintana laughed, and she leaned her head against his chest. "He's supposed to say she doesn't have a big nose."

"I know, but Finnikin was brought up by men. If it wasn't the Guard for the first ten years, it was Sir Topher for the next nine. He knows very little about women."

"So what do you say when the queen of Lumatere comments about her nose?"

He flicked a finger at her nose. "I tell her I've seen much bigger."

"You are a smart man, Dafar of Abroi."

He shuddered with pleasure to hear his name spoken by her.

"Froi?"

"Yes."

"I don't trust the Avanosh party," she whispered. She moved closer to his ear. "I've allowed them to believe that all is civil between us, but I think they are planning something wicked. There's too much whispering, and Feliciano doesn't seem to have control. His uncle does. He reminds me of Bestiano."

She shuddered, and Froi held her closer.

"Don't let them take away our little king, Froi. Not the Avanosh people or Bestiano. I'm begging you, Froi."

That she had to speak the words broke something inside of him.

"I will protect you," he whispered. "I will never let anything happen to you or our child."

And he would come to realize sooner rather than later that it was the greatest lie he had ever spoken aloud.

CHAPTER 39

He went to see Gargarin in his chamber the next morning. It was almost a miniature compound, with two bedrooms and a library. Gargarin was writing with vigor, and Froi could hear Lirah pottering around in the other room. They'd be safe and comfortable here. Despite his bitterness, at least he could take that away with him.

"I don't trust the people of Avanosh," Gargarin said, his head still bent as he wrote.

"Nor do I."

Gargarin sighed, and their eyes met. Froi saw relief in Gargarin's. "Good. I have a plan."

Froi shook his head. "I have a plan. I'm taking her. Probably to Turla."

"Excellent. My plan exactly. If anyone can hide us, it's Ariston. We can leave—"

"I'm taking her alone."

Froi heard a sound behind him and saw Lirah standing at the dividing door. She looked at Gargarin.

"I can't look after you," Froi said. "I can't protect you and Lirah and Quintana."

"But I can protect you, Froi," Gargarin said. "I've written to every *provincaro*. Every ambassador. I've attempted to contact every Mountain tribe. We can build an army, bigger than Bestiano and Nebia's. Her army, Froi. Without one, she has no power."

Froi shook his head. "You'll slow us down," he said bluntly.

"But if we get caught, you will be protected by my name," Gargarin said. "I'm beginning to realize that at a time like this it means something."

"Your name is nothing," Froi argued. "You can't protect me. Neither of you can. You never did!"

Lirah stood watching them. "We stay together. We need you both," she said firmly.

"He can't even protect himself," Froi shouted. "Did he save you from harm? Or me? Do you want to know what they did to me in Sarnak, Gargarin? Do you want to know what they made me do?"

Tears of rage spilled from Froi's eyes. Because he loved them and he hated them. Because he wanted them safe and he wanted to hurt them beyond anything else. So he spoke the words he had never dared to speak aloud. About the men who controlled the backstreets of the Sarnak capital and made him sing on street corners because his voice was sweet and high and a gift from the gods. How the rich merchants would pay to take him home. And he spoke of the time in that stable in Sorel when he tried to take Isaboe of Lumatere. He watched Lirah and Gargarin flinch, as though his words were Gargarin's cane beating them over and over again until nothing much was left of Gargarin's and Lirah's spirits.

"You couldn't protect me, so why would I trust you with Quintana and my son?"

* * *

He knocked on Olivier's door moments later. The last born of Sebastabol looked worse for the wear, having had little sleep the night before.

"Let's talk about what we spoke of last night in the inn," Froi said.

Olivier looked down the hallway and ushered him in.

"When can you be ready?"

"We are ready."

They planned to meet the others in the courtyard under the pretense of an excursion into the *vicinata*. They were to take no possessions with them, for it would draw attention and cause suspicion, and Grijio felt it best that they invite Feliciano along as well.

"We're going to see the last days of the greatest show in the kingdom," Grijio called out with a wave to his father on the balcony, beside the uncle from Avanosh.

Froi felt De Lancey's eyes on him, and there was something in his stare that told Froi he knew what would take place. That Gargarin had already spoken to him.

"Grij?" De Lancey called out. They were almost out the gate and they nervously looked back up at the *provincaro*.

"If you and Tippideaux aren't back in time, I'll send the guards to come search for you."

It was a father's warning. That whatever the plan was, it would not involve his children.

As they traveled down the road to the *vicinata,* Tippideaux clutched Quintana's arm.

"I'm not feeling myself today," Tippideaux sniffed, and Froi could see she was weeping, truly weeping and not just acting out her part in their charade. "All this anger from Father about your nonsense, Grij. It's upset us all. Upset the queen."

Grijio stopped and held out a hand to Quintana. She took it, and he pressed a kiss to it. In the eyes of Feliciano, it was an apology. In the eyes of the others, a farewell.

"You've never offered anything but friendship, Grijio," Quintana said. "One day I'll repay it tenfold despite your poor form these past nights."

Quintana turned her attention back to Feliciano and linked her arm with his, while taking one moment more to clutch Tippideaux's fingers before walking ahead with the heir of Avanosh.

When they reached the lane that would take them into the *vicinata,* Olivier indicated the fletcher's cottage with a slight toss of his head.

"Be safe, friends," Grijio said, quickly embracing Froi and Olivier.

"Everything is for Charyn," Olivier said somberly, his voice breaking from emotion. *"Everything."*

Tippideaux quickly hugged Froi. "Keep her warm. She's awfully bad-tempered when she's cold."

And then they all caught up with Quintana and Feliciano, full of pretend laughter and talk of the greatest show in the kingdom.

"Feliciano," Tippideaux said in a hushed tone, with a wink toward the stalls they could see at the entrance of the *vicinata.* "Trinkets. A perfect gift for a blushing betrothed."

He nodded, unaware of what was brewing, and Tippideaux dragged him away.

Froi grabbed Quintana's hand, and then they were running for the fletcher's cottage.

"Can we trust this man?" Froi asked Olivier.

"Just trust that he will do anything to protect the princess and the babe," Olivier said as they entered the house.

"This way," they heard someone say.

Froi followed the voice down into the cellar, his hand never letting go of Quintana's. An oil lamp was lit, and he saw the fletcher and his wife standing before them.

"Quick. Help me with this," the fletcher said.

It took the weight of Olivier, Froi, and the fletcher combined to push aside the stone, revealing a tunnel that would lead to the hills just outside the province to the north.

"It will take you no longer than a day," the man said. "I'll travel behind you soon to replace the stones."

Olivier handed over a purse of coins.

"Paladozza must not fall," Olivier said firmly.

The fletcher's wife took the purse of coins from her husband.

"Can I see?" she asked, reaching out a hand to Quintana. Froi froze. *Don't touch her,* he prayed. The last thing they needed was Quintana's savage strangeness frightening those who were here to help. But Quintana took the woman's hand and pressed it against her belly and the woman wept. In return, she placed the purse of coins inside Quintana's hands.

"Keep them," the fletcher's wife said. "They will come to good use. You can return the favor when you're settled in the palace with the heir."

"We need to go," Olivier said.

"Weapons?" the man asked.

"I have a sword and two daggers," Froi said.

"We're wasting time," Olivier hissed, pulling Froi and Quintana away.

"Here," the man said, giving Froi and Olivier a bow each and a quiver of arrows. "Protect her with your life, lads."

CHAPTER 40

Beatriss traveled through the Flatlands with Tarah and Samuel to see how her villagers were faring. They were scattered across the kingdom, some as far away as the Rock village, quarrying stone, or the River villages, gutting fish. Most expressed sadness when they heard she would be moving into the palace with Vestie. "Always thought we'd be able to return to you," they said. "We may have work here, but we don't have a home, Lady Beatriss."

As they passed the road that led to the village of Fenton, she saw a crowd. The Queen's Guard was there as well, and among them Trevanion sat astride his horse. Beatriss remembered Isaboe's words the day the queen visited and they had traveled back to the palace together. That she was not to expect Trevanion to reveal his feelings of the past. "They're not like us women, Beatriss. For all their strength and might, any talk of the past pains them, and if you're waiting for him to speak words you want to hear, then make the decision to live without him now. For you may never hear them."

"What do you think is happening there?" she asked Samuel.

"Why, the palace is auctioning the village, Lady Beatriss,"

Samuel said gently. "Did you not know? The surviving Fenton villagers will all receive ten pieces of gold to resettle elsewhere or stay if they wish. The queen says it's what Lord Selric would have wanted."

"The queen and Finnikin mentioned as much. What are the villagers saying?"

Tarah made a rude sound. "Those of Lord Freychinet's village are saying they wished he was dead in a ditch someplace in Charyn and they had ten apiece."

"Doubt anyone will stay in Fenton, though," Samuel said. "Not if Lord Nettice buys."

Beatriss shuddered at the thought.

"Let's stop awhile," she said quietly. "I see dear friends."

She approached Abian and August, who kept their distance from the other lords and ladies. Abian hugged her tightly.

"Sad day," August said. "If they waited until spring, I'd have the money from the crop. Selric would have hated any of that lot getting hold of his land and people."

Beatriss knew from Abian that August felt he had let his neighbor down. She squeezed his arm. "You've taken on more of his villagers than you can afford to, August. He would have been grateful."

They watched Lord Nettice and his cronies, who were laughing among themselves. Already they were thumping Nettice's back with congratulations, as though he already owned Fenton.

"What I don't understand is where he got his gold from," Lady Abian said, bitterness in her voice.

"He made his money shamelessly under the impostor king's rule," Beatriss said quietly.

Her eyes met Genova's. She was huddled with her husband, Makli, and the survivors of Fenton. As was the case with Sennington, the village of Fenton once boasted sixty-four people and was now down to twenty-eight. Most had died in the Charyn plague. What was ten pieces of gold worth to them when they were still grieving the loss of neighbors?

A moment later, Trevanion approached and dismounted. Beatriss felt her face warming up under the intensity of his stare.

"Honestly, Trevanion, can't you arrest them for their smugness?" August said.

Abian's fury could hardly be contained. "If any of their wives come near me to boast the purchase, you're going to have to bail me out of the palace dungeon tonight, Augie, because I don't know what I'll do to them."

Trevanion laughed. He looked at Beatriss. "Would you like me to arrest Lord Nettice for purely existing, Beatriss?"

Beatriss's stomach churned at the mention of his name. She was unable to join in the jest, and all too soon Trevanion's smile was gone and he was off to oversee the growing crowd.

It was all a farce, really. The poor Fenton lot had pooled together their promised amount, deciding that perhaps they would try to buy it together, but Lord Nettice doubled the amount the moment it began and it was humiliating to watch. Humiliating. Beatriss stared at the man, the word thundering inside her head. Humiliating. *Humiliating.* Her anger grew. She felt its rage, but there was no longer shame in it.

What had her fellow Lumaterans said about her during those early years of the impostor king's cruel reign? That she gave them courage. That each time his men ruined her land, Beatriss the Bold refused to stop planting.

"Four hundred pieces of gold," she shouted. It was what the priest-king had promised her for Sennington.

There was a stunned silence around her. August and Abian stared at her as if she had lost her senses. It wasn't that they doubted she had money, but to buy a village? Beatriss looked across at where Lord Nettice stood with his wife alongside Lord Freychinet and their acquaintances.

"Five hundred," Lord Nettice said, and her heart dropped.

Every person standing on the field stared back at her, but Beatriss knew she could not match the price. The auctioneer waited.

"Five hundred and ten, Lady Beatriss?" the auctioneer called out, searching for her through the crowd. "Perhaps another go?"

"End this," Lord Nettice shouted at the man, but the auctioneer refused to be rushed.

Suddenly Makli and Genova were there beside Beatriss, as were the rest of the Fenton villagers.

"End this," they heard Lord Nettice shout again.

"Lady Beatriss," the auctioneer called out, his voice anxious. "Another bid, perhaps."

"We have two hundred and eighty coins between us," Genova said. "Use it, Lady Beatriss. Use it all. If he wins the bid, Fenton is lost to us. The pride of Lord Selric and his beloved girls are lost to us."

Beatriss caught Makli's eye and she saw sorrow there and before she could stop herself, she pushed through the crowd and reached the front, her stare fixed on Lord Nettice.

"I bid six hundred and eighty pieces of gold!" she said. "Do you have the nerve to outbid me, Lord Nettice?"

"Nerve?" Lord Freychinet laughed, looking at his friend. "What has nerve to do with it? I'll lend you the rest, Nettice."

Lord Nettice hesitated, and Beatriss dared the coward to be the first to look away. For it would not be her. Never again would she look away from this man. She stepped closer, until she was almost nose to nose with him.

"I defy you to outbid me," she said. "I defy you."

There was a hush from the crowd, filled with confusion and anticipation and hope.

"Sold to Lady Beatriss for six hundred and eighty pieces of gold," the auctioneer shouted, his words slicing through the silence.

"What?" There was outrage from Lord Freychinet and their companions.

"Too fast," Lord Freychinet shouted at the man. "Too fast."

"End this. End this," the auctioneer mimicked. "Is that not what you shouted? Make up your mind. I'm finished for the day."

"This is an outrage!" Lady Milla said.

"Nettice! Do something," his wife said.

"Leave it," Lord Nettice said to his entourage, his tone cold and bitter. "Leave it. She's paid too much for it, anyway. Fenton was always the runt of the villages."

Through the crowd Beatriss could see Trevanion, his eyes on Nettice as if he wanted to tear the man apart. But a moment later, she was surrounded by those of Fenton and lost sight of him. Abian and August were there too, as were Tarah and Samuel and anyone present from Sennington. They all seemed stunned at the quick outcome of the day's events. Beatriss could hardly find the words to speak.

"Did I just buy a village?" she asked.

Then Makli laughed. "You did indeed, Lady Beatriss. You did indeed."

That afternoon her home was filled to the brim with those from Sennington and Fenton. Even the auctioneer had returned with them when he heard of the ale and the sweets to be served.

"May I make a toast?" Beatriss called out when the sun was beginning to set and it was time for her guests to leave. Silence came over the room.

"A toast to Lord Selric and Lady Milla and Lady Hera and

Frana and Lentro. And a toast to those others we lost from Fonton and Sennington." Beatriss's eyes blazed with tears. "We won't have a moment's rest this coming year, dear friends. Not a moment's rest, but we break our backs in their names."

There was a cheer for her words, and she stood among them overwhelmed with fear and exhilaration. What had she gotten herself into? What would people say? One moment refusing to step outside her house, next moment buying a village.

Later, the man who had conducted the sale approached and took her hand, and she smiled.

"I gather you weren't a big supporter of Lord Nettice after what you did today?" she asked. "Did he do you wrong, sir?"

The auctioneer, named Pollock, shook his head. "I'm not interested in those who do me wrong, Lady Beatriss. There's not enough time in the day for them. But my daughter spent five safe years in the cloisters because of you and that mad Tesadora. Won't be forgotten by me and my wife. I can tell you that."

She stood awhile and watched them all go, but as she turned, she heard the sound of a horse coming down the road. Samuel stepped out beside her.

"It's the captain," she said quietly. "I'm safe, Samuel."

She waited for Trevanion to dismount, and without a word, he followed her into the house.

"Was it him?" he asked, and she heard the barely contained rage in his voice.

She sighed, pouring him a cider and cutting him a slice of cake.

"And what are you going to do to him if it was?" she asked.

"Kill him," he said through clenched teeth.

"No, you won't," she said gently.

Trevanion kicked the stool out of the way, and it bounced off the wall and splintered. "I've killed traitors before, Beatriss. It's my job. In what way would this be any different?" he asked.

Beatriss calmly picked up what was left of the stool. "Because you don't have proof. Nettice was smart in that way. He would come to this house often in the early days to talk about the soldiers and his hatred for the impostor king. Later he'd tell me he was lonely. His wife kept a cold bed. I would send him away each time. And then suddenly he was a guest of the impostor king in the palace. A fact I knew because I was dragged down there often enough."

She caught Trevanion's wince of pain.

"Nettice would tell all who would listen that his visits to the palace were to make life easier for us, but the only families who had an easy life were those who collaborated."

She swallowed, trying to keep down the bile that always rose when she thought of those years.

"He must have made a deal with the impostor king and somehow I became part of that bargain because the king and his men didn't touch me again. And do you want to know the truth, Trevanion?" she asked. "I felt relief. Each time he came up that path, I felt relief. Better a demon I knew, better one man than any of the others in the palace. Relief," she cried. "Nothing more. Nothing. And that relief shamed me and he knew, trading on that shame all these years."

Trevanion closed his eyes, his expression so pained that she wanted some kind of magic to take away all their suffering. But that type of magic didn't exist.

"He stopped the visits when I was carrying Vestie, and then, of course, there was Tesadora. Nothing frightened those cowardly men more than Tesadora. Her friendship saved my life. It saved my spirit."

Beatriss began to clear away the plates and cakes. She looked away so she wouldn't have to see his face. Would there be judgment? Had it been easier for him to love Vestie knowing that the father was nowhere in their lives?

Trevanion stayed, his silence frightening. And there they sat opposite each other, two people who had grown older without the comfort of the other. She wanted to weep for the lost opportunities. But deep in the night, when she thought there would never be words between them again, he spoke.

"The reason I couldn't ask questions all this time is that I feared I'd have to respond to yours in return." His voice was low and hoarse. "That I'd have to speak of being imprisoned in the mines and my first months there and what I let them do to me and how I couldn't save those two brothers from the Rock who came to join me there."

He looked away, the tears biting at his eyes.

"We didn't let them do anything to us, Trevanion," Beatriss said fiercely. "They did it without our permission."

She walked to where he sat and placed her arms around him. He turned and buried his face against her waist and she thought she felt a sob against her, and they stayed wrapped around each other, bathed by the sounds of this house that had seen the worst and best of times. But all Beatriss had to hear was the sound of his breathing and her child mumbling in sleep to know that perhaps for tonight alone all was good in her world.

"Do you remember the day three years ago when we spoke at the babe's grave?" he asked. "Do you remember your words? Has anything changed? About how you can never go back to the way things were?"

She took his face in her hands. "I only remember the words that haven't changed, Trevanion."

She pressed her brow against his.

"I still wake with your name on my lips every morning."

CHAPTER 41

Froi's only consolation as they crawled through the underground caves of Paladozza was that the tunnels were too narrow and long to allow an army to invade. And in that way, Gargarin and Lirah would stay safe in Paladozza. Try as he might, he couldn't get their faces out of his head and already felt a strong sense of loss knowing he might never see them again.

They rested that night close to the stone that would take them out into the hills of the north. The space was too small for comfort, but Quintana curled against him, asleep in an instant. Froi couldn't help thinking of Isaboe when she was carrying Jasmina in her belly. The way everyone in the palace fussed over her. How Finn would prop her up against him and knead her shoulders and back while she gave Sir Topher instructions on how to deal with the merchants in the main village who refused to work with some of the Flatland lords. Froi couldn't count the amount of times he'd ride from Sayles to the palace on an errand for Lady Abian, who insisted that the queen have the best apples their orchard had to offer, or the days he had accompanied Finn to the mountains because the juiciest berries in the kingdom were grown there and Isaboe deserved the best.

"You are all becoming tiresome," she'd complain. "I'm carrying a child, not dying of an ailment."

And Froi wanted all of that for Quintana. He wanted to hear her complain how tiresome they all were with the attention they were giving and how she was sick of resting and sick of taking warm baths and sick of her people waiting on her hand and foot. Yet here Quintana was, crawling through the bowels of a city for a kingdom of people who would never truly understand what she had sacrificed for them.

Hours later, he gently shook her awake and their journey continued.

"I'll hurt the babe," Quintana said as they used their elbows to crawl along the jagged contours of the ground beneath.

"It won't be for too long, Your Highness," Olivier gasped. "My mother told me often that she took a tumble a time or two on the docks of Sebastabol when she was carrying me."

"That's no comfort, Olivier," Froi said. "You're an idiot most times."

The tunnel finally spilled out into a larger cave, and soon they'd be out in the hills. Froi felt the breeze come through the cracks in the stone, and he smelled their freedom. His eyes met Quintana's, and he saw hope there. The hills would be a safe enough refuge, and in days to come they would be back with the Turlan mountain goats. It made Froi laugh to think of it.

"When we get to Turla, Olivier, do not try to prove your manhood," he said as they followed the last born.

"I've never really been one to do that," Olivier said.

"Then you've not met the Turlans," Quintana said.

They reached the last stone and pushed it aside, shielding their eyes as light poured into the cave. Crawling out first, Froi could see they were in a small ravine with a stream between them and the hills on the other side. He climbed up to the cave top they had come from and saw the woodlands farther north.

When he jumped back down, he took Quintana's hand and they walked farther along the stream, ready to cross where the water was a trickle. Quintana looked out into the distance, and the rare smile she gave Froi lit up his heart.

"To the hills we go," she said. He pressed her palm to his cheek.

The arrow took him by surprise, and he grunted from the pain as it ripped through his thigh. Froi pulled Quintana down to him, crawling behind the closest rock. Olivier followed, and Froi could hear his ragged breath. He stole a look from their hiding place, and his blood ran cold. Men were scattered across the stream and throughout the hills, with their bows cocked, pointing down at them. At least fifty. Neither unprepared nor surprised. Waiting. Some were dressed in the uniform of the palace riders, and Froi knew that Bestiano's men had been waiting. They had been betrayed.

Froi took in his surroundings. He had to think fast. It was safer to climb the rock behind them and run for the woodlands than it was to return to the tunnel.

"There," he said, taking a quick painful breath and pointing to a large boulder.

Olivier was panicking. Froi could see from the sweat on the last born's brow and the tremble in his body.

"Olivier, help me with this," Froi gasped, placing a hand over the arrow in his thigh. He needed to get it out. But Olivier could only stare at it in horror.

"Squeamish? You idiot!"

Without Olivier's help, Froi placed both his hands around the arrow's base and pulled it free with a hoarse shout of pain. He stole a look again and saw that Bestiano's riders were still

waiting. He wondered if the three of them stood a chance.

"Froi, listen to me," Olivier said. Pleaded. "They'll protect her. And they won't kill you. I promise."

Froi froze. *No,* he thought. *Not Olivier.* He trusted this lad with his life. With Quintana's life and that of his unborn child. His eyes met the last born's, and he saw the truth there.

"Olivier?" Froi said the word, his voice broken. "Have you betrayed us? Have you led us into a trap?"

Quintana gasped, and Froi saw her horror and fear.

"Not a betrayal, friends," Olivier said. "A reprieve. You can't keep her safe, Froi. You can't. The Avanosh people almost took her from us. They would have made her a puppet to Sorel. Who will be the next lot to try to take her, Froi? At least Bestiano—"

Quintana cried out at the sound of Bestiano's name, her arms clutching her body as she wept with futile rage.

"How could you do this to your queen?" Froi bit out with fury.

"How could I not?" Olivier shouted back. "I love my kingdom, Froi, and I will keep it safe. It was the pledge I made to the men you sent to keep me prisoner while you became Olivier of Sebastabol. And they gave me worth. All my life a useless last born, and for once, I had purpose."

Froi took deep breaths to alleviate the pain and to think. *Think, Froi. Think.*

"Rafuel of Sebastabol despised the king and Bestiano, you fool," Froi said.

"No," Olivier said shaking his head emphatically. "Zabat said—"

"Zabat? Zabat was a traitor. He switched sides, Olivier. Took you with him without you even noticing. The men who kidnapped you belong to the priests of Trist, and Zabat betrayed them to the riders. Bestiano's men killed Tariq."

Olivier shook his head, refusing to believe.

Froi secured the bow and placed the quiver of arrows on his back.

"You are putting her life in danger, Froi!" Olivier said, a plea in his voice.

Froi snarled. "The first man who fires a bolt at Quintana and the child she carries puts her life in danger."

Froi held a hand to Quintana's frightened face. "She does not go to Bestiano," he promised.

He took in another deep breath of pain, his eyes fixed on Quintana's. "We're going to run up to that boulder," he said, pointing up. "They won't shoot at you, so don't stop until you reach it."

"But they'll shoot at you," she said.

"And I'll shoot back."

"You're putting both your lives at risk," Olivier cried.

"A curse on you, Olivier," Froi shouted. "A curse. You put both our lives at risk, and if I ever know that you've returned to Paladozza to taint the lives of Grij and Tippideaux and De Lancey and Lirah and Gargarin, I will hunt you down and tear you apart limb by limb."

Struggling to his feet, Froi looked at Quintana. He drew his bow, gave her a nod, and they both ran.

He never stood a chance. The arrows came for him. Another to his thigh. One to his calf. One to the side of his torso. All those drills in the meadows of Lumatere and all that instruction, but Froi never stood a chance. When they reached the boulder and she saw the arrows, Quintana's cry was full of rage and Froi could have sworn he felt the earth move around them. But the despair was also Froi's, the knowledge that he could not protect her and his child. It made him want to weep.

He pressed her down behind the rock, trying with all his might to keep the grimace of pain from his expression. Her

hands hovered around him, as if she had no idea where to place them. Froi reached out and gripped one of them.

"It's not that I liked you least," he croaked through his pain, "it's that I feared you most. The *reginita* taught me to like you. There was a strange joy to her that lifted my spirits. But you, Quintana of Charyn, you made me love you. And you're going to have to promise me something."

"Don't ask me to leave you," she cried through clenched teeth. "I can't do this on my own."

"You can. You did it before. That last day in the Citavita when you let go of my hand. You thought I was a threat to you, and you chose to protect the little king on your own rather than put him in danger. On your own, Quintana. You can do it again."

She shook her head over and over again.

"The moment I stand and begin lobbing my arrows, you run," he ordered, "and keep on running. Try to get to Turla. Keep away from the north. Satch has written to say there's plague in Desantos. But you run, Quintana, and you keep yourself alive."

"We'll do it together, Froi," she said with determination, pressing the skirt of her dress to the wound on his thigh to stop the bleeding.

He shook his head. Too much pain. Too much pain.

"I can't protect you," he gasped. "Not like this. I will slow you down, and Bestiano will take you. He will kill you the moment you birth the babe."

"But they'll kill you."

He shook his head, biting back the pain. "They would never chance a battle with Lumatere now. They know it will involve Belegonia and Osteria. Their orders are to shoot me to slow me down, but not to kill me. I know such orders, Quintana. I've followed them myself. I'm worth more to them alive than dead."

They both knew he was lying.

"I'm counting, Froi," she cried. "I'm counting in my head."

"Good girl."

He took her face in his bloody hands. "I'll come and find you wherever you are. I'll not stop breathing until I do. So you're going to have to promise me that you won't lose hope. That you will keep yourself alive."

He tried to wipe her tears, but there were too many.

"I heard your song the moment we were born," she sobbed. "And years later, it dragged me back from the lake of the half dead when all I wanted to do was die. Each time someone tried to kill me, it sang its tune and gave me hope."

She pressed cold lips against his, and they tasted the salt of each other's tears.

"Are you ready?" he asked.

She nodded.

"Run!"

Later, Froi would have sworn to anyone who listened that it was Tariq of Lascow who propped him up so Froi could shoot at anyone in those hills who stood to take aim at Quintana.

And while he thrashed with pain as seven barbs were removed from his body, he wondered if he truly heard the voice of the *reginita* in his ear. "You're coming the wrong way, Froi," she said indignantly. "Turn back!"

But what he knew to be true were those voices surrounding him now. Speaking of Quintana of Charyn.

How seven days had passed since she had disappeared from existence.

That it would take the eyes of the gods to find her.

Or the heart of the Lumateran exile.

CHAPTER 42

Lucian knew the moment he saw Jory's face that something was wrong. Because Jory was alone on the Lumateran side of the stream and Lucian knew the lad would never leave her. He was half in love with her himself.

"Where is she, Jory?" he asked, his voice harsh. He had decided just hours before to surprise Phaedra and ride down the valley to collect her earlier than usual. It was about time they went to the capital, he told Yata. They'd all go together and stay with Isaboe and Finnikin, and he'd properly introduce Phaedra to his queen. As his wife.

Jory jumped to his feet, holding his hand up as if to ward Lucian away.

"It's plague, Lucian."

"What?"

"Not the whole camp. They think they may have contained it. To one cave. But I don't want you to come near me in case I've got it."

The boy was wild-eyed. Full of fear, but not for himself.

"Talk to me, Jory," Lucian said, walking to the lad. "Don't be frightened. Just talk."

"Stay away, Lucian. I beg of you."

"Where's my wife, Jory? Where's Phaedra?"

Jory seemed confused. Dazed. He pointed back to the camp across the stream, then his arm dropped with a fatigue of spirit.

"When we arrived this morning, it was all so normal," Jory said, "and I stopped a moment, you know. I didn't mean to, but I stopped a moment to speak to Kasabian because I try so hard with him, Lucian. Phaedra had gone into Angry Cora's cave and later, when I went to enter, Phaedra yelled at me. 'Stop, Jory,' she said. 'We think it's plague. Call Matteo, who has seen plague himself.'"

Jory shuddered.

"Rafuel or Matteo or whoever he wants to be, he went to the cave but didn't go inside. I saw him from the entrance, Lucian. I saw his face. I thought his heart had stopped beating. He ordered the camp leaders and Harker and Kasabian and everyone away. 'Plague,' he shouted. 'Plague.'

"Harker had to be held back. 'You can't keep me away from my women,' he shouted. But Rafuel picked up a sword and said that the next person to pass him would die with a sword through his heart. 'Plague is plague,' he said. Everyone was ordered back to their caves. Rafuel told Donashe that the women had to be isolated. 'They can't just stay there in the middle of us all and spread their stinking disease.' He was like a madman, Rafuel was. Phaedra came to the entrance and said that she would take the women farther down the stream and that perhaps in that way, they'd contain it. And I called out to her, Lucian. Truly I did. I said, 'Phaedra, you've not been there long. You can stay with us because it can't catch you that fast. Not if you haven't touched them.' But she wouldn't come, Lucian. She said that if she returned with me and brought plague to the mountain and to the children, she would never forgive herself and nor would you, Lucian."

Jory looked back to the Charynite camp again, as if willing Phaedra to walk through the trees.

"So now they're downstream and Phaedra said that each day she'll write a message outside a cave wall up high with an ochre stick, the writing big and bold."

"Write what?" Lucian asked, horrified. But he didn't need to hear the answer.

Phaedra would write the numbers of the dead.

Despite Jory's pleas to keep away, Lucian crossed the stream and approached Rafuel, who was standing in a huddle with the rest of the camp dwellers. Lucian grabbed him, shaking him hard.

"How many of them are there?" he asked.

"Six."

"Take me to her."

"And what?" Rafuel spat. "Get yourself killed? Have you ever seen plague, Mont? I doubt that, in your cozy Osterian hills. If I take you to her cave, Lumatere will be annihilated within weeks. I was there six years ago. I lived through the last plague we had."

Rafuel turned to the others. "I say this to you all. The first man or woman who travels past me to that cave downstream will catch an arrow to the heart. The first man or woman who does not report a sign will catch an arrow to the heart."

"Are you camp leader all of a sudden, Matteo?" Lucian demanded.

Donashe stepped forward. "We stand by Matteo's threat," he said.

Rafuel stared at Lucian. "If you cross the stream again, then you're a bigger fool than I thought you were, Mont."

Lucian stayed with Jory on the Lumateran side of the stream for days. When he saw Yael coming down the mountain on the third day, he called out to his cousin to stay away. Although he strongly suspected that he and Jory were not in danger, he couldn't take the chance. The only good news was that none of the cave dwellers had reported symptoms, although there were those who, according to Rafuel, reported anything from a sneeze to an itch.

But on the fourth day, the true horror began. Downstream from where the women had moved, two markings on the outer wall of one of the caves appeared. Two dead. Lucian held his vigil with Jory. Across the stream he saw Harker and Kasabian and the husband of the lazy girl Ginny, waiting. Two days later, Rafuel reported two more markings on the cave walls. On the seventh day, Rafuel traveled to the caves with his body wrapped and every part of him covered but his eyes. Lucian and the world of the valley prayed, dreading the news. And later that afternoon, they all saw the flames from a distance.

"Not good," Kasabian muttered. "Not good."

Rafuel returned, and Lucian crossed the stream with Jory, to join Kasabian and Harker. He could see that Rafuel's face was ashen, his eyes everywhere but on the men who stood before him.

"Matteo?" Kasabian asked. "Speak, Matteo."

And the moment Rafuel's eyes met Lucian's, he knew.

"All of them?" Harker asked, his voice broken. Rafuel nodded. He looked around to where a crowd was gathering.

"But not Phaedra?" Lucian said.

"All of them, Mont."

Lucian shook his head, not wanting to believe.

"I want to see her," he said, pushing past Rafuel.

"You can't. The corpse of a plague victim carries disease. I had to burn them."

Jory grabbed Lucian, trying to drag him back.

"Mont, don't risk our lives," Donashe ordered.

The cries of fear and grief stopped Lucian.

"You had no right to do that," he accused Rafuel. "She was my wife. You had no right."

"I had every right in the world, Mont," Rafuel shouted. "What were you going to do? Bury her in the ground. We don't honor our dead in such a way."

"She was my wife!"

"She didn't belong to you anymore," Rafuel said. "She didn't belong to her father. She belonged to this valley, and I had every right in the world. These people are frightened. They've lost Phaedra, and they believe your queen will exile us for fear of spreading the plague."

"I want to see my wife," Harker said. "I want to see my daughter! Take me to them!"

Rafuel went to walk away. "You know that's not possible."

Harker leaped on Rafuel, beating him with a rage beyond anything Lucian had seen among these people. It took four men to drag him from Rafuel and they tied his hands and legs. *"You had no right to take them from me,"* Harker moaned. *"No right. I want to see my Florenza. I want to see my Jorja."*

In the mountains when Lucian and Jory returned, the Monts were waiting for them. Yael and his wife were there, overjoyed to see their son alive and well.

"Where's Phaedra?" Tesadora asked, and Lucian saw tears in the eyes of a woman he had believed would weep for no one.

"Lucian!" Japhra and Constance and the novices grabbed at the fleece of his coat as he walked toward his cottage. "Where is she, Lucian?"

He continued walking, leaving behind their cries.

Later, Yata and Tesadora came with supper and they ate it quietly.

"Foolish girl," Tesadora said. "Foolish girl."

Foolish man, Lucian thought, *who took a year to realize he loved his wife and never said the words to her.*

"Tomorrow you go to Alonso," Yata said quietly. "Her father needs to know."

As Lucian set off the next day, Jory and Yael were waiting for him outside Pitts's cottage.

"We thought we'd come with you, Lucian. To keep you company, cousin," Jory said, and Lucian thought how young he looked. Still a boy.

They traveled all day on horseback in silence. As they passed the caves where Phaedra died, he saw the four bold red lines marking the four out of six deaths. He wondered who died last with her. He hoped it was Cora. They would have been a comfort to each other in the end. He wondered if she had thought of him. If she'd realized that Lucian had grown to love her and that he had planned a bonding ceremony among the Monts unlike the one in Alonso, through which she had wept. He wondered if she imagined that Lotte and the fool Orly would build a shrine for her in his paddock and that Yata had the entrance of her house adorned with the shroud of grieving, refusing to accept visitors. And that Alda had her sons leave a posy of mountain wildflowers on the Charyn side of the stream and that Lucian had slept in her cot with her shawl clutched in his hands, the scent of her consuming his small cottage.

In Alonso they identified themselves at the gates and were escorted to the *provincaro*'s house, where Lucian met Sol of Alonso. The *provincaro* would have read the sorrow on their faces. Lucian knew the moment the man understood what they were doing there, but he spoke the words out loud regardless.

Phaedra was dead.

And for the second time in days, he saw the grief of a father for his daughter and he heard the fury spat at him as every man in the room tried to hold Sol of Alonso down.

"You were supposed to protect her! On your mountain! Your father pledged! Your father pledged he'd take care of my Phaedra! He pledged!"

Lucian realized the truth with bitterness. She had lied to the *provincaro*. Had led him to believe she was still living happily in the Mountains with her Mont husband since their bonding ceremony in Alonso. Did she not say that in her letters home each month? She had lied to all of them. Her father would never have refused to take his daughter back into his home. It had been Lucian's ignorance that had allowed him to believe that only a Lumateran father would not forsake his daughter.

And as they left the province walls, he heard the wails, the crying from the people grieving their beloved last born.

Phaedra of Alonso is dead.

When they arrived back at the valley, Lucian was numb. He didn't stop but kept on riding past Kasabian, who was on his hands and knees in the vegetable patch he had lovingly restored with his sister, Cora, after the Mont lads had destroyed it. Before Lucian or Yael could stop him, Jory dismounted and walked to the man and knelt in the earth beside him. Lucian watched his young kinsman reach out and embrace Kasabian, and for the first time since his father's death, Lucian wept.

CHAPTER 43

In the palace meeting room on the day of his father and Beatriss's bonding day, Finnikin stood with Isaboe and stared at the object placed before them.

"Just tell me he's alive, Sir Topher," Isaboe said. "That's all I want to hear."

Sir Topher stared at the ruby ring. "This is all there is to prove he was alive in early autumn. The man who brought it to us claims it was given to him as a trade during the events in the Citavita. He thought we might want it back. For a price."

"And?" Isaboe asked.

"Perri and Trevanion are interrogating him as we speak."

"Mercy," Finnikin muttered. "That's all we need. My father turning up to his bonding ceremony splattered in blood."

He stared out the window to where their people were setting up the trestle tables. There would be many absent faces today, especially from the Monts. Lucian's grief was fierce. The loss of his Charyn wife was felt across the mountain, and even Yata had declined to attend Trevanion and Beatriss's bonding day out of respect for the days of mourning. Finnikin was torn between his joy for Trevanion and his sadness for his friend. He had noticed during his last visit to the mountains that Lucian's feelings for the Charynite girl had changed. It was in the way the Mont's eyes had blazed with pride when Phaedra spoke with such ease to those around her and flashed with jealousy when she spoke about the handsome *provincaro* of Paladozza.

The death of Lucian's wife had come at the same time as the arrival of a Charynite through the Osterian border claiming to have a ruby ring belonging to the queen. The moment Finnikin and Isaboe had heard those words, they had suspected the worst.

"Have you heard news from the envoys, Sir Topher?" Finnikin asked. "About events in Charyn?"

"Only Celie. She's returned for the wedding. The Osterians are saying that the king's First Adviser has taken control of the kingdom with the Nebian army. The Belegonians are saying that a man named Gargarin of Abroi is holding the queen hostage with Paladozza's blessing. The Sorellians are saying that a Lumateran nobleman has kidnapped the queen. The Sarnaks are saying that she is in the hands of rebel priests in the Turlan mountains."

"Is anyone saying the same thing?" Isaboe asked.

"Yes," Sir Topher said. "Everyone is saying that the princess of Charyn is with child. Bestiano, the former king's First Adviser, has made contact with the Belegonians asking for their acknowledgment of his right to lead the heir. He claims the queen of Charyn is carrying his babe and that she has been kidnapped by Gargarin of Abroi. He says that the last thing Belegonia and Lumatere want is for Gargarin of Abroi to take control of the palace."

"As opposed to Bestiano, who was the savage king's First Adviser for ten years?" Isaboe asked bitterly.

"Yes, but appointed after the events of Lumatere, not before," Sir Topher said. "And that is where our interest lies. According to Bestiano and the Belegonians, Gargarin of Abroi was in the palace eighteen years ago. He was the king's brightest adviser."

Finnikin sat before Sir Topher.

"What is he implying?"

"That Gargarin of Abroi was the mastermind behind the attack on Lumatere. That it was years in the planning."

"Eighteen years ago?"

"Belegonia believes it to be true. Because what did Charyn need eighteen years ago more than anything else in the land?"

Finnikin and Isaboe exchanged looks.

"Women who could give birth," Sir Topher said. "Gargarin of Abroi, according to Bestiano, believed the curse lay with the women and not the men. What better way to prove that than to invade Lumatere and take its women?"

"Too ridiculous," Isaboe said. "And heinous."

Finnikin shook his head. "Not so ridiculous. There was widespread rape here, Isaboe," he reminded her quietly. "Despite the fact that it led to no births among us."

"Thank the goddess for the smallest of favors," she said.

"And you believe this Gargarin is staying in Paladozza?" Finnikin asked Sir Topher.

"According to the Belegonians, yes."

Isaboe stood and took Finnikin's hand. "What say you, my love? That it's about time we go in and get our lad back?"

He thought for a moment and nodded. "And we set a trap for Gargarin of Abroi."

They walked out into the main hall, where their people awaited them beyond the courtyard doors.

"We'll speak of this later," Isaboe said. "I will not have Beatriss and Trevanion's day ruined."

Jasmina burst through the doors dressed for the celebrations and they both knelt down and held out their arms to her.

"We do what needs to be done," Isaboe said quietly before Jasmina reached them. "We kill Gargarin of Abroi."

epilogue

Somewhere in Charyn, Froi woke to see Gargarin sitting beside his bed. Amid all the horror, he felt a sense of joy to see him here. After everything Froi had said to Gargarin and Lirah, his father had come to be with him.

"I'm sorry," Froi croaked, reaching out to take his hand. "I'm sorry for everything. I'm sorry for losing her."

Gargarin gripped Froi's hand, a gentle smile on his face.

"We'll do it your way, Gargarin. All of it. I'll never doubt you again."

Froi tried to sit up, but pain shot through almost every part of his body. Gargarin gently laid him back down, and Froi held on to him with a fierceness that spoke of never letting him go.

"Where's Lirah?" he whispered. "I want to see my mother. I want her forgiveness."

Gargarin cleared the emotion from his throat.

"You're in the mountains of Sebastabol, Froi. Someone left you here. Someone who didn't want you to die, no matter how many of their arrows pierced you."

Gargarin's voice was so tender it made Froi weep.

"I don't know where Lirah is, lad. Nor Gargarin."

Arjuro. *Froi reached out a hand and touched his face. The priestling's hair was cropped and his beard not so wild and his eyes more lucid than Froi had ever seen.*

"You're in a bad way, beloved ingrate," his uncle said. "But we are going to put you back together."

In the Flatlands of Lumatere, Beatriss and Trevanion walked home with Vestie between them. She swung their arms as if she had not a care in the world. Beatriss had never seen her child so happy, but despite it all, she knew that Trevanion would leave soon and she already felt the day's sadness.

"Are you going to go searching?" she asked quietly, having heard talk that day of Charyn.

"I have to," he replied. "I sent him, Beatriss, and I won't rest until he's returned to us."

"Who?" Vestie asked. "Are you going somewhere, Trevanion?"

"Father," he corrected gently.

Beatriss brushed hair out of her daughter's eyes. "The Guard has lost its . . . dearest pup, Vestie, and they're very sad without him, so Trevanion will travel soon to bring him home."

Trevanion lifted Beatriss's hand to his lips.

"You're stretching my arm, silly," Vestie said, giggling.

"We can't have that," he said, and lifted her into his arms.

Up ahead, Beatriss could see the family of Makli of the Flatlands approach on a horse and cart. They now had a future together, and although it would be a long while before she would forget Makli's harsh words, she had come to respect him. But as they rode by, Vestie poked out her tongue at Makli's boy.

"He's my father!" she bellowed, pointing to Trevanion.

"Vestie!" Beatriss said firmly, stopping to stare up at her. "I'll

snip at that tongue if I ever see it in such a way again! Trevanion, speak to her."

Vestie hung her head, shamefaced.

"Vestie," he said, his voice still gentle.

"Yes, Father."

"Shout it out louder, my love. Shout it out louder."

In the valley between two kingdoms, she sat on the rock face and waited for the day to begin. It was always at this hour that she thought of him and wondered how those they loved were faring. But she knew they had made the right decision. That what they were doing was for the greater good of Charyn, no matter how much heartbreak it brought.

"Do you think it will rain again?" a voice asked from within the cave.

"No," Phaedra of Alonso said, turning with a smile. "You should all come out. It's beautiful. I think I see the sun."

acknowledgments

A special thanks to my editor Amy Thomas for her intelligence and musical taste and for sometimes loving these characters as much as I did.

Also much thanks to Cathy Larsen, who made sense of my maps, Marina Messiha for yet another beautiful cover, and Jeanmarie Morosin for her proofreading.

To my manuscript readers, Barbara Barclay, Brenda Souter, and my mum, Adelina Marchetta, for dealing with early drafts. To Anna Musarra, for the tattoo that inspired the day of weeping.

Thanks always to the Penguin gang, especially my publisher, Laura Harris, to whom this novel is dedicated, and Kristin Gill, Anyez Lindop, and Erin Wamala.

For my U.S. editor, Deborah Wayshak, and everyone at Candlewick, and my agents, Sophie Hamley, Jill Grinberg, and Cheryl Pientka.

And thanks always to friends and family and the writers in my life who allow me to purge.

A note about the setting: *Finnikin of the Rock,* the first of the Lumatere Chronicles, was inspired by the landscape around the Dordogne area of France. It was during my visit to this region that the novel found the second half of its title. With *Froi of the Exiles,* I knew the physicality would have to have a different type of beauty. The town of Matera in Basilicata, Italy, with its amazing *gravina* (ravine) was the first place I researched when I knew that *Froi* would be set in a world of stone houses and cave frescoes. The rest of my research centered around the castle of Conwy in Wales and the truly sublime Cappadocia in Turkey, with its unique landscape and underground cities.

N

CHARYN

KEY
province walls
the capital
village